D1348875

Music in Contemporary British Fiction

Also by Gerry Smyth

THE NOVEL AND THE NATION: Studies in the New Irish Fiction

DECOLONISATION AND CRITICISM: The Construction of Irish Literature

SPACE AND THE IRISH CULTURAL IMAGINATION

NOISY ISLAND: A Short History of Irish Popular Music

Music in Contemporary British Fiction

Listening to the Novel

Gerry Smyth

palgrave
macmillan

First published 2008 by
PALGRAVE MACMILLAN

Palgrave Macmillan in the UK is an imprint of Macmillan Publishers Limited, registered in England, company number 785998, of Houndmills, Basingstoke, Hampshire RG21 6XS.

Palgrave Macmillan in the US is a division of St Martin's Press LLC, 175 Fifth Avenue, New York, NY 10010.

Palgrave Macmillan is the global academic imprint of the above companies and has companies and representatives throughout the world.

Palgrave® and Macmillan® are registered trademarks in the United States, the United Kingdom, Europe and other countries

ISBN-13: 978-0-230-57328-4   hardback
ISBN-10: 0-230-57328-2   hardback

This book is printed on paper suitable for recycling and made from fully managed and sustained forest sources. Logging, pulping and manufacturing processes are expected to conform to the environmental regulations of the country of origin.

A catalogue record for this book is available from the British Library.

Library of Congress Cataloging-in-Publication Data

Smyth, Gerry, 1961–
    Music in contemporary British fiction : listening to the novel /
    Gerry Smyth.
        p.   cm.
    Includes bibliographical references and index.
    ISBN 0-230-57328-2 (alk. paper)
    1. English fiction—20th century—History and criticism.   2. Music and
    literature.   3. English fiction—21st century—History and criticism.
    4. Music in literature.   5. Music—Social aspects—Great Britain.
    I. Title.

PR888.M87S69   2008
809'.933578—dc22   2008016423

10   9   8   7   6   5   4   3   2   1
17   16   15   14   13   12   11   10   09   08

For Stacey

Contents

PART II

Acknowledgements

I have discussed various aspects of this book with a wide range of friends, family and colleagues over a long period of time. Of the many who have helped with comments and constructive criticism I would particularly like to thank the following:

Writer and academic Jim Friel, in acknowledgement of the enthusiastic support that he offered for this project from an early stage, and also for sharing his extensive knowledge of contemporary British fiction;

Micheline Robinson, a brilliant artist who executed the commission for the cover of this book with humour and insight;

My colleagues in the Department of English at Liverpool John Moores University, for providing a stimulating intellectual context within which to undertake research;

My daughters Lizzie and Esther, for sharing my love of music and literature, and for indulging my 'interesting' tastes;

My friends Holly and Duncan, for helping me to keep the value of academic discourse in perspective.

I would also like to thank Jim Marshall for taking the cover photograph, and the Princess Grace Library in Monaco for appointing me Academic-in-Residence in September / October 2006, during which period much of the research for this project was undertaken.

Finally, and for reasons too simple to mention, I would like to thank my partner.

Introduction

Listening to the Novel

Music has played an important role in the development of the novel in Britain since the early eighteenth century. Anyone even passingly familiar with the history of that particular literary form will probably already be aware that music represents a significant consideration for many of the authors who have contributed to the tradition. A reader fully sensitised to the role and representation of music is bound to encounter it throughout the canon of British fiction.

Musical considerations may be incorporated into the novel in many different ways. In *Gerontius* (1988), for example, the author, James Hamilton-Paterson, provides a fictionalised account of an actual visit made by the British composer Edward Elgar to the Amazon rainforest in 1923. Reference is made throughout the novel to Elgar's compositions as well as to the general tradition of European art music within which his work is generally located. The novel is in some senses an interpretation of each (the music and the tradition). Feeling personally abandoned and aesthetically outmoded, the mature composer meditates on his past achievements even as he searches for inspiration amidst Brazil's unfamiliar environment. *Gerontius* thus incorporates a good deal of musical matter: it refers to certain works and composers of greater or lesser fame; it describes certain musical effects and practices; it reflects on the emergence (and subsequent decline) of certain musical fashions and tastes – and so on. It is a novel, in other words, in which the literary processes of interpretation (what the novel might mean) and pleasure (how enjoyable it might be to read) are thoroughly infused with matters of music.

Although *Espedair Street* (1989) by Iain Banks is in some ways a very different proposition, it too is saturated with musical concerns. This time the milieu is rock music – in fact the novel tells what is in many

1

ways the archetypal rock story of a poor white male who comes under the influence of this style of music at an early age and whose subsequent success in the medium precipitates an identity crisis. The young Danny Weir grows up on the eponymous street in Paisley, Scotland, during the early 1970s, listening to David Bowie, the Rolling Stones and Led Zeppelin, and nurturing vague dreams of emulating these rock gods. Like so many young British men of the era, Danny's world is turned upside down by the punk revolution of the mid-1970s: suddenly his unfashionable background and gauche personality are positive advantages for a career in popular music. The narrative describes the emotional journey taken by Danny over the course of his brief career, and links it with a spatial journey that takes him away from and then back to his Scottish Catholic working-class roots. At the same time, certain aspects of modern rock discourse are incorporated into the narrative – the process of composition and the dynamics of performance, for example, as well as various commercial and administrative aspects of the modern popular music industry.

Gerontius and *Espedair Street* raise many of the issues that might be considered likely to be of interest for a study of the role and representation of music in contemporary British fiction. Indeed, the alert reader may note that the brief comments introduced in the two previous paragraphs will recur in expanded fashion throughout this study. It will also be observed that these two examples immediately predate the period upon which I am going to focus in Part II of this book: 1990 to the time of writing (2008). It is my perception that the latter represents a period in which music has moved from being a kind of residual or background element within British fiction to being of increasingly central concern. The validity of this claim, as well as the reasons that might lie behind such a development, are matters that will emerge during the course of the study itself. In the meantime, it should be noted that if music has grown in significance within contemporary British fiction, this is a reflection of a shift within the critical and theoretical discourses attending the practice of novel-writing. In short, there are now many more interesting and sophisticated ways to talk about the role and representation of music in the novel than at any time since the emergence of the form.

As a point of departure, it is worth noting that 'noise' has emerged as an important analytical category within modern cultural studies. The key figure here is the French historian and cultural theorist Jacques Attali, who desired to place noise not only at the centre of human history, but also (and more radically) at the centre of *thinking* about human

history. 'For twenty-five centuries', he claimed in the opening to his celebrated study *Noise: The Political Economy of Music*, 'western knowledge
has tried to look upon the world. It has failed to understand that the
world is not for the beholding. It is for hearing. It is not legible, but
audible' (1985:1). Attali invites his readers to forego what he perceives
as a visionary bias encoded in western culture since ancient Greece and
begin instead to approach the world as an auditory phenomenon.

Music, moreover, has an especially important role to play in this
thesis: music, Attali declares, 'is prophesy. Its styles and economic organisation are ahead of the rest of society because it explores, much faster
than material reality can, the entire range of possibilities in a given
code' (12). What this means is that throughout history music has constituted both the clearest exercise of power and at the same time the
most available locus of resistance to, and subversion of, established discourses of power. Therein lies the source of its political importance:
'Music, the quintessential mass activity, like the crowd, is simultaneously a threat and a necessary source of legitimacy; trying to channel it
is a risk that every system of power must run' (14). The message of
Attali's study is that we ignore music at our peril, for at the same time
as it affords us an insight into how things really are, it offers us the most
enabling impressions of how things might be.

One might be forgiven for questioning the relevance of Attali's research
for a study of fiction. Although stories are occasionally read aloud for
an audience, and although the audio book is a viable commercial
prospect in the early twenty-first century, the fact remains that the
novel is first and foremost a legible form – one that is usually consumed alone and in silence. Moreover, the novel does not produce any
remarkable sound of itself, other than perhaps a rustle of pages as it is
being read or a dull thud as it is set aside or replaced on a shelf. In fact,
silence appears to be built in to the novel's historical, sociological and
commercial heritage. In this sense, anyone wishing to 'listen to the
novel' is going to be disappointed and will, moreover, appear a little
foolish.

Despite this, Attali's demand for an auditory engagement with cultural
history brings us back to the novel and to the way in which noise – more
specifically music – has featured in the evolution of the form. The novel
may be silent in and of itself, but the recurring recourse to music that is
discernible throughout British fiction since the eighteenth century represents an important aspect of the nation's socio-political development
when considered from an aural (as opposed to a visual) perspective.
'Listening to the novel' in this sense means contemplating the ways in

which music has impacted upon the formal and conceptual organisation of this perennially successful literary form; it means reflecting upon the value accorded to thematic material that is noisy by definition within a medium that is by definition silent; most importantly, it means attending to the ways in which music is represented in relation to a variety of social and subjective discourses over an extended period of time. It is my conviction that by 'listening' to the British novel in these ways, we can in fact uncover some of the most potent issues bearing upon the society in which we live, concerning both how it is organised and the means by which it may be understood.

Isolated scholars have been considering the relationship between music and literature for many years. Calvin S. Brown's *Music and Literature* (1948) and Alex Aronson's *Music and the Novel* (1980) are just two examples of pioneering work in the field (both have proved influential for the present study). Certainly, music was an issue of serious significance for many of the writer-critics of the nineteenth century. It was not until the last decades of the twentieth century, however, that a more systematic approach to the study of the music/literature nexus began to emerge. The reasons for this are many and varied; it seems reasonably clear, however, that radical changes within the parent disciplines of musicology and literary criticism were especially significant. Both these fields were undergoing a crisis during this time relating to the validity of established systems and received methodologies, and both responded by diversifying along various political, methodological and theoretical lines. One of the consequences of this was what might be termed the 'interdisciplinary turn' – that is, the emergence of 'culture' as a common object of study for formerly demarcated scholarly systems, and the attempt to bring such systems into mutually illuminating relief (Moran, 2001), leading to the emergence during the 1990s of Word and Music Studies.

As with all new academic initiatives there is contention surrounding more-or-less every element of Word and Music Studies – its institutional status, its methods, its archive, even its title. (The subtitle of an essay collection from 1999 – *Word and Music Studies: Defining the Field*, ed. W. Bernhart, S. Scher and W. Wolf – is revealing.) Many of the issues are broached in Werner Wolf's *The Musicalization of Fiction: A Study in the Theory and History of Intermediality* (1999). The author restricts his attention to what he calls 'musicalized fiction' – that is, the attempt on the part of literary authors to replicate or reproduce musical effects in their writing. Nevertheless, this is an extremely ambitious study, including musicological as well as literary critical discourse, a historical overview of the both fields, and numerous case studies. Wolf tries hard to contextualise all his analyses and to explain the specific historical function of every instance of musicalised fiction. Despite this, his approach is primarily formalist (by which I mean oriented towards the text) in as much as he seems very keen to define the terms of the debate, and is willing to go to exhaustive length to develop a viable critical discourse that will answer each and every instantiation of his preferred term.

The Musicalization of Fiction may represent the last, long word on one particular form of literary–musical connection. There are many such connections, however, and many different ways in which a critic might set about approaching and describing them. Wolf has nothing to say about the many different forms of music that have been incorporated into the novel since the form consolidated; how would he begin to approach *Espedair Street*, for example – a novel that is not 'musicalized' in any of the senses developed in his study, but one in which music (albeit of a form routinely dismissed as inconsequential in many influential accounts) is nevertheless absolutely central? Nor does Wolf seem particularly concerned with the multitude of ways in which musical matters bear upon the reader's engagement with the text. Do you have to have heard (or heard of) the music of David Bowie to 'get' Banks's novel? To what extent does a reader's knowledge of a musical text (or oeuvre, or figure, or event) bear upon their engagement with and understanding of developments within the fictional narrative?

At the same time, there appears to be a fundamental contradiction between Wolf's quasi-scientific discourse and the object of his analysis. Of course, certain methodological parameters are essential before any meaningful analysis may commence: we need a subject, a period, a debate, a critical language, and so on. In the present study, however, I have preferred to pursue what might be described as an immanent form of analysis, based primarily upon what emerges from the literary texts themselves. I wish, in other words, to allow my critical imagination to be led at least to some extent by the objects under consideration. These objects range from the self-conscious, fully committed 'musicalized novel' to those texts in which music functions as an incidental reference or casual pretext. Both can teach us something about the composition and the disposition of the society from which they emerge; likewise, both can teach us something about fiction's perennial recourse to music as a formal and conceptual influence.

There is another influential scholarly discourse that addresses itself to the relationship between music and language, a discourse particularly associated with the American critic Lawrence Kramer, who calls it 'cultural musicology'. Kramer represents a response from within traditional musicology itself to the theoretical challenges that have been presented to the academic world since the 1960s, and he has practised his approach in a series of influential publications covering a range of historical and geographical contexts (1990, 1995). He is clearly aligned with that process when he claims that music is, above all else, 'worldly': both in and of the world – composed of, referring to and influenced by matters that have observable consequences for a range of subjects in what, for better or worse, tends to be known as 'the real world'. This understanding is opposed to the more traditional one that sees music as being very much 'otherworldly': 'Because the sounds of music function in a non-denotative fashion and do not refer to the external world,' as John Shepherd puts it, 'music is thought of as being devoid of worldly significance, either "empty", or replete with formal properties, but none that would speak to the material and therefore social worlds' (1999: 162).

One of the principal ways in which music might be seen as worldly is its *wordiness* – that is, its amenability to linguistic, as opposed to purely musical, treatment. Music, we find, is always being talked about and written about, always being described in language of various kinds and registers and vocabularies. Crucially, music is always being reconstituted in language. Music may possess the ability to 'speak for itself' – 'on its "own" terms', as Kramer puts it (2003:124); I have no wish to dispute this, and am indeed keen to avoid the claim that musical meaning can only exist as a function of linguistic ascription. I do subscribe to the belief, however, that music inevitably speaks the language of those discourses within which it is invoked – which is to say, the linguistic discourses within which the sound of music is constantly encountered and re-encountered. 'Words', Kramer writes,

> situate music in a multiplicity of cultural contexts, both those to which the music 'belongs' in an immediate sense and those to which it stands adjacent in ways that often become apparent only once the words are in play . . . Musical meaning is produced less by the signs of a musical semiotics than by signs about music, signs whose grounding in historically specific forms of subjectivity is the source of their legitimation, not of their – literal – insignificance.[1]

The full challenge of cultural musicology will come into focus in Chapter 1 of this study when it is situated within the evolving history of literary-critical responses to music, in particular its relationship with language (including literary language). At this stage it is enough to note that in reconnecting music with the wider cultural contexts within which it is composed, performed and consumed, cultural musicology provides an imprimatur for interventions such as the present study, because, as I have already claimed (and as we shall see at length in Chapter 2), music looms surprisingly large in the history of British fiction. Novelists from every generation, working within every genre, have responded to the power of music by incorporating it into their narratives, by trying to harness its techniques and effects, and by attempting to recreate the emotions that come to be associated with particular musical styles, forms or texts. In fact, music represents a recurring feature of the canon – one ranging from those texts in which it plays a seemingly incidental (although usually strategically significant) role to those in which it permeates the formal and conceptual fabric of the literary text.

Another book that has been influenced by cultural musicology (and which has in turn proved influential for the present study) is Stephen Benson's *Literary Music: Writing Music in Contemporary Fiction* (2006). Although distancing himself (at least to some extent) from the formalism of Word and Music Studies, Benson does not necessarily subscribe to the historicism that has become one of the principal methodological tenets of cultural (or 'the new') musicology.[2] Of course, in as much as *Literary Music* was born of a particular moment in the history of critical theory and focuses on a selection of novels from the late twentieth century, its insights are as susceptible to historicisation as any other critical initiative. In his analysis of the role and representation of music in contemporary fiction, Benson does not seek a better understanding of the wider culture within which such fiction is being produced. Rather, he approaches contemporary fiction in search of 'paradigmatic instances of the ways in which such writing has sought an encounter with music . . . [The] object of real interest', in this sense, 'is the manner in which individual works or genres come to exemplify a particular construction of music' (2006: 7).

Benson's search for paradigmatic encounters between music and fiction leads him to restrict his attention to what are generally referred to as 'literary fiction' on the one hand and 'classical music' on the other. My goal for the present study is perhaps less ambitious in theoretical terms, although certainly more wide-ranging in methodological and archival terms. Perhaps this is the point at which to reveal that I am not a literary critic as such, but a cultural historian by training, inclination and profession – albeit one who continues to be primarily interested in the provenance and contemporary status of certain kinds of writing. This means that I am oriented in critical terms towards all forms of writing in a particular medium (in this case, prose fiction), not just one particular form (the 'literary novel', however one might care to define it). At the same time, and for the same reasons, I find myself drawn towards the cultural-musicological attitude that, as described by Kramer, 'destabilizes firm distinctions between cultivated and vernacular forms, and in principle takes all music as its province' (2003: 126).

These theoretical and methodological predilections have determined the structure of the present study. Part I comprises two chapters, the first of which provides a theoretical overview of the historical relationship between music and literature, with special emphasis on the novel. The intention, first of all, is to describe some of the ways in which that relationship has been addressed and characterised since it was invoked as part of a modernising critical discourse during the eighteenth century, and then to examine that discourse in relation to examples from both the wider tradition of European fiction and from the modern British tradition that will form the basis for Part II. Chapter 2 offers a practical critical overview of the tradition of British fiction from the mid-eighteenth century to 1991 with reference both to the theories described in Chapter 1, as well as to a variety of critical studies that have from time to time addressed themselves to the music/novel connection.

There are three chapters in Part II, the first two of which are organised in terms of the various genres that structure musical and novelistic discourse in contemporary Britain. Classical music is represented here, as are a number of other genres (including folk, jazz, hip-hop, etc.) that have clearly impacted upon the musical imagination of contemporary Britain. Equally, 'proper' literary writing does have a place, although it is ranged alongside other forms of fiction (fantasy, graphic, crime, and so on). In this way, my scepticism towards the paradigmatic exemplariness of classical music shall be shown to be of a piece with my scepticism towards the privileged status of literary fiction, for the fact is that there are many different forms of music abroad in contemporary Britain, as well as many different kinds of novel in which such music might be represented. Such representations are 'dialectical' in as much as each musical genre determines to some extent the kind of novel that tries to represent it in literary language; at the same time, each novelistic genre determines, to some extent, the meaning of the music that it looks to represent. Chapters 3 and 4 of the present study are a gesture towards this complex dialectical process.

The final chapter focuses upon some of the wider uses – social, political, philosophical, and so on – to which the literary representation of music has been put in contemporary Britain. Here again, the intention (and hence the methodology) clearly differs from Benson, as what is envisaged is something like a cultural history of the present – a section taken through society so as to reveal some of the most prominent concerns currently exercising the literary imagination of modern Britain. These particular concerns (history, nostalgia, silence and love) are facilitated in the first instance by the particular form of fiction that incorporates music into its formal or conceptual composition. The implications of each of these themes penetrate deep into the wider culture, responding to and in turn stimulating the patterns of experience (both emotional and physical) that characterise the era. The contemporary British music-novel is, in this sense, a portal (albeit one of many) through which we may access some of the defining concerns of our period.

The last sentence raises the issue of nomenclature – an issue that bedevils all interdisciplinary projects. Many different terms have been coined to describe this kind of novel: melopoetic fiction, musical fiction, the intermedial novel, the ekphrastic novel, interart discourse, verbal music, and so on (see Bernhart, Scher and Wolf, 1999). Both Aronson and Benson deliberately avoid the issue, presumably because the problems raised outnumber the problems solved by any particular formulation. Aronson refers to 'the musical experience in the modern novel' (1980: 32), while Benson never offers much more than the 'literary music' of his title. Wolf's 'musicalized fiction' refers to a particular kind of writing that he defines as 'the imitation of music in a narrative text' (1999: 51). This will do for some of the novels addressed in the present study, but by no means all.

My experience in teaching, researching and writing about these novels has led me to a term that, whatever its limitations or awkwardness, most accurately describes my theoretical and methodological requirements. I have settled on 'British music-novel' as the term that will hopefully achieve the most while offending the least. First of all, this formulation is obviously oriented to a specific national tradition. Fifteen years as an Irish Studies specialist leave me in no doubt as to the incredibly delicate nature of questions regarding what might or might not be considered 'British' in the light of the fraught relations between the various cultural traditions existing within the two main islands of the Atlantic archipelago. For me, Ireland's status seems clear enough: it represents a separate modern tradition, and any attempt to engage with it here would soon render matters untenable.[3] The question of autonomous Scottish and Welsh (and indeed English) traditions is more problematic. State-imposed political unity becomes undermined (perhaps to the point of worthlessness) the deeper one penetrates into the disparate cultures; and many are of the opinion that the idea of a modern 'British' literary tradition is in this sense an unwarranted organisational fiction. Nevertheless, it remains a useful fiction for the purposes of the current project, and for two reasons.

Firstly, the idea of 'Britain' retains a function in the various textual worlds created by the novelists themselves as well as in the 'real' world within which I write and you, reader (whatever your political persuasion or social orientation), read. The relationship between these realities (internal and external) is, I suggest, worthy of our attention. Secondly, the various texts have been brought together in terms of a specific subject – music – that, despite longstanding attempts to organise along sectional (including national, or nationalist) lines, is notoriously reckless in the matter of borders. Although the 'Britishness' of 'the British music-novel' remains problematic, the idea of 'music' contained in the latter term encourages us to be flexible in the way we organise the world for the purposes of analysis.

The term 'British music-novel' is also quite clearly form-specific. It conveys that the principal concern is not with shorter fiction, nor indeed with any of the other literary forms (poetry, for example) upon which musical considerations might be expected to have a bearing. Nor am I particularly concerned with a literary presence within music – the adaptation of literary texts for musical discourse (plays into opera, or poetry into song), for example. These are highly significant practices, of course, and I shall make reference throughout the study (especially in Chapter 1) to different literary forms as well as to the reciprocal relations between literature and music. My main focus, however, remains firmly upon the extended prose narrative form known as the novel, and in particular on the ways in which that form has engaged with and responded to music over the course of its evolution.

The term 'music-novel' covers cases in which music features as a significant theme within or inspiration for a particular text, as well as those in which it exercises a formal influence over the structure of the narrative or the style of the prose. At the same time, it covers cases in which music is intentionally introduced by a writer, as well as those in which the critic feels warranted to impute a musical element or presence, with or without authorial sanction. It refers to a specific strand within the tradition of British fiction as well as to a tendency to which all fiction-writing is prone. All in all, the term 'British music-novel' is precise enough to identify a particular field for the purposes of meaningful cultural analysis; at the same time, its eclectic composition demands a critical discourse that utilises a diverse array of interpretive strategies.

Underpinning all, however, is an attitude that accords with Lawrence Kramer's description of 'a full, open engagement with music as lived experience, experience rendered vivid and vivified by a host of overlapping cultural associations. Why', he asks, 'bother with anything less?' (2003: 134). Extending the sentiment to embrace the novel also, I join Kramer in asking why, indeed?

Part I

1

'All art constantly aspires towards the condition of music': The Music-Novel in Theory and Practice

Introduction

Enormous complexities face anyone attempting an overview of the role and representation of music in literature. The task is aided somewhat, however, by the restriction of the latter element of that relationship to a single form. As Calvin S. Brown (one of the pioneers of this brand of interdisciplinary scholarship) has stated: 'For fairly obvious reasons, music has exerted considerably more influence on poetry than on prose fiction' (1948: 208). Werner Wolf concurs, writing: 'In many poems the old affinity to song is still present' (1999: 3). Although poetry looms large in any consideration of music's influence on literature (Winn 1981), the focus of this book is that particular form of extended prose fiction that both commentators and practitioners since the early eighteenth century have learned to call 'the novel'.

With its use of musical effects and devices such as rhythm, versification, and repetition – with, above all, its semiotic excess in respect of 'normal' everyday language – it is not difficult to understand how poetry once dominated the question of music's impact upon literature. Since the period of its emergence as a recognisable form, however, the novel has impacted seriously upon the subsequent tenor and direction of that debate. In some ways, this is precisely because it is *not* poetic. On initial consideration, the 'prosaic' language of which it is composed appears to lack any obvious or intuitive link with music. Such, however, was discovered not to be the case. In fact, it is possible to identify any number of ways in which extended narrative fiction might fruitfully be understood with reference to music. It is the task of this chapter to introduce and describe at least some of the ways in which commentators over the past three centuries or so have approached the possibility of music in the novel.

But how to organise such an overview? How to condense forests of speculation into one moderately sized tree that the interested reader can regard and embrace? How to develop a coherent model that can reach from the natural philosophers of the eighteenth century to the cultural theoreticians of the twenty-first? What is required is some kind of structure into which the enormous amount of commentary, speculation, philosophising and downright propaganda can be fitted, so that the landscape of the music-novel can be mapped and 'read'.

Of course, all maps are 'fictions', so to speak; no matter how objective their makers claim them to be, maps always reflect the concerns of certain parties and certain ways of seeing; they are, moreover, always subject to revision once new interests and new technology render them obsolete. But we have to start from somewhere, and so I have decided to organise this chapter in terms of the tripartite structure described by William E. Grim in his essay 'Musical Form as a Problem in Literary Criticism' (1999). There he claims that '[generally] speaking, there are three ways in which music may influence the creation (and by extension, the critical reception) of literature' (237); these he terms the inspirational, the metaphorical and the formal.

Having accepted the impossibility of an objective map, my intention is to embrace this tripartite structure in order to see what it produces – in full expectation that there shall be omissions and oversights, and that I shall encounter contradictions and intersections along the way. Each of these 'fictions' will be followed by short analyses of one classic and one modern text, each of which may be understood to engage to some degree with the issues introduced in the theoretical sections. These analyses anticipate the remainder of the book in which the novel, rather than the theory, becomes the chief focus of attention.

Music as Inspiration I – Theories

On the role of music as inspiration for the literary text, Grim writes:

> A writer of fiction or poetry may simply be inspired by a particular piece of music in the act of creating a work of literature. This is a case of music being the writer's muse. At this level of influence the work of music is not utilized as subject matter or thematic material for the work of literature it inspires.
>
> (1999: 237)

It is an unfortunate person who has never been 'inspired' by music; indeed, the ability of music to inspire emotional responses amongst its listeners – which may in turn lead to observable consequences – has come to function as one of the principal 'meanings' of music in society. It has been a commonplace of western culture for over two hundred years that listening to the music of Beethoven, for example, can change the way you understand the world – can inspire you, in fact, to reorient yourself in relation to the world, to act and behave differently as a result of the sounds that have penetrated your brain by way of your ear.

At the same time, Grim's definition seems far too narrow to encompass the many and varied ways in which music may impact upon either the composition or the interpretation of the literary text. When one considers the seminal role that music has played in the development of a range of philosophical systems since the eighteenth century, and when one notes the impact of those systems upon generations of writers and readers, then it is necessary to acknowledge that music has indeed 'inspired' the novel – but often in ways that are far from simple, and much more than just acting as an occasional 'muse' for the writer in search of a spark. We need to acknowledge that music is linked to the novel first and foremost because they are both part of an ancient and ongoing process of inquiry into 'the human' – a process that encompasses such issues as the special role of language in the evolution of the species, the question of consciousness, the historical development of a moral imagination, and the role of creative culture in the apprehension of the human.

The roots of the modern philosophical engagement with music lie in the eighteenth century, and emerge in the first instance as part of a debate concerning the origins and function of language, and its role in the evolution of society. In his book *Music and the Origins of Language*, Downing A. Thomas describes how '[eighteenth-century] "musicology" became involved with theories of language and of the origin of society and culture'; at the same time, 'music accomplished theoretical work for eighteenth-century "anthropology"', linking together the argument and conceptual apparatus necessary to explain the origin of language' (1995: 47). It is from this time that music's emergence as the principal mode of aesthetic engagement with the world may be traced. During this period it was widely accepted that literature's closest artistic ally was painting, and that these two were in fact 'sister arts' – ways of representing the world that acknowledged the dominance of the eye and the primary role of vision in the understanding of nature. Jean H. Hagstrum puts what used to be the standard case:

The eighteenth century saw the culmination of the literary man's increasing sophistication in the visual arts. In no previous age did writers to the same extent see and understand paintings, possess such considerable collections of prints and engravings, and read so widely in the criticism and theory of the graphic arts. And in no previous period in English literature could a poet assume knowledge of great painting and statuary in the audience he was addressing.

(1958: 130)

It appears, however, that the idea of literature and painting as 'sister arts' was as much a critical imposition by later commentators as it ever was a contemporary reality. In fact, developments in Enlightenment philosophical discourse (in Britain certainly, but more influentially in France and Germany) – especially as it pertained to the understanding of language and its function as the medium in which the human subject comes to know, and eventually to represent, the world – had created a context for the emergence of an alternative paradigm in which music rather than painting came to be considered as the most significant artistic counterpart to literature.

Although it is perhaps too schematic a model to maintain, there is nevertheless some truth in the association of painting with neo-classical literature and music with Romantic literature. In his book *Language, Music and the Sign* (1987), Kevin Barry describes how a perceived 'tyranny of the visual' (a phrase associated with Coleridge, although the idea is rooted in the thought of John Locke) eventually crumbled in the face of growing scepticism regarding the representative powers of language. As literature was turning away from pictorial art, it was at the same time turning towards music – a form that had become the subject of increasingly intense speculation, not to say contention, as the century progressed. The battle was most fiercely joined in France and Germany, where philosopher-writers were developing theories (of human agency, of language, of nature, of society, and so on) which often turned on a particular understanding of what music was and how it worked.[1]

The new thinking regarding music emerged in the first instance as one aspect of the reaction against an empiricist orthodoxy embodied by Locke. This orthodoxy, it was felt, was based on an untenable notion that language was possessed of an immanent meaning which the mere utterance of the sound would unlock, but which failed to provide a space for the creative process whereby language is actively transformed into meaning by the imagination. Thus, language was uncertain, insecure, the means whereby the emancipated Romantic imagination could explore itself rather than the tool whereby the sincere neo-classical imagination could represent itself in relation to the world.

'The analogy for language, under such a sceptical and exploratory gaze,' Barry writes, 'is music' (178).[2] For music itself was changing – rapidly and profoundly, in theory·and in practice – during the eighteenth century, and such changes were both emanating from and impacting upon the wider philosophical landscape. The adoption of equal temperament had precipitated what was to all intents and purposes a tonal revolution, as exemplified in the first instance by the work of Bach and Handel. But that revolution had been brought to its fullest expression towards the end of the century by the development of the non-programmatic symphony, epitomized by Haydn and Mozart. The latter, especially, was responsible for the production of a kind of music that had a profound impact upon contemporary theories of expression and the role of language in the creation of meaning; moreover, Mozart, more than any other figure from the history of art music (excepting Beethoven), helped to elevate music to the dominant position in relation to the other arts that it has enjoyed ever since.

What Mozart's music appeared to confirm was the existence of a realm of experience beyond the ability of language to express: what, after all, did his 'Jupiter' Symphony (no.41 in C, K551) 'mean'? What did it represent, articulate, or communicate? Different things to different people, obviously; but did it possess a single, essential meaning – a 'master' meaning – capable of being transposed into (and therefore expressed in terms of) verbal language? Apparently not. To put it simply, during this period music goes from being the primordial 'representational' medium upon which all subsequent linguistic conventions are elaborated, to one which obviates the category of representation itself – which refuses, that is to say, the representational imperative in which one thing always stands for another. Barry writes: 'The meaning of music depends upon the enigmatic character of its signs, which, instead of replacing a source which they would imitate or express, turn the listener's attention to his own inventive subjectivity' (104). Or as Christopher Norris puts it, music at this time was in the process of becoming an 'empty' sign – 'a language whose very lack of determinate meaning gives it this peculiar power to awaken the listener's faculties, and thus to stimulate a level of productive involvement that exceeds all merely sensuous or passive understanding' (1990: 216). In short, music provided both a reminder and an example of what mere language could not say: form without content, expression without meaning – music was a message from God reminding us of our divine inheritance.

If the terms of the eighteenth-century debate on language were set in the main by the French philosophical tradition (dominated by Condillac, Diderot and Rousseau), then it was the work of contemporary German Romantic philosophers (most influentially Schiller, Schlegel and Goethe) that '[led] to an unprecedented hegemony of music in nineteenth-century aesthetics' (Wolf 1999: 101). It was this German Romantic tradition that introduced the profoundly influential idea of 'pure' or 'absolute' music during the early years of the nineteenth century. This amounted to a conviction that the best, the most effective, and the most truthful music disdained extra-musical programmes or functions of any kind but was autonomous and sufficient unto itself; further, that such music – devoid of a meaning reducible to mere words – provided access to the meaning of existence through the act of unmediated contemplation. The idea of 'absolute music' (as explained by Carl Dahlhaus in his book of that title, 1978) emerged in opposition to an evolving bourgeois sensibility that insisted on 'function' as a determining criterion in all judgements, aesthetic or otherwise. Against the dominant paradigm, Romantic thinkers argued that text-led forms (song, opera, oratorio, chorale, etc.) were all debased to some extent, for they deflected the listener's attention from the contemplation of 'music alone' (in Peter Kivy's influential formulation, 1990) onto the contemplation of meanings generated by linguistic and other non-musical means.

Dahlhaus reveals that the idea of the self-sufficient object, which represented nothing but itself, generated problems that could only be sustained by means of some extremely creative thinking. For one thing, 'pure' music struggled to avoid the bourgeois charge of uselessness, of being without purchase in the phenomenal world – a charge that has haunted the category of 'the aesthetic' since the eighteenth century. Then again, Romantic music (as we shall see later in this chapter) constantly deferred to 'the real', regardless of critical prescription.[3] More fundamentally, music (no less than any other form of intended human endeavour) could not out-manoeuvre the human will to interpret: a seemingly universal imperative to comprehend novel phenomena in terms of received narratives. Meaning, it appears, is everywhere and thus unavoidable: in the names and nicknames of tunes; in the associations of certain composers with certain effects and ideas; and in the emotions generated by music in each and every aspect of the musical event, from the lowliest score modifier to the most ambitious symphonic structure.

Despite these problems, Dahlhaus's study reveals the idea of 'pure' music to have had a decisive impact on subsequent aesthetic theory, and thus, by extension, on cultural and critical practices. The profound 'paradigm shift' (7) implemented by the early Romantics was taken up later in the nineteenth century by thinkers such as Arthur Schopenhauer and Friedrich Nietzsche, as well as artists such as Richard Wagner; and if Mozart was a key reference point for early proponents, Beethoven became the *sine qua non* for the later currency of 'absolute music'. As Dahlhaus writes:

> Around 1870, Beethoven's [late] quartets became the paradigm of the idea of absolute music that had been created around 1800 as a theory of the symphony: the idea that music is a revelation of the absolute, specifically because it 'dissolves' itself from the sensual, and finally even from the affective sphere.
>
> (1991: 17)

The philosophical coherence of absolute music as a concept remained at issue throughout the nineteenth century, especially in the intense aesthetic debates between *Symbolistes*, Wagnerians and other polemicists in the *fin de siècle*. One clear effect of such debates, however, was to elevate music to a position of predominance among contemporary art forms. It was in such an aesthetic context that nineteenth-century literary forms such as the novel traced their own anxious evolution; it is in terms of the plenitude of 'absolute music' that the question of literary language's 'adequacy' comes into focus; and it was against such a background (in which music merged into metaphysics) that the English art critic Walter Pater produced his famous dictum that '[all] art constantly aspires towards the condition of music' (1910: 35). The idea inspiring such an assertion was that, in saying nothing specific, music expressed everything that was essential.

So, questions of language, and (related) questions of meaning – or at least the range and limits of meaning – are the two principal means by which music has insinuated its way into the wider philosophical, aesthetic and creative consciousness since the eighteenth century. Issues of language have dominated humanistic thought in the West since the publication of Ferdinand de Saussure's *Course in General Linguistics* in 1915. The major literary-critical trends of the twentieth century – formalism, New Criticism, structuralism, semiotics, psychoanalysis, post-structuralism – were all focused to a greater or lesser extent on the role and status of language in the text. And because music was already implicated in linguistic analysis (due to its eighteenth- and nineteenth-century heritage as a key element within the philosophy of language) it is not too difficult to discern some of the ways in which music might be considered relevant for the great variety of language-driven literary theories produced during the twentieth century.

Such relevance is not in itself a subject for extended discussion in this study, although two hugely influential figures are worth mentioning very briefly at this stage: Jacques Derrida and Mikhail Bakhtin. Derrida is associated with the idea of 'deconstruction', which, he insisted, was not a technique or method brought to bear on the text by the critic, but a potential lying dormant within the text itself. A deconstructive reading, as Christopher Norris writes, consists

> not merely in *reversing* or *subverting* some established hierarchical order, but in showing how its terms are indissociably entwined in a strictly undecidable exchange of values and priorities . . . Deconstruction is a process of 'displacement' endlessly at work in [the] text, rather than an act of critical intervention that would come, so to speak, *from outside* and simply apply the standard technique for reversing some 'logocentric' order of priorities.
>
> (1987: 56, original emphases)

Derrida's scepticism towards the ontological (rather than the mere semantic) status of language resonates deeply within traditional debates regarding the status of music in relation to language. Indeed, those debates were explicitly engaged in the extended analysis of Rousseau's *Essay on the Origin of Languages*, which makes up Part II (and by far the bulk) of *Of Grammatology* (1976) – the study that, more than any other single text, launched the poststructuralist age upon an unsuspecting Anglophone academy. In fact, musicology and deconstruction haunt each other (to use a resonant Derridean metaphor): two centuries (and more) of speculation regarding the essential function of music in relation to language anticipates, and to some degree enables, the insights of deconstruction; at the same time, this latter concept invites us to approach the question of the literary representation of music with an ear towards the paradoxical silences of the text – what it cannot say, and what it cannot help saying, about music.

Along with Derrida, Mikhail Bakhtin was probably the most powerful influence on the development of English literary theory in the late twentieth century. Bakhtin is an important figure for the present study for two principal reasons, the first of which is his insistence on 'dialogism' as the absolute, inescapable condition of all acts of human communication. When writing of the novel (the literary genre on which his

work has had the most impact), Bakhtin utilised a musical term –
polyphony, meaning 'many voiced' – to refer to the way in which the
genre evolved specifically to incorporate and juxtapose a multitude of
'voices'. Such 'voices', moreover, are not reducible to metaphorical
effect or mere narrative device (and herein lies the second reason): each
voice in the text derives from, and at the same time represents, some
aspect of the socio-historical formation from which it emerges. The
word, for Bakhtin, is always unstable, always the site of a struggle to
define its meaning in relation to discourses of power observable both in
history (the fates of dialects and national languages, for example) and on
contemporary society (the fates of particular classes and class fractions,
for example).

Stephen Benson has pinpointed the passage within *Problems of
Dostoyevsky's Poetics* in which Bakhtin transposes musical concepts –
specifically, polyphony and counterpoint – into literary critical discourse.[4]
Against Bakhtin's contention that such a transposition represents 'a
graphic analogy, nothing more', Benson argues that a particular understanding of music (or at least of certain musical effects and properties)
was in fact vital to Bakhtin's imagination of novelistic discourse in every
aspect, from its (pre-)historical evolution to its consummation in 'the
multi-leveledness and multi-voicedness of the polyphonic novel' as
exemplified by the work of Dostoyevsky.[5]

The fact is that music in one form or another informs the work of perhaps the leading modern theorist of the novel. Music provides him with
concepts and tools for tracing the evolution of the genre and for
explaining its workings, and it locates the novel at the nexus of an
ongoing multidisciplinary debate incorporating issues of language,
meaning, history and consciousness. This both justifies and demands a
dedicated critical discourse focused on the role and representation of
music in the novel.

Music as Inspiration II – *Swann's Way* (1913) by Marcel Proust

Marcel Proust's *A la recherche du temps perdu* represents the fullest commitment in any novelistic tradition to the task of capturing human consciousness at a specific phase of its evolution: the process whereby the
individual consciousness emerges from an inscrutable intermingling of
sensory, emotional, social and psychological resources – the resource of
memory in particular. Proust's chosen form was the novel: but music
assumes a special role within his writing, and for very particular reasons.

For one thing, music has phenomenological presence: it is *in* the world and impacts upon the senses. The ubiquitous presence of music means that it is something that most humans encounter at some point in their lives; the social organisation of that encounter (in specific styles, genres, conventions, and so on) provides the novelist with a key mechanism for describing the particular regimes of meaning that obtain in various societies. Among other things, Proust's writing makes it clear that how a society listens to its music tells us a great deal about how that society understands itself, both in relation to its own past and in relation to other societies in the present.

At the same time, music is capable of eliciting intense emotional responses in the listener. This emotional economy – running (at least in the western tradition) from extreme joy to extreme sadness – provides a privileged window on the evolution of experiences (such as love) and practices (such as courtship) specific to a given society. Music thus becomes for Proust the measure of the subject's emotional life. Finally (and most significantly in this instance), music is locked in to the key category of memory, which appears to be one of the defining human faculties (although it is also present to some extent among other species). Memory provides us with key resources (such as narrative and subject roles within those narratives) for the imagination of desire. Again, music is especially sympathetic to that process.

Thus, the meaning of a piece of music is always a function of the complex negotiation between these three elements: the subject's phenomenological encounter with musical sound (however defined) in the present; the emotion excited by that sound (frequently accompanied by some kind of physical response); and the subsequent invocation of both sound and emotion through a process of remembering. Music offers the quintessential remembering experience – hence its supersignificance for a novel focused so centrally upon the artistic task of rendering the past through the faculty of memory.

All these elements are invoked in *Swann's Way*, the first of the seven-volume series that was to become *In Search of Lost Time*. As a not entirely welcome guest at a Parisian soirée, the eponymous character listens to a piano recital. This picks up a narrative strand – involving music, memory and desire – that the author will still be teasing out hundreds of pages later. It seems that before the narrative proper begins, Swann has been deeply affected by 'a little phrase' from a piece of music, which he now learns is a sonata for piano and violin by an uncelebrated composer named Vinteuil, who had been introduced earlier in the volume. The narrator goes into great detail to explain the manner in which Swann first experienced the little phrase, the effect it had on him at the time, and the meaning it came to have for him subsequently when, unable to identify the composer or locate the score, he was obliged to rely on memory to keep it alive in his imagination. The phrase becomes particularly associated with Odette, the woman with whom Swann becomes obsessed – it is 'the national anthem of their love' (1957: 256).

When the nature of that relationship begins to change, however, so too does the meaning of the music. Thus, both music and memory have clear narrative import in terms of Swann's evolving consciousness. In ways that have persisted into the present, and which have migrated into alternative artistic traditions, music features as a key element within the thematic development of the narrative. More than that, however, the fate of the 'little phrase' is revealed to be intimately linked to – indeed, an emblematic form of – the problem of memory identified in the 'Overture' (9–59) to the series;[6] and this is where the influence of Proust's magnum opus is felt most profoundly.

The 'little phrase' reappears in a long sequence towards the end of the first volume, when Swann, now estranged from Odette, sees her at a salon concert (377ff). The music sparks memories in him which in turn elicit strong emotions: loss, sadness, bitterness, despair, and eventually sympathy – for the composer, for himself and Odette, and for the human race which is so exiled, it seems to him, from happiness. (Music in general, and the little phrase in particular, will create a similar pattern of memory and emotion in the narrator 'Marcel' in later volumes.) As the prose runs on, however, and as the meditations which the little phrase induce in him begin to accumulate, it seems that Swann is getting further away from, rather than closer to, defining its effect.

Proust is meticulous in his attempt to detail Swann's precise emotional response to every recurrence of the little phrase; and yet there is always something more, something that cannot be said: a tacit melancholy residing in the gap between the music itself and the meanings ascribed to it. This is precisely what music affords the modernist novelist: the ability to invoke states of consciousness that are beyond the ability of language to render. With Proust in mind, Alex Aronson writes:

> [A] sequence of sounds played or sung at a certain pitch or rhythm or a change from major to minor key are found to evoke a variety of associations and memories, frequently, though not always, related to sense impressions received in the past. It is this complex interrelationship between the musical experience and the mental process it

initiates that stimulates the novelist to investigate the twilight where the encounter between music and human consciousness takes place.

(1980: 21)

Proust was heir to a European aesthetic tradition that regarded music as seminal to both the understanding of human experience and to the latter's rendering in artistic form. His work established music as a key resource for the novelist in search of a means to dramatise the dynamics of consciousness and the evolutionary changes to which consciousness – as much as any other biological process – was subject. Therein lies his seminal significance for the development of the music-novel, as well as the source of his continuing influence on contemporary practices.

Music as Inspiration III – *The Concert Pianist* (2006) by Conrad Williams

This novel concerns Philip Morahan, a fifty-something professional musician who is undergoing a crisis that is preventing him for performing. The roots of the crisis lie in his own past: in the fact of his adoption, in the deaths in a house fire of a family to which he was particularly close, and in the knowledge that an old girlfriend aborted his baby soon after their relationship ended. The crisis is compounded by a diagnosis of cancer, which remains unresolved at the end of the text. Worst of all, music – the idea to which Morahan has dedicated his life; indeed, the practice through which he has vicariously lived his life – appears to have deserted him.

With his reputation already very well established, Morahan's agent has booked a series of London concerts designed to elevate him to classical superstar status. On the night of the first performance, however, a combination of nerves, self-doubt and illness renders him unable to play. The central part of the narrative follows the pianist as he searches for resources of hope amidst the ruins of his life. Hope appears to arrive in the shape of Ursula, a beautiful woman half Morahan's age who works for his agent and who 'rescues' the ailing musician by virtue of her unstinted admiration for his musicianship, some astute advice about his career, and, eventually, sex. The narrative ends with Morahan's successful performance at one of the original London concerts, the culmination of which is his interpretation of Chopin's Piano Sonata no.3 in B minor, op.58.

The Concert Pianist incorporates a good deal of specialist knowledge about classical music. There are references to a great many composers, musicians, venues and other aspects of the field; the qualities of different musical styles and periods are broached, and the life of the modern professional pianist is described in some detail. The encoded reader is one who 'gets' these references – who understands what Chopin, for example, 'means' in terms of the history of piano composition, and who is familiar with the names and careers of the virtuosos whose careers Morahan is emulating. Above all, the reader must appreciate music's function as both a conduit and a vehicle for the expression of intense emotions. In a long passage towards the beginning of the book, Morahan describes the musician's worth in terms of a relationship between technical prowess and what he describes as 'emotional intelligence':

> Technique's not enough, of course . . . The repertoire engages an incredible range of experience: mystical, romantic, erotic, poetic, religious, what you need to discover emotionally and then convey, and that's a harder challenge because our modern lives are so comfortable and godless and insulated . . . It's only through a student's sentimental education that he makes the link between his inner life and the psychological truth of music – the truth of the way music structures emotion – which is why you never stop suddenly grasping what a familiar piece really means. Without emotional intelligence the biggest technician is just a bore. (29)

This is a version of a familiar story, gleaned from two centuries of intense philosophical speculation and transposed by degrees into a range of music-related discourses. The theorist, the critic, the composer, the musician, the audience, the novelist and the reader, all 'understand' that music comprehends a dialectical relationship between form (which must be realised through technical expertise) and content (which offers the subject an emotional range in terms of which they may – or may not – express themselves). This is the context in which Morahan experiences his breakdown, and it likewise dictates the semiotic realm in which he must search for both artistic and existential redemption.

The problem is that Morahan has been immersed in music, both aesthetically and practically, for so long that he has lost the ability to inhabit the reality that music supposedly 'expresses'. So when reality suddenly forces its way into his life, the musician finds himself hopelessly ill-equipped to cope. 'Life' in this instance takes the paradoxical form of 'death': of Morahan's friend Peter and his family; of his unborn child; of himself. As someone who has 'let music dictate [his] life' (9), who has embraced the life of the professional pianist with the obsessive dedication that it requires, Morahan now finds that music has deprived him of the resources to cope with death's inevitability. He faces the final period of his life without parents, siblings, partner or children. Grief, guilt and resentment battle within him at the loss of the people through whom he had achieved some vicarious measure of family life. And as his own life descends into turmoil, he finds the earlier pronouncements regarding the musician's 'sentimental education' have begun to ring hollow. Music may be about life and death, and about the emotions experienced as a result of these prospects; but what he now suspects is that the pursuit of these virtual experiences has denied him an authentic emotional life of his own.

Having initially turned away from music as being in some senses the cause of his breakdown, Morahan finds that he must return to it to find redemption. First, however, he needs to come to terms with the 'baggage' that he has been unknowingly accumulating and which has had such a disruptive impact upon his life. A visit to the site of the fire allows him to begin the process of grieving which he had initially avoided. A showdown with an ex-partner obliges him to acknowledge the cost of his dedication to music, and the perspective gained informs his developing relationship with Ursula. As for the shadow that lies over his lungs, since it cannot be avoided it must be confronted: that is the mature, the responsible, the only thing to do, and with Ursula's support it is what the afflicted musician intends to do. Finally back in touch with his own existence, Morahan is now ready to return to music to discover – possibly for the last time – what it can offer him and what he can offer it.

The book ends with an extended description of his performance of three well-known pieces from the classical piano repertoire: a prelude by Rachmaninov, an impromptu by Schubert, and the Chopin sonata. At the concert, Morahan plays the Rachmaninov and the Schubert competently but without the indefinable element that (he believes) can turn an excellent performance into something more than either the composer or the musician is alone capable of. But it is precisely such a transcendent moment that occurs during the Chopin. This great Romantic figure develops in significance over the course of the narrative. Not only was he a pioneer in the fields of piano composition and performance: Chopin's career encapsulates the life of the professional pianist who, through constant travel, practice and performance, must sacrifice 'normality' in the pursuit of musical transcendence. The intimations of mortality that suffuse his later work render Chopin especially significant for a contemporary pianist under sentence of an early death through ill health. Together, they realise a musical 'event' – which is to say, an empathetic conjunction of score and performance – that produces a 'victory' of some kind:

> throttling back for the final climb, the right hand travelling chromatically up, the left hand beating out that ominous figure for the last time, and then a spilling-over of glitter and sparkle; the final chords ratcheting, bass octaves thundering, straining to the ultimate cadence, deep B, summation, the last crash of octaves dispatched, skewered to victory, instrument ringing. Arms back. Wild release. Victory. (244)

The language, syntax and punctuation of this extended final section are organised in such a way as to attempt to reproduce the actual sound of the music in terms of its precipitous rush towards closure and release. The 'victory' of the performance (Morahan's triumph over the demons that have haunted him) is at the same time a 'victory' for the text – which is to say: the triumph of language over music, as the author deploys the resources of the former to encapsulate the emotion embodied in the latter. Whether such a victory is in fact available, however, remains far from clear.

Conrad Williams's novel is inspired by a vision of music which (as Stephen Benson remarks of a similar effort, Vikram Seth's *An Equal Music* [1999]) 'is predicated on value: the value of particular works and, by implication, the value of particular ways of experiencing and thinking about them' (2006: 117). In so far as this is the case, *The Concert Pianist* is locatable within a genealogy of music-fiction that features Marcel Proust as one of its most potent and most influential progenitors. In this tradition, music represents a privileged means for the subject to come to a sense of itself – a way of being in the world which language alone can never realise. The paradox whereby this insight is articulated in terms of a literary discourse represents the principal recurring attraction of the music-novel.

Speculation regarding the derivation and function of music has thoroughly permeated western thought since the Enlightenment, influencing ideas about fundamental human issues such as language, emotion and consciousness. Because this kind of speculation is such an established method within intellectual practice, it follows that imaginative writers concerned to engage with these fundamental human experiences stand a good chance of confronting the idea of music at some point. Music is, in fact, part of the aesthetic atmosphere breathed by the novelist, 'inspiring' them at times in ways they may not even recognise.

Music as Metaphor I – Theories

With music so central to a range of humanistic and social-scientific disciplines, it was inevitable that it would feature at the thematic level in various artistic media, even those that were primarily non-musical in orientation. Because they were born of the same philosophical matrix – the one that focuses on the relationship between language, experience and consciousness – literary discourse has proved especially receptive to music, incorporating it (as Grim puts it) 'as the subject matter, point of departure, or intertextual reference within the work of literature' (1999: 238). This might seem a natural adaptation in relation to poetic discourse: after all, poetry and music shared a common concern with rhythm, and they had been locked together through the practice of singing from an early point in the evolution of the species. However, it was in relation to the relatively new genre of the novel that music as metaphorical presence was to make its strongest and most enduring impact.

The modern Anglophone novel emerged during the same period as the great musicological debates of the eighteenth century, and was both formed and inspired by those same debates. This is not to say that the likes of Daniel Defoe, Henry Fielding and Samuel Richardson were self-consciously concerned in the first instance with matters such as the derivation of language or the dynamics of consciousness. They were, however, concerned both with the clear changes that were overtaking the world in which they lived, and with finding appropriate forms and languages for the representation of those changes. Such concerns led the novelists back towards the territory being mapped by contemporary philosophers and quasi-anthropologists, who were themselves so exercised by the subject of music. The contention thus is that both the fiction and the music-driven philosophy of the eighteenth century addressed themselves to the same set of issues (albeit approaching it from different angles) – which, at its simplest, connoted the human subject in relation to society, in relation to nature and in relation to God.

Chapter 2 of this study is focused in large part on the incorporation of music as a metaphorical presence within a representative range of novels from the mid-eighteenth century to the present day. By way of preparation for that survey (and developing some of the points introduced in the first section of the present chapter), I now wish to introduce three high-profile interventions – one each from a philosopher (Arthur Schopenhauer), a poet (Stéphane Mallarmé) and a novelist (Thomas Mann) – which exemplify some of the pressing issues raised by the incorporation of music as metaphor into narrative fiction.[7]

Schopenhauer is generally regarded as a pessimistic philosopher. He perceived the phenomenal world (both animate and non-animate) to be ordered according to a universal, ubiquitous will, which itself realised a ceaseless conflict between the competing energies of existence (desire) and non-existence (fulfilment – leading to absence – of desire). Besides presiding over the historical evolution of the species as a whole, this will manifests itself in the individual human subject, placing us constantly in conflict with ourselves and with each other. For Schopenhauer, the history of civilisation is one of evasion, of an inability (or an outright refusal) to face the truth – and what is that truth?

> [Much] and long suffering, constant struggle, *bellum omnium*, everything a hunter and everything hunted, pressure, want, need and anxiety, shrieking and howling; and this goes on *in saecula saeculorum* or until once again the crust of the planet breaks.
>
> (1969: II, 354)

In this view, pleasure can never be a positive force; it is, rather, merely a temporary absence of the pain brought about by internal and external contention; and this – pain and contention – is the essential principle of life itself.

Only aesthetic experience can provide us with a momentary respite from the otherwise remorseless will. For Schopenhauer, as Terry Eagleton explains, '[the] aesthetic is a temporary escape from [the] prison-house of subjectivity, in which all desire drops away from us and we are able, for a change, to see the phenomenon as it really is' (1990: 162–3). Schopenhauer regarded music as the pre-eminent form of aesthetic experience (an idea he inherited from the immediately preceding generation of German philosophers) and referred to it as 'the most powerful of all the arts' (1891: 232), constituting the purest form of that temporary respite.[8] Because it is not mortgaged to reason; because its primary function is to be rather than to represent; because it expresses nothing but its own structure; because it encourages us to step outside ourselves so as to observe the will rather than unconsciously to embody it – because of all these reasons, music offers us help for pain, albeit help that is haunted by its own imminent loss. Experiencing music can temporarily transcend the will, at that moment when the exhausting play of life (characterised by Schopenhauer as an unending narrative of desire, temporary gratification and inevitable frustration) is temporarily halted, and contemplation of the musical work's achieved order enables the subject to escape the fate into which they are otherwise permanently locked.

At the same time, music (as least western tonal music) actually mirrors the will in its fundamental dynamics: there is an 'analogue' (1891: I, 232) between its structure and the structure of life itself. The use of keynotes, modulation and other tonal and harmonic conventions is exactly analogous to the narrative of desire, gratification and frustration in which the subject is caught up – 'not an image of phenomena', Schopenhauer writes, 'but directly the *will itself*' (1891: I, 232, original emphasis). In this sense, music 'gives us nothing but the pure activity of the will' (Peckham 1962: 149) – when we hear it, we perceive the will at work. Music is thus both the paradoxical means whereby the will is simultaneously confirmed and abrogated: on the one hand, 'the effect of music is so very much more powerful and penetrating than is that of the other arts, for these others speak only of the shadow, but music of the essence' (Schopenhauer 1969: I, 257); on the other hand, aesthetic contemplation of music affords the subject temporary relief from the otherwise endless, ubiquitous presence of desire.

Music is a privileged category for Schopenhauer, then, as are the various social roles associated with it, including most importantly those of composer and musician. This is of a piece with (indeed, one of the principal sources for) the general prominence of music-related roles and practices throughout the aesthetic imagination of the nineteenth century. This in turn impacted upon the practice of fiction, in which the idea of music's supposedly heightened emotionalism was widely engaged for a range of narrative purposes. Schopenhauer, in other words, made a significant contribution to the process whereby music was rendered available for widespread metaphorical adaptation.

Schopenhauer was enormously influential in the latter part of the nineteenth century, in the fields of philosophy and aesthetics. His writings – and in particular the imagination of power he developed – impacted powerfully upon the work of Friedrich Nietzsche, for example, through the wide dissemination and adaptation of whose own philosophy Schopenhauer's ideas retain relevance into the present day (even if his influence is often neither realised nor acknowledged). Schopenhauer was also a major inspiration on the life and work of Richard Wagner, who may himself be regarded as the single most significant presence in late nineteenth-century art. We shall encounter Wagner's influence on contemporary Anglophone fiction in the final part of this chapter, and then again in some detail in Chapter 2. Here it is enough to note two things: first of all, the implicit presence of Schopenhauer's thought within the pre-eminent artistic system of the period; and secondly, his role in the elevation of music to a paramount position within the contemporary aesthetic imagination. Both of these have important ramifications for a consideration of the music-novel.

Another influential nineteenth-century figure who felt – who indeed envied to the point of resentment – the power of music was the French poet and man-of-letters Stéphane Mallarmé. Indeed, literary 'resentment' might not have been an unexpected response to over a century of marginalisation in the face of music's aesthetic domination: Mallarmé was only the most radical of those writers whose admiration for music was tinged with jealousy at its reputation – a 'sublime jealousy', as his fellow-*Symboliste* Paul Valéry wrote[9] – and who were openly covetous of its function. As Mary M. Breatnach puts it: 'Mallarmé was not interested in music for its own sake, and he listened to it, not with the ears of a music-lover, but with the heightened perceptions of a predator' (1999: 266).

Mallarmé was a prominent figure within the Symbolist movement of the late nineteenth century. Complex in provenance and identity though it was, Symbolism connoted a series of recognisable beliefs and prejudices, many of which come into focus in terms of ongoing debates regarding music and its relationship with language. One such prejudice concerned what contemporary poets regarded as the tragic fall of language in the modern world and its compromised status as a medium for poetic expression. Dahlhaus talks about the Symbolists' 'disgust with language that is threadbare and "besmirched" because everybody uses it every day' (1991: 148). Related to this was a conviction that form in art was everything; form, that is to say, was not just the passive vessel in which meaning was transported from the artist to the consumer; it was, rather, the place where truth – so far as it could be apprehended at all by the human mind – resided.

Mallarmé's ambivalent attitude towards music emerged as a result of his dedication to language, on the one hand, and his suspicion, on the other, that language's referential function (its status as a tool enabling us to negotiate day-to-day life) would always prevent the poet accessing a truth that was available only at a non-linguistic level. This, we recognise, was precisely the level at which non-programme music was believed to function. We are back, in other words, to the notion of 'absolute music', of music as a release from expression – at the very least, music as an indefinite response to life. One of the principal aims of Symbolism, as Edmund Wilson astutely put it, was 'to approximate the indefiniteness of music' (1961: 13). As mentioned in the previous section, however, such a notion had itself always attracted accusations of redundancy: specifically, the charge that in distancing itself from the language of the world, music could express nothing about the world. Besides, absolute music was always much more of an ideal than a reality. Romantic music was highly expressive: from the programmatic symphonies of Beethoven and Berlioz to the lieder of Schubert and Schumann and on, seemingly finally, to the 'total artwork' of Wagnerian opera, nineteenth-century art music was far from being the 'absolute' ideal of pure, expressionless form.

As a poet anxious about the condition of his medium, Mallarmé's problem was twofold. Firstly, there was the widely held, still influential notion of language's debasement in the face of music, and the latter's boast (or at least the boast made on its behalf) of being able to access truth in a way that the former never could. Faced with this assault upon the artistic medium to which he was dedicated, it is little wonder that the poet felt ambivalent towards the power of music; for even as it offered him an example of a consummate art form to which he could aspire, music – certainly the ideas surrounding the role and function of music in human society – seemed determined to prevent him from emulating that example.

Secondly, there was Wagner's recruitment of poetry for musical purposes, and his manipulation of music, language and gesture to produce emotional effects that language alone (so it was claimed) could not approach. In some senses, Wagnerian music drama represented the end of art: precisely because it was (or aspired to be) 'total', it left nothing to say, no space for mystery or intuition or creative misreading. Thus it was implicated (despite its seemingly impeccable Romantic credentials) in an ongoing Enlightenment project to 'dominate' nature by means of the rational manipulation of knowledge, power and representation; moreover, Wagnerian opera was culpable in the eyes of a poet such as Mallarmé, who was drawn away from the notion of 'totality' by both temperament and aesthetic conviction (Bucknell 2001: 31). At the same time, Mallarmé's dream of a poetry that blended musical and linguistic effects itself represented a kind of 'total' art in which all the binaries informing contemporary aesthetic debate – emotion and thought, music and language, inside and outside, sound and meaning, etc. – would achieve consummate balance. The key difference seems to be this: whereas Wagner's notion of 'total' art evolved as part of a search for truth that could be known, the ideal for Mallarmé appeared to be an art that embodied a truth that could be maintained as an ideal but which could not be known.

Mallarmé's complex, ongoing negotiation of all these issues (as described at length in Breatnach,1999, and Bucknell, 2001: 16–36, for example) need not detain us here. In very broad terms it may be seen that Symbolism *a la* Mallarmé represented the search for some kind of accommodation between music's formal properties and language's ineluctable will-to-reference; and that underpinning this search lay a suspicion (Schopenhauerian in derivation) that silence was in fact the ultimate truth that the human mind could know. This quest released powerful energies within European culture: energies that eventually fed into the structure of feeling known as Modernism. The Byzantine story of Symbolist poetry's relations with art music on the one hand, and literary fiction on the other, is likewise beyond our remit, although we shall touch on aspects of it in the next chapter.[10]

In some senses, Mallarmé's attitude could be regarded as typical French recalcitrance in the face of a century and more of German aesthetic polemic. Although there is certainly an element of nationalistic tradition informing these intense end-of-century debates, such a claim over-simplifies matters, for as Dahlhaus has shown (1991: 141–55), nineteenth-century German art was itself riven by passionate, often vitriolic, exchanges regarding the troubled relationship between literature and music – exchanges that anticipated and informed Mallarmé's own anxieties. What may be reasonably claimed is that his work represents an important stage in the literature/music nexus, and that because of the capital significance he afforded it, music came to assume a key role within the imagination of a number of writers who are now acknowledged as among the greatest and most influential of the modern era.

Music as Metaphor II – *Tonio Kröger* (1903) by Thomas Mann

Of all the many modern writers who incorporated music into their work, Thomas Mann was (with the possible exception of Anthony Burgess) the most committed. Enamoured of music in general (and of Wagner in particular) from an early age, widely read in modern philosophy (Schopenhauer and Nietzsche in particular), friend to composers, musicians and musicologists throughout his long life, Mann was clearly well-disposed towards the deployment of musical effects and themes in his writing. *Tonio Kröger* (1903), a novella published early in his career, established themes and issues that he was to continue to address in all his future work.

It was in *Tonio Kröger*, Mann claimed, that he 'first learned to employ music as a shaping influence in my art' (quoted in Brown 1948: 212). This 'shaping influence' refers in particular to two aspects of Mann's technique that we shall encounter in detail in the final section of this chapter ('Music and Form'), and which will feature throughout Part II of this study: the adaptation of sonata form and Wagnerian leitmotif for literary purposes. As part of his pioneering study of music and literature, Calvin S. Brown convincingly demonstrated how Mann utilised these techniques in *Tonio Kröger*.[11] Highly suggestive as these dimensions are, however, they should not lead us to overlook the thematic (or metaphoric) function of music within the narrative; for the fact is that music possesses an important narrative function in the text, regardless of its impact upon technique.

Mann's *Künstlerroman* focuses on key moments in the artistic evolution of the eponymous hero. This evolution is represented in terms of the relationship between an artistic sensibility, which needs to be free of bourgeois restrictions, and a bourgeois sensibility, which in some respects is inimical to true art, although it nevertheless provides the human materials (emotions, characters, situations) from which true art is made.

The mature Tonio of the latter part of the novel suspects that dedication to art (in his case, literature) has functioned to deny him access to life and love – the essential human experiences from which art itself springs (in which condition he anticipates Philip Morahan in Conrad Williams's *The Concert Pianist*, examined above). Tonio believes that he experienced life and love when, as a boy, he gave his heart in turn to a school-friend named Hans Hansen (as described in the opening chapter of the book) and a sometime dancing partner named Ingeborg Holm (introduced in the second chapter). Music plays a subtle yet crucial role in each of these relationships. Tonio experiences his love for Hans as part of a general response to life, a response which although intellectual in inspiration is in fact musical in expression:

[He] wandered round his own room with his violin (for he played the violin) and drew from it notes of such tenderness as only he could draw, notes which he mingled with the rippling sounds of the fountain down in the garden as it leapt and danced under the branches of the old walnut tree. (139)

Two years later, he knows that despite the pain his love for Inge will cause him, 'it would enrich him and make him more fully alive' (147). At dancing class, Tonio makes a mistake while performing a quadrille, drawing the sarcasm of his teacher and the amusement of his fellow students, including Inge. The music is unsympathetic and uninspired, played on the piano with 'a dry professional air' by the 'bony hands' of Herr Heinzelmann; such music is, nevertheless, fully implicated in the life-force that the younger Tonio (of the first chapter) had already recognised. This opening section of the text shows how the banality of the music he hears is offset by the intensity of the emotion he feels; in the following chapters (three to seven), the reader learns how Tonio's chosen career leads him to disdain banality of technique, but at the cost of emotional intensity.

Now a successful writer, Tonio nevertheless feels jaded and empty. His pursuit of artistic truth has brought him to a life of indulgence, one at odds with the bourgeois values of his youth: 'The life he lived was exhausting, tormented by remorse, extravagant, dissipated and monstrous, and one which Tonio Kröger himself in his heart of hearts abhorred' (154). He leaves Munich and travels to the northern landscape he identifies with Hans and Inge. It is once again in and through music that he comes to acknowledge the life-affirming values that they represent. Somehow over the years, his own art of writing has become associated with the functional materialism of his father, while 'his dark, fiery mother, who played the piano and the mandolin so enchantingly' (140) represents a positive attitude towards everyday life that has been squandered due to Tonio's absolute identification with *la vie artistique*. It is fitting that his former home has now become a library, full of books about, but at the same time removed from, life.

Tonio escapes to a small seaside hotel in an attempt either to avoid or to confront (the narrative is not forthcoming as to which) his artistic crisis. There he encounters two people who remind him of his adolescent loves. From a dark veranda he watches 'Inge' and 'Hans' dance and socialise in the brightly lit room from which he feels excluded. Again, the quality of the music is suspect: 'the musicians were doing their best. There was even a trumpeter among them, blowing on his instrument rather diffidently and cautiously – it seemed to be afraid of its own voice, which despite all efforts kept breaking and tripping over itself' (188).

Despite its poor quality, Tonio feels himself 'irresistibly drawn towards the foolish, happily lilting music' (187). In this context, music provides an occasion for flirting, for imagination, for the confirmation of the individual's role in relation to the community and the community's reciprocal provision of a space wherein the individual can 'be'. The music, that is to say, both enables and represents life and love – precisely those experiences from which Tonio has come to feel cut off. It is this music that returns to haunt Tonio in the darkness of his room later that night:

> He remembered the dissolute adventures in which his senses, his nervous system and his mind had indulged; he saw himself corroded by irony and intellect, laid waste and paralysed by insight, almost exhausted by the fevers and chills of creation, helplessly and contritely tossed to and fro between gross extremes, between saintly austerity and lust – oversophisticated and impoverished, worn out by cold, rare, artificial ecstasies, lost, ravaged, racked and sick – and he sobbed with remorse and nostalgia.
>
> Round about him there was silence and darkness. But lilting up to him from below came the faint music, the sweet trivial waltz rhythm of life. (193)

In many respects, Tonio Kröger is a prototype for the composer Adrian Leverkühn, the central character of Mann's *Doctor Faustus* (1947). The feelings of dissolution, corrosion, paralysis and exhaustion felt by the Kröger as he listens to 'the sweet trivial waltz rhythm of life' drifting up from below anticipate the feelings experienced by Faustus as he drifts towards disease and death. Whereas the narrator (in the 'coda' that closes *Doctor Faustus*) finds resources of hope that enable him to move forward, it is clear that Leverkühn is doomed and damned. The latter's fate functions as much more than an allegory of syphilis, however. It is also the story of a country decadently regressing towards barbarism, and how music is implicated in the process. For if Mann's democratic sympathies were at odds with Nazi Germany, this was an analogue of his humanistic antipathy towards serialism, the compositional technique 'invented' by Leverkühn.[12] As syphilis corrupts the body, so fascism corrupts the political – and serialism the musical – imagination. Which is to say: in *Doctor Faustus*, music becomes both the semiotic symbol of, and the hermeneutic key to, history itself.

In as much as any novel is about music – incorporating music as a thematic or formal element within its discourse – it is always intertextually linked with the work of writers such as Proust and Mann – novelists for whom music was of such central importance. We can demonstrate this by looking at a contemporary text in which music possesses thematic, formal and metaphoric significance.

Music as Metaphor III – *Art & Lies: A Piece for Three Voices and a Bawd* (1995) by Jeanette Winterson

Like *Tonio Kröger*, Winterson's book reflects self-consciously upon the role and function of art in relation to society and to individual identity. The title reference to 'three voices' immediately establishes the polyphonic nature of this text – the fact that the writing is comprised of different (though probably interlinked) voices articulating different (also probably interlinked) responses to the material introduced in the text. At the same time, a number of paratextual signals – the use of an ampersand in the main title (instead of a 'proper' word) and the introduction of a subtitle (an unusual. although not unknown, convention in novelistic discourse), as well as the metafictional description of the text as a 'piece' (a long-established synonym for a musical work of indeterminate form) – alerts us to the uncertain nature of this particular 'literary' text: although it *looks* like a novel, and we may recognise the author as a familiar name from literary circles, the material contained therein might not necessarily conform to the form of the conventional novel. And so it proves to be.

Art & Lies is organised into sections entitled 'Handel', 'Picasso' and 'Sappho' – names that appear to refer to 'characters' featuring within several overlapping narratives. These are also, of course, the names of three famous artists in the fields of music, painting and poetry respectively, although those historical figures appear to exist not as 'real' textual presences but as remote references or influences suggested by the names. These three also provide the 'three voices' of the subtitle, brought together in dramatic 'conversation' near the end of the text. The idea of three connected, overlapping voices is then recapitulated by the inclusion of nine pages from the score of Richard Strauss's opera *Der Rosenkavalier* (1911), detailing the orchestral and vocal parts for a passage in which three of the principal characters from the opera (Sophie, her lover Octavian, and *his* lover, the Marschallin) sing with each other.

It would be difficult to say with any great certainty what *Art & Lies* is 'about' at the level of plot, although the novel does give the reader plenty of scope for speculation. Each of the 'characters' experiences a crisis – of faith, of sexuality, of love – which in each case is resolved (and the characters thereby redeemed) by art. Such crises occur in the first place, the text suggests, because of the human inability to be 'at home' either in time or in language; at one point the 'presence' called Handel asks: 'Can I speak my mind or am I dumb inside a borrowed language, captive of bastard thoughts? What of me is mine?' (22–3). More than two centuries of speculation and scepticism regarding the ability of language to represent the world (or the subject in the world) has made the asking of such questions possible; but does this particular text have room for any of the potential answers that have been offered during that time?

Art & Lies works to show that identity crisis is in fact the 'natural' human condition, the message being that we are all permanently displaced in time and in language. But there is hope: 'Two things significantly distinguish human beings from the other animals; an interest in the past and the possibility of language. Brought together they make a third: Art' (137). Contemplation of the remorseless vacuity at the heart of human experience leads Winterson to assert the Proustian notion that '[art] defeats time' (67) – which is to say, that both the creation and the contemplation of the work of art offers us, if not outright redemption, then at least the possibility of temporary respite from the sin of knowledge into which we have fallen. The characters of Handel, Picasso and Sappho, suffused as they are with the influence of their artistic inspirations, move through their narrative crises towards this possibility. At one point the three are united in an image celebrating the effusive joy of light, sound and language conjoined:

> In its effect the light was choral. Harmonies of power simultaneously achieved, a depth of light, not one note but many, notes of light sung together. In its high register, far above the ears of man, the music of the spheres, vibrating light noted in its own frequency. Light seen and heard. Light that writes on tablets of stone. Light that glories what it touches. Solemn self-delighting light. (26)

If 'lies' represent the fallen condition that is our human inheritance, 'art' represents the immemorial search for integration, for the re-harmonisation of experience, language and meaning. The 'Handel' of *Art & Lies* does not explicitly invoke, or even refer to, the eighteenth-century German composer whose work feature in the canon of western art music; that historical figure's presence is felt, however, as a representative of the idea of music and its role as one element of an artistic triumvirate (with painting and poetry) whose role it is to maintain the possibility of transcendence active within the human imagination.

This is an idea we recognise to be descended, via many adaptations and modifications, from eighteenth-century philosophical speculation regarding the derivation and the role of music. It is not necessary for the author to make explicit reference to this discourse; suffice to say that music (as well as musicological speculation) has 'inspired' the ideas underpinning the text in a number of ways, most significantly in the representation of the characters as contrapuntal 'voices' and the reiteration of this effect in the score extract from Strauss that closes the text.

This last element presents a serious formal problem, however, one that might be regarded as working against the salvific idea of art developed at a conceptual level throughout *Art & Lies*. This problem arises from the fact that, as Benson puts it, 'the prevalence of score extracts in the texts of music analysis is a sign not only of a particular critical approach, but also of a particular conception of music itself' (2006: 109). That 'particular conception of music' is founded on a conventional model in which various activities – composition, performance, listening and interpreting, for example – are locked into specific relationships of power, with the score itself acting as the final arbiter with regard to the 'meaning' of the music. This does not preclude the possibility of deconstructive uses of score extracts in texts that are not themselves primarily musical in orientation or intention. In Winterson's case, however, the nine-page musical paratext from Strauss appears to be at odds with the experimental 'writerly' discourse contained in the main body of the text; this is because it possesses, in its unmediated form, a conventional 'realist' aura that militates against the idea of art's ability to induce within the listener a transcendent experience.

The score fragment from *Der Rosenkavalier* is expected to 'speak for itself' in ways that are unavailable in verbal language; what it actually 'says' (or tries to say) is that meaning resides within the written score, and this 'meaning' is impervious to considerations arising from contextual discourses of performance, consumption or interpretation.[13] Authority, which has been thoroughly interrogated at the level of 'story', is thus quietly reinstated at the level of form. But, written music does not – has never, never will – 'speak for itself'. The conversion of sound into meaning always necessitates a negotiation with verbal language; by attempting to obviate this process (by providing the 'real' meaning as contained in the score), Winterson undoes the ideological work undertaken in the 'narrative' proper – as Benson says: 'Rather than corroborate and exemplify the novel's aesthetic, the score fragment works in precisely the opposite direction. Its resolute silence and textuality withhold music from the reader, drawing attention to the necessary dependencies of art' (117).

Novelists have incorporated music into their texts for all sorts of reasons since the inception of the modern form in the eighteenth century, and will no doubt continue to do so as long as the novel survives. One of the key things that music appears to offer the novelist, however, is an opportunity to reflect upon their own medium: language. At various stages in the history of the novel, music has functioned as a metaphor by means of which the writer dramatises the ability of language to represent human experience. Much of the time, music itself represents, stands for, the ineffable that subsists outwith language – or at least outwith the human ability to articulate, if not to imagine. In this section we have considered some of the philosophical and aesthetic sources of this idea. At this stage, it is time to turn to matters of form: musical form and literary form and the relationship between them.

Music and Form I – Theories

Suppose that you are a novelist inspired by music and that you wish to incorporate music into your writing: how are you going to do it? One response, both obvious and valid, might be to introduce it at the thematic level – that is to say, by making it an element of greater or lesser narrative significance within the plot. But such a response raises another question: might not what you say about music have implications for how you say it? In other words, is it possible that fiction about music always has a tendency towards musicalised fiction – that is, a kind of writing that attempts to recreate some aspect of the musical material that has been invoked at a thematic level?

These questions arise in the context of a consideration of how a novelist's concern with music as inspiration or metaphor impacts upon the formal structure of the text – how, to continue with Grim's tripartite characterisation, 'the work of literature utilizes or attempts to imitate musical forms and/or compositional procedures within a literary context' (1999: 238). All art embodies a negotiation between what it represents and how it represents it; but this is complicated in the case of the music-novel because music has traditionally been regarded as the art wherein form and matter, theme and expression, are most thoroughly enmeshed. It was, as we have seen, precisely the inseparability of form and content that caused music to be elevated to a position of dominance among the arts.

Pater's argument is worth quoting at length:

> It is the art of music which most completely realises this artistic ideal, this perfect identification of matter and form. In its consummate moments, the end is not distinct from the means, the form from the matter, the subject from the expression; they inhere in and completely saturate each other; and to it, therefore, to the condition of its perfect moments, all the arts may be supposed constantly to tend and aspire . . . Therefore, although each art has its incommunicable element, its untranslatable order of impressions, its unique mode of reaching the 'imaginative reason', yet the arts may be represented as continually struggling after the law or principle of music, to a condition which music alone completely realises. (138–9)

According to this theory, any novel approaches 'the law or principle of music' in so far as it attempts to 'obliterate' the division between form and content. The novel about music functions as a special case, however, in so far as its subject matter (music) is precisely the practice wherein the form/matter division is widely perceived to be always already collapsed. What this means is that every such text realises a tension between different (possibly opposing) levels of musical influence: one general, emerging from what may be regarded as an historical tendency among all the arts towards a specifically musical effect (the 'perfect identification of matter and form'); one specific, emerging from the textual event-in-progress, in which the music represented at the level of plot is revealed to have a bearing on the organisation of the narrative.

The situation with regard to the music-novel is complicated still further by the impact of yet another tier of significance: textual criticism. This raises the question: must the occurrence of musical effects and features in the novel always be the result of authorial intention, or may it appear without the intention or even the knowledge of the writer? For example, a novel might incorporate any number of formal techniques – rhythm, repetition, counterpoint, leitmotif, theme and variation, and so on – that could be identified as having a musical function. Is it legitimate, if the author was not aware of or did not intend those functions, to interpret the text with reference to musical discourse? To what extent is the presence of music in the novel a matter of critical ascription, as opposed to authorial inscription? Anyone could 'discover' musical effects or influences in a novel. For example, it may seem bizarre, or just plain wrong (it is certainly anachronistic), to describe *Finnegans Wake* as a 'punk' novel, but it seems clear that in some respects Joyce's text does offer itself up for such an interpretation. It seems equally clear, however, that such a characterisation would raise more questions – regarding value, legitimacy, method, and so on – than it could ever answer.[14]

The question of form in the music-novel is extraordinarily complex, because there are a number of different forces operating constantly (although not necessarily equally) upon the text: the forces of history, of narrative and of criticism. Moreover, the apprehension of form introduces a self-reflexive element into any critical discourse that takes as its object the music-novel, because every individual project will be obliged to incorporate, with a greater or lesser degree of self-consciousness, a theory of how musical content might be related to literary form. Likewise, every such project will be obliged to acknowledge that to some extent the critical separation of form from content is, at best, conventional, if not illusory – and (worst of all) possibly contrary to the spirit of the literary text under analysis. In the case of the present study, it has been a struggle thus far to write about the role of music in fiction without invoking the matter of form; strictly speaking, it should be an impossible task. To discuss music as inspiration for the novel with reference to Dahlhaus, Bakhtin and Proust; to discuss music as metaphor within the novel with reference to Schopenahuer, Mallarmé and Mann: such critical strategies only truly come into focus when it is perceived that both inspiration and metaphor – issues, that is to say, that apparently feature at the thematic level – are in fact thoroughly enmeshed with questions of form.

So, to return to the question with which this section opened: in what ways may music feature at a formal level in novelistic discourse? There is in theory no end to the comparisons that could be made between the novel and the vast number of musical forms that have emerged during the modern era. In the sphere of popular music (which will feature widely in Part II of this study), for example, one could argue that every oeuvre, every album, indeed every individual song contains tendencies – in terms of the characters they feature, the narratives they relate and the ways in which they are narrated – that might be interpreted with reference to novelistic discourse. There is, however, one particular musical form that consolidated during the eighteenth century (during the same period, that is, as the emergence of the modern novel), and whose subsequent influence in the field of western art music has been so powerful that it demands attention for any comparative project: sonata form.[15]

'Reducing sonata form to its simplest terms,' writes Calvin S. Brown, 'we may summarily describe it as the statement of a first subject, a contrasting second subject, and a closing subject; the development of this thematic material; and finally its restatement' (1948: 163). Rather more technically, Grim describes sonata form as 'a three-part (or ternary) thematic plan with a two-part (or binary) harmonic outline' (1999: 238). The 'three-part (or ternary) thematic plan' refers to the structure of exposition, development and recapitulation that gives sonata form its characteristic ABA shape. Such a structure allows for the dramatisation of the 'two-part (or binary) harmonic outline' – what Brown describes as the first and contrasting second subjects. In fact, drama suffuses sonata form from beginning to end: in the declarative statement of the first subject; in the introduction of the second subject and the exploration of its harmonic relationship with its fellow; in the modulation from a 'home' or 'tonic' key to the dominant and back again; in the expansive vista of the development, in which ideas (some of them seemingly marginal or incidental) introduced earlier are now explored with energy and commitment; in the variation of rhythm and tempo between sections; and in the willed closure of the recapitulation, in which the various temporal, tonal, instrumental and melodic discourses are reconciled.

Sonata form developed in the context of certain trends that were impacting upon the class structure and the related leisure practices of eighteenth-century Europe. For those without formal musical training, it offered a means to engage with a valuable form of cultural capital. Knowledge of sonata form enabled listeners to 'imagine' the shape of the music and to locate themselves in relation to it.

As time went by, sonata form proved itself to be 'almost infinitely flexible' (Grim 1999: 238); a genius such as Mozart could manipulate the basic binary/ternary precepts in any number of ways so that what might be regarded as a crude structuring device became in his hands an immensely sophisticated prospect for those who performed it and a highly rewarding experience for those who listened to it.

At some point around about the beginning of the nineteenth century, and for reasons related to those described in earlier sections of this chapter, a change overtook sonata form – or at least, the perception of sonata form. The emphasis shifted and became less an aid to audience interpretation and more a vehicle for the composer to articulate a sophisticated personal response to life – or for the critic to infer such a response. This was possible because, despite the apparent simplicity of its structure, sonata form in fact embodies two fundamental elements or aspects of human experience. The first (relating to the binary element – that is, the relationship between primary and secondary themes) connotes the possibility of 'the subject' and its relationship with another subject designated 'other'. The second (relating to the ternary structure) connotes the possibility of 'home' and the journey that takes the subject away from, but ultimately back to, that home. Together these musical elements articulate the fundamental identity/difference binary that has played such a significant role in the evolution of human culture, while at the same time rehearsing some of the most primordial emotions (belonging, exclusion, fear, desire, etc.) of which the species is capable.

In other words, sonata form seems to tap into the deep mythic structures underpinning human history, structures that may be observed informing (or at least acting upon) both the evolution of culture itself as well as specific cultural practices.[16] This in turn leads us to a consideration of the relationship between sonata form and the novel.

Various critics have attempted to describe the ways in which sonata form may be understood to have influenced specific novels.[17] Whatever the success or failure of such critical manoeuvres, they are in some senses redundant in so far as the two discourses would appear to be already linked at a deep structural level. Consider for a moment the form of the modern novel, and in particular two of its defining characteristics: it is always subject-centred – which is to say, it always realises a relationship between 'identity' and 'otherness' in some or other form; and it always incorporates into its structure the spatial co-ordinates of 'home' and 'away' in some (literal, psychological, symbolic or other) form. Such characteristics account for many of the genre's distinguishing features, especially 'character' and 'narrative'. Indeed, these latter terms have proved crucial for the social and historical organisation of the novel as a form, influencing the evolution of subgenres (for example, the *bildungsroman* and the detective novel) within the field and feeding back into novelistic discourse through intermedial forms such as television and cinema.

From the present perspective, however, the main point to note is that the novel appears to have evolved from the same fundamental human concerns that characterise sonata form, regardless of the intentions of the writer or the subsequent ingenuity of the critic. The 'dualism' of sonata form functions as a counterpart to (in some accounts, as an effect of) 'the dualism inherent in human nature', and that is precisely what makes it 'so eminently suitable a model for the contemporary novelist' (Aronson 1980: 66). The character/narrative disposition of the one echoes the binary/ternary disposition of the other, with both seemingly emerging from primordial concerns with the function and the limits of human consciousness.

It was with the music of Beethoven, and in particular his symphonies and late string quartets, that the archetypal properties of sonata form began to impact upon both creative and critical practices.[18] The formal 'voice' of sonata form is transformed into the Beethovian romantic persona: a presence or discursive agency within the music who may or may not be identified with the composer himself but who over a period of time comes to function as the subject through and around whom the 'meaning' of the music may be organised.[19] At the same time, the temporal structure of sonata form, especially when adapted into the expansive form of the symphony, appeared to lend itself to various kinds of narrative interpretation. Even in the absence of a clear programme (a text or a title, or a statement by the composer, to let the listener know what the music is 'about') it was possible to infer meaning in the musical work by referring to certain archetypal narrative structures seemingly embedded in the form itself.[20] In other words, with the advent of Romanticism it is possible to discern a discursive landscape wherein music and the novel might begin to be mapped in relation to each other.

Now, such a model clearly runs contrary to the idea of 'absolute music' encountered earlier in this chapter – which is to say, music removed from anything so quotidian as 'character', or indeed anything so banal as 'story'. The stand-off between 'purists' and those for whom music always 'means' (or is made to mean, or should mean) continued throughout the nineteenth century, and in some ways it continues to dictate the terms of the debate as to the function of music.[21] If, as Grim maintains, '[all] dramatic situations in literature could be construed as sonata forms' (1999: 241), how useful is the analogy, either for the novelist or for the critic? Be that as it may, there was a musical form – opera – that grew in popularity during the Romantic era, that was specifically organised around the process of telling stories about characters, and which in the hands of its master theorist and practitioner, Wagner, became one of the dominant influences on European art (including the novel) during the late nineteenth and early twentieth centuries.

I shall have a good deal to say about opera generally, and Wagner specifically, in Chapters 2 and 5. Here, it is enough to note the survival, indeed the thriving, of opera in the face of both 'absolute' and non-textual 'programmatic' music. It seems that the bourgeois appetite for edifying art was always going to be matched by the bourgeois appetite for an engaging narrative. Although regarded by many as a somewhat vulgar medium, tainted by a penchant for the spectacular (both in visual and aural terms) and determined in the final instance by economic rather than artistic considerations, the opera nevertheless continued to grow in popularity during the first half of the nineteenth century. For some, opera was the embodiment of all those material distractions that diverted the musician from his divine purpose (Davies 1970: 17–39); for many more, however, it was both a living and an entertainment. Here, after all, was a practice in which music's referential capacities were not eschewed for the better apprehension of the 'absolute', not buried in the binary and ternary elements of the form, but clearly and creatively utilised for the purposes of storytelling.

It is with this latter faculty – the compulsion to narrative – that a clear parallel emerged between the novel and the opera. Considered in their most basic terms, they both tell stories about characters, and this allows for the emergence of a comparative imagination that would address itself to the two fields in terms of their commonalities, differences and interrelations.

In some respects, Wagnerian music drama represented an attempt to salvage a relationship between the different artistic tendencies of which it was born. The vision, ambition and scale of the work were monumental, while the narratives were archetypal in scope and vision. Wagner harnessed the power of music to tell stories that drew upon, and in turn contributed to, human history (or at least a Germanic variation on that history); in those terms, he was clearly concerned with the referential capacities of music and the ways in which it could be sympathetically deployed in relation to the opera's other signifying discourses (the libretto and the spectacle). At the same time, his conceptualisation of the leitmotif (a short musical phrase intended to represent a particular presence – whether character, object or idea – within the continuing action of the story) maintained links with the Romantic 'voice' (and with its post-Beethovian variants), which itself drew upon the archetypal propensities of sonata form. Wagner deployed the high seriousness of art music in the service of spectacle – in other words, creating a new art form out of ideas and elements that already existed within the European musical imagination.

Much of the highly specialised debate (both during his own lifetime – to which he contributed – and since his death) attending Wagner's work has concerned the relationship between his musical imagination and the wider impulses (artistic and political) that animated him. Those are debates with which this study cannot engage at any length (although see the section on A. N. Wilson's *Winnie and Wolf* in Chapter 5). What may be suggested with some degree of confidence is that, if philosophical discourse since the eighteenth century had established music as the art form *par excellence*, Wagner's consummate artistry confirmed and extended that dominance; and his influence – both in terms of what he wrote about, and how he wrote about it – proved extremely powerful on the subsequent history of European art, including the history of the novel.[22] Indeed, it might be claimed that if Schopenhauer is the musician's philosopher, then Wagner is the novelist's composer, providing an example in terms of vision and achievement with which many of the writers whom literary history has canonised as 'significant' felt themselves obliged to come to terms.

Wagner's example led to the development of the leitmotif as a technique within literary discourse, and as a consequence he is implicated in the general consideration of rhythm in the novel. The leitmotif was one of the characteristics of the 'Wagnerian novel' that emerged during the last decades of the nineteenth century; Calvin S. Brown defined it as:

> a verbal formula which is deliberately repeated, which is easily recognized at each recurrence, and which serves, by means of this recognition, to link the context in which the repetition occurs with earlier contexts in which the motive had appeared. Perhaps we should add that in both music and literature the Leitmotiv has to be comparatively short and must have a programmatic association – must refer to something beyond the tones or words which it contains.
>
> (1948: 211)

To qualify as a leitmotif, then, a 'verbal formula' must be repeated at least once, although in practice it tends to recur throughout the text. As with its musical source, moreover, the literary leitmotif accrues levels of resonance with each instantiation – which is to say, each repetition modifies the meaning of the leitmotif itself and its function in relation to the text as a whole. Each repetition also contributes to the text's rhythmical sense, which according to E. M. Forster operates in two ways. The first – which he calls 'easy rhythm' and defines as 'repetition plus variation' (1981: 148–9) – functions within the fabric of the text, as it were, and is created by the judicious recurrence of a 'verbal formula'. Although he does not use the term, Forster is clearly referring here to the leitmotif, which had functioned as a self-conscious element within European novelistic discourse since at least the 1880s. His example of 'easy rhythm' is Vinteuil's 'little phrase' from *À la recherche du temps perdu*, although he might have equally referred to the Mann's highly controlled manipulation of certain scenes, images and language in *Tonio Kröger*.

Forster also suggests, however, that fiction may in theory comprehend a 'difficult rhythm', which is discernible in music (at least in larger works of musical composition: Beethoven's Fifth Symphony is the example he mentions) and which may have a bearing upon both the creation and the understanding of the novel. The 'difficult rhythm' occurs at a more architectonic level; it is a function of 'the relation between . . . movements – which some people can hear but no one can tap to' (1981: 146). This 'difficult rhythm' is what strikes the listener when the symphony as a whole, rather than its constituent parts, is realised. What Forster appears to be referring to here is the deep structure that inheres within the musical work and which coalesces into a 'common entity' which the mind apprehends as the 'meaning' of the piece. Forster raises the possibility of achieving such a rhythm in the novel, although he produces no examples (apart from some very tentative speculations regarding Tolstoy's *War and Peace*) as to how it might actually be realised.

The question of rhythm must feature strongly in any theoretical consideration of the role and representation of music in the novel. Rhythm comprehends the related concept of repetition, which is itself fraught with philosophical and aesthetic difficulties. The very concept of repetition depends upon the concept of an original instance – 'original' in the sense of 'first', but also in the sense of 'new', something brought into the world by a creative agent. But where would such an 'original' come from, and how could it be identified? Can anything (an idea, sound, event or image) ever be repeated, or does every attempt at repetition create – perhaps unwillingly, perhaps only marginally – something new? If everything is always already a part of something else, is the possibility of originality (and hence of repetition) categorically obviated? Does rhythm really function at the 'easy' (which is to say, local textual) and 'difficult' (underlying structural) levels identified by Forster, and if so, what is the relation between these effects? What aesthetic or political ideologies have invested in different models of repetition, and what is the provenance – and indeed the wider implications – of such ideologies?[23]

While theoretical questions proliferate, we find in practice that musicians and novelists incorporate rhythm and repetition into their work in a great variety of ways. Repetition may be, as Grim claims, 'an essential element in the construction of a work of literature in the experience of the reader' (1999: 242); we may need repetition to orient ourselves in relation to the narrative, and it does indeed appear to offer an author a means of creating or implying levels of meaning beyond the level of the plot. Too much repetition or its too obvious use can be tedious, however, and that is something which no artist can risk. Forster acknowledges this when he says: 'Done badly, rhythm is most boring, it hardens into a symbol, and instead of carrying us on it trips us up'; when handled by a master like Proust, however, the leitmotif of the 'little phrase' assumes an organic function in the text, 'not . . . there all the time like a pattern, but by its lovely waxing and waning [filling] us with surprise and freshness and hope' (1981: 148).

In any event, it would appear that such issues arise 'naturally' in musical discourse – they are a seminal element of the human organisation of sound that is universally understood as 'music'. In fiction, however, the techniques of rhythm and repetition feature in a far less intuitive fashion. They may be present at a deep structural level – encoded into the narrative at part of its 'natural' architecture. To function as a deliberate part of any meaning-making discourse, however, techniques of rhythm and repetition have to be perceived, understood, learnt and applied; and this will happen in different ways at different times. In late nineteenth-century and early twentieth-century Europe, the process was facilitated by more than a century of speculation on the special role of music in human affairs, and by the emergence of a number of writers (such as Forster, Proust and Mann) who, through training and predilection, were especially receptive to music as a paradigm for their own artistic endeavours. To this list of musically inspired novelists, we must add one more.

Music and Form II – 'Sirens' (from *Ulysses*, 1922) by James Joyce

James Joyce has emerged as the quintessential Anglophone Modernist in a number of ways, none more so than in his recalcitrant attitude towards received literary discourses, and more specifically in his attempt to bring literary and musical discourses into some kind of fructifying relationship. Building on the insights and achievements of previous experiments, Joyce was intent on re-animating the field of prose fiction so that it was answerable to his understanding of art and its role in human experience. As a talented amateur singer, moreover, he was well-disposed towards a consideration of music as an aesthetic system through which such a radical project could be broached. Together with Proust and Mann, Joyce was responsible for 'musicalising' the European novel in ways, and to an extent, with which the genre is still coming to terms.

A number of stories in the collection *Dubliners* (1914) signal the emblematic role that music came to play later in Joyce's art. Sometimes – as with the seemingly throwaway references in 'Eveline' and 'After the Race' – music appears incidental, although as generations of dedicated researchers have shown, every reference is thoroughly enmeshed in the complex narrative webs woven by the author. In other stories ('A Painful Case' and 'A Mother', for example), music assumes a more central narrative role. It is in the final story, 'The Dead', however, that Joyce's preoccupation becomes apparent. The significance of music for the group gathered in a house in Dublin on a winter night at the beginning of the twentieth century is signalled in a variety of ways: it is an accompaniment to dancing, one of the main activities of the evening; all three hosts are involved in music in some form or other – as performers, organisers or teachers; it forms the major topic for discussion during dinner, as different styles, periods and performers are introduced and evaluated. As Joyce shows, in fact, music is woven into the fabric of contemporary Dublin life in a manner that both reflects and comments upon a supposed innate national proclivity.

Music is incorporated as part of Joyce's critique of contemporary Ireland, and its bland, disappointing imitation of the English culture from which it was ostensibly attempting to differentiate itself. It would be erroneous to maintain, however, that 'any discussion of Joyce's "musical" technique in fiction writing need not concern itself with references to actual music, heard or performed in his novels, but with the musical experience as a metaphor for life and for the novelist's attempt to translate this metaphor into words' (Aronson 1980: 39). In fact, Joyce is one of the few writers for whom thematic references to music are at least as significant as experiments with transposing musical into literary discourse, something that is borne out in his most daring and most elaborate experiment with musical fiction: 'Sirens'.

Incorporated as Chapter 11 of *Ulysses*, 'Sirens' is generally recognised as an extraordinary achievement, '[containing] remarkable analogies to musical microstructures and general compositional techniques as well as some fine word music' (Wolf 1999: 138). The story of Joyce's ambitions for this piece of writing has been told often enough, and I have neither the desire nor the space to repeat it here. Critics since Stuart Gilbert have followed the author's direction in regarding the chapter's 'art' as music, its 'organ' as the ear, and its 'technic' as the *'fuga per canonem'* – this latter term translating as something like 'fugue according to rule' (Joyce 1993: 875). Basically, in his desire to incorporate Ulysses's encounter with the Sirens in the Homeric original, Joyce produced an extended piece of writing in which he attempts to render written language according to the precepts of music – using techniques (such as onomatopoeia, puns, neologisms and extensive repetition) that militate against language's traditional signifying function. The result, as Gilbert wrote, was a chapter 'which both in structure and in diction goes far beyond all previous experiments in the adaptation of musical technique and timbres to a work of literature' (1952: 239).

Generations of critics have devised many ingenious ways of interpreting the product of Joyce's musical imagination.[24] Among all the critical responses 'Sirens' has elicited, however, two points are worth stressing for present purposes. Firstly, even as Joyce was extending the possibilities of literary music, he was at the same time revealing its limitations and insisting (by example if not by intention) on the referential powers of language and narrative above and beyond 'pure music'. It may be, as Wolf suggests, that 'the higher the degree of musicalness the less a text is recognisable as narrative fiction' (1999: 78). Nevertheless, as the editor-critic Jeri Johnson writes:

> If Joyce takes Pater seriously in pushing narrative as far as it might go toward imitating the form/matter dissolution in music, he also parodically pushes Pater into an admission that the sensible words formed into narratives which are novels necessarily refuse the decomposition into pure sound required in music. For Ulysses (and no less *Ulysses*) resists the Sirens' song.
>
> (1993: 876)

It would appear, in other words, that written language retains an ineluctable 'will to signify', no matter the extent to which such a will is deliberately alienated as the artist pursues some form or level of experience that cannot be expressed by means of 'normal' language. It seems clear that Joyce belonged (with critical retrospection, perhaps, but certainly also self-consciously to a certain extent) to a Modernist movement intent on deconstructing not only an entire range of received narratives, but the very category of narrative itself. Nevertheless, narrative subsists within 'Sirens' – with familiar characters and locations, dialogue, themes, plot developments, and so on. Time moves, characters meet, the story advances – all the stuff of the traditional mimetic novel is present, even if remotely. As Aronson says, 'his allegiance to words never faltered' (1980: 40). Joyce, it seems, retained an investment in 'story', no matter the pioneering lengths to which he was willing to go to mitigate the effects of traditional mimesis.

The second point is a general critical-theoretical one, but one which, I would maintain, has its origin in musicological discourse. We have noted that the attempt to render human consciousness led many Modernist writers – either by deliberate analogy or by accident – to approximate music. As William Freedman writes:

> Simultaneity, the impingement of past and future on present and vice versa, the interrelationship, repetition, and overlapping of ideas, the intricate and mysterious associations of those ideas, and the sudden or prepared transitions between thoughts, attitudes, and emotions – all are characteristic of the processes of interior experience, all are characteristic of the processes of musical development.
>
> (1978: 49)

As a writer dedicated to capturing inner consciousness in novel ways, Joyce turned – sometimes deliberately (as in 'Sirens'), sometimes without apparent purpose or intention – to a cultural medium that both his education and his inclination led him to believe was equipped for the task by Nature itself. In doing so, Joyce advanced the possibilities of the music-novel beyond anything previously attempted, and his impact on future experiments has been inescapable. I want to suggest, however, that the influence of *Ulysses* in general, and of 'Sirens' in particular, extends both forwards and backwards. If since its publication the text has obliged every musically inclined novelist to reassess their motivation and their method, its presence may be discerned in all musical fiction, including that which predates it, as a kind of imagined ideal 'text', as yet unwritten but providing sanction and example on every new experiment in the field. As the full development always resides within the musical note or phrase, so the music-novel always resides within the first tentative uses of musical effects to mitigate narrative discourse. Thus, Laurence Sterne's *Tristram Shandy* (1760–7), for example, resonates more clearly after 'Sirens', because the former was 'composed' in anticipation of the latter – that is to say, in anticipation of what a fully dedicated music-novel would be.

Music and Form III – *Cloud Atlas* (2004) by David Mitchell

How do sonata form and 'Sirens' impact upon subsequent music-fiction in terms of composition and interpretation? Let us briefly consider an example which, in keeping with its author's reputation as an innovative writer who is also interested in music, has a unique form. David

Mitchell's third novel, *Cloud Atlas*, is designed as if six novellas (each about eighty pages long) were opened more or less in the middle and then laid down one on top of the other so that the first halves of each of the first five were encountered one after another, followed by the sixth in its entirety, followed by the second parts of each text, although this time in descending order. The stories are dispersed in time (beginning in the nineteenth century and progressing to a distant dystopian future) and space (moving in the main between the Pacific Rim and Europe). Each story, moreover, is linked to every other, both in terms of certain recurring details and in terms of the central theme, which might be described as the persistence of hope in the face of a rampant will to power discernible everywhere throughout history.

This theme is established in the opening section, entitled 'The Pacific Journal of Adam Ewing', and it functions on both an inter-personal and a wider socio-cultural level. Returning home to San Francisco after a period working in New South Wales, an American notary is appalled by the violence of the island tribes who conduct their wars with savage relish, and who regularly slaughter each other to the point of genocide. During the course of his journey, Ewing's faith in the power of Christian love as a force for good is shaken by the cynicism and brutality of his fellow whites. Implicitly convinced of their moral and cultural superiority, sailors and missionaries alike are bent on exploitation and domination. This general point then comes home to roost in as much as the narrator learns that he has been slowly poisoned, to expedite robbery, by a charlatan who has 'befriended' him. It is in fact this character, the quack doctor Henry Goose, who most clearly articulates the informing rationale of the separate stories, as he taunts (what he believes to be) the dying Ewing:

> He mimicked my voice, very well. 'But why *me*, Henry, are we not friends?' Well, Adam, even friends are made of meat. 'Tis absurdly simple. I need money & in your trunk, I am told, is an entire estate, so I have killed you for it. Where is the mystery? 'But, Henry, this is wicked!' But, Adam, the world *is* wicked. Maoris prey on Moriori, Whites prey on darker-hued cousins, fleas prey on mice, cats prey on rats, Christians on infidels, first-mates on cabin-boys, Death on Living. 'The weak are meat, the strong do eat.'
>
> (523–4, original emphases)

Ewing is rescued by Autua, a Moriori slave whom he had somewhat unwillingly saved from certain death in the opening section of the book. The 'return' of this altruistic gift leads Ewing, from his location at the 'beginning' of history (which is actually the end of the text) and in terms which resonate throughout all the stories, to insist that the survival of the species depends, firstly, on an acknowledgement of human interdependence, and secondly, on the capital importance of the individual who acts in good faith.

Mitchell is Schopenhauerian in his delineation of the species' capacity for evil; nor does he attempt to avoid the spectre of hopelessness that haunts so much of human history. The novel is replete with war, murder, disease, exploitation, egotism, ignorance, hatred and prejudice. Into this narrative of pain, however, the author introduces the possibility of music as a means to begin to imagine an alternative to what Ewing describes as 'the "natural" (oh, weaselly word!) order of things' (528). He does so, moreover, at both a formal and a thematic level.

The key to *Cloud Atlas* is provided by the second story, 'Letters from Zedelghem', which concerns the relationship between two English composers in the early 1930s. The first (who is also the narrator) – young, bisexual Robert Frobisher – travels to Belgium in the hope of meeting, being employed by, and hopefully getting himself into a position to exploit, the second – Vyvyan Ayrs (clearly based on Frederick Delius, 1862–1934), an established figure within the world of art music who, awaiting the ignominy of a syphilitic death, is eking out his final years in frightened, cantankerous exile.[25] The narrative is comprised of Frobisher's letters to an English friend named Sixsmith, who features in the third story.

Neither of the composers is particularly endearing; the possibility of salvation through music appears remote in the face of their devious, self-serving, mutually exploitative attitudes. Nevertheless, music is revealed to be a highly developed, highly sensitive means of engaging with the world. Self-conscious 'cad' though he be, Frobisher constantly thinks in sound, more specifically in music – a facility that encourages him to organise the banalities of everyday life into musical form. It is these random moments of artistic endeavour that he eventually pulls together into the piece that will be his monument, and that achieves emblematic status within the fictional text in which he features as a character:

> Spent the fortnight gone in the music room, reworking my year's fragments into a 'sextet for overlapping soloists': piano, clarinet, 'cello, flute, oboe and violin, each in its own language of key, scale and colour. In the 1st set, each solo is interrupted by its successor: in

the 2nd, each interruption is recontinued, in order. Revolutionary or
gimmicky? (463)

Frobisher calls this piece the *Cloud Atlas Sextet*, and for him it represents
a victory for art over human nature (including his own): 'People are
obscenities', he claims shortly after; 'Would rather be music than be a
mass of tubes squeezing semi-solids around itself for a few decades
before becoming so dribblesome it'll no longer function' (489). At the
same time, Frobisher's 'sextet for overlapping soloists' is also quite
clearly a description of *Cloud Atlas* the novel, which is also comprised of
six overlapping parts that cohere – despite their discrete identities (what
Frobisher refers to as 'its own language of key, scale and colour') – to
form a unit that is greater than the sum of its parts.

The key role of music in the text is established in two principal ways.
In the first place, the title (as we have seen) refers to Frobisher's composition, which itself anticipates an idea explained by the narrator of
the central story, 'Sloosha's Crossin' an' Ev'rythin' After', who says:

I watched clouds awobbly from the floor o'that kayak. Souls cross
ages like clouds cross skies, an' tho' a cloud's shape nor hue nor size
don't stay the same it's still a cloud an' so is a soul. Who can say
where the cloud's blowed from or who the soul'll be 'morrow? Only
Sonmi the east an' the west an' the compass an' the atlas, yay, the
atlas o' clouds. (324)

A 'cloud atlas' is a particularly fitting metaphor for the idea of souls per-
sisting through time and space, an idea which itself resonates at both a
political and an artistic (more particularly, a musical) level. The conjunction of nature (clouds) and culture (atlas) symbolises the immemorial human endeavour to find a place for itself in a seemingly random
and hostile universe. If such an endeavour gives rise to the beliefs and
practices which inform so much of the abhorrent behaviour in *Cloud
Atlas*, it also connotes ideas of interdependence and good faith which,
as Ewing insists, constitute the best hope for the survival of the species.
At the same time, the notion of a 'cloud atlas' invokes the tension
between form and formlessness which animates cultural activity in general, but which finds its ultimate articulation in music – an idea, as we
have observed, with a distinguished pedigree in both philosophical and
novelistic discourse.

Music's importance in the text is established, secondly, by its recurrence as a motif within all six stories; and as a corollary of this, by the

installation of 'recurrence' itself as a structuring principle within the text as a whole. The 'bee-like "hum"' (6), which Ewing notes during the flogging of Autua in the opening pages, and which is associated at this stage with the savage rituals of the Pacific island natives, anticipates Frobisher's 'cultured' propensity to convert random noise into musical form. The sextet motif returns in later stories: the composition itself becomes an important clue for Luisa Rey (120–1), and a jazz sextet plays at a party attended by a character named Timothy Cavendish (149). The artificial life-form Sonri 451 works for a company called 'Papa Song' (187), during an era in which the end of year holiday period is referred to as a 'Sextet' (199); later she wonders why birds sing (213), and is fascinated by the sound of a human choir (226); later still, the song her 'sisters' sing as they make their way unknowingly towards obliteration '[interweaves] with background hydraulics' (358), much in the same way that Frobisher, on his journey to Ostend, 'listened to the distant brass of the engine room and sketched a repetitive passage for trombone based on the ship's rhythms' (46). And so on; in these and many other instances, music is signalled throughout the text as a peculiarly significant means for humans – and quasi-humans – to experience and to represent the world.

The various narratives that comprise *Cloud Atlas* 'overlap' in structural terms – one begins before the other ends; but they also 'overlap' (as we have just observed with the example of the Sextet) through the recurrence of a wealth of minor detail which is constantly both recalling and anticipating other iterations, other contexts and other meanings. This effect is exacerbated, moreover, by the double structure of the text: a reference from the second part of 'The Pacific Diary of Adam Ewing' (say, the oblique allusions to sodomy on page 493) might predate the references to homosexuality in all the other stories, but actually postdates them in textual terms. This makes for an extremely fluid narrative in which the reader's attention is constantly drawn to parallels between the otherwise disparate stories. In this respect, the six stories represent not only different overlapping 'voices' with their own keys, scales and colours: they also resemble the separate 'movements' of a larger, organic work – movements which constantly recall and anticipate each other, using leitmotif as a technique to evoke particular ideas and emotions which are themselves dispersed over time and space.

The persistence of certain key human impulses, regardless of geographical or historical setting, is precisely the theme of *Cloud Atlas*; and it is precisely music's ability to embody and to represent those impulses that accounts for the central role it is afforded in this particular text, and in the general tradition of the novel.

2

The Role and Representation of Music in the Novel from Lawrence Sterne to Anthony Burgess

+ some backdrop

Introduction

In Chapter 1 we encountered some of the theoretical and philosophical issues encompassed by the concept of the music-novel, and we developed a rough working distinction between three main tendencies: music as inspiration, as metaphor and as formal influence. It was suggested that throughout the modern period all three of these tendencies have been enmeshed with a fundamental and recurring debate concerning the relationship between aesthetic discourse and a number of related areas of enquiry, including culture, nature, biology, philosophy and politics.

This chapter attempts to flesh out that theoretical structure by examining a small selection of high-profile British novels in the light of this rough working model (which is itself a fiction of sorts). One of the premises underpinning this book is that the music-novel is not a marginal practice – it is more than simply one of any number of 'special interest' ways of approaching literary history; the suggestion here, rather, is that music has been fundamental to the evolution of the modern British novel, and therefore it remains fundamental to the understanding of that discourse down to the present day.

More than that, this chapter is an examination of music-inspired literary criticism in action. The fact is that music's central role in novelistic discourse has not always been recognised in the field's attendant critical discourses: indeed, we might describe some of the engagements that have occurred as misrecognitions. At the very least, we can say that over the years several critics have attempted to arrive at different conclusions about the novel's use of music; much of the commentary has been ad hoc and throwaway, although of late (as mentioned in the

59

introduction) more systematic interventions have been attempted. Before commencing an analysis of the role and representation of music in contemporary British fiction it behoves us to examine some of those engagements, so that alongside the theoretical issues introduced in Chapter 1, and patterns within the fiction itself (identified in Chapters 3 to 5), we can observe recurring themes and techniques within the critical tradition. Such, in any event, is the intention of this whistle-stop tour of some of the great monuments of the canon.

Lawrence Sterne, *Tristram Shandy* (1760–7)

Sterne's infamous novel figures in most accounts and surveys of British fiction; the fact that he was born and spent the first decade of his life in Ireland has occasionally earned him a place in that island's literary history also (Welch 1996: 539–40). Generations of readers have been charmed, puzzled or disgusted by *Tristram Shandy* – both for what it is and, more frequently, for what it is not. For here, near the outset of the modern Anglophone tradition, we appear to have a text that brilliantly and comically exposes the bad faith upon which the novel as a form relies. *Tristram Shandy* is likely to disappoint (and bore, and probably offend) readers and critics for whom the novel should not be an endless, seemingly aimless, catalogue of digressions and interruptions, but rather a story containing characters who do and say things in places and for reasons that 'we' can recognise as corresponding more or less to the way things are said and done in 'the real world'. Sterne's novel, in fact, might be seen as a blow against the future hegemony of 'realism', before that paradigm had even established itself.

Although it remains more read about than read, *Tristram Shandy* initiated a sceptical anti-tradition in British fiction – a tradition for which neither 'we' nor 'the real world' were ever the unproblematic prospects so assiduously endorsed by the mainstream realist tradition. It is in this sense that some critics remark Sterne's affinity with writers such as James Joyce and Virginia Woolf – both of whom share (among other things) their predecessor's recalcitrant attitude towards conventional representations of the subject. More ambitiously, we might say that the eighteenth-century *Tristram Shandy* also bears comparison with some aspects of the work of such writers as Samuel Beckett and Thomas Pynchon, both of whom expend considerable numbers of words to reveal the lengths – the absurd, pathetic, self-contradictory lengths – to which the human subject will go to rationalise their existence. Sterne is thus both 'modernist' and 'postmodernist' *avant les lettres* – a precedent for those novelists whose self-appointed task is the search for a reality beyond realism.

This task is reminiscent of some of the claims regarding music that were discussed in Chapter 1 – the idea that music affords the human subject access to levels of experience, as well as a means to express those experiences, that are denied by other forms of communication, including language. This claim raises the possibility of calling *Tristram Shandy* a music-novel, as the critic William Freedman does in his book *Lawrence Sterne and the Origins of the Musical Novel* (1978). Freedman suggests that Sterne, like many others during that questioning century, was intrigued by the manner in which the human mind processed external reality, and was intent on using the novel to explore the paradoxes of being and consciousness (although Sterne certainly would not have employed such terminology). Freedman further suggests that Sterne found in music a topical means to experiment with the exploration and expression of such paradoxes:

> [Much] of what Sterne's novel is and does and much of what modern fiction has derived from him is distinctively musical in character. Sterne's principal concerns and contributions are in the realm of time, process, the flow of consciousness, communication, and form; and each of these facets of his fertile originality is inseparable from yet another: the transmutation of musical rhetoric, principles, and structure to literature. (5–6)

Sterne was a keen amateur musician who lived during a period when the idea of music was the subject of intense negotiations in all walks of life – in philosophy, in society, and (crucially) in terms of its relationship with other art forms (Barry 1987; Thomas 1995). For Freedman, music 'permeates' (186) *Tristram Shandy* at the level of plot and imagery – in the image of the process of narration as a kind of 'humming' or 'fiddling' (Sterne 1980: 221, 261), for example, as well as in other self-conscious metaphors of composition and performance. Much more importantly, however, Sterne self-consciously utilises techniques adapted from contemporary musical practice (in the works of contemporary composers such as Handel and C. P. E. Bach, for example) to structure his novel – techniques such as repetition, embellishment, ornamentation, extemporisation, digression, improvisation, modulation, and thematic statement and development. Music has evolved these techniques (according to Freedman) because of its special role in relation to human perception – which is to say, these techniques reflect the human way of being in the world better than do the techniques available at the time to other art forms, especially those reliant on language. 'Sterne is at war with mere words', says Freedman, 'because they cannot do his work' (184).

Thus, for Freedman, Sterne wrote the first great music-novel. By '[bringing] to fiction an architectural structure analogous to that of music' (46), Sterne resisted the literary impulse towards narrative and placed the question of perception at the centre of novelistic discourse in Britain (hence the noted affinities with Joyce, Woolf and others). He also developed specific techniques that would prove to be profoundly influential upon the future course of British fiction.

Werner Wolf, however, is of a contrary opinion. Although 'it cannot be denied that *Tristram Shandy* does contain elements of intermedial attempts as a musicalization of fiction . . . Freedman's book', Wolf argues, 'may in large parts be regarded as a typical example of the dubious "metaphorical impressionism" that is often to be observed in the use of musical terms in literary criticism' (1999: 86). Sterne may have incorporated musical elements or effects into his writing – as, for example, Parson Yorick's use of musical terms to describe his own sermons (1980: 300–2) or the self-reflexive metaphor of narrative as 'humming' mentioned above. It would be an error, however, (at least, it would be so according to the strict formal criteria described by Wolf in his study) to impute any intention on Sterne's part to musicalise 'the novel as a whole' (1999: 86) or to draw conclusions upon such a tendentious imputation. Although '*Tristram Shandy* is no musicalized *novel*', he concludes, 'it contains early elements of a musicalization of fictional *passages*' (1999: 92, original emphases).

For Wolf, music remains a haphazard and non-systematic presence within *Tristram Shandy*. Any 'evidence' to the contrary is more likely to result either from the ubiquity of music as an analogy available within all human endeavour – that is, the fact that music can be invoked in one form or another to describe or understand more or less anything and everything – or from the extratextual impositions of a reader-critic who is supersensitised to that analogy and who adapts the 'hardware' of the text to his or her particular 'software' program (intermediality and musicalisation). Thus, music either emerges from the text or is imposed upon it; neither scenario – at least to Wolf's way of thinking – renders it a music-novel, although he does admit that *Tristram Shandy* represents a significant moment in the evolution of such a form.

Jane Austen, *Pride and Prejudice* (1813)

Music pervades the world depicted in Jane Austen's fiction, and nowhere more so than in the novel traditionally regarded as her finest achievement. In *Pride and Prejudice* Austen deploys the complex social practice of contemporary music to expedite the complex aesthetic processes of contemporary fiction. The result is a novelistic milieu in which every response to, as well as every representation of, music is highly resonant in terms of the development and modification of the narrative. Music functions in the first instance as a kind of social emollient: whenever people are gathered together there is playing and dancing and singing, and this is one of the most important ways in which this society regards and remakes itself. At the same time, music is a guide to the moral standing of each character in terms of how they regard each other, how the narrator regards them, and, therefore, how the reader is invited to regard them.

To take one example: in Chapter 31 a group of people are gathered in the drawing room of a grand country residence called Rosings Park. The principal tension of the scene (here as throughout the text) is provided by the interaction between the characters of Elizabeth Bennett and Mr Darcy. Early in the chapter, Darcy's cousin, Mr Fitzwilliam, is questioned by Lady Catherine de Burgh as to what he and Elizabeth are discussing among themselves in a different part of the room, to which he replies 'We are speaking of music, Madam' (1972: 207). 'Of music!' she says:

> Then pray speak aloud. It is of all subjects my delight. I must have my share in the conversation, if you are speaking of music. There are few people in England, I suppose, who have more true enjoyment of music than myself, or a better natural taste. If I had ever learnt, I should have been a great proficient. And so would Anne [her daughter], if her health had allowed her to apply. I am confident that she would have performed delightfully.

This speech, and the scene in which it takes place, provides the reader with a lot of important information about the characters and the story. For one thing, Lady Catherine's outrageous boasting clearly reveals her 'confident' character to be in fact ignorant and domineering; she senses that music represents valuable cultural capital and attempts to lay claim to it without the necessary knowledge or competence. Her exploitative response to the idea of music also registers in a wider sense, however, as an example of a kind of materialistic social discourse (also represented by Mr Bingley's sisters) from which Darcy will have to distance himself if he is to win Lizzie's love. Lady Catherine's invitation to Lizzie to practise on a piano in the servants' quarter at Rosings exemplifies a kind of attitude (characterised as 'pride' in the title and throughout the text) that employs social privilege to indulge reprehensible character traits (as determined within the moral terms of the narrative) such as selfishness and jealousy.

Lizzie Bennett plays and sings, but not to any great standard; rather than detracting from her moral worth, however, this contributes to the fullness and humanity of her character. Later in the same scene, Lizzie uses her own lack of proficiency at the piano to score a point in the ongoing love-war with Darcy: if she herself practised harder she would play better, she maintains – it is her own fault that she does not; just so, if Darcy practised at being sociable he would socialise better – it is his own fault, not a lifelong sentence to which an immutable personality has condemned him. This is an important point in the search for an accommodation between his pride and her prejudice, and it is made in terms of a musical conceit that will continue to accrue resonance over the entire course of the text.

More than this, however, Lizzie's deficiency as a musician bespeaks her proficiency as a woman. It is interesting that the women (for example, Mary Bennett, Caroline Bingley and Georgiana Darcy) who do aspire towards musical proficiency – that is, towards a kind of acquired excellence – are all deficient or defective in one or another personal sense. Mary affiliates herself with beautiful music so as to deflect the mortification she feels at her own lack of physical beauty in comparison with her sisters. Uncertain of her own attractions, Caroline uses music as an aggressive weapon in her battle with Elizabeth for Darcy's attention. In Georgiana's case the inference is that music is performing a convalescent function, channelling the passions precipitously awakened by her would-be seducer Mr Wickham. In each case, music is implicitly linked with the subject's sexual identity and thus with the wider social status of gender.

Touching on issues that were to exercise George Eliot later in the century, Austen depicts the exemplary character of Lizzie as pursuing a sensible path between affirmation (music as an index of civilised society wherein woman can both establish her presence and assert her identity) and denial (music as a distraction from unrealised female sexuality). Lizzie loves and enjoys music, and is thus associated with its positive social capital; but she is too much of a person – too much of a woman – to be entirely identified with it, for that would detract from her principal object, which is the captivation of the most eligible man in her circle.

Even a cursory consideration reveals that *Pride and Prejudice* is a novel in which music, as well as various ideas relating to music, plays a crucial role. More integrated and ambitious theories of the role of music in relation to Austen's fiction have also been developed. The thesis of Robert K. Wallace's *Jane Austen and Mozart: Classical Equilibrium in Fiction and Music* (1983) is that Austen's writing is – not metaphorically but actually – the literary analogue of Mozart's. The 'classical equilibrium' of the title describes an ideal that dominated European culture (especially the arts) before the onset of Romanticism. Besides the overarching quality of 'equilibrium', neoclassical art (according to Wallace) emphasised values such as balance, proportion, symmetry, restraint, clarity and wit. These values, he avers, find expression in various 'terms, themes and tendencies' (1983: 17), with the emphasis always on tropes of accommodation, stability and closure; and they are nowhere better exemplified than in the music of Mozart and the fiction of Austen.

Wallace points out that literary critics have always drawn comparisons between Austen and Mozart (2); his intention is to formalise these ad hoc observations by conducting direct, extended comparisons between three of her novels (*Pride and Prejudice, Emma* and *Persuasion*) and three of his most celebrated works: the Piano Concertos Nos. 9, 25 and 27. Such an analysis will, he suggests, emphasise the methodological strengths of the relevant disciplines (musicology and literary criticism) while offsetting their traditional weaknesses. Musicology is strong on 'the significance of the form' but weak on 'the humanity of the spirit' (5); literary criticism, on the other hand, remains weak (despite nearly a century of formalist literary theory) on matters of form, but strong on matters concerning the 'human spirit'. Thus, a formal analysis of the structure of Mozart's Piano Concerto No. 9 provides a model for 'a more precise description of the fictional structure [of *Pride and Prejudice*] (and of the relations among its component parts) than literary analysis alone has provided'. Similarly, a study of Elizabeth Bennett in terms of personality, maturity and her relations with 'society at large . . . makes possible a more detailed account of certain human and social dynamics in the concertos than music criticism alone has provided' (6).

Wallace's experiment with interdisciplinary criticism has been described as 'misconceived' by Kramer (1986: 277) (quoted in Scher 1999: 16) and as 'problematic' by Wolf (1999: 36). *Classical Equilibrium in Fiction and Music* is clearly a speculative work; in any event, such a study was never likely to satisfy those requiring more rigorous theories of how music figures in literary discourse and of how to approach the material so identified. Nevertheless, such scepticism was not enough to prevent Wallace essaying a similar methodology in relation to another literary classic.

Emily Brontë, *Wuthering Heights* (1847)

Following the pattern established in his comparative analysis of Austen and Mozart, Wallace turned his attention to an extended comparison between Brontë's celebrated novel, *Wuthering Heights* (1847), and a selection of musical works by Beethoven (in *Romantic Equilibrium in Fiction and Music*, 1986). Such an exercise is valid, he maintains, in so far as 'the "meaning" of their art is commensurate. That meaning', he continues,

is comparable to the extent that 'the motions of the spirit' are comparable. The motions of the spirit that make these two artists unique within their separate artistic traditions are those that make them most similar to each other. This study is devoted to characterizing – in emotional, spiritual, and stylistic terms – the extent to which the meaning of their art, the human experience it expresses and induces, is comparable. (1)

The thesis here, as with the Austen/Mozart study, is that Brontë and Beethoven share 'emotional, spiritual and stylistic' concerns which render a comparison between them more revelatory and more relevant than a comparison conducted along 'proper' disciplinary lines (that is, in terms of literary history or musicology). Both these artists, he claims, articulate a dominant strain of Romantic art which, while defining itself (implicitly or explicitly) in opposition to the classical dispensation that preceded it, withdraws from the radical subjectivism that characterised the work of certain other artists working in what is more or less recognisable as a 'Romantic' idiom (Poe in literature, for example, or Schumann in music). Beethoven and Brontë achieve, Wallace claims, a new equilibrium to succeed the classical precursor – the 'romantic equilibrium' of his title. It matters not that one worked in music and one in fiction: sympathetic analysis will bypass the discrepancies of mere media in order to discern the deep structural resonances that obtain between different artists articulating the same 'truth' in different works of art.

Lacking the extended Austen canon in this instance, Wallace focuses instead on the three endings he discerns in *Wuthering Heights*. These three endings, he goes on to suggest, 'correspond to the endings of . . . three Beethoven [piano] sonatas' (20). Thus, the 'conventional', happy ending with which the novel closes (the marriage between Cathy Linton and Hareton Earnshaw) is compared with the Piano Sonata in C minor, op.13 (*Pathétique*); the 'essential ending . . . [which] seems to be Catherine's death and Heathcliff being left alone without her' (20) is compared with the Sonata in F minor, op.57 (*Appassionata*); and finally, the 'marriage' of Catherine and Heathcliff in death and their survival as 'ghosts' in local folk-memory is compared to Sonata in C minor, op.111 – Beethoven's last sonata. In its ironic treatment of conventional closure, and its emphasis upon the ultimate transcendence of passion by the peace of death, this ternary structure encapsulates the essence of the 'Romantic equilibrium' expressed in words by Brontë and in music by Beethoven, and which 'derives in each case from a powerful ability to combine equilibrium with tension, vehemence with restraint, clarity with ambiguity, sanity with madness, the classical with the Romantic' (5).

Werner Wolf has argued that '[as] long as [nineteenth-century] fiction remained rooted in the aesthetics of (realist) mimesis, fictional experiments with establishing intermedial relations with music as a predominantly a-referential art are hardly to be expected to any major extent' (1999: 124). Because of its opposition to realism in a number of key respects, however, Romanticism offered a different case in point, as Wolf shows with his analysis of a Thomas de Quincey fragment entitled 'Dream Fugue' (first published in 1849, incidentally, and therefore very much of an era with *Wuthering Heights*). Even so, Wolf by and large restricts his musical analysis of the de Quincey text to formal and structural matters, since he finds no attempt at 'word music' on the author's part, while the 'content analogies to music' (114) are limited to the 'fugue' of the title.

This seems of a piece with Wallace's analysis of Brontë's novel, in which he finds little overt reference to music at all; the music, such as it is, resides not in the detail of the plot but in the 'spirit' and the 'structure' – what the critic refers to as the 'imaginative plane of *Wuthering Heights*' (21). It is certainly true that the text does not immediately strike the reader as a particularly sympathetic one for a music-oriented analysis. Wallace points out (175) that music appears on the surface level of the plot on only two occasions. The first is a reference to the fiddle that Hindley Earnshaw requests his father to bring him as a present from a trip to Liverpool – but the instrument is 'crushed to morsels in the greatcoat' (1965: 78) when Mr Earnshaw rescues and carries home the destitute child who will become Heathcliff. The latter thus immediately interrupts the 'natural' succession from father to son symbolised by the gift of music, and one might reasonably contend that it is with the consequences of this destructive, 'unnatural' disturbance that the remainder of the text is concerned.

Beyond this crude, Freudian episode, Heathcliff's introduction of disharmony into the domestic sphere of the Heights is interesting, if we accept Terry Eagleton's suggestion that this famous fictional character might be an amalgam of the male Brontë sibling – the feckless, alcoholic Branwell who died young and unsuccessful – and the impoverished Irish immigrants whom Branwell himself would have encountered on a trip to Liverpool on the eve of the Great Famine in 1845. Music and Irishness have been closely associated since medieval times, and the association remained strong during the early Victorian period when *Wuthering Heights* was written. But if that association was benign and familiar on the one hand – represented, for example, in the crafted songs of Thomas Moore, which remained popular in middle-class England throughout the nineteenth century – on the other hand it was dangerous and alien, possessed of passionate intensities born of fear and frustrated desire.[1] Such emotions were difficult to accommodate in the kind of stable society so assiduously pursued by Victorian England. One increasingly successful forum for exploring such disruptive energies and the means to contain them was the novel, which is of course what renders *Wuthering Heights* such a typical, and at the same time such a unique, prospect.

Heathcliff's obliteration of conventional music (even that associated with the fiddle, a very 'Irish' instrument in some respects) symbolises both his defiance vis-à-vis established practices and his refusal to be implicated in the complacent consolations of English bourgeois society. As Eagleton says: 'There is an archaic weight of history with which English society has become entangled, and which is threatening to drag it down, and its name is Heathcliff, or Ireland' (1995: 21). He is thus equated with a kind of 'bad' Irishness, which repudiates all invitations (in both contemporary political and cultural discourse) to enter into the bourgeois British 'family', or (in musical terms) to attend to prevailing harmonic practices. The 'music' he will make with Catherine will be of an altogether different kind, one not answerable to, nor comprehensible by, received standards, but as elemental and as unpredictable as the wind.[2]

This is borne out in the other 'overt' musical scene noted by Wallace, in which Heathcliff is locked in a garret on Christmas Day after attacking Edgar Linton for a perceived slight. He thus misses out on the after-dinner dancing (for which, presumably, there must have been some music, although we are not enlightened as to how it was provided), and the subsequent arrival of the fifteen-strong Gimmerton band, who provide 'carols . . . songs and glees' for a company who 'esteemed it a first-rate treat to hear them' (100). Not only is Heathcliff at odds with the social 'harmony' down below, but he implicates Cathy in his dissent, for despite the fact that she loves the music, she is drawn up the stairs to where she can 'hold communion with' the disgraced boy. Cathy's youthful association with 'singing'[3] is gradually subsumed by an alternative music, one associated with Heathcliff and symbolised in the wind that wuthers constantly around the house. The 'communion' entered into by Heathcliff and Cathy thus represents an alternative music – a kind of 'primeval' music that is anterior and superior to the artifice of conventional musical discourse.

It is not quite true to say, then (as Wallace does), that '[in] *Wuthering Heights* music does not play any significant role in the plot itself' (176). The Brontë/Beethoven comparisons are certainly suggestive, and the exercise contributes another dimension to the process of intermedial analysis which is the focus of this study. By broadening the definition of music to incorporate the category of 'noise', however, and by looking a little deeper and a little further into the text's immediate contexts, critics will invariably find music – and the bundle of issues comprehended by that concept – awaiting them.

George Eliot, *Middlemarch* (1871–2)

George Eliot is one of the most musically engaged writers (in any language or tradition) in the history of the novel. In *George Eliot, Music and Victorian Culture*, Delia da Sousa Correa convincingly argues that 'musical allusion . . . works across and between Eliot's novels', and that 'music remained a vital source of reference and inspiration throughout [her] development as a writer' (2003: 2, 3). Da Sousa Correa's study also reveals the extent to which Eliot embraced intellectual life, becoming entirely engaged with the artistic, but also the scientific, debates of her day. She was personally acquainted with some of the most important composers of the era, including Franz Liszt and Richard Wagner; indeed, she appears to have been the first English writer to offer a favourable critical response (in a review of 1855) to the latter's music. Her appreciation of Wagner's work confirmed her regard for German (or at least Germanic) cultural history, a regard that led her back through a long list of great male composers, but also embraced a patriarchal canon of philosopher-writers such as Feuerbach, Schopenhauer, Schlegel, Kant, Herder, Goethe and Schiller – all of whom, not coincidentally, made telling contributions to the debate on the special role of music in human experience.[4] Also of particular influence upon Eliot's intellectual development was her friend Herbert Spencer, whose pseudo-scientific writings on the derivation and function of music were fully engaged with contemporary debates regarding human evolution.

The contemporary artistic, philosophical and scientific debates to which Eliot was exposed provided the range of contexts within which her novels developed, impacting upon her characters and the situations they are obliged to negotiate. Central to all this was the question of music: where does it come from? how did it develop? what does it express? is it a language, or is it the end (the goal or the death) of language? Eliot was highly sensitised to contemporary musical aesthetics, which seemed to her (as indeed it did to many artists working in non-musical media) to be the discourse wherein the great questions – regarding art and life, behaviour and faith, and so on – were being most assiduously and most daringly considered. Given her deep immersion in contemporary intellectual discourse, in fact, it would be surprising if Eliot had not incorporated music into her work in some or other form. As it happened, she clearly devised ways and means of featuring her response to contemporary ideas regarding music into her fiction. If *The Mill on the Floss* (1860) and *Daniel Deronda* (1876) are her two most 'intensely musical novels' (da Sousa Correa 2003: 192), *Middlemarch* remains her most successful and characteristic book, and as such, the one wherein her literary treatment of music should be considered for the purposes of a survey such as this.

We noted in relation to the character of Lizzie Bennett in *Pride and Prejudice* that music was an ambiguous accomplishment for a woman. By Eliot's time, the category of gender had become wrapped up in scientific and medical debates that spilled over (through the work of Spencer and others) into popular debates regarding the 'nature' of women and their relationship with music. On the one hand, the female – given her 'naturally' heightened emotional status – was preternaturally disposed towards music. Both articulated – and both implicitly understood – the language of the emotions. The female resisted 'reality' in the same manner in which music resisted the world as experienced by the senses; in this way, an ideal bio-cultural category ('woman') and an ideal bio-cultural medium ('music') came to be implicitly affiliated in the Victorian cultural imagination. The benign association between women and music (encapsulated in the ubiquitous image of the woman seated at the piano) contributed in turn to the overarching domestic ideal that played such a central role in nineteenth-century ideology.

It was precisely the importance of this ideology, however, that gave rise to an anxiety regarding the female identification with music. If music could be 'an agent of social progress' on the one hand, it could also be 'a cause of sexual havoc', on the other (da Sousa Correa 2003: 60). Music's fast-track to the emotions could easily unbalance those who used it unconsciously, or who could not control its affective powers. The immediate danger was that the musically sensitised, piano-playing woman could deflect the listener's attention away from the spiritual, unleashing a range of emotions (within themselves and their listeners) that would militate against the ideal of domestic harmony. Music, in other words, could just as easily lead towards the body as towards the spirit; the female's emotionality rendered her especially vulnerable to music's insidious potential. In this regard, even the very physicality of woman's relationship with the musical instrument was a challenge to her 'natural' role as wife, mother and home-maker.

This basic dichotomy informs Eliot's depiction of music in the two main relationships explored in *Middlemarch*. The first significant exchange between Tertius Lydgate and Rosamond Vincy is a conversation about music, followed soon after by a performance at the piano:

> Rosamond played admirably . . . A hidden soul seemed to be flowing forth from [her] fingers; and so indeed it was, since souls live on in perpetual echoes, and to all fine expression there goes somewhere an originating activity, if it be only that of an interpreter. Lydgate was taken possession of, and began to believe in her as something exceptional.
>
> (1977: 190)

Although taking place in the idealised domestic environment of the Vincy's drawing-room, there are ominous, 'discordant' overtones to this scene which speak to the widespread anxiety – clearly shared in some significant respects by Eliot – regarding the social function of music. Rosamond plays 'admirably', but the term registers here in a technical, rather than a moral, sense: she is a 'good' musician, but not necessarily a 'good' woman. Eliot reveals how the character uses her technical accomplishments here for ends that are at best dangerous, at worst dishonest. Rosamond assumes the power encoded in the music, the 'hidden soul' echoed in her performance. This is one of the dangers of music: it allows the 'interpreter' to assume the 'soul' encoded within the music without the knowledge or the experience that informed its composition. Rosamond is not 'being herself' when playing the piano, and the moral economy of the novel demands that such a deception will have to be redressed at some stage.

Lydgate is 'taken possession of' – that is, he loses his true 'self' under the emotional impact of the music. To adapt a familiar narrative that will grow in resonance over the course of this study, Lydgate is here like Ulysses, journeying home (at least symbolically) for reasons of duty and honour; Rosamond is the Siren, using the mesmeric, alienating power of music to deflect the hero from his path. A related image is evoked later in the novel when Lydgate begins to understand the fundamental unsuitability of his marriage:

> [How] far he had travelled from his old dreamland, in which Rosamond Vincy appeared to be that perfect piece of womanhood who would reverence her husband's mind after the fashion of an accomplished mermaid, using her comb and looking-glass and singing her song for the relaxation of his adored wisdom alone. (628)

Although frustrated for so long by convention and custom, the relationship between Dorothea and Will Ladislaw is far healthier, incorporating as it does an internalised musicality that eschews artifice of any kind or degree, including (as remarked above in relation to Rosamond's 'echoes') amateur performance. Dorothea's uncle, on the other hand, adheres to the 'benign' model of female musicality, seeing it as a harmless accomplishment to which women are naturally suited. Thus, in an early scene he questions Mr Casaubon about the wisdom of exposing Dorothea to 'deep studies':

> [There] is a lightness about the feminine mind – a touch and go – music, the fine arts, that kind of thing – they should study those up to a certain point, women should; but in a light way, you know. A woman should be able to sit down and play you or sing you a good old English tune. That is what I like; though I have heard most things – been at the opera in Vienna; Gluck, Mozart, everything of that sort. But I'm a conservative in music – it's not like ideas, you know. I stick to the good old tunes. (89)

Dorothea has a 'slight regard for domestic music', and this accords with Eliot's disdain for the 'small tinkling' and 'good old tunes' (89) that characterised so much of the English domestic musical repertoire during the nineteenth century. If Dorothea is unmoved by Thomas Moore's 'The Last Rose of Summer' (89), however, neither is she particularly likely to identify with the purveyors (such as Gluck or Mozart) of traditional opera in the Italian/Viennese tradition. Her 'soul', rather, resonates to an older, more authentic and more natural music, symbolised in the image of an 'aeolian harp' that Ladislaw invokes at both of their first two meetings (105, 241).[5] This elemental music is implicitly linked in Eliot's vision with a 'new' music that is itself paradoxically older and deeper than the available alternatives. I refer to the operatic style developed and brought to its fullest articulation by Richard Wagner, the composer championed by Eliot throughout her artistic life. This in turn leads us to the question of Wagner's influence on late nineteenth-century art, and in particular the evolution of what literary history has come to refer to as the 'Wagnerian novel'.[6]

Thomas Hardy, *Jude the Obscure* (1985)

Eliot brought one tradition of English fiction to a kind of perfection: the long, multi-layered narrative possessed of an extensive list of characters whose thoughts, words, deeds and relationships reflect upon the wider socio-political contexts of the period in which the action is set (in the case of *Middlemarch*, middle England in the period leading up to the first Reform Bill of 1832), and of the period in which the text was written and published. In this achievement, as we have observed, she was profoundly influenced by contemporary debates about the role of music in human experience, and in particular by the musical philosophy (for so such a highly integrated artistic system deserves to be called) of her contemporary Richard Wagner.

While it is certainly true that Eliot felt Wagner's influence as strongly as any writer then or since, and that she crafted her novels as a response to the intellectual challenges set by his music, it is not at all clear that her imaginative writing qualifies as 'Wagnerian fiction'. For one thing, the author's vital role within her own work (in the complex figure of the omniscient, interventionist narrator), might be regarded as militating against Wagnerian method, in which the narrative is organised in terms of a complex system of relations between 'Wagner' – the composer and librettist – and a cluster of other subject positions including the conductor, director, singers, orchestra and chorus. A second discrepancy derives from the tradition of English domestic fiction, which remains a strong presence within all Eliot's work. This tradition lends the fictional worlds she creates a resolutely non-epic, and certainly non-Wagnerian, aura. Finally, there is the issue of realism, which – although too large to broach here – is clearly the animating aesthetic informing Eliot's fiction, and places her in clear opposition to the arch-Romantic Wagner in a number of important respects.

In some senses, then, the provincial England of *Middlemarch* is a very long way from the epic theatre of the the Rhineland gods. If one were searching for the roots of a response within the British literary tradition to the Wagner phenomenon, however, one could do worse than turn to another English novelist: Thomas Hardy.

In his study *Thomas Hardy, Metaphysics and Music*, Mark Asquith has shown the extent to which Hardy was influenced by music in general, and in particular by the example of Wagner, who was moving into a position of aesthetic dominance just as Hardy himself was setting out on his career as novelist. For Asquith, 'music forms a web which weaves together the events unfolding in the narratives into a unified expression of [Hardy's] gloomily coherent metaphysical vision' (2005: 7). This vision was typical in some respects of the anxiety that has long been recognised as afflicting the late-Victorian period. Such anxiety derived in part from widely perceived feelings of loss (of God, as well as of other traditional systems and values) following the Darwinian crisis and the rise of industrialisation, and it found formal expression in the work of many contemporary artists, including the fiction of Charles Dickens and the poetry of Matthew Arnold. In Hardy's case, however, his characteristic angst was systematically underpinned in a much more permanent way by the philosophy of Schopenhauer, for whom earthly pleasure could offer only temporary respite from the underlying reality of the will and its constant, contradictory striving for a peace that can only ever be realised in death.

For Schopenhauer, music constitutes the purest form of that temporary respite. Because it is not mortgaged to reason, because its primary function is to be rather than to represent, music encapsulates the process of desire, gratification and frustration – what we call 'life' – into which the subject is locked. Music, he writes, 'is not an image of phenomena . . . but a direct image of the will itself' (1891: 312). In this sense, music 'gives us nothing but the pure activity of the will' (Peckham 1962: 149); when we hear music, we hear the will at work. At the same time, the musical experience can temporarily transcend the will, at that moment when the subject contemplates the musical work's achieved order, when the exhausting play of 'life' (desire, gratification, frustration) is halted. Music is thus both exemplar and mitigation of the will, encapsulating the 'inner essence' (Schopenhauer 1891: 328) of things far more powerfully than any other art form, and for that very reason, affording us relief from its otherwise constant influence.

Wagnerian aesthetics were clearly locked into Schopenhauerian philosophy in a number of important respects. Besides establishing the influence of these two formidable German figures upon his subject, however, Asquith also explores how Hardy's lifelong amenability to music clearly primed him for considering it 'as an expression of his conception of man's place in the universe.'[7] Hardy's narratives are locatable in material time and place for the sake of novelistic convention; like those of Wagner, however, they are expressive of an essential, universal human drama, the 'reality' of which subsists beneath all merely material phenomena. And just as Wagner developed techniques to enable him to tap into this 'reality', to explore and express it in a customised art form specially developed for the purpose, so Hardy – learning from the composer and adopting many of his techniques – developed a type of fiction that answered the requirements both of his philosophical vision and his aesthetic needs.

Music pervades Hardy's fiction in its use as a metaphor for both sexual attraction and community relations in *Under the Greenwood Tree* (1872), in the technical description of the wind on Egdon Heath in *The Return of the Native* (1878), and in its highly focused role in the later tragedies, such as *The Mayor of Casterbridge* (1886) and *Tess of the D'Urbervilles* (1891). As Asquith shows, moreover, this music is Schopenhauerian in inspiration and Wagnerian in articulation, incorporating effects such as the tone-setting prelude, the implacable music that acts as a chorus in relation to the unfolding drama, and the translation of the individual's immediate plight into the idiom of a species myth.

As a gesture towards the extent and the complexity of Hardy's musical fiction, we might consider the leitmotif of the Christminster bells in *Jude the Obscure* (1895). This technique is especially associated with Wagner's great opera cycle *Der Ring des Nibelungen*, although there are self-conscious precedents throughout the history of art music going back at least as far as Beethoven, and arguably much further. As we observed in Chapter 1, the leitmotif (variously translated as 'leading motive' or 'representative theme') is a short musical phrase intended to denote a character, object, or abstract idea within the world of the narrative. As the musical leitmotif punctuates the unfolding operatic drama, creating effects of remembrance and expectation within the listener, so the literary leitmotif punctuates the unfolding novelistic drama, accruing layers of signification that assume an organic function beyond the mere consumption of narrative. Calvin S. Brown's description of the literary leitmotif still holds good:

One might say that it is a verbal formula which is deliberately repeated, which is easily recognized at each recurrence, and which serves, by means of this recognition, to link the context in which the repetition occurs with earlier contexts in which the motive had appeared ... Perhaps we should add that in both music and literature the Leitmotiv has to be comparatively short and must have a programmatic association – must refer to something beyond the tones or words which it contains.

(1948: 211)

Jude first hears the bells when taking an evening walk to a hill outside the village of Marygreen so as to be able to see the lights of the city of Christminster whence the schoolteacher Phillotson has gone:

Suddenly there came along the wind something towards him – a message from the place – from some soul residing there, it seemed. Surely it was the sound of bells, the voice of the city, faint and musical, calling to him, 'We are happy here!'

He had become entirely lost to his bodily situation during this mental leap, and only got back to it by a rough recalling.

(1985: 63)

The bells stir a desire within Jude that will lead to tragedy, for himself and for many of those associated with him. At this point, however, focalised from the perspective of a naïve young boy, they represent the immemorial emotions of hope and happiness. In fact, the bells here represent a kind of music, and Jude a kind of audience, momentarily submerging his personal will in the universal will. It is in essence an aesthetic experience of the kind constantly sought by the artist (such as Wagner). In a movement that encapsulates the contradictory nature of Schopenhauerian Will, Jude's physical self – his 'bodily situation' – is 'entirely lost' for the duration of the encounter with the bells; which is to say, as he perceives the prospect of satisfied desire, he momentarily frees himself from it, and experiences a kind of ecstasy as a result.

Having broached the 'gratification' of a contemplative life, Hardy depicts the process of its defeat in remorseless detail. Jude's relinquishment of his Christminster dream in favour of the disastrous relationship with Arabella is symbolised by 'the chime of church bells ... reduced to one note, which quickened, and stopped' (99). By the time the Christminster bells are next invoked as a specific theme, he has experienced nearly twenty years of disappointment and frustration.

The dream proved vain, his ecstasy more temporary and more elusive than he might have feared. Jude wanders around the town in the rain with Sue and three children looking for accommodation:

> Two or three of the houses had notices of rooms to let, and the new-comers knocked at the door of one, which a woman opened.
> 'Ah – listen!' said Jude suddenly, instead of addressing her.
> 'What?'
> 'Why the bells – what church can that be? The tones are familiar.'
> 'I don't know!' said the landlady tartly. 'Did you knock to ask that?'
> Another peal of bells had begun to sound out at some distance off.
> 'No; for lodgings,' said Jude, coming to himself. (402)

In Wagnerian practise, although the leitmotif remains the same basic organisation of sounds, its meaning in relation to the surrounding sounds alters, so that what had once sounded as unproblematically positive, for example, can, through inventive uses of colour, harmony and other effects, sound ambivalent or even negative. Moreover, once heard in this fashion, it is impossible for the listener to return to the original 'pure' connotation; any future rendition will always retain the possibility of the revised meaning. This is borne out by Hardy's use of the bells in this instance. Irrespective of whether these are the actual bells that called to him all those years ago, '[the] tones are familiar' indeed, because they remind him (and the reader) of what they once connoted. In a cruel echo of the earlier experience, Jude is once again transported out of his body, but this time there is no hope of regaining that experience in any more permanent or formal way: the doors of Christminster remain firmly closed to him, and Jude knows that he is destined to be 'obscure', to be 'an outsider to the end of [his] days' (401).

Moreover, we should note that this passage is presaged by two short references, one to a 'peal of six bells' (398), the other to 'the peals of the organ' (399) – the latter being a description one would not normally associate with the sound of an organ. Again, this recalls the Wagnerian technique of repeating leitmotif materials in different forms throughout the entire texture of the music, as different instruments assume the theme (in totality or in part) in different registers.

The bells make a final appearance as Jude lies dying, watched over by the impatient Arabella:

> Certain sounds from without revealed that the town was in festivity, though little of the festival, whatever it might have been, could be

seen here. Bells began to ring, and the notes came into the room through the open window, and travelled around Jude's head in a hum. They made her restless, and at last she said to herself: 'Why ever doesn't father come!' (484)

The bells repeat their primary function of making the hearer 'restless' with the promise of happiness, but this time Jude is not physically capable of answering the old call, and it is left to Arabella to take to the streets of Christminster in pursuit of the promised pleasure. His death song (485–6) is a bitterly ironic duet composed of the 'learning' that betrayed him to such a miserable end, punctuated by the cheers of those – students and dons – to whom the bells apparently did not lie. In a usage that uncannily imitates the sound of bells as they cease ringing, the final thematic appearance (on page 484) is followed by two faint echoes which recall both the articulation and the frustration of the first association long ago in Marygreen. As Arabella calls to the sexton to see about the bell for Jude's funeral, '[through] the partly opened window the joyous throb of a waltz entered from the ball-room at Cardinal' (489); while on their last appearance, '[the] bells struck out joyously; and their reverberations travelled round the bedroom' (490). This 'joy' is not the expression of a vindictive God celebrating the demise of yet another over-reacher, however; it is simply a function of the 'bellness' of the bells, which, in themselves, remain indifferent to the human drama being enacted within their sonic range.[8]

E. M. Forster, *Howards End* (1910)

George Moore was the Anglophone writer most heavily influenced by Wagner. The novel *Evelyn Innes* (1898) and its sequel *Sister Theresa* (1901) are 'saturated' (Blissett 1968: 58) with Wagnerian associations at both the formal and conceptual levels, while Richard Cave regards *The Lake* (1905) as 'the Wagnerian novel perfected' (1978: 165). Moore had lived in Paris after the Franco-Prussian War of 1870–1, witnessing at first hand the onset of French literary Wagnerism in the wake of the publication of Charles Baudelaire's influential essay of 1861 entitled 'Richard Wagner and Tannhäuser in Paris' (1992: 222–35). The young Anglo-Irishman became acquainted with many of the leading European writers who gathered in the city, including the novelists Gabriele d'Annunzio, Joris-Karl Huysmans and Edouard Dujardin, as well as the poets Stéphane Mallarmé and Paul Verlaine. All of these figures were heavily implicated in Wagnerism, even if much of the time (as, for example, in the case of

Mallarmé) those implications were fraught with ambiguity. Moore was especially friendly with Dujardin, who edited the *Revue Wagnerienne* between 1883 and 1886, and who encouraged discussion of the possibility of adapting the great composer's example for literature. Dujardin later admitted that the interior monologue 'technique in his famous novel [*Les Lauriers sont coupés* (1887–8)] had been devised as an attempt to achieve in literature the effect of Wagnerian music' (Blissett 1968: 61).

Although Eliot and Hardy were certainly inspired by Germanic theories to some degree, and although the impact of the Francophone response to Wagner gradually began to emerge through the likes of Moore and of his friend the critic A. W. Symons, it is true to say that English-language literature was relatively slow to respond to the Wagnerian revolution. It was left to another writer-critic to reflect upon the implications for English literature of the European musico-literary debates of the late nineteenth century and to begin the process of forging a response to those debates within his own imaginative work.

E. M. Forster is an interesting figure in the evolution of the Anglophone music-novel. As a critic he discussed the transposition of various musical techniques and effects into novelistic discourse, although his tone – almost dilettantish, certainly non-systematic – was a very English rejoinder to the passionate philosophical pronouncements of the continentals. As a novelist, he attempted to practise what he preached; or perhaps it would be more accurate to say that in *Aspects of the Novel*, first published in 1927, he preached what he had been attempting to practise since the outset of his writing career. E. K. Brown's *Rhythm in the Novel* (1950) was largely inspired by Forster's frustratingly curtailed comments on the use of 'easy' and 'hard' rhythm in fiction. Brown suggests that the interested reader should turn to Forster's own fiction, and particularly to his final novel, to discern his meaning:

> Three big blocks of sound – that was Forster's account of rhythm in the Fifth Symphony. Three big blocks of sound – that is what *A Passage to India* consists of . . . [It] is a prophetic novel, a singing in the halls of fiction: the infinite resourcefulness of Forster has given it a rhythmic form that enables us to respond to it as prophesy and song; to pass beyond character, story, and setting, and attend, delightedly, to the grouping and ungrouping of ideas and emotions.
>
> (Brown 1967: 113, 115)

In fact, Forster's experiments with rhythm – indeed, his general engagement with matters musical – may be traced to the beginning of his career; it was certainly a factor in *Howards End*, in many ways his break-through novel and one some consider to be his greatest achievement, despite the epic ambitions of *A Passage to India*.

Rhythm functions in Forster's novel at both the micro and the macro levels. Focusing on the former for present purposes, the reader observes the recurrence of certain terms and phrases that are clearly intended to invoke certain ideas and emotions. One such cluster of phrases is asso-ciated with the Wilcox family, and suggests a general competence and confidence vis-à-vis the 'real world'. Thus, there is a retrospective irony attached to Aunt Juley's description of Helen's affair with Paul Wilcox as a 'business' (1960: 8, 10); for it becomes clear during the course of the narrative that the Wilcox family regard even matters of the heart in terms of a materialist discourse in which 'value' is the key criterion in any exchange. Mr Wilcox's assertion, 'that one sound man of business did more good to the world than a dozen of your social reformers' (24), claims the word for his discourse, and sets up a regime of meaning that will recur throughout the text.[9] Echoes of this regime – modified and mitigated though it be by the intervening plot – may still be discerned in Paul's explanation towards the end of the text that he has 'come home to look after the business' (317).

English materialism is opposed, at least initially, by German idealism in the form of the Schlegel family and their identification with what Aunt Juley characterises as 'Literature and Art'. The importance of this phrase is emphasised by the fact that it is repeated within a short space of narrative time early in the text (10). When it next appears, however, in a passage in which Mr Wilcox is being quoted in free indirect dis-course, the phrase has been inverted ('Art and Literature', 24). This process recalls the musical technique whereby a particular phrase is repeated in some altered form (inversion is common), so as to suggest not only the original connotation but also a range of alternative mean-ings lying dormant within the phrase, which will be liberated by its rep-etition in a different setting. It also recalls Bakhtin's strictures regarding the implicit dialogism of novelistic discourse – which is to say, that every phrase realises a contest between different discourses that attempt to claim the phrase within their own terms, thereby imposing their interpretations upon it.

Caught between the worlds of 'business' and 'Art and Literature' is the lowly clerk Leonard Bast; once again, ironies amass around the repeti-tion of certain words and phrases. So, whereas the Schlegels have been intimidated by the fact that the Wilcox family seemed 'to have their hands on all the ropes' (27), Leonard is intimidated by the Schlegels for the very same reason and in the very same terms (53). *Howards End* is in fact a meditation on the existence of these different worlds, on the different discourses within which they express themselves, and on the possibility of connection between them. The key point for present purposes is the manner in which music comes to figure within all three aspects of this meditation.

Forster's concerns with the possibility of connection are clearly signalled in Chapter 5, which opens with his description of a performance of Beethoven's Fifth Symphony – or rather, with the author's description of various characters' responses to that work, in particular the character Helen Schlegel who, impetuous romantic that she is, responds impetuously and romantically to the performance, discerning a quasi-Wagnerian (and thus anachronistic) narrative involving gods and goblins within the music, where no such programme was in fact nominated by the composer. Her sister Margaret explains Helen's response to the suggestible Leonard Bast in terms that engage with recent musico-literary debates, and which reflect back on Forster's own concerns in this novel:

> Now, this very symphony that we've just been having – she won't let it alone. She labels it with meanings from start to finish; turns it into literature. I wonder if the day will ever return when music will be treated as music . . . But, of course, the real villain is Wagner. He has done more than any man in the nineteenth century towards the muddling of the arts. I do feel that music is in very serious state just now, though extraordinarily interesting. Every now and then in history there do come these terrible geniuses, like Wagner, who stir up all the wells of thought at once. For a moment it's splendid. Such a splash as never was. But afterwards – such a lot of mud; and the wells – as it were, they communicate with each other too easily now, and not one of them will run quite clear. That's what Wagner's done.
>
> (1960: 38–9)

Wagner is identified as the figure responsible for the muddling of the arts, although whether the ensuing 'communication' between them is to be welcomed or not is unclear. In the meantime, the possibility of 'connection' has implications both for the fictional world of the narrative and for the 'real' world of the narration. Helen's desire to turn music into literature accords with her general concern (one produced by a combination of temperament, class and education) to find 'connections' between disparate phenomena, including people. It is this concern, to 'only connect', which provides both the impetus and the drama for the narrative, for it is precisely the politics of connection – between the Schegels and the Wilcoxes, between the world of 'business' and 'Art and Literature', between Germany and England – that drives the plot.

At the same time, the passage is a microcosm of the text itself in which the possibility of connection – in this case medial connection between two different art forms – is broached. Helen's desire to understand music in terms of literature raises the possibility of understanding literature – this specific literary instance, in fact – in terms of music. In other words, *Howards End* is possessed of a metafictional dimension in as much as the social and political elements, which are engaged at the level of plot, are seen to emerge from, and at the same time have implications for, the process of narration itself. The passage quoted above represents a *mise en abyme* – which is to say, it is a scene that both reflects and reflects upon the text's larger concerns.[10] It is thus one of the earliest examples from the British novelistic tradition of the tendency to suspend mimesis in order to question the possibility of the text itself, and to extend that interrogative gesture into the world of the narrative as well as into the 'real' world outside the text. (The influence of Sterne is of course discernible.) It is not the last time, however, that the putative 'otherness' of music will be recruited as part of the novelist's reflection on the possibility of the text-in-process.

Aldous Huxley, *Point Counter Point* (1928)

Point Counter Point appears to be the first novel from any tradition in which '[the] musicalization of fiction' (Huxley 1965: 301) is invoked as a specific, self-conscious topic. The title is a bit of a giveaway: as Calvin S. Brown explains, it is 'a literal translation of the *punctum contra punctum*, or "note against note" of the early theorists' (1948: 209). The twenty-second chapter of the text is an extended metafictional meditation in which the character Philip Quarles (a novelist) ponders (in the form of a journal entry) the possibility of writing a novel that would subscribe to musical aesthetics. He imagines a novel that could replicate the subtleties and the suppleness of musical structure; that could incorporate variation and modulation of theme; that could develop techniques to enable simultaneity of perspective – to develop, that is to say, a means of adopting the quintessential musical effect of counterpoint for literary discourse.[11]

Quarles is drawn to this revolutionary form of the novel because of the peculiar way in which he understands the world to function. In chapter 14, when he discusses the role of contemporary fiction with his wife, he identifies 'the essence of the new way of looking [as] multiplicity. Multiplicity of eyes and multiplicity of aspects seen' (197). It is no longer possible for the true artist, he insists, to see or to represent the world from one perspective, or to assume the outmoded rights and privileges of a uni-ocular god who could master the panorama beneath his all-seeing eye. No less than Joyce or any of his fellow Modernists, Huxley was aware that the period in which he was living had witnessed a revolution in the sheer ubiquity of sensory phenomena, a revolution facilitated by the technical diversification of representative media – in a nutshell, there was simply more 'stuff' in the world: more stuff to read, to listen to, to look at. As reality changes, so must the means of representing it; and as someone whose business is the comprehension and representation of reality, Quarles realises that the novelist must acknowledge that revolution and respond accordingly.

This early passage is dominated by a visual metaphor. Quarles and Elinor talk about seeing 'with religious eyes, economic eyes . . . [loving] eyes too'; transposed into fiction, 'the result [would be] a very queer picture indeed.' The aesthetic breakthrough Quarles achieves between Chapters 14 and 22 is the realisation that music (at least, the European art music he references) rather than pictorial art is better suited to the adaptation of 'multiplicity' for literary discourse, and to the exploration of 'multiplicity' in relation to the human subject at this particular point in history. European art music has properties – in particular, sonata form and the related techniques of harmony and counterpoint – that militate against singularity and which invite the listener to locate the subject (or the idea of subjectivity) in relation to other subjects (or the idea of multi-subjectivity). Such relationships may be harmonic or dissonant, sympathetic or antagonistic; what they always offer, however, is both a reminder and an example of the dialogic nature underpinning all human endeavour – the fact that the 'one' only comes to a sense of itself in terms of its relationship with the 'many'. It is unsurprising, therefore, that music is incorporated into the aesthetic systems of the fictional author Philip Quarles, and indeed, into that of his creator, Aldous Huxley.

Point Counter Point is the contrapuntal novel imagined by Philip Quarles in Chapter 22. The narrative is comprised of a large number of characters (thirty-eight, according to one estimate[12]), each of whom represents a 'voice' that is incorporated into the main body of the work. Some of these 'voices' are stronger than others, just as some instruments can dominate an orchestral composition. These 'voices', moreover, overlap in various groupings and clusters; each is recognisable by characteristics analogous to the musical qualities of tone, timbre, pitch and loudness (for example, the phonetic representation of various accents in the text, or the association of a particular vocabulary with a particular character). Themes are introduced – desire, love, authority and death, for example – each of which has, in the manner of a musical theme, its peculiar identity, a 'shape' or 'form' which differentiates one from the other, but which also links them in some respects. These themes are dramatised with reference to various situations, and then 'developed' as we observe different characters responding to a similar situation (say, the situation of being trapped in an unsatisfactory relationship, or of coming to terms with the death of a loved one) in different ways. The text 'modulates' through a number of moods, each theme being treated with reference to the peculiarities of the different 'voices'. Philip Quarles' notions of desire, love and authority, for example, are different, and recognisably so, from those of his father Sydney. At the same time, they are not as dissimilar as either thinks, and for all their recognisable differences, remote strains of the father's 'voice' may be discerned in that of the son.

All in all, then, *Point Counter Point* offers an extended example of 'the musicalization of fiction' – the attempt to incorporate musical forms and effects into literary discourse. At the same time, music features throughout the text at a thematic level, and not only in the metafictional musings of Philip Quarles. The narrative is framed by two musical encounters: the first, a live performance of Bach's Suite in B minor at a party held in the home of Lord and Lady Edward Tantamount; the second a gramophone version of the third movement from Beethoven's String Quartet no.15 in A minor, played in the home of Maurice Spandrell as he, unbeknownst to his guests Mark and Mary Rampion, awaits the death he has arranged for himself at the hands of some political assassins. It is in Huxley's descriptions of the various characters' different responses to these pieces of music that the implications of 'multiplicity' as both a force in the world and an aesthetic concept are fully realised.

We notice, first of all, that there is no sign of Wagner here or anywhere throughout the novel, unless it be in the monomania of the charismatic fascist leader Everard Webley. It is clear, in fact, that Huxley has travelled a long way in method and intention from the Wagnerian novelists of the late nineteenth century.[13] There are some obvious parallels between *Point Counter Point* and a novel such as *Jude the Obscure*, not least in the bleak outlook of many of the characters and the unhappy fate that overtakes them. Huxley has no room for the Wagnerian hero, however, or indeed for most of the formal and conceptual qualities that characterise that composer's aesthetic vision. Instead, we are back to 'absolute music', sound uninfected by the language of the singer or the gesture of the actor; for it is there, in the unadulterated sonic imagination of Bach and Beethoven, that we may perceive something of the truth of the human condition.[14]

The Bach suite anticipates the theme of individuality-in-multiplicity that will exercise the thoughts and actions of a number of characters, while at the same time impacting upon the form of the novel itself. Each instrument utters its own truth, occasionally combining

> to create a seemingly final and perfected harmony, only to break apart again. Each is always alone and separate and individual. 'I am I,' asserts the violin; 'the world revolves round me.' 'Round me,' calls the cello. 'Round me,' the flute insists. And all are equally right and equally wrong; and none of them will listen to the others. (26)

The narrator likens this effect to 'the human fugue' in which every voice in the world is encouraged to assume that 'I am I . . . the world revolves round me'. The role of the artist is to set these individual voices (or a selection thereof) in counterpoint, so that from the resulting 'sound' something of the paradoxical 'truth' of the human condition may be communicated. As interpreted by the narrator, the Bach represents a form of beauty that the human can recognise and aspire to, but only infrequently and temporarily realise. This point is then concretised in the different responses to the music of various members of the audience: the painter John Bidlake is bored, because his aesthetic sense is primarily visual (27); the widow Fanny Logan is moved because the music offers her a consoling vision of her husband, at once sad and comforting (28); the scientist Lord Edward is fascinated because of music's affinity with mathematics (37). No single vision is privileged; each response – like the beauty envisioned in the music itself – is shown to be contingent, temporary, one element of a contrapuntal response of which the individual voice is not necessarily aware, but which the artist has drawn together for the purposes of communicating a contingent, temporary 'truth'.

If Bach's music offers the reader of *Point Counter Point* an image of the paradox of existence, Beethoven's music offers to resolve that paradox. Maurice Spandrell is in search of a reason for existence, and believes he may have found it in the long third movement of the A minor quartet, which Beethoven famously described in an annotation at the head of the original manuscript as 'a restored one's holy song of thanksgiving to God, in the Lydian mode'. Spandrell's interpretation is resisted by the artist Mark Rampion, however, who, while acknowledging the music's power and beauty, disdains its promise of metaphysical redemption.[15] Huxley 'orchestrates' the scene brilliantly, describing the music itself in some detail while at the same time observing the impact of its emotional development upon the listening characters. Again, the truth communicated by the music is paradoxical: 'an active calm, an almost passionate serenity. The miraculous paradox of eternal life and eternal repose was musically realized' (439). Having once perceived the paradox, however, Spandrell is ready for the peace that follows, and he embraces his own murder with alacrity:

> Through the open door came the sound of the music. The passion had begun to fade from the celestial melody. Heaven, in those long-drawn notes, became once more the place of absolute rest, of still and blissful convalescence. Long notes, a chord repeated, protracted, bright and pure, hanging, floating, effortlessly soaring on and on. And then suddenly there was no more music; only the scratching of the needle on the revolving disc. (439–40)

Music, then, provides Huxley with both an interpretation of the human dilemma and an image of its resolution: on the one hand, the 'counterpoint' that characterises human existence and its search for an assurance of beauty 'in spite of squalor and stupidity . . . in spite of all the evil' (26); on the other hand, the inevitable 'point' of resolution, the home key, that we crave in the face of this constant struggle.

Colin MacInnes, *Absolute Beginners* (1959)

Although set in the same city and published only thirty-one years apart, *Absolute Beginners* and *Point Counter Point* are in many respects very different prospects, both in terms of the worlds they represent and the aesthetic assumptions underpinning each text. Whereas the earlier novel self-consciously incorporates music and musical aesthetics as part of its own structure, Colin MacInnes's interest in music appears to reside firmly at the level of plot: what the characters say about it, how they use it, what it represents as cultural value within the moral economy of the story. With its four-part structure (each part given over to a particular month), its array of characters orchestrated by the limited perspective of the unnamed narrator, and its argot of 'hip' language, it might be possible to infer musical structures and effects within the novel; this seems beside the point, however, when the author has invested so much in the idea of music within the textual world itself.

Set over four months during the summer of 1958, MacInnes's cult novel offers a perspective on British culture during a period of intense change. The country was still recovering in many respects after the Second World War: food rationing did not end until 1954, and the impact of bombing remained evident in many cities – none more so than London. Even when matters started to pick up economically, the social and cultural legacy of the war remained strong among the generation that had been forced to endure it. The Suez crisis of 1956 had severely demoralised national confidence in Britain's imperial status. Just as the country was renegotiating its international status, a different form of 'otherness' had appeared at home with the influx of economic migrants from the West Indies and other former colonies. At the same time, two socio-cultural trends were combining to undermine traditional British values: the 'invention' of the teenager and the global hegemony of American popular culture.

MacInnes incorporates many of these issues into his novel. Tension rises between old and new Britain throughout the summer, culminating in the race riots represented towards the end of the story. As befits his confused state, the narrator is ambivalent towards the country (and especially the city) in which he lives: on the one hand, he thinks 'my God, how horrible this country is, how dreary, how lifeless, how blind and busy over trifles!' (1992: 44); on the other hand, London is his home and he moves around its spaces in a proprietorial and occasionally affectionate manner. The socio-political crisis that emerges around the narrator politicises him against his will, for he comes to realise that he cannot simply opt out of 'adult' issues such as racism. In this sense *Absolute Beginners* is clearly a kind of *Bildungsroman* in which the young hero undergoes a spiritual and emotional education precipitated by the narrative crisis in which he is unavoidably implicated.

This is borne out by the fact that the civic conflict provides a backdrop for a series of personal crises that the narrator is experiencing over the same period of time. For the fact is that adolescents get older: the narrator is in his final teenage year and is facing the prospect of leaving behind not just that period of his life but the values and the lifestyle associated with it. One set of problems relates to his friendship with 'the Wizard' and his relationship with sometime girlfriend 'Crêpe Suzette'. The former turns seriously sour as the Wizard's innately exploitative nature is revealed over the course of the narrative. The latter is more complex, as the narrator finds himself jealous of Suzette's sexual predilection for black men and frustrated by her engagement to Henley, a much older man who offers her financial security. Averse as he is to such 'adult' emotions, these responses contribute to his sense of disorientation as the summer progresses. All these crises, moreover, are locked in to the related issues of age and music that inform the novel throughout.

To the narrator, established British culture appears exhausted, worn out by its exertions, and unequal to the challenge of the new world it helped to create. He celebrates the category of youth for its freshness, its power, its lack of identification with the war and all the suffering and austerity that it entailed. At the same time, youth's immaturity is disdained by those in search of some form of 'authentic' cultural capital appropriate to their new separate identity.

At the period in question, many young people were seeking this cultural capital in music. While some turned to the family of styles related to rock 'n' roll and others embraced a resurgent folk movement, a significant section of contemporary British youth came to identify with a musical genre that was part of a living, maturing tradition, that appeared to be uncontaminated by issues of 'popularity', and that seemed to impart to listeners some of the hipness that distinguished its performers: that music was jazz.

As an invention of African-American culture, jazz tended to feature in the cultural traditions of that community and that country; its enthusiastic adaptation in the United Kingdom, especially in the years after the war, assumed an unavoidably belated air, and this was as true of the textual representations of the genre as it was of the music itself. In *Absolute Beginners* there can be no doubting the narrator's genuine affection for jazz, however, and his identification with its values and principles. The process whereby a young white English boy makes an empathetic leap between his own experience and those (for example) of African-American jazz divas such as Ella Fitzgerald and Billie Holiday highlights some of the enduring attractions of modern popular music: its endless adaptability, its importance as a readily available site of identity formation, and its ability to create communities outwith those sanctioned by official state formations.

'[Youth] is international', claims the narrator; and throughout the novel 'the teenager' is acknowledged as a special, separate category. Precisely because of this separate status, however, the teenager is vulnerable to exploitation. The novel opens with the narrator and Wizard bemoaning the commercialisation of 'the teenager' as manifested in the contemporary popular song 'He's Got the Whole World in His Hands', which was a number one British hit in April 1958 for a fourteen-year-old singer named Laurie London. The difference between Laurie London and Ella Fitzgerald – which is to say, between a form of music detested for its manipulative commercialism and one cherished for its supposed authenticity – creates an economy of meaning and value in terms of which the narrator can organise his life, providing him with a seemingly stable field of value within a world that is being turned upside down.

The narrator of *Absolute Beginners* represents a type that we shall encounter frequently in Part II of this study: a young male metropolitan who believes in the supreme importance of music in general, and of the music of his era in particular. In this case the music may be jazz, but the dedication is familiar in terms of its vehemence and its utter commitment:

> Now, you can think what you like about the art of jazz – quite frankly, I don't really care *what* you think, because jazz is a thing so wonderful that if anybody doesn't rave about it, all you can feel for them is pity.
> (1992: 61, original emphasis)

Music offers the narrator a 'home' – an absolute centre of value and meaning that remains stable – to which he believes he can always (re)turn, no matter the changes overtaking his country, his city, or himself. This is the power of music's attraction to youth culture and to novels such as this. The prospect of loss remains strong, however, and despite the strength of their convictions regarding the music, these subjects tend to be always in or on the point of crisis. Such crises arise in part from the wider socio-political context, and in part from the ineluctable human process of ageing. However, they arise also from the inability of any cultural discourse – including music – to 'embody' or 'represent' a stable system of values. The meaning of a cultural practice or object is always a function of its relationship with an engaging subject – a subject who is always changing physically, psychologically, emotionally, politically, and so on. What MacInnes captured at this early stage in the emergence of youth-oriented culture was the fact that the teenager is always under pressure, always attempting to define an identity, even as they are forced to face the prospect of leaving that identity behind.

Anthony Burgess, *Mozart and the Wolf Gang* (1991)

Anthony Burgess is widely regarded as the writer who brought the serious artistic intent of Modernism into the Postmodern era. A novelist who was also a composer, Burgess dedicated much of his artistic life to thinking about, and experimenting with, the possibility of representing music in literary form. This interest (which was to become an obsession) is apparent in what remains his most famous novel, *A Clockwork Orange* (1962). The narrator, Alex, disdains the popular music of the day, regarding it as sentimental and shallow. The classical music he prefers (a combination of fictitious and actual works) is not a calming or civilizing influence, however: rather, its emotional intensity inspires him to extremes of violence – the 'ultra-violent' sprees in which he leads his gang of 'droogs'. Beethoven emerges as an especially complex figure. Alex already associates the composer with violence as when, for example, he listens to the Ninth Symphony while raping two young girls in his bedroom (2000: 39). This association is made explicit in the aversion treatment to which Alex is subjected, when the Fifth Symphony is used as a soundtrack for the shocking Nazi film he is made to watch. Thereafter, he cannot hear classical music (especially Beethoven) without feeling acutely ill.

When Alex overcomes the treatment, he listens again to the Ninth Symphony, but it is clear that the 'freedom' he embraces is the freedom to be violent:

> Oh, it was gorgeosity and yumyumyum. When it came to the Scherzo I could viddy myself very clear running and running on like very light and mysterious nogas, carving the whole litso of the creeching world with my cut-throat britva. (139)

Burgess was clearly alert to the role of music in wider cultural discourse, including his own fiction. It was this sensitivity that he was to test to the limit in *Napoleon Symphony* (1974) – as Werner Wolf describes it, 'one of the clearest cases of a novel informed by a musicalizing intention' (1999: 197). Burgess explains his ambitions for this novel in 'An Epistle to the Reader', a rhyming apologia which is inserted at the end of the text:

> I was brought up on music and compose
> Bad music still, but ever since I chose
> The novelist's métier one mad idea
> Has haunted me, and I fulfil it here
> Or try to – it is this: somehow to give
> Symphonic shape to verbal narrative,
> Impose on life, though nerves scream and resist
> The abstract patterns of the symphonist
> (1974: 348).

Napoleon Symphony represents the first attempt in the history of literature to write an extended prose fiction in the form of, or at least with
sustained reference to, a pre-existing musical work – in this case,
Beethoven's Third Symphony in E flat (1805), entitled *Eroica*, which the
composer originally dedicated to his contemporary Napoleon Bonaparte.
Burgess uses the epistle to explain how he attempted to convert both
the structure of Beethoven's composition and the emotions contained
in or expressed by that structure into novelistic form.

Wolf's analysis reveals some of the devices employed by the author to
achieve this, including: the use of repeated motifs (such as the phrase
'ensanguinated tyrant') throughout the text, each repetition developing
and modifying previous articulations; the use of typographical innovation to suggest polyphony and create counterpoint, emphasis, and other
musical effects; the four-part structure modelled (in mood, duration and
ratio) after the structure of *Eroica*; the further structuring of each chapter in terms of the thematic development of each part of the symphony;
and so on.

Wolf claims that 'Burgess manages to create a piece of verbal music
that continually reminds the reader of the musical pretext and keeps
the impression alive that here indeed "verbal narrative" is given "symphonic shape"' (1999: 207). Is this the most that may be said for
Burgess's grand experiment, however? Does '[keeping] the impression
alive' really represent the culmination of two centuries of experiment
with musical fiction? The author himself demurs, freely admitting the
failure of his 'mad idea': despite the structural analogies, the battery of
overt and covert references, and all the other ingenious devices, it is
simply not possible, he maintains, for prose fiction to capture 'music's
formal essence' (350) in a literary medium. In this regard, *Napoleon
Symphony* is a monument to its own failure, and to the failure of the idea
of the music-novel as it has evolved since *Tristram Shandy*.

Because Mozart predated Beethoven, it is counterintuitive to imagine
the former's work as a rejoinder to the latter's. Temporal logic (as well as
cultural history) suggests that Romanticism evolved from classicism,
developing the structural and thematic concerns of the earlier period in
response to new technologies and different socio-political contexts. Yet
there are elements in Mozart that anticipate and qualify Beethoven, and
not merely in a technical sense. What the two composers offer are alternative visions – occasionally overlapping but always distinguishable – of
what it means to be human. In very broad terms, one might characterise
the relationship between the two great composers as a dialectic of
hope and resignation, or perhaps of desire and the surrender of desire;

the one constantly haunts the other, insinuating himself into the other's imagination and its articulation in musical form. To turn to Mozart after Beethoven is thus not necessarily a return, but a reorientation of the economy of desire within which the human subject is bound to trade.

I mention this because of Burgess's (re)turn to Mozart in one of his last 'novels', certainly his last sustained attempt to realise – or at least invoke – the idea of musical fiction. *Mozart and the Wolf Gang* (1991) is clearly 'musicalised' in a number of recognisable ways – in its title and its content, as well as in the deployment of various 'musical' forms. The text is far from being a traditional novel – there is no attempt to construct a plausible, developmental plot enacted by plausible, consistent characters. Rather, *Mozart and the Wolf Gang* is comprised of 'a parodic conglomerate of dramatic dialogue, libretto, symphonic text, mock-Socratic dialogue, film script and essay' (Muller-Muth 1999: 249). It opens with a discussion – about music in general and Mozart in particular – conducted in the form of a conversation between a number of famous composers from history, including the two 'masters' against whom Mozart is traditionally ranged in terms of vision and achievement: Beethoven and Wagner. There follows a mock *opera buffa* libretto in three acts which, besides featuring Mozart himself and various contemporaries, continues the discussion broached in the opening – this time introducing a novelist (Henry James) and a librettist (Lorenzo Da Ponte, who collaborated with Mozart on some of his most successful operas) as well as the twentieth-century composers Arnold Schoenberg and George Gershwin.

The centrepiece of the text is 'K550 (1788)' (81–91) – ten pages of text in which the author apparently attempts to produce a prose rendition of Mozart's Symphony no.40 in G minor. This piece of writing is less ambitious than *Napoleon Symphony*, perhaps, but is nonetheless 'composed' with the same serious intent of transposing music into literary discourse. The result, as 'Anthony' remarks to 'Burgess' at the beginning of the following section, is 'gibberish'; the latter agrees, admitting '[there's] a musical structure underneath, filched from Mozart, but one art cannot do the work of another' (92). The author appears, in other words, not to have progressed beyond the point he reached at the end of *Napoleon Symphony*: he is capable of suggesting a musical analogy through the use of allusion and various non-standard literary devices, but ultimately he has to admit the impossibility of his 'mad idea'.

Such a conclusion might appear to bode ill for an academic study of musical fiction such as this. If the most sustained and ambitious efforts to incorporate music into fiction are 'gibberish', then analysis can only comprise a series of descriptions of the ways in which various authors have failed in the same endeavour. To this implicit indictment there are two responses, the first of which is the straightforward one that not all writers imagine music in the same way, nor do they attempt to incorporate it into their writing in the same way. Burgess's high ambition for music-fiction was born out of a concern with the evolving human subject and its capacity to create and communicate meaning. That ambition represents only one use of music within fiction, however; the task of this book is to consider, describe and account for the very different reasons that writers choose to incorporate music – at either a thematic or a formal level – into their novels. As Stephen Benson writes: 'The central point about [literary] music is not the success or otherwise of the evocation, but the nature of the performance: the question of how and why music is staged, and to what desired end' (2006: 4).

The second response is suggested by a reading of *Mozart and the Wolf Gang* itself. As Burgess explains in the essay that concludes the book, he returned to Mozart after a lifetime's immersion in Romanticism and Modernism in an effort to reaffirm not one or another particular ideological vision, but the very principles of human endeavour and creativity. Despite cynicism, scepticism and the shame and ignobility that characterised twentieth-century history in particular, Burgess insists that the music of Mozart can function to remind us that 'noble visions only exist because they can be realised' (148). It is in such a spirit that he turned once again to the music-novel after the 'failure' of *Napoleon Symphony* – to fail inevitably, once again. It is in the same spirit that I now invite the reader to broach the inevitable 'failure' of the contemporary British music-novel, to celebrate the 'noble visions' that inspire such endeavours, and to insist upon their potential 'realisation' in the face of cynicism and doubt.

Part II

3
'It Ain't What You Do . . .':
Musical Genre in the Novel

Introduction

It will have been noted that the various debates attending the music-novel thus far have been conducted (with one or two exceptions) with reference to a specific genre of music: the European art tradition. This is entirely understandable, of course; historically, the creative practices of musical and novelistic composition, as well as the critical one that reflected on the relationship between music and fiction, would have been the province of those with the resources (wealth, education, leisure) and the desire to indulge such 'non-essential' activities. All of these elements are located some way from the vernacular practices (themselves emerging from older paradigms and practices) that gave rise in the twentieth century to a wide range of 'popular' musical styles and traditions. The days when 'music' signified a single, if diverse, field of high cultural activity are, for better or worse, over. In the early twenty-first century the term 'music' is in practice invariably modified with other terms ('rock', 'folk', etc.) so that the particular style in question may be contextualised and thus sensibly discussed.

The 'popular' styles ands traditions that make up this new approach to music have, moreover, found sanction in the form of organised institutional attention.[1] A student may now opt to study jazz, rock, pop, folk, hip-hop, world, dance or a range of other 'popular' (that is, non-art) music genres; that student may further opt to specialise in any one of a number of sub-disciplines emphasising matters of production, organisation, consumption, and so on. The reasons for the emergence of Popular Music Studies since about 1980 are beyond the remit of this study; they involve complex changes in the organisation of various pedagogical and political institutions, and concomitant changes in critical philosophy

(Bennett et al 1993; Lochhead and Auner 2001). In short, the study of popular music became possible, and then seemingly inevitable, in the years around the turn of the millennium; and during that same period the study of popular music has become as complex (if not yet as culturally or institutionally entrenched) as the study of art music.

One of the effects of the emergence of a range of popular styles within the wider critical-cultural landscape has been the greater availability of such styles for novelisation. It is practically impossible to say which came first – the validity of the popular music experience or the legitimisation of the cultural institutions. In any event, popular music has become both a valid and a legitimate experience within the British cultural imagination; as a consequence it comes as no surprise that it has begun to emerge as a significant recurring theme within the wider cultural landscape, and especially in the contemporary British novel. Given the theoretical and literary-historical material encountered in Part I of this study, it should likewise seem likely that when thus invoked, popular music raises a number of important issues with regard to the role of (popular) music and fiction, to the relationship between these practices, and to the wider array of human concerns within which, as we have seen, such practices are locked.

If the first element of the music/novel dyad has become unstable, the second has also mutated and evolved in various directions. Following on from the period of Modernist innovation and experimentation, the novel during the twentieth century became a highly protean form, subject to a great variety of endeavours (on the part of idealistic writers) and prescriptions (on the part of ideological critics). It is fair to say that there has been no dominant impulse within British fiction-writing during the period covered by this study; instead, a wide range of ideas and influences have made themselves felt (Bradford 2007; Mengham 2003). The resulting fiction is, as a glance over the field reveals, diverse in terms of its formal and conceptual concerns and, indeed, in the descriptive titles it has attracted. One conspicuous factor, however, (and it is the idea upon which this study is premised) is the clear and obvious presence of music as a recurring element within a range of otherwise quite diverse texts.

The possible reasons for this phenomenon, as I suggested in the introduction, are many and various. Certainly, one could claim an atavistic function: the novel itself has evolved to a point at which the musical elements, which (as we saw at length in Chapter 2) were always implicit within the form, are now re-emerging, as they did during the high Modernist period at the beginning of the twentieth century. But why (if this is the case) are they re-emerging? What social, political or sector-specific factors pushed music to the forefront of the British novelistic imagination during the last decades of the twentieth century and maintained it there into the new millennium?

The changing fortunes of the art and popular traditions may account to some degree for the high profile that music has assumed in contemporary British fiction. For some, the waning of art music as a factor within the cultural landscape jeopardises a crucial means of knowing and being in the world. Its weakening presence is the most potent symbol there is of the profound changes currently impacting upon the western world; and novelists – as some of the most visible and vocal intellectuals in the public domain – inevitably pick up on this. Should we be surprised if music is thematised in the work of writers anxious about the fate of art music and the form of cultural capital that it represents?[2]

On the other hand, the increasing profile of popular music is, as I have just suggested, a factor of at least equal consideration. We should consider the timescale of this particular narrative: jazz and folk were already established as areas of scholarly interest by the middle of the twentieth century; then rock and other forms of popular music begin to attract serious attention (albeit mostly in the form of journalism) during the 1960s and 1970s. The emergence of punk in the middle of the 1970s, however, was an era-defining phenomenon, its influence spreading far beyond the distinctive music that (along with the accompanying fashion) was its clearest manifestation. Arguably, popular music had been 'crucial' in the lives of young British people since at least the end of the Second World War (as we saw in relation to *Absolute Beginners* in Chapter 2). The medial ubiquity of punk, allied with the 'democratisation' of taste and the growing institutional validation of popular culture itself, brought a new dimension to this obsession: the fact is that popular music became valuable cultural capital in and of itself, and that beyond the subcultural cachet it once possessed, popular music developed into a highly significant factor – in the experience of many, the single most influential factor – in the lives of a whole generation of British youth (Christenson and Roberts 1998). It is within this cultural milieu, and from this generation, that the crop of novelists writing at the turn of the millennium emerged; and it is my contention that this is a major contributing factor to the presence of popular music as a significant, recurring element within the imagination of so many contemporary British writers.

We shall encounter the impact of the punk 'revolution' at length in Chapter 5. Before that, however, and in the light of these opening remarks, I wish to consider the role and representation of a range of musical genres in a selection of contemporary novels, with the intention of examining how these texts deploy different musical forms to explore different experiences and issues.

Folk: *Captain Corelli's Mandolin* (1994) by Louis de Berniéres

We turn first of all to a genre that pre-existed the art tradition, that has shadowed the latter throughout the period of its institutional hegemony, and that arguably functions as the primary genre from which all other musical forms and practices derive.

It might be argued that the music made by the human species as it evolved was the prototypical folk music, as in every instance it appears to have been closely attuned to nature and to the rituals that accompanied the rise of vernacular culture. Among other things, folk music emerges from, and is based upon, the experiences, emotions and practices that most humans can expect to encounter at some point during their lives: work, love, achievement, loss, death, etc. It can appear to be simple both lyrically and musically – indeed, such attributes tend to serve as the basis for its dismissal in accounts that confuse complexity of expression with sophistication of experience. In fact, folk music is extraordinarily complex in all its aspects, replete with protocols and subtleties that only long exposure to the genre can uncover.

Above all, folk music relies on tradition for its power and for its survival. The elements that make up the tradition – including songs and song variations, regional and individual styles, performance and reception protocols, particular tonalities, and so on – all these function with reference to a complex process of authorised inheritance and individual renewal. The emotive power of the music derives from the ritualised repetition of the sounds that animated former generations and from the evocation of shared, apparently elemental, phenomena. At the same time, the music only survives because it is constantly remade in terms of the new contextual concerns (including, quite centrally, new technology) that bear upon each new generation (Rosenberg 1993).

Given that the subject matter of most fiction tends to be drawn from a common store of human experience, one can infer a 'folk' element in many novels from the British tradition. Indeed, it is to such music, rather than to the European art tradition, that one should probably look for formal correspondences between the media. A text such as Thomas Hardy's *Far From the Madding Crowd* (1874), for example, resonates strongly in terms of various ballad traditions: those involving the betrayal of a virgin by a soldier (as in the Troy/Fanny relationship), say, or those concerning the love of a 'common' working man (the shepherd Gabriel Oak) for a 'lady' (Bathsheba Everdene). One could extend these formal resonances to cover a large proportion of the canon of British fiction (especially those with pastoral settings). Given the elemental nature of the themes shared by folk music and fiction, however, the usefulness of such an exercise must very soon be considered questionable. After all, one might say that all stories (literary and musical) are 'about' desire, but that is not necessarily the most interesting or the most useful way to organise a comparative study.

What is more interesting, however, is the relative absence from British literary history of novels incorporating anything resembling folk music as a thematic element within their narratives.[3] The proportion is further diminished if we discount Ireland, where folk music has historically been (and arguably remains) much more integrated into the national cultural consciousness. Even in Ireland, however, novels about (or even incorporating) folk music are relatively rare,[4] and this is something that may lead us to suspect a fundamental incompatibility between this particular literary form and this particular musical genre. Formal analogies aside, folk music does not appear to be an especially attractive topic for the novelist. Speculation as to why this might be so (if indeed it is so) belongs elsewhere; as a first response one might suggest competition from other, apparently more compelling or more exciting, musical genres such as classical or rock. Whatever the truth of the matter, one thing remains clear: folk music does not feature strongly in – has, indeed, been virtually absent from – British fiction during the period covered in this study.

If we were looking for a text to begin to explore the role and representation of folk music in fiction, however, we could call upon the novel that in many ways exemplifies the 'musical turn' in contemporary British fiction: *Captain Corelli's Mandolin* (1994) by Louis de Berniéres.[5] In this very successful and much-loved book, an Italian officer is billeted with a Greek family on the island of Cephallonia during the early years of the Second World War. Antonio Corelli is a man 'full of mirth, his mind whirling with mandolins' (100). Ostensibly an enemy soldier, he nonetheless charms the local community with his lively personality and his musicianship – as one of the locals says of him: '[the] man's mad, and he's a wop, but he's got nightingales in his fingers' (287). These attributes are also instrumental in his winning – eventually, after much resistance and soul-searching on both sides – the love of Pelagia, the fiery daughter of the house in which he is staying. Through misunderstanding and the general chaos fostered by war, their love remains unrequited, and the story ends in modern Cephallonia with the aged 'lovers' reunited after lifetimes apart.

Pelagia initially resists Corelli not only because he is an enemy soldier but also because she is betrothed to Mandras, a local fisherman who has joined the partisans after the defeat of the Greek army. Mandras is associated in the early stages of the narrative with a kind of folk music which, arising from the local culture and focused on familiar themes and motifs, is available for improvisation in accordance with the demands of the context – '[they] make them up as they go along . . . [never] the same twice' (296), Pelagia explains to the impressed Corelli. In this manner, Mandras adapts a traditional fisherman's song (an appeal to dolphins to aid the work) in terms of his pursuit of Pelagia (67); a little later, a local quarryman invents a song in honour of the miracle associated with a local saint (78). It is this dialectic of familiarity and extempore creativity that, as suggested above, constitutes the enduring attraction of folk music as a quasi-universal cultural form.

A powerful, attractive and useful form of music is already in place before the arrival of Corelli, then. This music is part of a deeply embedded culture; simultaneously emerging from and expressive of local practices, it helps to order and organise the lives of Pelagia and her fellow Cephallonians, informing both the perceptual ways with which they understand the world and the physical ways they can be in the world. Mandras represents Cephallonia, which is not just a place but an 'idea'; there is a sound – a set of musical practices – that articulates the man, the place and the idea, and it is this sound, this music, that dominates Pelagia's imagination before the coming of Corelli.

War changes everything, however, including people, landscapes and ideas. It also changes the music – or at least the meaning of the music – that supposedly 'represents' these things. In the world depicted by de Berniéres, music comes to function as an alterative notion of communication, one based on harmony, empathy, sympathy – these and many of the other human faculties that it is the specific purpose of war (especially one overtly conducted along racist principles) to eradicate. So identified is Corelli with this alternative notion that he names his mandolin 'Antonia', because he feels that it 'is the other half of himself' (157). Music shapes his view of the world, and especially his view of Pelagia, whom he comes to regard in terms of both the shape and the sound of his mandolin (248ff).

Corelli's musical imagination is profoundly programmatic – which is to say, it is based upon the notion of a correspondence of greater or lesser degree between particular sounds and particular events or emotions. As noted in Chapter 1, the concept of programmatic correspondence (as opposed to 'pure' or 'absolute' music) has remained a significant force within the art tradition throughout the modern era. It would be fair to say, however, that it is in essence an effect of the folk imagination. Considered thus, it represents a means by which Corelli may begin to experience, and then to understand, and then to articulate, and finally to share, his love for Pelagia. A tune he composes 'portrays' and 'implies' certain aspects of her character; even the fact that it is a march in 2/2 time 'corresponds' in some sense to her strident personality. Shortly after, as he meditates on his growing attachment, a specific mandolin chord elicits her response: 'That was exactly how I was feeling. How did you know?'; to which he answers in his mind: 'Pelagia, I love you, and that is how I know' (250). When, at the end of the book, Pelagia listens to Corelli's first concerto, she imagines every musical effect in terms of their shared history. Music, in other words, offers these 'enemies' an opportunity for connection in a situation in which they are being pulled inexorably apart.

Ultimately, music for Corelli provides insights that are not available elsewhere: and it is his close identification with this power that constitutes the captain's attractiveness – to his fellow soldiers and members of 'La Scala', the opera society he has founded; to Günther Weber, the 'good Nazi', who feels himself drawn to Corelli's life-affirming music despite its subversive implications; and to Pelagia herself who, although not 'understanding' the music in any technical sense, finds herself responding both to the power embedded within it and to the captain's ability to release that power through his playing. Because it comes to represent hope within an increasingly hopeless world, it is in effect Corelli's musicality with which Pelagia falls in love.

Some measure of reconciliation is still demanded, however – some acknowledgement of the world that war has swept aside, and it comes in the form of Corelli's adaptation of the folk tunes to which he was exposed during his time on the island. Despite his penchant for the mandolin, Corelli is not, after all, in essence a folk musician. The musical world to which he defers in the first instance is the European classical one in which the likes of Bach, Beethoven and Bartok (all invoked during the course of the narrative) are currency. Thus, he is familiar with the canon (limited though it be) of mandolin art music; he discusses and appreciates theoretical niceties beyond the scope of any other character in the book; and he has aspirations to be a performer/composer for his beloved instrument. Such indeed is the career he takes up after the war.

As Corelli explains, however, the music he composes is based on a sympathetic union of the folk and art traditions: 'I took old folk tunes, like some Greek ones, and I set them for unusual instruments' (427). Moreover, he discovers what he believes to be a deep structural congruence between the two traditions, for the folk tunes are 'in the same form, with the same kind of development, as you'd find in Mozart or Haydn or whatever' (427). The power of art music, Corelli appears to be claiming, is based on the adaptation of formal properties that emerge much more organically within the folk tradition. In his own compositional practice, therefore, he is looking to bridge the gap between a number of conjoined opposites: the folk music of Mandras and the art music of Mozart; Pelagia and himself; Italy and Greece.

Jazz: *Trumpet* (1998) by Jackie Kay

From its beginnings in New Orleans around about the turn of the twentieth century, jazz has become one of the most global and most influential of popular musical styles in history. Because of its radically eclectic roots (no other popular form can claim so vast an array of formal or stylistic influences), jazz has demonstrated an amazing evolutionary capacity. The idea of jazz comprehends a number of continua, running from the appealingly simple to the dauntingly complex, from unashamed commercial product to high artistic intention, from a racially delimited historicism (an expression of African-American culture at a particular point in its history) to a universal human faculty (a propensity of the species to express intense emotion in the form of musical improvisations that require at least some degree of technical virtuosity). Moreover, while every generation remakes jazz in its own image and in response to its own requirements, every movement retains its aficionados (and in some cases its practitioners), so that all the dominant styles of the past – trad, swing, bebop, modal, fusion, etc. – remain in currency to some extent (Ake 2002; Cooke 1997).

It was inevitable that a phenomenon so widespread and so polarising as jazz would eventually begin to influence other art forms (Appel 2002). As explored at length in Part I, music tends to impact upon the novel in one or a combination of three principal ways: as inspiration, as metaphor, or as form – and so it has proved to be with jazz. Dorothy Baker's *Young Man with a Horn* (1938), based on the life of the cornet player Bix Beiderbecke, is a celebrated early example; but the number of American novels incorporating jazz as subject or inspiration of greater or lesser significance is now considerable (Albert 1996). More subtly, jazz may be said to have influenced the formal development of the twentieth-century North American novel in a number of recognisable ways, in areas such as narrative structure, focalisation and language. Toni Morrison's *Jazz* (1992), for example, is as much about a means of relating the world as it is about a means of relating *to* the world. The novel concerns the lives of various African-American characters during the early decades of the twentieth century and, not unexpectedly, jazz features as an element of some significance. Beyond this thematic level, however, Morrison incorporates a variety of formal techniques associated with jazz (solo improvisation, tempo, call and response, and so on) into her narrative, so that rather than merely telling the reader about jazz, it shows how that particular music genre functions as an aesthetic system.[6]

It may be that jazz owes its global success to its coincidence with the development of global media such as cinema, radio and television, as well as the various playback technologies (from the horned phonograph to the MP3 player) that have shadowed its evolution. Whatever the historical factors involved, jazz spread to Europe during the 1920s where, despite certain curatorial tendencies that have remained strong, it began to mutate in interesting directions. France was at the forefront of European jazz (Jackson 2003), although it also began to make an impact in Britain (Moore 2007; Parsonage 2005). That impact was consolidated during and after the Second World War, with the influx of American servicemen and the advent of American Forces Network radio. And as elsewhere, jazz was capable of exciting extreme responses among British people (as we saw in Chapter 2 in relation to *Absolute Beginners*): while for some it embodied the decline of civilization consequent upon the rise of American cultural hegemony, for others it was simply the sound of freedom – the sound of individual self-expression in the face of massed opposing forces.

One other aspect of jazz (and indeed of popular music in general) bears specifically upon present concerns: gender configuration. It comes as no surprise that the industry itself and the subculture to which it gave rise were overwhelmingly male-oriented. There have in fact been relatively few first-rate female jazz instrumentalists, and fewer women still involved in management and related matters. There have been a number of prominent female jazz singers, but both the musical personae and the extra-musical representation of these figures have tended to reproduce rather than to challenge the stereotypical gender discourses at large within twentieth-century western society. The iconic figure here is Billie Holiday (1915–59) whose impoverished, sexually-abused childhood was apparently realised in the unique singing style for which she became celebrated in later life. The value of Holiday's music continues to be widely regarded as a function of the intense emotion with which she invested it; less frequently remarked is the fact that this emotionality was the product of a specific history of gender relations, which was itself characterised by implicit female subservience (Citron 1993; McClary 1991; Whiteley 2000).

It was precisely such a discourse that Morrison attempted to deconstruct in *Jazz*. By and large, however, the pattern described above tends to be reproduced in jazz fiction, including the fiction that has emerged as part of Britain's late but nonetheless committed response to this particular field of music. The young male narrators of John Murray's *Jazz Etc.* (2003) and Fraser Harrison's *Minotaur in Love* (2007), for example, are every bit as enamoured of jazz as the narrator of *Absolute Beginners*. And as with MacInnes's novel, Murray and Harrison use their narrators' obsession with a certain style of music to explore ideas of identity, friendship, love and change. It is true that the later books – informed at least to some degree by a 'post-feminist' sensibility (whether conscious or otherwise) – are less overtly sexist than *Absolute Beginners*; nevertheless, the quality of femininity is still regarded in these texts as a function of the central male character and his quest (with jazz featuring as both a medium and a commentary) for full identity.

These issues come into focus in Jackie Kay's well-regarded debut novel, which tells the story of a celebrated jazz musician who, having lived his adult life as a man with a wife and child, is revealed after death to be female. The central character (who is absent for most of the narrative) grows up as a mixed-race girl named Josephine Moore in the small Scottish town of Greenock in the years either side of the Second World War. By the time she meets her future 'wife' in 1955, however, she has become Joss Moody, male jazz musician. Many of the issues tackled in this novel have also featured in Kay's poetry and other writings, and they resonate with some of the most radical concerns of the cultural theory of the time: the borderlands of race and sexuality, for example, as well as the politics of 'drag' and the use of masks in the construction of identity (Butler 1999; hooks 1991). Into this already volatile mix of themes and influences the author added the highly potent ingredient of music.

The Scottish background to the story may seem discordant on first analysis. London, with its immense population and its increased cultural opportunities, would appear to offer far greater possibilities for the novelist looking to write about jazz. Indeed, the action moves there at various stages throughout the narrative. It is clear, however, that the emotional core of the story is located in rural and small-town Scotland – removed from the complex, anonymous cities (even large Scottish cities such as Glasgow and Edinburgh) that are in some senses Moody's proper locus. Literary jazz, in the USA and elsewhere, has been predominantly an urban discourse; it is among the streets and within the clubs of the great cities that jazz comes into focus as both narrative element and formal influence. Kay's novel works to show, however, that jazz may be regarded as less about any specific place than about a state of mind – comprising a way of looking at, responding to and engaging with the world; and these faculties are just as available in Greenock as they are in London, or indeed in Chicago or New Orleans.

Jazz music impacts at both the formal and the conceptual levels of Kay's novel. With regard to the first of these elements, it may be observed how the narrative technique resists the notion of any stable position from which to approach Moody's experience, and how this is 'attuned', as it were, to one of the themes of the novel: the relationship between appearance and reality. Instead, the story is narrated from diverse perspectives. Some of these are 'major': Millie, the loving wife learning to grieve; Colman, the resentful son journeying towards understanding; Sophie Stones, the unscrupulous journalist bent on 'exposing' the truth. Joss Moody makes a contribution in the form of a letter towards the end of the text. There are besides a number of 'minor' voices – 'people' whose partial perspectives (which are conveyed in free indirect discourse) contribute significantly to the overall impression: a doctor (42), a registrar (73), a funeral director (101), a drummer (144), a cleaner (171), and an old school friend (245). These sections are 'orchestrated' by an anonymous narrator who interprets the action from time to time (131, 278), but whose voice is never in danger of hardening into the final word on any aspect of the story.

Such a narrative technique compares to jazz music in a number of obvious respects: the avoidance of a narratorial 'score'; the pattern of theme and quasi-improvised variation; and the idea of different 'voices', each the modifying the overall theme in terms of its own special colour and texture. The ultimate sanction, however, is provided by the subject matter of the text: jazz as the medium through which the central character comes to a sense of his/her identity. This is signalled in a chapter located at the centre of the text and entitled 'Music'. In a sustained piece of prose (131–6) Kay attempts to describe the physical, the cultural, and ultimately the existential nature of Moody's relationship with jazz:

> The music is his blood. His cells. But the odd bit is that down at the bottom, the blood doesn't matter after all . . . He unwraps himself

with his trumpet. Down at the bottom, face to face with the fact that he is nobody. The more he can be nobody the more he can play the horn. Playing the horn is not about being somebody coming from something. It is about being nobody coming from nothing. The horn ruthlessly strips him bare till he ends up with no body, no past, nothing. (135)

Kay does not wish to avoid cultural ascription: Moody's race, lineage and socialisation have contributed to his relationship with the music. At the same time, jazz is not a means of gaining or asserting an identity, but a release from the strictures that insist on 'identity' as the sine qua non of subjectivity itself. This notion – of a mask being employed to disguise the fundamental absence that undermines the very concept of subjectivity – chimes with some of contemporary cultural theory's most radical claims. It is all the more forceful in this instance because of its expression in relation to a discourse – music – that has functioned as one of the prime cultural locations in which the idea of subjectivity has taken root in the modern world. Moody embraces this 'nothing', this ruthless stripping away of an identity manacled to the real world; in that sense, the experience of playing jazz is enabling and celebratory. However, the characterisation here could just as easily be glossed as an acknowledgement of a terrifying abyss at the heart of human consciousness. The enigma of Moody's life and his response to music is in that sense the enigma of human consciousness itself: we may turn to music to find ourselves, but what shall we do, and whom shall we blame, if we find nothing there?

Pop: *Personality* (2003) by Andrew O'Hagan

In as much as they have been actively sought out and enjoyed by significant numbers of people at different times, many different styles of music qualify to be described as 'popular'. The two genres introduced above, for example, have been and remain extremely popular among certain niche audiences throughout Britain, although it would be fair to say that neither folk nor jazz, however they are defined, have endured as mainstream pursuits (if indeed they ever were). As a consequence, it is very important to differentiate between 'popular' and 'pop' music. The latter refers less to a particular musical style (although there are certain recurring characteristics to which one could point) than to a particular attitude towards the practice of music-making and music consumption. Pop music, that is to say, lays emphasis on certain values that are implicit within all forms of music-making – values such as accessibility, entertainment, professionalism, clarity, interpretation, and so on. Pop tends towards conventional tonal patterns and (in song format) quasi-universal narratives; taken together, these elements offer the listener shorts bursts of undemanding pleasure which confirm certain standardised limits of recognition or concentration (Frith 1981: 32–8; Warner 2003).

It would be a mistake, however, to simply dismiss pop music (as so many commentators and musicians from various traditions have done) as infantile or regressive. For the fact is that pop accumulates so many layers of significance during each stage of its realisation – from composition to performance to consumption – that it stands as an extremely complex phenomenon within any society's wider cultural landscape (Savage 1995). This is especially the case with regard to the latter element – consumption – and more specifically in respect of the faculty of memory with which consumption is ineluctably entwined as both a social and a subjective category. How do listeners 'hear' the song? What does it mean to them? How are they 'realised' in its terms? What emotional or physical responses does it elicit, and in terms of what sociopolitical discourses are such responses expressed? Most pressingly, how does the subject remember the song – immediately after it has finished and later with the passing of time? In short, although generally avoiding any self-conscious agenda in itself, pop music instantiates some of the most intense issues facing the modern subject.

Here we find the source of pop's attraction for the novelist – an attraction it shares with music in general but which assumes a specific focus when the novelist engages (either centrally or as background) with issues of relatively recent popular culture. When it is incorporated as part of the fabric of a novel, the pop song can develop signifying possibilities beyond its original (invariably banal) context. This is certainly the case with Andrew O'Hagan's *Personality*, which uses pop music as a vehicle to meditate upon various aspects of modern British culture.

O'Hagan's novel is loosely based on the life and career of Lena Zavaroni, a Scottish woman of Italian descent, from the Isle of Bute, who came to national prominence as a child during the 1970s when she won a televised talent show called *Opportunity Knocks*. Zavaroni became a pop sensation, receiving high-profile media exposure in the UK and elsewhere (including the USA – the 'promised land' for generations of British entertainers). The young performer seemed set for a long and successful career, when she began to manifest the symptoms of the eating disorder anorexia nervosa.[7] Zavaroni spent the remainder of her life battling this condition, making occasional 'comebacks' during periods of relatively better health but never regaining her initial level of success. She died in Cardiff on 1 October 1999, aged 35, following an operation to try to cure her condition.

Zavaroni's experience would appear to offer itself for interpretation with reference to one of the enduring myths of modern popular culture (itself based on a paradigm that is seemingly encoded into civilisation itself). The story of youthful success followed by alienation and precipitant, self-induced demise crops up in many different musical genres; versions of it subsist, for example, within country, rock and jazz (consider, for example, the careers of Hank Williams, Keith Moon and Bix Beiderbecke, respectively). Pop music can claim the exemplary modern redaction, however, encapsulated in the figure of Elvis Presley, whose ignominious end in 1977 (also linked to an eating disorder) coincided with the first wavering of Zavaroni's success. Certain narrative elements recur within this myth: precocious talent; the thrill of performance; the loneliness of success; shifting priorities; confusion between on- and off-stage identity; the public's insatiable appetite for 'personality'; and finally, the self-destruction that ensues from a life lived larger and faster than it should be. The moral of this myth is that we needs stars, but our attention may force these superhumans to destroy themselves – in some ways, indeed, we hope it will.[8]

Maria Tambini is the central figure of O'Hagan's novel, and her experience accords with that of Zavaroni in many key respects. Rather than the stark strokes in which the myth is usually rendered, however, the author provides a series of detailed contexts – family, community, social, cultural and political – which together form a backdrop for Maria's story. Music is signalled as an important presence within her life from an early age, but also within the lives of the immigrant Italian community into which she is born. (Her experience bears comparison with Enzo Mori, the central character of John Murray's *Jazz Etc.* whose Italian father also emigrated to the north-west of Britain after the Second World War.) Maria is revealed as the product of many different forces and influences, some of which (such as her unique singing style, incorporating a powerful voice and an ability to convincingly 'inhabit' whatever song she sings) are entirely inscrutable, and some of which (such as her grandmother's wartime affair with an Italian singer) she is unaware of. One of the obvious goals of *Personality* is to fill in the gaps left by the public perception, to provide the details obviated by the narrative writ large.

Central to the novel is the hijacking of Maria's 'identity' by the concept of 'personality'. The latter refers, in this instance, not to an individual's distinctive attitudes and characteristics, but to a particular blend of charisma, talent and personal beauty that has been fetishised in pop discourse since the onset of mass media in the early twentieth century. Interestingly, Lena Zavaroni's second hit was a song entitled 'Personality' the lyrics of which (reproduced in part in O'Hagan's novel on pages 162–3) play out a discursive encounter between these competing definitions. The novel traces the gradual submission of Maria's identity – which we observe in clear if incipient detail in the early parts of the text – to a pop rationale in which 'personality' is the key element.

This process is brilliantly illustrated in the chapter entitled 'The Evolution of Distance' (133–41), which comprises a series of letters exchanged over a two-and-a-half-year period between Maria and her childhood chum Kalpana. The latter's gradual maturation is reflected in her changing tastes, especially in the books and music she enjoys as the months go by. Her favourite bands include the Jam, the Police and Dexy's Midnight Runners – all leading post-punk acts of the period and all far removed in attitude and sound from the world of popular light entertainment in which Maria is stuck. Kalpana, in other words, is going through the necessary process of growing – realising herself in relation to various texts, practices and ideas at large within the community.

Maria's letters, meanwhile, reveal her initial wonder turning slowly to alienation and eventually an inability to escape the 'personality' into which she has been moulded. The letters reveal a classic instance of arrested development and the attempt to assert control through morbid self-discipline. For Maria, the intensity of performance has come to replace the banality – the absolutely necessary banality – of everyday life as reflected in Kalpana's letters. Maria's life, which ran parallel to Kalpana's before she moved to London, is now lived vicariously through the pop songs she sings and the 'personality' she has developed. Communication with her former best friend begins to take the form of impersonal beauty tips, signed 'Yours sincerely, Maria Tambini'. Kalpana continues to write but it is too late: the 'real' Maria is now lost, replaced by 'Maria Tambini', personality and pop singer.

O'Hagan's response to Lena Zavaroni's tragic life is to override the fantasy of pop with the fantasy of literary narrative (in which respect it resembles Gordon Burn's fictional treatment of the 1950s singer Alma Cogan in the eponymous novel of 1991). Thus, Maria succumbs neither to her illness nor to Kevin Goss, the 'fan' who stalks her throughout the latter stages of the novel, and whose volatile love/hate attitude towards Maria encapsulates in some senses the general public attitude towards stardom – what the text calls 'the brutal lie of his affection' (309).

The gesture with which she resists Goss's physical assault represents the re-emergence of Maria's identity in the face of those who retain an emotional investment in her personality (it is her rendition of the song 'Personality' that Goss listens to as he stalks Maria and her boyfriend Michael). Maria escapes with her true love, leaving Goss to bleed to death on the floor of a public toilet at Victoria Railway Station. While the ending is deliberately fictional in respect of Lena Zavaroni's experience, the ignominious fate of the pop fan carries an effective message: music retains a power to break down the walls between realities, and this power is dangerous and enabling in equal measures.

Rock: *The Ground Beneath Her Feet* (1999) by Salman Rushdie

A three-cornered relationship also provides the structural framework for Salman Rushdie's long seventh novel. Vina Apsara meets Ormus Cama in Bombay in the 1950s. Compulsively attracted to each other from the outset, they begin a life-long love affair against the background of a new style of popular music that was beginning to make its presence felt even in far-flung corners of the old British Empire. Vina and Ormus become pop, and then rock, musicians – she singing, he writing and playing. The novel traces their growing success at home, in Britain and then the USA and the rest of the world. *The Ground Beneath Her Feet* is nothing less than an odyssey through rock 'n' roll mythology from its inception in the 1950s down to the time of writing. The twist is that rock music in this instance is regarded through a post-colonial Indian lens, and that its rebellious attitude towards 'normal' or 'straight' society comes as a consequence even more into focus.

That journey is related by the photographer Umeed Merchant, the third pillar of the structure and a character who emerges over the course of the book as an extremely interventionist narrator. As he pursues Vina across time and space, Umeed hears and describes the unfolding soundtrack of his generation, and it is a story that will be familiar to anyone possessed of even a passing familiarity with contemporary popular culture. At the same time, he maintains a professional interest in pictorial imagery, and this sets in train a sensory dialectic that permeates the text, oscillating between the ear and the eye, the heard and the seen – eventually, between the competing ideologies of sound and silence.

Before we can begin to address the significance of these issues, some fundamental questions present themselves: what is this music, this industry, this attitude known as rock? What myths and legends does it draw upon? And what character roles does it make available for participants?

Rock music emerged as a transatlantic phenomenon during the mid-1960s, evolving from earlier popular styles such as rock 'n' roll, urban blues, beat, garage, and rhythm 'n' blues. Although initially characterised as a rebellious, countercultural, youth-oriented subculture, certain strands of rock soon began to aspire towards the romantic values associated with bourgeois art – especially the key romantic proposition of the individual artist articulating an original response to the world. This move initiated a creative and critical dialectic in which the meaning of rock music has tended to be organised in relation to one or another set of values: the first stressing the body, movement, rebellion, noise and related faculties, the second stressing the intellect, discernment, affiliation, sound and related faculties.

The punk rock 'revolution' of the mid-1970s was characterised at the time as an assault upon the orthodoxy of progressive rock, a turn away from what was regarded as a collusive cerebralism, and a return to rock's roots in corporeal practices (styles of noise and movement, for example) that were intended to be offensive to previous generations. In retrospect, punk may be regarded as simply one moment (albeit one that has left an enduring legacy) in an ongoing history of radicalism and reaction, as the genre moves between different impulses. As rock has aged, moreover, its adherents have become more self-conscious regarding its history, and this self-consciousness has been incorporated as a recognisable, recurring gesture within the rock idiom. Every generation since 1966 has predicted rock's fall; every generation has remade the style in its own image. The pattern has been for initiates to revisit previous iterations, raiding old styles for various sonic and lifestyle elements, and employing new technology to adapt these elements to the new circumstances. In this way, rock music has managed to survive long after the disappearance of the technological and socio-political context in which it first emerged.

This brief and extremely partial narrative is reflected in *The Ground Beneath Her Feet*. Each stage in the rock's stylistic evolution, from the swinging sixties in London to the postmodern nineties in the USA and elsewhere, is encountered. The evolving careers and protracted love affair of Vina and Ormus mirror (and self-consciously recall) the experiences of many familiar names from the rock canon: Madonna, Elvis Presley, the Beatles, John and Yoko, Bob Dylan, Paul Simon, U2, and so on.[9] For example, 'The Swimmer', a song written by Ormus about his relationship with Vina, contains the line 'swim to me' (131); this repeats a line from Tim Buckley's 'Song to the Siren' (1970), a celebrated composition from the rock canon that articulates a range of generally negative emotions: frustrated desire, pain, fear, etc. Buckley's extratextual presence is invoked for atmospheric purposes, certainly, but it also contributes to the virtual soundtrack that the novel, precisely because if its literariness, cannot provide. If the reader knows 'Song to the Siren', they will know something of Ormus's feelings at this stage and something of how he articulates those feelings in music. Of course, this virtual soundtrack depends on the extent of the reader's familiarity with the rock canon, as well as an ability to catch the frequently opaque references and allusions. In this way, the text assumes a much more active presence within the reader's imagination, offering pleasures (of identification and comparison, for example) without which the long trawl through modern popular culture might become tedious.

'Song to the Siren' fortuitously raises the issue of myth, something which Rushdie has worked hard to embed into the fabric of his story. The central myth upon which the novel draws (indeed, which arguably all music-based narrative draws to some extent) is that of Orpheus. In Greek legend, Orpheus was a musician so skilled that he could charm wild beasts. There are two principal associations with this mythological figure: firstly, he played for the Argonauts when the Sirens attempted to distract Jason and his men from their search for the Golden Fleece; secondly, he descended to the Underworld to recover his dead wife, Euridice. This latter legend is organised in terms of a series of elemental binaries (life and death, sky and earth, male and female, etc.), and this allows for virtually unrestricted adaptation and interpretation. The fact that music is at the centre of the narrative has proved especially interesting for musicians, however, with the result that the Orpheus legend has been revisited and reworked in more or less every generation since the emergence of secular art music.

The Ground Beneath Her Feet is the Orpheus legend novelised and adapted for the rock generation. The story of Ormus and Vina clearly recalls – and is intended to recall – the legend of lovers separated by death, the intense emotions that this causes, and the desperate actions taken by the living in an attempt to recover what has been lost. The intention is signalled in the extract from Rilke's *Sonnets to Orpheus* that precedes the text: 'We should not trouble about other names. Once and for all it's Orpheus when they're singing'. This reference is taken up early in the text itself, when Umeed comments wryly on the liberties taken by the composer Gluck and his librettist Calzabigi with their celebrated operatic treatment of the legend, *Orfeo ed Euridice*, first produced in Vienna in 1762 (12). This is also a metafictional moment (a *mise en abyme*) in which Rushdie identifies his narrative progenitor and introduces the possibilities of fidelity to or deviation from the original. For the question is posed: how will *The Ground Beneath Her Feet* orient itself in relation to the tragic 'original' and the 'happy' variation introduced by Gluck?

Moments after she sings the aria with which Gluck's opera triumphantly closes, Vina is swallowed by an earthquake, just as Euridice was swallowed by the earth after her death. The narrative then returns to the beginning of the Vina/Ormus relationship, tracing the long evolution of their love against the background of the emerging rock scene. After she is lost, Ormus pines for her as Orpheus pined for Euridice. Towards the end of the novel we find him travelling around the world with the most expensive rock show in history (strongly reminiscent of U2's unprecedented *Zoo TV* tour of the early 1990s), searching for ways to reunite with his dead lover or, failing that, to evade the reality of her loss. Unable to bring Vina back from the underworld, he joins her there permanently after he is assassinated outside his New York hotel. (The parallels with the murder of John Lennon are clear.)

Music and the absence of music take on specific resonances within the moral economy of the novel. As Umeed (whose names translates as 'hope') tells us: 'Sound and silence, silence and sound. This is a story of lives pulled together and pushed apart by what happens in (and between) our ears' (47). Silence is associated here with death, an absence of hope, the inevitable end towards which the human subject is constantly moving. Sound, on the other hand, represents civilisation's relentless striving for something beyond itself; it represents endeavour, faith, community – a signal that we are in the world and trying to understand it.[10] As Ormus puts it: '*Music will save us, and love*' (353, original emphasis), and this message is confirmed at the end of the text when Umeed invokes music and love as bastions against the 'mayhem' (575) of life.

One of the ways in which humans try to understand the world is by making reference to stories – to the myths and legends that enable ordinary people to orient themselves in relation to the world. That is what the legend of Orpheus and Euridice provides; that is what the love story of Ormus and Vina provides in the world depicted in *The Ground Beneath Her Feet*. And that, Rushdie appears to suggest, is what rock itself provides: despite its tawdriness, its materialism, even despite its not infrequent banality, rock music is sound made by the stars on our behalf, and it is set rebelliously against the awaiting, inevitable silence.

Hip-Hop: *On Beauty* (2005) by Zadie Smith

Zadie Smith's third novel, *On Beauty*, resets in a modern context
E. M. Forster's *Howards End* (which we examined in Chapter 2). Forster,
as we noted in Chapter 1, engaged with music at both a formal and
a thematic level. The former connotes matters of 'easy' and 'difficult'
rhythm, and the deployment of Wagnerian leitmotif. With regard to
the thematic level, Forster incorporated classical music as an index of a
certain kind of cultural value that some characters (the Schlegel sisters)
possessed, others (Leonard Bast) desired and others still (the Wilcoxes)
disdained. The attitudes and values associated with art music have not
disappeared in Smith's rewrite; Mozart, for example, still functions as an
index of a certain privileged way of thinking about, as well as being in,
the world. The musical range has expanded, however, and now Mozart
must be ranged alongside other styles, other attitudes and other values.
The most significant of these alternative music styles is hip-hop, a genre
that comprehends an aesthetic far removed (in terms of composition,
performance and consumption) from art music, and indeed from any of
the other styles encountered so far in this chapter.

Like jazz, the roots of hip-hop lie in certain aspects of the African-
American culture of the United States. From its roots in the New York borough of the Bronx in the 1970s, hip-hop has come to refer more than
simply to a particular style of music but to a subculture connoting certain
lifestyle choices involving fashion, technology and modes of communication (verbal and otherwise), as well as particular attitudes and behavioural
patterns. Hip-hop music itself incorporates various elements – particular
technologies and production styles, for example – that together comprise
its characteristic aesthetic. In the main, however, the form is usually associated with a specific form of vocal performance known as 'rapping',
which utilises properties from a range of musical and literary styles such
as poetry, jazz improvisation and popular song. Like its parent, hip-hop,
rap derives from many different sources and has proved extremely adaptable. Over the course of its existence rap has grown in popularity and
influence, so that by the opening decade of the new millennium it was
an extremely successful music genre.

And not just in the United States. As with jazz, France was the first
European country to respond positively to hip-hop culture, producing its
own exponents and a genuine 'scene' relatively early in the evolution of
the style. Britain eventually followed suit, although it is generally agreed
that it was not until the 1990s that an authentic scene emerged complete
with local and regional styles.

Benjamin Zephaniah tackles British hip-hop in his 'teenage' novel *Gangsta Rap* (2004). Set in London among feuding adolescent 'crews', the narrative describes hip-hop's role in the lives of young men who feel excluded from mainstream culture on account of their ethnicity and class. More positively, it reveals how rap music offers these young men opportunities for creative self-expression that they would otherwise never have. *Gangsta Rap* introduces the competing negative and positive forces that animate hip-hop itself: the former, aggressive and rebarbative, is impelled by feelings of exclusion and redress; the latter is productive and ameliorative, inspired by the possibility of articulating an original response to the world. While incorporating the negative for the purposes of narrative tension, Zephaniah accentuates the positive force of hip-hop culture in the lives of his young protagonists. The didacticism is understandable given the wanton 'misreading' of hip-hop among many of its adherents, especially those who come to it late and subscribe to a media-led agenda that is inimical to the music's positive message; however, it is by no means certain that the novel as a form can sustain the pressure of such moralising.[11]

Despite this, Zephaniah's novel raises two issues that bear upon an analysis of Smith's *On Beauty*: the limitations of hip-hop as a credible theme for a British-set novel, and the technical question (recurring throughout this study) that attends the relationship between music represented at a thematic level and the literary form though which such representation is attempted. Smith addresses the first by locating the action of her novel in the United States, albeit in a city region less obviously sympathetic to hip-hop culture than New York or Los Angeles. The second issue goes to the heart of the novel, raising questions regarding the nature of 'beauty', its role within human experience, the many different forms it takes and the various personal and institutional means we have devised to respond to it. Such questions, we recall, are of a kind with those that exercised E. M. Forster nearly a century ago; and it is in relation to this cluster of issues that the parallels with *Howards End* are most clearly signalled by the author.

In *On Beauty*, Smith revisits many of the themes and issues broached in her first two novels, especially the award-winning debut, *White Teeth* (2000). Attention is focused in the main on the Belsey family: father Howard (a British academic now teaching at a fictitious East Coast American college named Wellington, clearly modelled on Harvard University, where Smith was resident when she wrote much of the novel), his wife Kiki (an overweight African-American woman), and their three children (Jerome, Zora and Levi), each of whom is alienated to some degree from their parents' preferred lifestyle. Entwined with the Belseys is the Kipps family – parents Monty and Carlene, children Victoria and Michael – Trinidadian in origin but now resident in London where Monty has assumed a public profile as a conservative academic. When the latter takes up a visiting professorship at Howard's university, the scene is set for a clash between the two families and the various moral, aesthetic and lifestyle values to which they subscribe.

One such set of values comes to be associated with Levi Belsey, a teenage boy of mixed-race parentage who closely identifies with hip-hop culture. Levi is anxious about his own identity, which in terms of both race and class seems removed from the valuable subcultural capital represented by hip-hop. Levi, we are informed:

> loved rap music; its beauty, ingenuity and humanity were neither obscure nor unlikely to him, and he could argue a case for its equal greatness against any of the artistic products of the human species. Half an hour of a customer's time spent with Levi expressing this enthusiasm would be like listening to Harold Bloom wax lyrical about Falstaff. (181–2)

The reference to Harold Bloom (a pre-eminent contemporary literary critic) and Falstaff (a character from various plays by Shakespeare) raises an issue that has animated commentators on popular culture throughout the modern era, but especially since the 1960s when the matter became overtly politicised: the value of popular culture relative to established canons of taste. The questions proliferate: Must the popular cultural text be likened to the icons of high culture? Must the terms of the debate be set by those in command of a particular critical discourse? Most significantly of all, who gets to set the criteria regarding what is beautiful and what is not?

As it is set in and around a university, these issues exercise many of the characters in Smith's novel, none more so than Howard Belsey, whose disagreement with Monty Kipps regarding the 'meaning' of Rembrandt is merely the aesthetic expression of deeply opposed socio-political values. It is in terms of music, however, that the debate regarding beauty is most fiercely joined. Early in the text the Belsey family attends an outdoor concert of Mozart's Requiem – described in a manner (69–71) that clearly recalls Forster's technique in the corresponding scene from *Howards End* when the Schelgel family attended a concert of Beethoven's Fifth Symphony at a London concert hall. Father and son, Howard and Levi, disdain Mozart's music for apparently different reasons – for the one it is surreptitiously authoritarian, for the other it is not 'street' or 'scene', which is to say, not valued by the subculture to which Levi aspires. In fact, both question the music's relevance and the criteria whereby it is institutionally valued.

Whereas Howard Belsey struggles to find an alternative source of value to which he can subscribe in good conscience, his son firmly believes that he has found such a source in hip-hop. His faith is endorsed by Carl Thomas (a character corresponding to Leonard Bast in *Howards End*), an African-American slightly older than himself, whom Levi first encounters at the Mozart concert and who turns out to be a consummate rap performer. Carl participates in a 'spoken word' night at a local venue where his brilliance brings him to the attention of Claire Malcolm, a poet and teacher at Wellington College with whom Howard had a brief extramarital affair. The description 'like Keats with a knapsack' (230) again invokes the culture wars raging both inside and outside the university since the 1960s. Carl brings the worlds of classical music and hip-hop together in a practical sense, when he describes to Zora how he recorded himself rapping over a sample taken from the *Requiem* (136). His identification of Mozart as a fellow musician brings only a patronising smile from Zora, for, like Howard and Levi – indeed, like Claire Malcolm, for all her liberal attitudinising – she is too identified with one particular voice to be able to make connections between different voices.

On Beauty is a homage to *Howards End* rather than an attempt slavishly to update it, for there are choices facing Smith's protagonists that simply were not available or relevant during Forster's time. The Schlegel sisters' attempt to live out the meaning of their beliefs – to connect the various sundered elements of their existence – was ultimately defeated by a combination of personal bad faith and social convention. Music was fully implicated in that process – as desirable cultural capital, as a certain way of regarding and understanding the world, and not least as part of the storyteller's art. In Smith's novel, Levi and Carl have musical options that Leonard Bast did not, although those options entail a range of extramusical implications that the text works hard to expose. Over the course of the novel, hip-hop comes to represent both a means to connect and a system of values in and of itself with which other systems have to learn to connect. Or not, as the case may be.

Dance: *Morvern Callar* (1995) by Alan Warner

Alan Warner's debut novel, *Morvern Caller*, was one of the first novels to attempt to engage with the phenomenon of rave culture that swept through parts of Britain after the late 1980s. If it had done no more, *Morvern Callar* would retain interest as documentary evidence of one of the most important and influential subcultures to have appeared in the country in recent times. The novel achieves much more than that, however. In highlighting one of the prominent practical 'applications' of music in society – dancing – Warner's novel reminds us that music, contrary to this study's emphasis thus far, frequently elicits a physical, as well as an intellectual, response, and that such a response would appear to be as deeply encoded into human culture as is the linguistic facility. Indeed, it is the eponymous character's overwhelmingly physical engagement with the world, as opposed to a more intellectual one – connoted, for example, by the writing and reading of novels – that forms one of the main themes of the book.

A simplistic reading might say that the history of music comprehends a fully-fledged war between the imagination (which attempts to understand sound in terms of it structural and tonal properties) and the body (which responds to sound for a variety of non-musical reasons – say, religious ritual or sexual courtship). Such a simplistic binary deployment would be false, however, for it is clear that the process of understanding involves a physical dimension of some kind or degree (even if it is only an appreciation of how particular gestures create particular sounds), while the physical response to music incorporates a degree of imaginative understanding (as when specific sounds elicit specific movements). It is probably safer (as it is invariably is in such matters) to speak of historical tendencies rather than essential properties when it comes to a consideration of the human response to music.

Dance has been a particularly significant element of British popular culture since at least the Second World War, when developments in various media and playback technology increased the number and variety of music genres to which the public was exposed. Many of the major popular music styles have had particular forms of dancing associated with them.[12] Disco was a major phenomenon of the 1970s, but it only paved the way for the revolution that was ushered in with the onset of rave culture in the late 1980s and the various musical forms and social practices that were attached to it. Initially, a 'rave' was a party in which large groups of people came together in improvised venues for the purpose of dancing. The music at these parties was played on powerful mobile systems and was usually based on the house and techno styles that had begun to emerge in the USA during the 1980s. The practice caused a moral panic in the UK when it was revealed that drug use was widespread at these events; the music itself, however, also came in for vilification, and not just from 'concerned' authorities for whom it represented a kind of neo-savagery. Dance music was also widely abused in the popular music industry, for among the romantic terms that continued to dominate music-making, categories such as 'composer', 'performer' and 'listener' still reigned supreme. The new dance music was comprised of electronically manipulated samples (both rhythmic and melodic); it was purveyed by DJ-producers rather than by 'proper' singers or instrumentalists; and it deliberately elicited a physical rather than an intellectual response – all factors which militated against its identity as a form of 'music' at all.

The eponymous heroine of Warner's novel has an eclectic musical taste; what is more, she is constantly sharing that taste with the reader by relaying the names of artists, albums or even individual tracks to which she is listening. This information is often communicated at the most inopportune time: shortly after discovering the body of her boyfriend in their flat, Morvern prepares to go out for a drink with her friends from the supermarket where she works:

> I put the Walkman in the pocket and the plugs in my ears after fitting the long ear-rings on. I took some cassettes: new ambient, queer jazzish, darkside hardcore and that C60 I'd made with Pablo Casals doing Nana on his cello again and again. (4)

There are a number of important things happening here. In the first place, it seems quite clear that the development of the personal stereo system (in Morvern's case the Walkman – a portable, personal cassette player) represented a revolution in the consumption of music as least as significant as anything that had occurred in the history of the production of music itself. It might be argued that the ability to be able to control certain aspects of your sensory disposition represented a blow against those elements looking to dominate every aspect of public space – what you see, where you go, what you hear. In that respect, Morvern is only one of a veritable army of Walkman-users who took advantage of a relatively minor technological development to win back some element of control over their own identities: the indulgence of private taste in the public domain.

One could counter by saying that the technology is irrelevant if the sound entering the ear is already compromised. All music, it might be suggested, is available in the public domain only as a consequence of compromises and decisions far removed in location and in influence from the consuming subject. Yes, you are free to choose this genre rather than that one, this artist, this album, this particular track: the exercise of control is an illusion, however, if the availability (or unavailability) of material is determined by vested interests.

Morvern Callar was written and published just before the revolution in music consumption precipitated by the onset of large-scale downloading, the development of the MP3 personal playback system, and the online superstore facilitating access to more or less the complete archive of popular music with the touch of a few buttons on a computer keyboard. It is widely accepted that this revolution has effected a fundamental change in the discourse of popular music (in terms of meaning, value, originality, and a host of other effects and concepts) – a change that we in the new millennium are still trying to understand. Warner's novel is located in the interstices between two dispensations – one in which music is possessed of an auratic presence that is linked to an older bourgeois model of art, and one in which the possibility of universal availability has profoundly altered the relationship between sound, listener and meaning.

Morvern's Walkman accompanies her throughout the early stages of the novel, and she provides detailed references to her preferred choice of music. As remarked above, her tastes are diverse, although she clearly tends towards what might be described as 'darker' material, much of it jazz-inflected, avant-garde and cultish. In this, as in so many contemporary music-novels, there is a complex negotiation between the world of the narrative, in which certain musical materials are invoked to expedite some element of the narrative, and the world of the consumer, to whom none, some, or all of those materials will be familiar. Most readers could be expected to recognise artists such as Pablo Casals or Miles Davis; fewer will be familiar with Music Revelation Ensemble, and fewer still with the Mutoid Waste Company. It is not only the fact that music is such a central part of Morvern's life – something she uses to moderate aspects of her physical and emotional response to the world – the reader's knowledge or ignorance of the musical materials cited by Morvern impacts upon their response to her, and hence upon the meaning of the story.

It is in relation to the dance music that she encounters after moving to Ibiza, however, that Morvern's relationship with music is most fully revealed. Throughout the text she has revealed herself to be primarily and unapologetically body-oriented. When confronted by her boyfriend's novel, she says: 'You had to read to get to the end; you couldnt see the point in reading through all that just to get to an end' (82). Here, once again, is a *mise en abyme* in which the act of novel reading is exposed in terms of its intellectual conventions and indicted in terms of its bad faith. In this respect, it is revealing that an unnamed 'author' figure – elder, educated, male, middle-class – dies before the beginning of the text. We might see this as the 'real' author attempting to allow Morvern space to tell her own story in her own way; although this is a fiction within a fiction (Warner wrote the book, not Morvern), it is an effective way to dramatise the issues of power implicit in the process of story-telling. It becomes clear that music provides Morvern with a much more intuitive form of narrative experience, one closely linked to rhythms and requirements of her body. This is the aesthetic she pursues in the Ibizan nightclubs:

> The way Sacea [the DJ] was doing it the music was just a huge journey in that darkness. When we needed brought down to rest the ambient let us relax then he slowly built us up again until we were back in hardcore again and he pushed the 'core as long as I could take it before much softer synth waves were beaming across us . . . You didnt really have your body as your own, it was part of the dance, the music, the rave. (203)

This music also has an 'author' – the DJ Sacea – who through his skill, imagination and personality regulates the relationship between the narrative material (in this case, the music) and the consumer/reader (in this case, the dancer). The conventional intellectual response to music is rejected because it represents a privileged (and thus limited) response to experience, and because it elevates the faculty of understanding above that of use. Moreover, the novel as a form is implicated in this sensory politics because it also privileges certain ways of responding to the world while implicitly marginalising others. Morvern experiences her life not like a novel but like a dance, which makes the rendering of her experience in the novel *Morvern Callar* all the more ironic.

World: *Psychoraag* (2004) by Suhayl Saadi

Music is of such seminal importance in Suhayl Saadi's debut novel that the text comes with its own playlist and discography. As with all the other novels in this section, *Psychoraag* deploys specific genres of music for specific inspirational, metaphoric and formal ends. Music is transformed from a mere leisure accessory or an ethnic identifier into the single most important principle underlying human experience.

The story concerns a young Glaswegian of Asian descent named Zaf, who works as a late-night DJ on a local radio station. The author employs an intriguing device to structure his novel: the entire action (some 419 pages) takes place in a studio between midnight and 6.00am on the night of the station's final broadcast (it has lost council funding), although many different times and places are broached over the course of the evening. Zaf talks and thinks all through the night, covering a bizarre range of subjects from his personal life, the history of his own family and the cultural politics of contemporary Glasgow. He intersperses his ramblings with an eclectic selection of music, a list of which is provided as a paratextual appendix to the novel 'proper'. Besides 'mainstream' western bands such as the Yardbirds, the Byrds and the Beatles, Zaf plays a variety of Anglo-Asian musicians (Asian Dub Foundation, Cornershop) as well as a number of lesser-known artists purveying a kind of music that has come to be labelled in contemporary popular music discourse as 'world music'.

The provenance of world music as a commercial prospect is complex, and its specification in aesthetic terms is fraught with many difficulties (Miller and Shahriari 2005). One way to consider it, however, is as part of a process of postmodern 'de-differentiation' (Lash 1990: 11–15). Besides the collapse of traditional boundaries between various social realms (for example, the political, the cultural, the aesthetic), de-differentiation also describes the processes of communication and assimilation that takes place both between and within cultures. The category of world music was invented during the 1980s at a time when various 'ethnic' traditions began to increase in visibility in the highly calibrated societies of the West (especially the USA and the UK). Reasons for the growth of interest in different forms of music remain speculative, although certainly one suspects the increased levels of tourism to 'exotic' destinations and the development of a truly global media network.

At the same time, the 'centre' was experiencing high levels of interpenetration between the various ethnicities of which it was increasingly comprised. As George Lipsitz has suggested: 'Once immigrants from the Indian subcontinent or the Caribbean arrive in the UK, they transform the nature of British society and culture in many ways, changing the nature of the "inside" into which newer immigrants are expected to assimilate' (1994: 126). In Britain, for example, musicians and composers used new technology to bring various 'ethnic' traditions into fructifying relationship with each other, as well as with the western styles that tended to dominate the realm of 'popular' music. The result was some extraordinarily vibrant hybrids by artists such as Nitin Sawhney and Talvin Singh.

The complexity of this form of music, and of the various western responses to it, is confronted in Mark Hudson's *The Music in My Head*

(1999), a novel set in the fictional African city of N'Galam. This latter is a thin disguise of the Senegalese capital and world music hotbed, Dakar, where the narrator, independent producer and A&R man Andrew 'Litch' Litchfield, is on a field trip to re-establish contact with 'his' main act. As an increasingly unstable Englishman overwhelmed by a foreign culture that his arrogance led him to believe he knew thoroughly, Litch's experience symbolises some of the pleasures, and at the same time some of the dangers, to which world music is prone. His position is in some senses a direct inversion of Zaf's – an 'outsider' who has become an 'insider' by dint of domicile and an extensive acquaintance with British popular music. Both characters experience intense pressure over the course of the narrative; indeed, both experience breakdowns of a kind. It is difficult, it appears, to operate across the boundaries that have been established by long use and vested interests, especially those boundaries that are employed to differentiate between specific genres and national traditions.

As a Scots-Asian, Zaf represents a hybrid, hyphenated identity, something that is reflected in his cultural tastes and his language. The many Urdu words and phrases he employs (both on air and in his own head) throughout the night are incorporated as a ten-page glossary (421–30) at the end of the book, located just before the playlist and discography. The existence of these paratexts speaks to a discrepancy between the established literary forms (such as the novel) and the new identities and narratives that such forms are being employed to articulate.

At the same time, Zaf is Glaswegian born and bred, and one would expect his language to reflect that. Saadi subscribes to a modern tradition that attempts to reproduce a Scottish accent in prose.[13] The conjunction of these two impulses makes for an extraordinarily flamboyant style:

> Dunno boot yous oot there but Ah know Ah've always been a Dubber. Awright, tonight? That wis the first an there's lots mair tae come! Dum-dee-dee-dum-dee-dee-dum. Hey! It's sivin meenuts past midnight, Saturday night. This is *The Junnune Show* and Ah'm Zaf – that's zed ay eff. Can ye spell? *Salaam alaikum, sat sri akaal, namashkar.* Welcome again.
>
> (2004: 16)

Especially when he is in broadcast mode, Zaf traverses a dauntingly complex linguistic terrain; and just as he expects his listeners to follow him, so it would seem that Saadi is expecting his readers to appreciate the political and cultural issues at stake in his deployment (or avoidance, as the case may be) of particular languages. This is something that reflects in turn on the representation of music within the text.

Zaf's playlist for the evening includes a selection of 'authentic' music from Pakistan, India and Bangladesh, and this is one of the means by which he articulates the Asian dimension of his identity. At the same time, he has been socialised within a non-Asian cultural milieu, and his identification with the pleasures of the western rock text is reflected in his choice of a number of representative acts working within that genre. But it is the hybrid forms to which he is most drawn, and which over the course of the night come to represent for Zaf a truth underlying not only his own experience but a general political principle – although one with a specific aesthetic provenance. And what is that principle? It is the radical unavailability of pure forms; and its correlative – the inevitability of influence.

Zaf articulates this notion most clearly when he is speaking to his public:

> [We're] playin a real mix ae auld an new, of Eastern an Western an aw points in between. An beyond. Or, tae be mair accurate, the soangs that let us hear the truth ae the fact that the waruld is aw wan. That thur's nae 'East' and nae 'West' – that's jist a great big lie cooked up by those who, even if they wantit tae, could nivir hear *the real music* [added emphasis] . . . this is the music that Ah've been listening tae for years. It's the *mausaki* ae me life. It's made me whit Ah am . . . Very cosmic, eh? (132)

His privileged (in aesthetic terms) location 'at home' within two worlds leads Zaf to subscribe to a form of 'crossover' politics in which the geo-historical categories through which certain identities and practices are organised (eastern and western) are revealed to be a discursive fabrication – merely an effect of a particular way of understanding the world rather than the implicit truth of the world expressed in material form. Such a politics is itself linked with specific cultural attitudes and forms, and this is what Zaf refers to as 'the real music' – an interpenetration of, or harmony between, 'voices' which is directly at odds with the notion of the single voice articulating its own 'melodic' truth.

So, the aesthetic principles of 'world music' impact on Zaf's imagination, causing him to modify the way he understands the world and himself in relation to it. More than that, however, the music he favours reflects back upon the text in which his story is being articulated.

In Chapter 1 we noted a dialectic between musical and literary form, and how certain binary and ternary principles appear to be encoded into successful western genres such as the novel and sonata form. But *Psychoraag* is only partially 'western'; it also subscribes to aesthetic principles (including musical principles) which are alien to the established binary/ternary precepts of the western cultural imagination. What this means is that Saadi's novel is itself only partially engaged with the established genre, that there are other principles (relating most centrally to narrative and character) that bear upon its aesthetic composition.

Psychoraag may look like a typical postmodern British novel, with its playful use of drawings and alternative typographies, its incorporation of a range of paratextual materials, and its employment of various temporalities (including 'real-time' and 'flashback') to unsettle the reading experience (Bradford 2007: 47–78). It is important to note the divergent provenances of different traditions, especially ones that locate themselves at odds with some putative mainstream tradition such as 'the British novel'. For DJ Zaf, music itself represents a positive force in the world, an insistent principle of communication and harmony in the face of those who would fetishise difference. However, some forms of music express that principle more readily – for example, those emerging from the hybridisation of different, sometimes opposed, socio-cultural traditions. Although he values both artists, then, the music of Nitin Sawney speaks to some aspects of Zaf's experience in a way that the music of the Beatles, for all its brilliance, can not.

The same pattern applies to the text itself. The novel offers a specialised means for purveying narratives that reflect upon society, and it is a form which Saadi obviously values, having invested considerable amounts of time and thought in the composition of *Psychoraag*. But the form itself must answer the requirements of the world he is attempting to represent. After all, the book is not called *Psychosymphony* or *Psychosonata*; and if there is a particular musical form which Saadi attempts to invoke it is the 'raag' of the title rather than any of the forms available within the western remit.[14] There is no stable binary or ternary structure to guide the reader through Zaf's story; rather, his night-time odyssey through time, emotion and music recalls the dauntingly complex response of the trained Asian musician to the 'raag', which, as defined in the glossary at the end of the text, is

a pattern of notes in Indian music used as the basis for melodies and improvisations . . . Personalised descriptions of a raag enable a musician to meditate on its characteristics and to unite his or her personality with a particular mood and, thereby, instil the same mood in the audience. (428)

The parallels with Zaf's experience are clear. Yes, the novel is 'musical', but the forms of music it invokes (arising from his particular circumstances as an Asian-Scot) impact upon the way the story may be told. By the same token: yes, this novel is experimental, but not in the way that 'mainstream postmodernism' (if it may be so termed) is experimental. Sometimes the same or similar effects can be introduced, although arising from very different conditions and often with very different intentions in mind.

Classical: *Amsterdam* (1998) by Ian McEwan

Finally we (re)turn to the genre that dominated Part I of this study – the western art tradition – here represented in Ian McEwan's Booker Prize-winning novel *Amsterdam*. This controversial book by one of Britain's most celebrated post-war writers is approachable in terms of the tripartite model described at length in Chapter 1, in so far as music (in this case, the European art tradition commonly known as 'classical music') is incorporated into the book as inspiration, as metaphor, and as formal influence.

With regard to the first two elements, classical music features strongly at the thematic level. One of the main characters is a successful contemporary composer named Clive Linley, and much of the novel is taken up with his attempts – technical and otherwise – to describe the music he hears, composes and contemplates during the course of the narrative. Linley considers himself to be the latest in a line of distinguished modern (though certainly not Modernist) English composers running from Elgar through Vaughan Williams and Britten. His fetishisation of the artistic process is exposed, however, when, as he is walking in the Lake District in search of inspiration for a commissioned work, he is 'gifted' by nature with a signature theme for the piece, only to immediately come upon a scene of what appears to be male-on-female violence. Faced with the choice of whether to intervene or to retire and pursue the elusive melody, Linley opts for the latter, convinced that the long-term ramifications of his art outweigh an altercation that is likely to be (so he convinces himself) squalid and inconsequential. When he learns that what he in fact witnessed was the prelude to a rape, Linley's moral conscience – that which had allowed him to condemn a publisher colleague's use of 'private' photographs for political ends – is compromised.

His world, in which morality, philosophy and aesthetics have been forged into an integrated system, topples, and it comes as no surprise when his new symphony, which he had imagined as a kind of Beethovian salutation to the new century, fails.

As with the central character in Conrad Williams' *The Concert Pianist* (2006) and the eponymous hero of Thomas Mann's *Tonio Kröger* (1903), Linley has allowed himself to become too immersed in his art. Music for him is an end, a form of reality in and of itself; more or less anything can be justified in the name of the greater good to be achieved by those talented enough to imagine and construct beauty. The real world – which provides the materials (in terms of narratives, characters, media, and so on) from which art emerges – is a distraction. The real world is chaotic and casual; although it serves as the putative pretext for art, for Linley it is more likely to hinder than to inspire the artistic process. And as with Morahan and Kröger, the gap that emerges between the artistic persona and the 'real' world that artists are obliged to inhabit precipitates a pattern of dilemma, crisis and resolution. The difference with *Amsterdam* is that in Linley's case the latter element of this pattern proves terminal.

The irony here is that in literally turning away from a situation involving real human conflict, Linley has metaphorically turned away from the humanistic creed to which he claims to subscribe (21–3). His philosophy of music is based on two conjoined principles: the evolving tradition with which the contemporary genius (the 'individual talent' famously described by T. S. Eliot) is obliged to engage if they wish to articulate something meaningful in their chosen medium; and the human being's genetic predisposition towards certain basic elements such as rhythm, pitch and melody. These tenets are set resolutely against modernist scepticism towards received aesthetic principles (linear narrative, for example) and its transposition of experimentalism from a question of artistic option to one of political necessity. For Linley (as indeed for many critics and artists in reality), these latter tendencies lead down a blind alley in which what he refers to as 'music's essential communicativeness' (22) is sacrificed to dogma and formalism.

Music in *Amsterdam* becomes a metaphor, then, for a particular means of regarding the world, one that is privileged and therefore dangerous, especially when it encourages an amoral detachment from the rest of humanity. Although the book is not 'inspired' by music as such, the dynamics of musical inspiration are incorporated into the narrative as an important theme; for, despite his insistence on the necessity for tradition and his Platonic avowal of the human predisposition towards beauty, Linley is in fact obsessed with inspiration – with capturing the elusive combination of chance and readiness that is capable of producing the memorable moments of genius with which the history of human endeavour is unevenly spotted.

As the story begins, Linley is under pressure to finish a symphony that he has been commissioned to write to celebrate the millennium. Using his skill and experience, the basic architecture of the piece has been put in place. The final element is missing, however: 'an inspired invention – the final melody, in its first and simplest form' (24). This elusive melody begins to assume epic proportions, for not only will it constitute the 'lyrical summit' (26) of the symphony itself: Linley intends that it should become as closely associated with him as the signature melody from the Ninth Symphony is associated with Beethoven (76). And like that famously hummable tune, his melody is intended to encapsulate both the essence of the age that has just passed and something of the promise of the age that has just begun. Properly conceived and executed, these elusive few notes will cap his career, while at the same time confirming him as a dominant force in contemporary art music.

The melody is proving elusive, however, and life in London is as demanding as ever. The early, ignominious death of his former lover has depressed Linley, while his reacquaintance with the journalist Vernon Halliday both distracts and exhausts him. It is for this reason that he decides to leave London and travel north (to the Cumbrian Lake District) in search of inspiration. This spatial turn to the narrative recalls a pattern familiar within British culture since at least the eighteenth century, in which the sophisticated metropolitan seeks spiritual and cultural reinvigoration in the 'primitive' reaches of the archipelago. In this instance, Cumbria is a kind of honorary Celtic margin alongside Scotland, Wales and Ireland (and Cornwall, to some extent).[15] In one variant, the world-weary artist forsakes the infected city only to rediscover their inspiration amongst the denizens of a simpler environment.

Part 3, Chapter 3, of *Amsterdam* (76–90) represents McEwan's sustained attempt to delineate the creative process. The narrative focuses on Linley as his mood dips and rises along with the surrounding topography and as he waits impatiently for his unconscious imagination to supply the artistic matter so desired by his conscious mind. Having avoided the human drama that threatened to frustrate that desire, Linley rushes back to London to get to work on converting the raw material of the melody into the high artifice of the symphony. Once there, plot complications overtake him and the narrative moves inexorably towards its grimly comic conclusion. The final shame is the posthumous cancellation of his new symphony which, it turns out, is a 'dud' – as one character says: 'Apparently there's a tune at the end, shameless copy of Beethoven's Ode to Joy, give or take a note or two' (176). So intent was Linley on replicating Beethoven's achievement that he ended up replicating his work; obsession with music, in other words, has blinded Linley to his artistic, as well as to his moral, responsibilities.

So, Linley leaves London (the centre of power), travels north (to a 'green' environment), and then returns again. The plot, meantime, traces his degenerating relationship with 'old friend' Vernon Halliday, who McEwan depicts negotiating his own professional/moral crisis throughout the text. Halliday and Linley are linked in many ways, not least in the fact that they are both in search of something (one a story, the other a melody) that will justify their professional careers (to themselves as much as to their peers). The 'resolution' they reach entails mutual destruction, as each arranges the other's murder.

It is interesting to observe how this basic plot structure rehearses the ternary/binary configuration of sonata form, as described above in the 'Music and Form' section of Chapter 1. Linley's movements (from and back to London) recall the ABA structure of exposition, development and recapitulation; while the two principal characters represent the first and contrasting subjects – different yet linked, moving towards a harmonic closure in which each may be accommodated. The fact that the accommodation achieved in this particular instance is death, and that it takes place not in London but in the 'alien' textual space of Amsterdam, suggests a fundamental incompatibility between traditional sonata form and the post-Romantic world as depicted in the novel. This in turn reflects on Clive Linley's artistic pretensions, and sets a question mark over the claims – aesthetic, moral and otherwise – made on behalf of the art form that he embodies.

Amsterdam's 'blatant critique of a decadent Romanticism' (Benson 2006: 132) brings us to the end of our trawl through some of the musical genres represented in contemporary British fiction. It is now time to consider the issue from a more literary perspective, and to observe the various ways in which music is represented – as well as the various roles it is recruited to play – in a range of contemporary novelistic genres.

4

'. . . It's The Way That You Do It': Music and the Genres of Fiction

Introduction

The simple word 'music' comprehends a multitude of sounds, as well as the multitude of practices that go towards making those sounds and the meanings that have historically been attached to them. If music is protean in its ability to represent different things at different times to different people, it is also both powerful and volatile in terms of the social, political and interpersonal tasks for which it is recruited. During the contemporary period with which are concerned here, music has continued to permeate British society, performing important ideological work in the formation of subjects, in the provision of certain valuable experiences and attributes, and in the perpetuation of various institutions. Music – in one form or another – is everywhere, a ubiquitous accompaniment (whether in the forefront or the background) to the business of living in Britain in the early twenty-first century.

As we saw in Chapter 3, one of the means by which the great amount of music is organised in contemporary Britain is through the identification of generic categories. At least since the Renaissance, it has been widely believed that music's different properties correspond in some way or other to various human capacities; furthermore, that these properties elicit certain responses in human subjects because they articulate matters, (physiological, psychological and emotional, that are deeply encoded in the species. These musical properties include the principal ones of melody, rhythm and harmony, but also a range of other influencing (but perhaps less obvious) factors, such as timbre, colour, tempo, tonality, intonation and narrative theme. The complex deployment of these properties gave rise in time to the phenomenon of genre – which is to say, the emergence of specific kinds of music that may be identified in terms of their distinctive organisation of properties into a recognisable type. And with the concept of genre came affiliated concepts such as classification, stratification, taste and propriety – in other words, the notion of a relationship between musical genre and the contexts in which it was composed, performed and consumed.

The concept of genre has also impacted, and continues to have an impact, upon the evolution of the novel in terms of its social and institutional organisation. Like music, the novel has certain fundamental properties that render it identifiable in medial terms: it is generally an extended prose narrative featuring the actions and words of characters. Most people could differentiate between a novel and a poem or a play. Once you begin to refine that basic definition (which itself is far from straightforward), however, you also begin to introduce the possibility of genre – that is, the idea that particular emphases (which is to say, particular kinds of narrative, of character, of language, and so on) entail a categorical difference. Changes and innovations are introduced which reflect developments in the real world (for example, shifts in technology, or education, or politics) and which modify both the formal and the conceptual remit of the novel. The term 'novel', in fact, becomes inadequate in either critical or descriptive terms, and new classifications have to be invented to describe the variations that emerge.

'Genre fiction' is a somewhat dismissive term regularly used to describe non-literary fiction; but of course 'literary fiction' – however one defines it – is also a genre, albeit one that tends to be institutionally sanctioned. In Part I, we noted how a range of ideas attending one particular kind of music (classical) came to influence British fiction from the mid-eighteenth century down to the end of the twentieth century; it would be surprising if that process was confined to the upper echelons of British society – to those possessed of the time, the resources and the desire to engage with classical music in all its emotional and philosophical complexity. As music itself has diversified, so too has the novel. It is incumbent upon any overview of the music-novel to engage with the range of novelistic subgenres in which music is engaged as a thematic or formal influence.

Chapter 3 introduced various genres prominent in the musical life of contemporary Britain and observed the manner in which they elicited different novelistic engagements. It is the task of this chapter to introduce various genres of fiction in order to observe the manner in which music is invoked in relation to the different formal and conceptual concerns of each. If the previous chapter revealed the various kinds of music about which contemporary British novelists are writing, this chapter should go some way towards revealing the various kinds of novel in which music features as an element of greater or lesser significance.

Adolescent: *Starseeker* (2002) by Tim Bowler

Part I of this study joined the story of humankind's intellectual engagement with music during the eighteenth century, observing and commenting on the formulation of new ideas regarding both the derivation of music and its function in relation to the individual subject as well as to the world inhabited by that subject. It is important to remember that such activities were part of an ongoing response to more than two thousand years of speculation upon the same issues, and that some highly complex and influential ideas had emerged over the centuries. Perhaps the most influential idea was *musica universalis* – 'the music of the spheres' – a proposition that had its basis in the thought of the ancient Greek philosopher Pythagoras and which came (though many stages and adaptations) to dominate the understanding of music throughout the Middle Ages (Godwin 1993; James 1995).

Among other things, *musica universalis* proposed an affinity between music and mathematics. Harmony was essentially a mathematical principle, produced by the manipulation (whether intended or accidental) of different masses and ratios in relation to each other (Harkleroad 2006). The celestial bodies (sun, moon and stars) described a similar mathematical relationship, both with regard to each other and to the earth from which such observations were made. These relationships were harmonic in an actual rather than a metaphorical sense; and although inaudible during the course of everyday life, the idea of a celestial music which in certain circumstances might be heard remained an important concept throughout the Middle Ages.[1] It was the widespread, implicit belief in the existence of this harmony that gave rise in time to the notion of a universe in which music was the central informing principle. While such a conviction helps to account for the high significance that music assumed in pre-Enlightenment thought, it also provides the context for the Romantic developments in the field of musical thought described in Chapter 1.

Tim Bowler's *Starseeker* harks back to the ancient notion of a universe informed by music at a deep level. It proposes, moreover, that some human subjects are equipped with special faculties that enable them to hear the music that most of us cannot. These people act like aerials through which the music of the spheres resonates; they enable those within their ambit to experience a touch of the universal, while at the same time maintaining the idea of the universal as an active force within the general culture. It will be admitted that this is an ambitious agenda for a book aimed in the first instance at readers in and around the age bracket of the central character, Luke Stanton, aged fourteen.

The genre of 'adolescent fiction' emerged during the latter part of the nineteenth century, at which point it developed a didactic function that was locked into the wider cultural and political fabric of British society. The imperial adventure narrative, for example, invariably described the formation of British male identity as a practical realisation of the values and practices inculcated during childhood and in opposition to those confronted in a variety of 'alien' contexts (Bristow 1991). In other words, the narrative teaches the implied reader how to be 'good', offering him the reward of closure upon a fully calibrated identity such as that located within the narrative itself. Despite radical changes to the notion of adolescence since the era of classic adventure, this didactic function has remained influential to a significant degree.

It would seem that music has been an important aspect of adolescent experience at least since the emergence of classical music (and probably long before that): such, after all, is the age at which the rewards, both material and emotional, of music begin to impact upon the subject's imagination, and at which any facility in the areas of understanding, vision or technique begin to present themselves. The biographies of most of the 'great' composers relate a similar tale of exposure to music during childhood, followed by a relationship of greater complexity, sophistication and reward during adolescence and early maturity as they search for an authentic, individual 'voice'. It is really with the rise of popular forms during the twentieth century, however, that the adolescent fixation with music becomes most apparent – so much so, in fact, that music becomes one of the key identifying features of the adolescent experience (Christenson and Roberts 1998).

Adolescent obsession with music was broached in texts such as *Absolute Beginners*, *A Clockwork Orange*, *Gangsta Rap*, *On Beauty*, *Morvern Callar* and *Psychoraag*, and we shall be encountering it again at various points throughout the remainder of this study. Even when not specifically aimed at a specific pre-adult readership, it appears that music is one of the standard means by which the theme of adolescent struggle for identity may be introduced into a narrative. As we shall see in relation to texts such as *The Rotters' Club* and *The Buddha of Suburbia*, the vagaries of taste afforded by a complex cultural system such as popular music is capable of creating tension between teenage contemporaries as well as between generations. Moreover, traces of the didacticism associated with adolescent fiction can still exert an influence; in some of these texts (regardless of whether they are aimed at adolescents or merely incorporate them as part of a wider age range), music is introduced in order to help the as-yet-unformed subject learn valuable lessons about who they are.

In *Starseeker*, Luke Stanton is precisely such a subject-in-formation, one for whom music will provide the key experience as he searches for his true identity. Luke's father was a professional concert pianist before he died of cancer, approximately two years before the narrative begins. Luke shares his father's musical prowess; as the story unfolds we learn that he has also inherited his father's ability to hear music in everything – the primordial music of the spheres that subsists in every living thing in the universe. But Luke's anger at the loss of his father has alienated him from his mother, his education and his musical calling. It has alienated Luke from his true self, in fact, and it is only when he comes to terms with this anger that he can assume his full and proper identity as Luke Stanton, musician.

The central role of music is signalled in a paratextual quotation that reads: 'The universe is composed not of matter but of music'. It is this ancient notion, played out in a contemporary rural English setting, that the narrative works to realise. Luke is a trained musician who is familiar with the classical canon: during the course of the narrative he performs or encounters music by Grieg, Gluck, Schubert, Schumann, Debussy, Ravel and Scriabin. He is capable of interpreting these works with enviable technique and emotional insight; indeed, typical of the music-novel as a genre, a live performance of representative material from the art canon provides the climax of *Starseeker*. Also typical is the manner in which the text works to invest certain pieces (for example, 'Peace of the Forest' by Grieg or Scriabin's Etude, op.2 no.1) with special resonance, as if the values and meanings attached to these pieces in the real world can be imported and thereupon impact upon the world within the narrative. Familiarity with 'Peace of the Forest' will contribute to the reader's understanding of Luke's plight – in some ways, it is a crucial element of the reading experience, and thus a crucial part of the process whereby certain preferred meanings are communicated.

The narrative also finds Luke rehearsing with Miranda – a plodder in musical terms, but someone (like his mother and his erstwhile music teacher Mr Harding) who is attempting to help Luke to rediscover his purpose after the death of his father. As part of this process he will have to dissociate himself from the village gang with which he has been running and help to sort out the plot strand involving Mrs Little and Natalie/Barley, the mentally handicapped child she has kidnapped. Both of these elements involve music. The first introduces a kind of anti-musical ignorance whose basis in an undeserving working class is hinted at but never fully engaged: the gang leader Skin is, it seems, a villain and the son of a villain, just as Luke is a musician and the son of a musician. There is nothing much that either of them can do about it. The second plotline introduces two interrelated and recurring elements of the music-novel, the first of which is a widespread tendency (consummated, as we observed, in Proust) to link music and memory. Mrs Little's identification of the Scriabin piece with her husband, who died in the war, finds resolution in Luke's performance of the piece in concert. The other element relates to Natalie/Barley, and introduces the notion of music's curative powers. The child is at her calmest and most responsive when listening to Luke play piano; when she touches his arm as he plays the little girl is afforded access to realms of meaning and experience otherwise denied her. Music's elemental nature, it appears, is capable of producing a sympathetic response in anyone willing to listen.

'Real' music features strongly throughout the narrative, but there is another 'music' constantly vying for Luke's attention: it is the music of 'things', and, as his mother explains, the ability to hear this music is a faculty that Luke has inherited directly from his father:

> It's something your dad believed in very strongly. He used to say that every single thing in creation – every human being, every creature, every flower, every tree, every blade of grass, every speck of sand – has its own special song, different from all other songs. He said you can hear those songs if you listen hard enough. (172)

As Mr Harding informs him, Luke is one of the rare humans capable of hearing the music of which the universe is composed (54). Amidst all the sound, one particular strain recurs: it is 'a strange unfinished melody' (93) that Luke comes to associate with his father and which, he eventually realises, is his father communicating with him from his now altered state. He remembers his father composing the melody and dedicating it to Luke himself as a younger child (177); and over the course of the narrative he realises that in order to come to terms with his father's death and to achieve his own sense of identity he must finish the melody. As in many similar scenes, the prose style becomes heightened during the description of this process, as if the author is attempting to imitate the creative/performative process itself:

> The old melody ran out and the new melody ran in, hesitantly at first, then with greater strength until finally it was a river of sound that

would not be stopped. He played and played, not knowing where the music was leading him or what it meant, only that it seemed both to drain and quench him at the same time. He played on and on until the music mastered him and he knew nothing else. (301)

The language flows, just as the music flows; and in losing himself in the music in this fashion, Luke paradoxically finds himself. In listening to the music of the universe, in other words, Luke discovers the music inside himself, and this becomes a metaphor for the adolescent's achievement of the fully calibrated identity that he had been in search of, and which it is the text's role to provide.

Graphic: *Horace Dorlan* (2007) by Andrzej Klimowski

'Semi-graphic' would be a better description of this book; whereas 'graphic fiction' tends to describe novel-length stories characterised by the extensive use of stylised hand-drawn images and minimal amounts of text (including dialogue and description), Andrzej Klimowski's *Horace Dorlan* seems primarily to be a prose narrative into which a number of pencil-drawn, black and white images have been interpolated. The relationship between the images and the prose is far from straightforward, however. While there do appear to be correspondences of some kind, these do not support each other in the manner of standard graphic fiction, (in which a particular image is clearly related to a particular piece of narration or a particular exchange) – nor, indeed, do they with reference to the standard myths or narratives with which we would normally be encouraged to interpret narrative, whether graphic or literary.

Into this complex medial relationship, moreover, Klimowski has introduced the question of music, and this complicates matters still further. For if the relationship between word and image is shown to be fraught with difficulties – difficulties born of the media themselves as well as the conventional attributes they have accrued since the evolution of the species – the relations between word, image and music makes for highly disconcerting reading, as each medium appears to unsettle, and to some extent undo, the narrative logic pursued by the others.

The text concerns an eminent London-based entomologist who is due to travel to Pisa to deliver an important lecture. If Horace Dorlan has begun to acting strangely, however, this is because strange things have begun to happen to him. The text opens with him receiving a mysterious telephone call insisting that 'we' help 'them' because they are in danger of disappearing 'like us, into thin air, never to be seen again' (10).

The caller sounds like his wife Angela (who features significantly throughout the book) but Dorlan is not sure. Focalisation changes from third- to first-person, as team-member Ed describes the apparent disappearance of Angela, and Dorlan's increasingly odd behaviour.

Literary narrative switches to graphic imagery to depict a sequence in which Dorlan spots a woman on the street outside his house whose appearance seems to resemble the picture of an insect that he is drawing at that very moment. The woman is wearing glasses and a small backpack, while an elaborate haircut makes her look as if she had antennae sticking out from the top of her head. Dorlan follows her to the Institute of Entomology where, in a secret room off the library, he comes across what appears to be a medical procedure in progress. In fact, the five white-coated men apprehend Dorlan and conduct some kind of operation whereby he is turned into the insect woman that he was pursuing, complete with backpack (containing wings), antennae pigtails and Dorlan's own glasses. As 'she' leaves the building, the images depict Dorlan gazing from the window back in the Institute where he is attending a meeting. The sequence ends with a colleague lending Dorlan a small mirror so that he may observe the antennae that have sprouted from his head.

Horace Dorlan is not the first character from literary history to turn into an insect. Franz Kafka's 'Metamorphosis' opens with the famous line: 'As Gregor Samsa awoke one morning from uneasy dreams he found himself transformed in his bed into a gigantic insect' (2007: 85). Even the name 'Horace Dorlan' recalls the iambic stress of Kafka's character; and the worlds depicted by the two authors are in fact similar in many respects. The same aura of a surreally subverted normality infuses each text, while the grotesque physical changes suffered by the respective central characters seem in each case intended to suggest various forms of social, psychological and cultural alienation.

Another interesting parallel is suggested by Kafka's troubled relationship with music. Unlike many of his modernist contemporaries, Kafka was not particularly disposed towards music – in fact, he described himself as 'completely unmusical, of a completeness which in my experience doesn't exist elsewhere' (quoted in Benson 2006: 149). Yet he was not unaffected by the general literary zeitgeist in which music (as we observed at length in Part I) functioned so centrally; and as Benson has shown, in stories such as 'Josefine, the Singer or the Mouse Folk' (2006: 264–83) and indeed in 'Metamorphosis' itself, Kafka confronted the challenge of music. Indeed, according to Bennett, Kafka represents both a literary and a philosophical riposte to writers such as Mann, Proust and Joyce, for whom music functioned so centrally and in such a variety of ways: as solace, as aesthetic example, as corrective to the vacancy of language and, above all, as a phenomenon in the world (outside the text) that was capable of affecting the emotions and the perceptions of the listening subject. Bennett suggests that Kafka's engagement with music resists these notions, for '[in] place of an imagined "real" music after which the text strains in the course of its celebration, we have either textual music whose real presence is not permitted to be anything other than imagined, or the imagination of a music that is ultimately withheld' (2006: 157).

The incorporation of music in *Horace Dorlan* might be described as 'Kafkaesque' in these terms. Dorlan loses his voice after an accident, and as he lies in hospital he begins to draw incessantly. Once recovered, he informs his research team that he wishes to incorporate music in the forthcoming lecture – specifically, an opera singer named George who will 'interpret' his hospital drawings and a jazz quintet featuring a sax-ophonist named Aniela who bears a striking resemblance to Dorlan's own wife. Not everyone is happy with this assault on established principles, however. 'Where's the science?' (104) asks one disgruntled aide; indeed, from a more familiar perspective, one of the issues the text seems to be raising is the traditional stand-off between scientific and non-scientific discourses. Music, in this reading, represents the realm of the affective, the emotional, that which cannot be encompassed by traditional scientific method.

In fact, music's presence in the text is far less straightforward and far more disturbing than that. The lecture-performance goes ahead, although Dorlan is disappointed with its reception. The audience's failure to 'get' the event is of a piece with the text's failure to represent it; for untypically of most music-novels, *Horace Dorlan* avoids the climactic concert scene – the extended textual description of a central musical 'event' around which the discourses of value and meaning in the text are organised.[2] Instead, different forms of music begin to encroach upon the text. As Dorlan attempts to dance with his wife to a tune playing on the radio, we learn that the jazz ensemble hired for the lecture is now somehow ensconced in miniature form inside the radio. Meanwhile, Dorlan continues to confuse his piano-playing wife, Angela, with the sax-playing musician Aniela. They attend a nightclub where an acquaintance named Alexei Naco is playing jazz piano; he tells the story of how his former musical career was curtailed when he was electrocuted by his Hawaiian guitar. At this point, language gives way once again to imagery, and the reader is presented with drawings of a transported Naco playing the piano and Dorlan dancing intimately with Angela.

All in all, *Horace Dorlan* is as unsettled a prospect as 'Horace Dorlan'; which is to say, the latter represents the fiction around which the action of the book appears to coalesce. The narrative proceeds according to a logic that has more in common with dream association than with the patterns of cause and effect familiar from the real world. It is possible, moreover, that Dorlan may not even be the active dreaming subject: he himself could be a presence dreamt up by Ed the technician or Naco the musician or any of the other peripheral characters in the text. We are back, in other words, in the realm of philosophical speculation as to the 'reality' of the world, the identity of the subject, the possibility of agency. Most significantly for present purposes, we are back to the issue of the artistic media we employ both to interpret and to represent the world.

Generations of theorists have established the complex, conventional nature of literary narrative – the fact that it is not a naturally occurring phenomenon but the product of certain institutional, technical and socio-political factors. Likewise, the interpretation of a visual image – even one with a supposed narrative intent – is never a straightforward prospect. Conventional, institutionally sanctioned responses dominate at various times and in various places, so that the viewer may assume a preferred relationship with the text. There is always the possibility of 'mis-viewing', however – of altering the meaning of the image by altering the perspective from which one looks or the emphasis one places upon the elements that comprise the image.

The asynchronous juxtaposition of text and imagery in *Horace Dorlan* subverts the conventional reading process. There is another level to this subversion, however: for between the letter and the image comes the sound – represented in this instance by the recurring evocation of music within the text. The author introduces the possibility of music as an alternative narrative form, with its conventional modes of articulation, interpretation and subjective response. Then (in a gesture that recalls Kafka), he simultaneously undoes those conventions and that possibility. Music permeates the text, certainly, but the text is not forthcoming on what music means. There is no climactic epiphany, no moment in which the narrative is re-organised in terms of a musical (as opposed to a verbal or visual) discourse. The text refuses the classic gesture in which music is imported in order to re-organise the process of signification and to 'harmonise' a hitherto dissonant narrative. Instead, *Horace Dorlan* closes with a meta-narrative image in which various 'characters' gaze out of the text at the reader, as if demanding to know what they make of it all.

Celebrity: *Crystal* (2007) by Katie Price

Certain writers (such as Terry Pratchett and Ian Rankin) are 'popular' in the sense that their books tend to sell relatively well and the authors themselves develop significant extra-literary profiles. (The work of Pratchett and Rankin, for example, has been adapted for other media.) It is not at all clear, however, that this 'popularity' translates unproblematically from an economic register (in which it signifies sales rankings, high profile, and so on) to an aesthetic register (in which the term 'popularity' has somewhat different connotations). It is entirely necessary, in other words, to make a distinction between fiction which is popular and 'popular fiction', however invidious or unwelcome such a critical manoeuvre may seem.

'Popularity' is a notoriously difficult concept to engage, especially in relation to cultural practices (Storey 1993), and even more so in relation to the novel (Gelder 2004). Problems arise immediately one attempts to define the concept. Is it, for example, a question of style (the manner in which a text is written) or subject matter? Are some themes likely to be considered more 'popular' than others? Is popularity defined by sales figures? What is the process whereby what was once defined as popular becomes something else – becomes the 'literary', for example? What moral, social or political values have been, and continue to be, attached to the concept of popularity? And (this is the key question) what has the 'popular' been defined against over the course of its career as a cultural possibility?

One familiar answer to this last question is: 'the literary'. At least since the writings of Matthew Arnold in the latter part of the nineteenth century, the 'popular' and the 'literary' have been characterised in some influential theoretical discourses to be locked in constant combat, one battle in a larger war that has been fought throughout the modern era for control of the British cultural imagination. In this discourse, popular literature has been generally regarded as, at best, innocuous and ineffective, and at worst, politically culpable and morally repugnant (depending on the critical context within which the question is posed). The 'literary', on the other hand, remains the arena of the effective and the potentially truthful; it represents a form of cultural practice capable of encapsulating underlying realities and of producing effects in the readers, regardless of political affiliation or moral tendency, that will lead them to modify their understanding of the world and themselves in relation to it.

The relationship between popular and literary fiction is complicated still further when music is introduced into the mix. Traditionally, 'serious' literary fiction has tended to deal with 'serious' art music, as if there was some form of 'natural' correspondence between the 'higher' tendencies in each medium. Many of the texts addressed in this study adhere to such a pattern – which is to say, they are 'literary' novels (not 'popular' or 'genre' fiction) that engage in some ways or to some degree with art music. Increasingly, however, there has been a trend (as we noted in relation to a number of texts in the previous chapter) for 'literary' novels about popular music. The reasons for this are many and various. A general postmodernist sensibility within the cultural institutions has certainly extended the possibility of what it is possible to write. Also postmodernist is the central tendency of such novels (*Personality* and *Morvern Callar*, for example) to self-consciously highlight the seemingly contradictory relationship between 'popular' music and the 'literary' means used to represent it.

Conversely, there is the possibility of 'popular' fiction set in or focused on the world of art music, as we shall observe shortly in relation to the genre of detective fiction, for example. A typical scenario would involve the murder of a musician during a festival and the gradual revelation of means and motive by a detective figure who is in some form or to some degree implicated in the musical community (a performer or reviewer or such like). In such texts music tends to function as the occasion or the scene rather than the central theme; at most it retains a vague symbolic weight within the narrative. Certainly, such texts tend not to have pretensions towards the 'musicalisation' of fiction – which is to say, the attempt to reproduce musical form or effects in novelistic discourse. The music, rather, forms a backdrop – referenced occasionally and usually only in the most general terms – against which the generic narrative is played out.

Another example of popular fiction set in the world of classical music is provided by Jilly Cooper's *Appassionata* (1996) – described in one back-cover review as 'a boisterous tale of sex and Chopin'.[3] The latter phrase is a pun on 'sex-and-shopping' – a highly successful subgenre which is in turn related to other socio-literary trends such as 'chick lit', 'celebrity fiction', and the emergence of 'camp' as an aesthetic sensibility.[4] The modern 'sex-and-shopping' novel has its roots in the work of US-based writers such as Jacqueline Susann and Jackie Collins. Gelder describes it as an 'anti-romantic' (2004: 129) discourse in so far as it rejects (or at least radically questions) the traditional notion of fulfilment through romantic love. Collins's *The Stud* (1969) is typical in that it features a strong, sexually proactive woman attempting to make her mark in a professional environment. The fact that the environment in question is oriented towards the entertainment industry – in which music invariably plays a part – is suggestive.[5] So too is the fact that the 'sex-and-shopping' genre emerged alongside – and in some ways as a direct response to – developments in international feminism, with its deep suspicion of any form of female agency in a world in which both the material infrastructure, as well as the terms of the entire debate, are still determined in the last instance by male desire.

Cooper's long novel (891 pages) is an exception to the rule stated above regarding popular fiction's general disinterest in the musicalisation of fiction. The narrative begins with an 'overture' (33–125) and proceeds through six 'movements'. This structure is entirely nominal, however, and relates in no way to any musical discourse embedded within the text. In every other respect, in fact, *Appassionata* adheres to the precepts of contemporary popular romantic fiction. The book takes its title from the nickname of the character Abigail Rosen, an American violinist who, following an unlikely series of events, finds herself as conductor of the fictitious Rutminster Symphony Orchestra in rural England. Typically of Cooper's other 'bonkbusters', there is a good deal of sexual activity as the characters attempt to find their place among the large field of available partners. At the same time, Abigail and a number of other female characters also have to work hard to establish themselves within the world of classical music – as conductors, performers, writers and administrators. These two narrative threads form the main point of tension within the text: on the one hand, an older traditional model based on the search for, and endorsement of, romantic love; on the other, a discourse of female empowerment with its roots in an anti-romantic 'sex-and-shopping' genre.[6]

Katie Price's *Crystal* (2007) concentrates many of the trends introduced above. The author is the model also known as 'Jordan', who achieved a significant profile in British popular culture during the early years of the decade. Although the text was released under her real name, the publishers traded on her celebrity by including the line 'Jordan's sensational new novel' on the front cover.[7] This has the effect of directly linking the text with the kind of extra-literary practices and values with which the model is associated. This is borne out by the narrative, which, with its depiction of TV talent shows, 'glamour' modelling and 'celebrity' marriages, evokes the world of manufactured minor celebrity that came to dominate British popular culture in the opening years of the new millennium. On one level, Price's book offers to do for this world what Susann and Collins did for Hollywood and what (with different focus but with a similarly populist impulse) Cooper's book did for the world of the classical orchestra – that is, to expose the perennial human propensities (all variations on fear and desire, as it happens) that subsist beneath the glamour. On another level, *Crystal* functions as an implicit vindication, not to say celebration, of the lifestyle it represents.[8]

The eponymous heroine of Price's 'sensational' novel faces the same dilemma as her forebears: to discover the optimum balance between romantic love and self-fulfilment through work. Some, such as the anti-romantic Fontaine in Collins' *The Stud*, disdain the former in their ruthless pursuit of the latter. Some, such as Cooper's Abigail Rosen, demand both – a desire that brings much grief to the character and much artificial tension to the narrative itself. Crystal also believes that she can enjoy a fully realised relationship with the alpha male while at the same time achieving success in the popular music industry. In this conviction, however, it becomes apparent that the fictional character whom she most resembles is the one known as 'Jordan' who, from being a fully committed player within the world of manufactured celebrity, re-invented her public profile in the middle years of the noughties as wife, mother and novelist.

In the context of the present study, questions regarding the quality or value of *Crystal* as a literary text are in danger of missing the point – that being: the text incorporates music in certain ways and for certain ends that are related to long-established trends within the history of fiction. One could argue that the language is cliché-ridden, the narrative predictable, and even the main characters one-dimensional; some of the espoused values (regarding age, gender, body image, fashion sense, and so on) appear questionable (if not downright distasteful) when considered from a progressive perspective. And yet, Crystal's desire to express the strong emotions she experiences in original musical compositions remains a perfectly valid manoeuvre – a recurring trope, in fact, within a long and distinguished tradition of novelistic discourse. It is a long way from Price to Proust, no doubt, but in at least one respect – their characters' heightened response to music – they may be regarded as launched upon the same trajectory.

Fantasy: *Soul Music* (1994) by Terry Pratchett

In *Starseeker*, Luke Stanton and his father (see above), share a conviction that the process of creation was noisy – some variation on the 'big bang'; they believe, furthermore, that such noise continues to resonate throughout the universe. Even if most people cannot hear it, there is a background hum to life, which is described as 'the sound of the engine that started creation' (168). A similar idea, although refined in various ways, runs through Terry Pratchett's *Soul Music*:

> It was wrong to call it a big bang. That would just be noise, and all that noise could create is more noise and a cosmos full of random particles. Matter exploded into being, apparently as chaos, but in fact as a chord. The ultimate power chord. Everything, all together, streaming out in one huge rush that contained within itself, like reverse fossils, everything that it was going to be.
>
> And, zigzagging through the expanding cloud, alive, that first wild live music. (362)

Although cast in different terms, and although worlds apart in many senses, these two novels are remarkably similar in terms of the way in which they imagine music coming into existence and how it continues to function in 'the present' (whenever and wherever that may be).

Soul Music is the sixteenth title in Pratchett's 'Discworld' series. It tells the story of Imp y Celyn, a harp-playing bard from Llamedos – a place-name that spells 'sod em all' when reversed. The allusion to Dylan Thomas's 'Llareggub' (from *Under Milk Wood*) is just one of the ways in which Imp's 'Welshness' is suggested. It is also one of the many ways in which the author deliberately links the strange, 'impossible' world of the narrative with the familiar, 'possible' world of the reader, and suggests connections between them.

Having won a new harp at the local eisteddfod, Imp rows with his father and leaves for the big city of Ankh-Morpork, vowing to become the world's greatest musician. Once there he forms a band with a troll and a dwarf who, like himself, cannot meet the various fees demanded by the Guild of Musicians in order to practise as legitimate musicians. When his prize harp is accidentally destroyed by the troll, Imp acquires a guitar-like instrument from a mysterious shop. With the troll banging rocks to provide rhythm and the dwarf on horn, the band play their first gig, with extraordinary results. The sound produced by the three musicians seems to have a profoundly unsettling effect on anyone who hears it:

> It made you want to kick down walls and ascend the sky on steps of fire. It made you want to pull all the switches and throw all the levers and stick your fingers in the electric socket of the universe to see what happened next. It made you want to paint your bedroom wall black and cover it with posters. (114)

'Music With Rocks In' (as the style comes to be called) becomes a phenomenon on Discworld. Other bands emerge who wish to emulate the originals; the agents of the Guild are determined to crush this challenge to their monopoly; the band acquires a manager who wishes to exploit the fashion as quickly and as fully as possible. The Archchancellor of the Unseen University (whose normally staid staff have fallen under the spell of the music) begins an investigation into the mass hysteria, and begins to move towards an understanding of its causes.

Imp, meanwhile, changes his name to Buddy and begins to act very strangely, alarming even his fellow band members with his behaviour. (The 'strange' behaviour is, of course, relative when placed in the context of the strange world in which the narrative is set.) This is caused in part by the power of the music, but also by the fact that he is officially dead. In a parallel plotline, the character of Death has gone missing, with his duties being reluctantly assumed by his teenage granddaughter Susan. At the moment when Imp is due to die, two things happen: Susan fails to wield the scythe that traditionally severs the soul from the dead body; instead she attempts to stop the movement (a random axe thrown by a member of the audience) that would have caused Imp's untimely demise. At the exact same time, Imp plays a power chord on his new instrument. The two gestures conjoin to produce an unusual effect: the sand in Imp's hourglass (representing his life expectancy) is replaced with a blue light which, it becomes apparent, is an emanation of the music that from this point onwards begins to dominate his personality.

The 'Discworld' series represents one of the most successful publication projects in history. Genre fiction has always been 'popular' in the sense that it tends to sell well in comparison with 'literary' fiction – hence the ubiquity of the multi-volume fantasy franchise for which the modern avatar is J. R. R. Tolkein's *The Lord of the Rings* (1954–5). Since the 1960s, however, the multifaceted revolution in literary theory, allied with the anti-canonical sensibilities encouraged under its dispensation, has facilitated the entry of genre fiction into the academy. The current chapter is in part a response to that general process. Fantasy fiction, for example – once dismissed as mere adolescent escapism – has come to be regarded as a complex literary form that rivals the traditional 'literary' novel in terms of its formal and conceptual discourses (Armitt 2005; Freedman 2000).

Two aspects of fantasy fiction are relevant for current purposes. The first is the tendency (which it shares with science fiction) to realise a kind of dual aesthetic: whereas the imaginary setting is prized for its originality and credibility on the one hand, on the other, engagement with that setting invariably defers to the 'real' world and to scenarios and characters familiar from human history. In other words, there would appear to be an unavoidable allegorical impulse to fantasy fiction.

Some writers embrace this impulse with the clear intention of drawing parallels between the world of the narrative and the world in which the narrative is consumed. We observed this impulse at work in *Cloud Atlas* (see Chapter 1 above), in which the values and practices of various future worlds were invoked with reference to parallel contexts in both the past and the present. That, indeed, was the point. Even when a writer goes out of their way to avoid allegory, however, it is difficult to obviate the seemingly universal human tendency to apprehend the unfamiliar in terms of the familiar. Thus, despite Tolkien's frequent pronouncements to the contrary, *The Lord of the Rings* continues to be widely regarded as an allegory of certain aspects of twentieth-century history (Garth 2003).

Tolkien's epic is relevant in relation to the other aspect of fantasy fiction that it is worth mentioning here: Middle Earth is a profoundly musical world. Each race has its own music, from the drinking ballads and walking songs of the hobbits to the epic lays and death dirges of the elves and the various forms and styles practised by men, dwarves, ents and orcs. As a scholar of language and literature, Tolkien would have been aware that music features as a central element of all complex cultures; and his deployment of a complex, multifaceted musical discourse throughout *The Lord of the Rings* adds to the text's internal credibility. Its constant presence contributes to the sense of a multifarious reality that has been calibrated over an extended period of time. In short, music is central to the integrity – and thus the pleasure – of the text.[9]

Part of the pleasure of *Soul Music* lies in spotting correspondences between the music culture described in the narrative and a form of music from the real world with which the intended reader will be more or less familiar. Thus, 'Music With Rocks In' is obviously a version of rock music; Imp y Celyn supposedly translates as 'Bud y Holly', recalling the iconic figure whose early death in an aeroplane accident secured him a place within modern popular folklore; songs such as 'Don't Tread on My New Blue Boots' and 'Good Gracious Miss Polly' comically evoke well-known songs from the rock 'n' roll canon; and so on. It turns out that music in the Discworld is uncannily like music in the 'real' world – and therein lies both the power and the appeal of the text. Encountering the (more or less) familiar in this fantastic context encourages the reader to reconsider both the thing itself and their own relationship with it. So, the strange behaviour of the inhabitants of Ankh-Morpork after listening to Music With Rocks In invokes a recurring pattern familiar from our reality in which new musical movements (for example, rock 'n' roll, mod, punk or rave) induce vehement emotional responses among their adherents, the strength of which creates anxiety (often panic) among those with an investment in the status quo. Likewise, Imp's constant insistence that 'music should be free' resonates in a world such as ours, where music is in fact subject to intense regulation.

This allegorical correspondence between the world of the text and the world of the reader bears also upon the issue of music's deeper function in relation to life itself as both a physical and a metaphysical possibility. The idea of the universe beginning with a count-in followed by a power chord may seem absurd; it emanates from and speaks to a world – the Discworld – where life is similar to, but at the same time significantly different from, life as experienced in 'the real world'. The related ideas – of music being alive, powerful, and contained within all matter – are not at all absurd, however. Such ideas emanate from and speak to concerns that have been both active and influential within the human imagination since ancient times, which grew considerably in significance during the eighteenth and nineteenth centuries, and which continue in one form or another to bear upon the species' sense of itself down to the present day.

Science: *Sing the Body Electric: A Novel in Five Movements* (1993) by Adam Lively

A stroll through any of Britain's major bookstores reveals that science fiction is one of the country's most popular literary genres. Although characteristic aspects of the discourse may be discerned throughout literary history, the roots of modern science fiction lie in the latter part of the nineteenth century, during which period writers began to speculate on the evolving relationship between technology and the human species as it was then understood. Radical developments in the fields of natural history (Darwin), philosophy (Nietzsche), politics (Marx), psychology (Freud) and sociology (Durkheim) combined with a series of new inventions (the telephone, the machine gun, the motor car – followed soon after by the aeroplane) to put severe pressure upon established notions of the human subject and the scheme within which that subject was traditionally located. What constituted 'reality' appeared to be changing so rapidly and so radically, that the means of representing it needed to undergo change also (Trotter 1993).

One result of all this pressure was the pan-artistic movement known as modernism, and another was the development of science fiction.

While it might be possible to regard the latter as part of a general modernist sensibility at large in western culture at a certain point in history, there is another sense in which these discourses are clearly at odds with each other. Characterised by elitism and difficulty, modernism disdained the new literary genres that started to emerge in the latter part of the nineteenth century to cater for a new mass readership. The reading public had fragmented irrevocably, and the debasement of language consequent upon this was one of the precise problems with the modern world. This, we recall from Chapter 1, is one of the reasons why modernism embraced literature's musical tendencies so assiduously: it provided signifying possibilities beyond those traditional literary elements (narrative and language) that had been so compromised by the new times.

Science fiction, on the other hand, seemed specifically designed to confront the new times head on. Compared to their modernist contemporaries, its early practitioners seemed to have a less elevated sense of their profession. Indeed, science fiction is often represented as a kind of trade – entertaining, no doubt, but capable of being learned and practised by artisans; whereas literary fiction tends to retain an older Romantic sensibility of writing as a quasi-religious calling. This stereotype belies both the sophistication and the seriousness of science fiction, in which regard the key figure is perhaps H. G. Wells who, in a series of stunning publications at the outset of his career, introduced many of the thematic and formal elements that animated the genre throughout the twentieth century.[10]

Music does not feature particularly strongly in Wells's work, nor does it in the literary tradition that followed his lead. Occasionally a writer will deploy music to authenticate an unfamiliar setting or to reference experiences or emotions associated with a particular musical discourse. In Robert A. Heinlein's influential short story collection entitled *The Green Hills of Earth* (1951), for example, various earth-born characters express their love for their home planet in the ancient song form of the ballad as they roam across the solar system. The invocation of an established musical form in the context of this particular literary form lends depth and resonance to the story. But the influence is far from unidirectional. As remarked in footnote 9 to this chapter, the 'filk' musical subculture remains enormously popular, while science fiction has also proved enduringly attractive to popular musicians. A key figure in this regard is David Bowie (see Chapter 3, footnote 9), who has regularly used science fiction imagery (from 'Space Oddity', 1969, to 'New Killer Star', 2003) to reflect on personal and political issues in the present.

Music and British science fiction encounter each other in spectacular fashion in the work of the Manchester-based writer Jeff Noon. Beginning with *Vurt* (1993) – a novel that is in some obvious respects a retelling of the Orpheus legend – Noon has incorporated a regard for music throughout his literary output. The connection was cemented with the publication of *Needle in the Groove* (2000), set in a Manchester of the near future and telling the story of a down-and-out bass player who gets embroiled in a conspiracy to which music provides the key. In this particular text, moreover, the author disdains traditional novelistic structure; instead, the narrative is organised in terms of various techniques (most clearly, sampling and remixing) associated with certain modern musical trends. As the narrative of Suhayl Saadi's *Psychoraag* follows the logic of DJ Zaf's on-air performance (see Chapter 3), so the narrative of *Needle in the Groove* progresses as an analogue of the remix – that is, a musical 'text' in which every presence is subject to modification by the presences surrounding it and in which narrative structure is determined not by authorial intention or plausibility but by atmosphere, coincidence and improvisation.

Adam Lively's *Sing the Body Electric: A Novel in Five Movements* is another novel in which the structure is self-consciously inspired, if not determined, by musical form – in this case the form (five movements in this case) of the classical symphony. This is clearly signalled in the text's subtitle, as well as at various points throughout the text, when parallels between musical and literary form are self-consciously evoked (30ff, 64, 86, 104, 152, 196, 413, 438). As one might expect, a literary form based on the aesthetics of the symphony is very different from one based on the aesthetics of the remix, although in each case the structure is intended to correlate with issues broached at a conceptual level within the narrative.

Because it is set in the future and focuses on the impact of technology upon received ideas, Lively's novel qualifies to be described as 'science fiction'. At the same time, it retains clear links with the modernist tradition that shadowed the emergence of science fiction. The plot features a 'newly invented' device called a 'neurorch' (which locates the text within a 'cyber' tradition that stretches at least as far back as Mary Shelley's *Frankenstein,* and which finds seminal modern articulation in texts such as *Neuromancer* (1984) by the American writer William Gibson). The career of the novel's lead character, composer Paul Clearwater, and his response to the neurorch, however, also clearly recalls the figure of the doomed artist-hero that featured so strongly in modernist aesthetics. The key reference in this regard is Adrian Leverkühn, the central character of

Thomas Mann's epic mid-century novel *Doctor Faustus* (1947; see Chapter 1); and the similarities between Clearwater and his German forebear (who sells his soul to the devil in exchange for musical mastery) develop over the course of the narrative.

Each of the novel's five 'movements' is narrated from a different perspective and uses a different style. The first is made up of the letters of Paul Clearwater, who has moved to a coastal town named Wellfleet (loosely modelled on Hastings) in order to escape the distractions of New Venice (a city conceived and designed by his music-hating father). The year is 2064, and the world, although different in many important respects, is still recognisable as the Britain of the 1990s in which Lively's novel was published. Clearwater is working on a 'sea symphony' in five movements, and meditates at length on the musical and philosophical traditions with which he is engaged.[11] He keeps getting distracted by local matters, however, not least of which is the town's impoverished music provision. Soon, however, a more pressing distraction impinges upon his life.

The novel's second movement is comprised of recordings sent to Clearwater by his mother, his father and his sister, Jean. The latter tells him of a new craze overtaking New Venice: a manufacturing company named the Synergise Corporation had been using Walt Whitman's famous phrase 'Sing the Body Electric'[12] as a teaser campaign for the neurorch (short for 'neural orchestra') – a device that apparently gives the wearer access to the never-ending, immeasurably complex neural activity of the brain and enables them to express it in musical form. The rest of the book explores the implications of this devastating invention.

The Clearwater children react to the neurorch in different ways. Paul finds himself having to deal with the aesthetic implications of a device that could render him obsolete overnight. After all, he approaches the process of composition with a firm belief in 'the transcendence of music . . . Those unheard harmonies, the architecture of the universe . . . That was what he was trying to articulate . . . the "music of the spheres" – the universal and transcendent music that animated all visible matter' (Lively 233). The model to which the composer adheres at this stage is profoundly modernist; in other words, the composer-genius trains himself to hear those 'unheard harmonies' and thereafter transposes them into a musical form that would be apprehensible – and thus meaningful – to the listener. At least three important questions are begged by such an aesthetic model. Firstly, if the music of the spheres is 'universal', why do we not all hear it? Secondly, does not the composer's transposition of 'natural' music into conventional form represent a diminishment of its pristine existence? And finally, is the cerebral nature of the process of transposition (from nature to culture) at odds with music's sheer otherness – is there something inherently contradictory, in other words, in the attempt to bestow physical form upon a metaphysical concept?

All the cracks in the traditional aesthetic model to which Paul Clearwater subscribes are exposed by the invention of the neurorch. If everybody has access to the technology, and everybody is thus potentially both a composer and a musician, what impact does this have on the notion of the individual genius? Composition and musicianship, moreover, are now unmediated by metaphor or convention; neurorch composition literally expresses the activity of the mind into a sonic form that is representative of itself and nothing else. Typically of science fiction discourse, then, Clearwater's ambition to create a piece of art that would 'embody' or 'express' or 'represent' nature has been superseded by a technological innovation. Faced with a crisis that threatens his aesthetic calling, however, he decides to embrace rather than reject the neurorch. The latter part of the text finds Paul back in Wellfleet, a wasted old man, addicted to a device that he now describes as 'an instrument for everything that is true and noble and good' (405).[13]

Jean Clearwater, Paul's sister, is also reintroduced in the novel's final movement, which is set some thirty-five years after the invention of the neurorch and is narrated by a painter named Malcolm Abrahams, who has moved to Wellfleet with his wife and daughter. After an encounter with the old composer, Abrahams goes in search of Jean, whom he finds living in a community called New Harmony in a remote part of northern California. She explains the principles of a new movement based on the supposedly liberating technology of the neurorch:

> Ever since the Tower of Babel, people have dreamt of a natural universal language. And why did they have that dream? Because they knew that the actual languages – all those separate babbling tongues that people talk – are the root cause of human misery. It's the languages that divide people, twist them into lying to themselves and each other, draw them into hiding themselves from each other. They cause wars, they set people against each other, they stop people understanding each other. (433–4)

To Abrahams's accusation that the New Harmony philosophy sounds like political brainwashing, she replies: 'The neurorch doesn't destroy individuality; it helps you express it. It helps others understand it. And when everything's understood, everything's forgiven' (434). So, whereas Paul regards the neurorch as an unprecedented opportunity to sing, literally, the 'song of myself', his sister regards it as the basis of a new form of socio-political organisation characterised by full, transparent and unmediated communication. These different responses encompass the great polarities of human history: art versus politics, the individual versus the community, expression versus communication, male versus female.

If New Harmony recalls some of the radical lifestyle philosophies of the 1960s, the device on which the community is based is clearly born of the 1990s. Specifically, it represents a response to the advent of digitalisation and to advances on various scientific and medical fronts. If it has become possible to manipulate both matter and data at a microscopic level, and if the human body itself has been revealed to be nothing more than a temporary collection of electrochemical data, then there are profound consequences for the very idea of the human, as well as for the long-established systems wherein that idea is constantly reconfirmed and refashioned. *Sing the Body Electric* acknowledges that one of the most important of those systems has traditionally been music; at the same time, the novel offers a vision of the future as seen from a musical perspective. That future comes down to a choice between Paul and Jean, neither of whom is presented in a particularly sympathetic light; and of course, the reader's preference in this matter refers not to a future in which the technology is real and available, but to a present in which it is a product of the author's imagination.

Thriller: *Johnny Come Home* (2006) by Jake Arnott

As a genre, the thriller is related to the crime field, which we shall encounter shortly; however, it also retains links with a number of other popular genres, such as the spy and adventure novel. This eclectic literary inheritance, as well as its intrinsic adaptability, has given rise to a large number of subgenres that also draw in some sense or to some degree on the conventions of the thriller. These are the texts that tend to make up the bulk of the stock in airport and railway station bookshops: spy thrillers, political thrillers, psychological thrillers, techno-thrillers, eco-thrillers, and so on. These are the texts, also, that tend to be the most popular in the wide field of 'popular fiction', and which have the most potential for intermedial crossover (for example, film and television adaptation).[14]

The thriller is also generally regarded as the popular genre with the greatest pretensions towards proper 'literary' status (however that may be defined). There are, no doubt, a number of reasons for this; one, certainly, is the fact that the thriller may be regarded as an accentuation of certain formal and conceptual elements inherent within the modern novel as it has evolved since the early eighteenth century: conflict between characters and values; the search for identity; the economy of crisis and resolution; the relationship between the individual and a community variously defined; the manipulation of time for purposes of tension and surprise; and so on. In some senses and to some extent, the literary novel is always already a thriller; and such relations as do exist may be located in their common obligation to the exigencies of narrative – the need to engage the reader and retain their emotional and intellectual investment in the fictional world. What this points to is the fact that 'the literary' is not so much a genre in and of itself (although it continues to function as such in certain contexts and in answer to certain extra-literary agendas) as a continuously evolving system of values according to which different kinds of writing may be evaluated.

There are a number of elements that point to a potential correspondence between the literary thriller and music, the principal of which is their mutual investment in the category of narrative. Opera seems the obvious counterpart here, especially the melodramatic plotting and high emotional content of Romantic opera. If *Pride and Prejudice* and *Wuthering Heights* may in some senses be regarded as prototype thrillers, then so too may *La traviata* and *Tristan und Isolde*. The deeper one delves, however, the more possibilities arise; and this returns us to the notion of a correspondence between literary narrative and sonata form and the common elements of which they are composed: a dualistic relationship (alternating identity and difference) on the one hand, on the other a spatial model encompassing the nodal elements of home, departure and return, and the vast array of associations brought into play by such elements.

As always, the interest in critical discourse comes in noting the discrepancies between the theory and the text. *Johnny Come Home* concerns a number of characters living in London in the early years of the 1970s, many of whom have fetched up there from elsewhere in the Atlantic archipelago. The city is depicted in the throes of a post-sixties hangover, with all the optimism and colour of the previous decade dissipated in a welter of confusion and frustration. Political activism takes the form of a few loose cannons – the rump of the self-styled Angry Brigade – whose attempts to realise the radical social philosophy of Debord and Marcuse led only to a few impotent gestures against the state.[15] Meanwhile, the sexual revolution has resulted for the most part in exploitation and self-abnegation. All the main characters in the novel are gay or engage in homosexual practices, but all are confused about both the nature and the expression of their sexuality; and this is to be expected in a society which has only partially acknowledged the principle of sexual freedom, and in which homosexuality is still largely regarded as aberrant. Even Nina – who, as an educated middle-class agent is the most sexually aware character in the story – is confused, finding that she can only reach orgasm with her lesbian lover by fantasising about the teenage rent boy named Sweet Thing.

It was in the field of popular music, however, that developments within the wider zeitgeist were most apparent. In musical terms the sixties was a decade of experimentation and innovation. British rock represented, among other things, a search for a musical culture (comprising all the usual elements of composition, performance, reception, and so on) that was both authentic and alternative, and which would both reflect and express a widespread desire for change in the wider sociopolitical fabric. The animating spirit of that desire soon faltered, for a number of reasons: its disparate identity and inherent suspicion of authority; its antipathy to the idea of systematic activity of any kind, even oppositional activity; and the strong establishment reaction to it. And as the social and political energy of the sixties dissipated, so too did the musical energy.

Rock historians have generally been unsympathetic towards the form of popular music that appeared to fill the vacuum left by the disappearance of classic late-sixties rock.[16] 'Glam' is widely regarded as an aberration that occurred between the twin authenticities of rock and punk. At its best (as represented by the likes David Bowie, Marc Bolan and Roxy Music) it produced only thin echoes of former glories or decadent meditations on rock music itself, in which latter regard Bowie's album *The Rise and Fall of Ziggy Stardust and the Spiders from Mars* (1972) represents the key document of the era. At its worst (and the list is long), glam was exploitative and opportunistic, a clear move on the part of management and career 'artistes' (represented in the text by Joe Berkovitch and Johnny Chrome – the latter a very thinly disguised portrait of Gary Glitter) to occupy the ground cleared by the rock artists of the late 1960s. Arnott's novel works to show that things were never that simple, however, and that glam rock was always a much more complex prospect than has been depicted in the dominant narratives. This brings us back to the questions of genre and narrative.

An analysis of *Johnny Come Home* based on the deep structural correspondences between literary narrative and sonata form would have to admit the absence of a strong central relationship at the core of the text. There are, rather, a number of overlapping relationships between various characters, each liaison forming a temporary dyad that has the potential to evolve into the emotional core of the narrative, but none of which ever really does. If the notion of one central informing relationship is unavailable within the text, then this is a reflection of a time (the early 1970s) and a place (London) in which the idea of an informed relationship between one self-aware identity and its significant other is similarly under pressure. All the characters in Arnott's novel are uncertain; all are militating in some way or other against the various identities that they might have been expected to adopt, whether they be defined in terms of class, race, gender or sexuality.

It is likewise clear that the classical journey away from, and back towards, home is absent from this world. All the characters are displaced to a greater or lesser extent – an experience symbolised and indeed embodied in the squat that is inhabited by various characters over the course of the narrative. London is the place to which they have come, but not necessarily the place from which they will return. It is, rather, a kind of inferno in which they all obliged to circulate constantly. The emotions generated by the tripartite structure of leaving, arriving and departing – emotions such as excitement, disillusionment, nostalgia, anticipation, and so on – are unavailable, as the city simply absorbs those who flock to it without offering the consolation of closure.

In this world, glam becomes a symbol of uncertainty, atomisation, alienation and the dangers besetting any society in which such forces are prevalent. For the Bomb Squad detective, Walker, glam is the cultural logic of the society of the spectacle: politics turned into entertainment, but always retaining the potential to segue back into politics again. Introducing the line that will become standard, the old showbiz trooper Berkovitch regards glam as simply 'stripped down and over-produced rock 'n' roll. Boogie-woogie in a bit of make-up' (40). For many of the other characters, however, it offers a mode of being – that is, a means of entering into and understanding the contemporary world and themselves in relation to it. Glam may have offered a release from the onerous authenticity of rock; the price, however, was a potential loss of conviction, a loss, indeed, of the self – something which all the major characters in the text confront sooner or later.

The delusions that lead the naïve Stephen Pearson to plant a bomb in a central London entertainment arcade are of a piece with the delusions that beset Nina, Sweet Thing and Johnny Chrome.[17] Pearson is searching for a sense of himself in the wake of his lover's suicide and subsequent revelations as to the latter's political treachery. The gesture gives him a sense of agency which he is otherwise lacking; it is clear, however, that his actions were animated by a crisis brought on by the gap between the person he believed himself to be and the person he has discovered himself to be – that is, the gap between his 'fictional' and 'real' identities. Sweet Thing and Johnny Chrome are likewise 'fictional' characters in the sense that they have been invented (hence the aliases) and subsequently fully adopted by subjects whose own identities are as a result compromised. (The parallels with Andrew O'Hagan's *Personality* are clear – see Chapter 3 above.) The John Evans who was born in Swansea in 1941 is permanently eclipsed as his alter-ego, Johnny Chrome, manages to lose himself in a ritual of sexual self-abnegation. There is still hope for Sweet Thing, however, as, groping his way across the roof back towards Nina and safety in the final scene of the novel, he reveals his real name to her. But the text is not forthcoming as to fate of this Stewart Laing 'character' once the glam persona of Sweet Thing has been abandoned.

Crime: *Exit Music* (2007) by Ian Rankin

There exists a large, long-established subtradition of crime fiction set in and around the world of classical music. Many of the 600-plus titles in the 'Bibliography of Musical Fiction' compiled by John R. Gibbs for the University of Washington Libraries clearly belong to this 'whodunit' subtradition, as revealed by titles such as *Murder on the Downbeat, Death at the Opera, Murder in C Major, Deadly Sonata*, and *Murder, Maestro, Please*.[18]

The emergence of this subtradition should not be regarded as particularly surprising. At least since the development of the Viennese classical tradition during the late eighteenth century, the world of art music has been characterised by the presence of strong, dynamic personalities – composers, musicians, conductors, impresarios and so on – who tend to combine great talent with great drive; by a heightened affective atmosphere in which (as we observed at length in Chapter 1) music is widely believed to induce intense emotional experiences and responses; and by an infrastructure increasingly dominated by financial considerations at almost every level. These and related features rendered the world of classical music eminently adaptable for a genre of Anglophone fiction that began to emerge in the middle of the nineteenth century and which has maintained its popularity down to the present day: crime and detection. A typical scenario involves the development of tension between interested parties (performers, composers, administrators, etc.) in relation to a specific musical event or composition. The perpetration of violence (up to and including murder) resulting from this tension has to be redressed, frequently by a central figure who, if not an actual detective, is capable of bringing the disparate elements of the crime together in a coherent narrative that both solves the mystery and releases the pressure that precipitated it.[19]

Even when music provides neither a pretext nor a context for the criminal act, it continues to hover around the edges of the detective genre. The key figure in this regard is Sherlock Holmes, the detective created by Sir Arthur Conan Doyle, who has been so influential on the development of the genre. Music is implicated in some of Holmes's adventures: 'A Scandal in Bohemia', 'The Solitary Cyclist' and 'The Mazarin Stone' for example (Conan Doyle 1981: 161–76; 526–38; 1012–23). By and large, however, music is incorporated into the Holmes canon for purposes of atmosphere and character development. Incidental references to contemporary performers and performances contribute to the construction of a coherent, familiar world; they are but one element of the literary technique that made Holmes such a vibrant character, and which rendered the fictional world he inhabited so compelling for so many readers.

At the same time, the fact that the great detective is both a music scholar and a musician reveals much about his temperament and personality, which in turn have a bearing upon the successful method of detection based on research and observation, which he supposedly developed. Whether practising on his own Stradivarius (1981: 22, *passim*) or attending concerts in Covent Garden (1981: 766, 913), music helps to establish the atmosphere in which Holmes may apply his method. Conan Doyle is not forthcoming on whether this is an effect of the actual process of listening itself – as if familiarity with the rules of melody, harmony and counterpoint which characterise western art music can somehow point Holmes towards the solution to whatever problem he happens to be grappling with at the moment. It does become clear over the course of the extended Holmes canon, however, that music is an integral element of his personality and, as such, is implicated in the methodology that enables him to process criminal acts into coherent narratives of cause and effect.

These two variations ran parallel during the 'golden age' of British crime fiction stretching from the 1920s to the 1950s, whose principal figures included the so-called 'Queens of Crime': Agatha Christie, Ngaio Marsh, Margery Allingham and Dorothy L. Sayers.[20] It would appear, however, that whereas the murder mystery set specifically in the world of professional music has tended to become more of a specialist category – as, for example, with the Italian opera setting of Lindsay Townsend's

Voices in the Dark (1995) – the general tendency to introduce music into the detective novel for purposes of contextualisation, character development and atmosphere has grown. Such were the conclusions of the Scottish crime writer Ian Rankin when in March 2006 he hosted a three-part programme on BBC Radio 4 entitled *Music to Die For*, the subject of which was the use of music in contemporary crime fiction. It emerged that whereas music was a more significant device for some contemporary authors (John Harvey, Bill Moody and James Sallis, for example) than for others (such as Mark Billingham, Robert Crais, Karin Slaughter, George Pelecanos, James Lee Burke and John Connolly), all subscribed to the notion of music as a particularly useful means for the crime writer to establish atmosphere and to communicate impressions about various characters.

Neither Rankin nor his interviewees, however, touch upon what is perhaps the most significant effect of music in the crime text. Information has always been the key to the genre, as the reader observes the detective figure working to establish motive and means for the central criminal event. The narrative proceeds by means of the economical presentation of information and the establishment of both a practical and a moral rationale: the reader gradually learns that the crime took place 'in this way' and 'for these reasons'. Musical references provide a means for the narrator to introduce these issues without the risk of a full-blown authorial intervention, which, given the supersensitive nature of the detective narrative, could unbalance the text and alienate the reader. If the reader does not 'get' the reference, it still functions in terms of atmosphere and character development; if they do 'get' it, however, an entire alternative apparatus becomes available, one in which the extratextual life of the music – with its own narrative logic and morality – becomes active.

Rankin is responsible for one of the most successful crime series in modern British publishing: the 'Inspector Rebus' novels. It would be true to say that Rankin's vision was born of the brutal world of mid-twentieth-century American crime fiction rather than the highly mannered world of his immediate British forebears such as Christie and Sayers; John Rebus has much more in common with Sam Spade and Philip Marlowe than with Hercule Poirot or Lord Peter Wimsey. Nevertheless, Rankin's work has been in the vanguard of what has become to all intents and purposes a second 'golden age' of British crime writing.

The plot of *Exit Music*, like all the 'Rebus' novels, is convoluted and resistant to synopsis. That is as it should be: in his drive to make the world of the text as realistic and as believable as possible, Rankin depicts a large cast of characters, an extended urban landscape (Edinburgh and its environs), and a complex, multifaceted narrative in which it is not always clear on first reading how objects, actions and characters relate to each other. Rebus himself is likewise a complex, multifaceted character whose personality has developed in real time over the course of the publication of the series. *Exit Music* draws to some extent on the reader's knowledge of that personality as it has been established over the previous seventeen volumes, but it also functions as a stand-alone crime-and-detection mystery. This creates the possibility of winning new devotees for the series with each new publication.

In an entry on his website,[21] dated July 2007, Rankin describes the music to which he was listening while writing *Exit Music*, which he claims to be the 'last' novel in the 'Rebus' series. It is interesting in this regard that the author appears to have a much broader taste than the character he has created. Rebus is first and foremost a fan of classic guitar-oriented rock – what is commonly referred to in popular music circles as 'dad-rock'; the music of the Rolling Stones, for example, remains a key reference point throughout the series, as indicated by the fact that a number of the texts share titles with albums by that band.[22] Rankin, on the other hand, lists an eclectic selection in his web page, including many lesser-known artists ranging over a variety of genres. That, it seems, is the point: just as it is Rebus's character to be linked with a certain kind of music and with the extra-textual attributes and associations of that music, so it is also his character to resist other forms of music (those introduced to him by his colleague Siobhan Clarke, for example, whose taste more closely approximates that of Rankin himself).

Rankin's acknowledgement of the importance of music in the 'Rebus' series is signalled by his incorporation of it within the title of what is supposedly the final volume. *Exit Music* is littered with musical references of the kind described above. Specific songs are invoked, in other words, for purposes of character development, atmosphere, credibility and commentary. Examples include 'Lift Up Every Stone' by John Hiatt (12, as a description of Rebus's exhaustive method of detection); 'Jolly Coppers on Parade' by Randy Newman (209, a swipe at the politics of policing in contemporary Scotland); 'Sinner Boy' by Rory Gallagher (377, an appropriate handle for Rebus's villainous alter-ego Big Ger Cafferty). However, music also provides levels of significance beyond these merely indicative properties. Thus, at one point Rebus, listening to the John Martyn album *Grace and Danger*, remarks that the Scottish singer/songwriter is 'singing my whole life story' (222). It is a throwaway observation, but one that nevertheless communicates something of the detective's habits, tastes and state of mind at a particular point of the narrative. Familiarity with the album – with its sound, its lyrics and the 'story' behind it (it is a classic 'breaking-up' album) – add layers of meaning that interact in a highly complex fashion with these apparent intentions.

Similarly, a suspect's 'love' (39) for music – or rather, for a particular kind of music – impacts upon Rebus's response to him in ways that are not clear even to the detective. Initially sympathetic towards a fellow music-lover, he finds himself alienated to some degree by the suspect's music of choice (contemporary 'indie' rock for the most part), and this is an important clue as to how matters will develop. Another suspect belies his youth by expressing a regard for 'old stuff' (198), but once again the waters are muddied: the music is 'good' (at least Rebus thinks so), but the character is 'bad' – which is to say, culpable, at least to some degree, in terms of the moral discourse created within the text.

The fact is that the music referenced throughout *Exit Music* is fully implicated in the complex moral milieu that Rebus inhabits and which is the stock-in-trade of the entire series. On one level, musical taste is little more than a matter of affectionate banter between the two principal characters; on another, it is an indication of the moral frailties to which all the characters are susceptible – none more so than Detective Inspector John Rebus himself.

Biographical: *Clara* (2002) by Janice Galloway

Biographical fiction is a well-established and successful subgenre at the outset of the twenty-first century. As the name suggests, it is an amalgam of two different literary types – the biography and the novel: the first being a rendering of the life of a person (living or dead, usually famous to some degree) in a written narrative; the second being that form of extended prose fiction which evolved during the eighteenth century from earlier narrative forms. Not only does the biographical novel draw on generic traits proper to each of its parent forms; it also reveals their common investment in the category of narrative – this latter concept connoting the transposition of human culture into textual events of various kinds. What this means is that although the biography purports to be 'true' (based on research, common knowledge and observable fact) and the novel has historically been regarded as a 'fictional' genre, both forms tell stories about human life; both offer structured (typically developmental and accretive) accounts of individuals in relation to each other and in relation to communities variously defined; and both use the resources of language to create or encourage a variety of responses to those narratives on the part of their readers.[23]

The biographical novel is a form that blurs the boundaries between reality and imagination, between fact and fiction. We know that novelistic discourse is implicitly moralistic and meaning-driven: that is to say, the novel offers the reader an implicit vantage point from which to interpret the events, characters and relationships that make up the fictional world. Biography, on the other hand, is a quasi-academic genre that relies heavily on research; and although the biographical novel organises its narrative strategies in terms of the novel, by and large it retains that investment in research. The result is a hybrid form in which different impulses – towards 'truth' on the one hand, and 'interpretation' on the other – subsist within a finely balanced discursive economy. The message of the biographical novel tends to be: 'here' are the facts – and 'here' is what they mean.

The subjects of biographical fiction tend to be exemplary individuals whose lives and careers possess an interest beyond their immediate (temporal and spatial) range of influence. Besides royalty, politicians and sportspeople, 'artists' of various kinds have been perennial favourites for the biographical novelist. One of the most successful practitioners of the genre, the American Irving Stone (1903–89), wrote *Lust for Life* (1934) based on the life of the nineteenth-century Dutch painter Vincent van Gogh, and *The Agony and the Ecstasy* (1961) about the Italian Renaissance artist Michelangelo. Musicians and music-related subjects have also featured in this trend. In the sphere of popular music we have already mentioned fictional treatments of the lives of Lena Zavaroni, Alma Cogan and Bix Beiderbecke; there are also many thinly disguised portrayals of actual historical musical figures hovering around the edges of some texts. At the same time, novels about the great composers and musicians of the classical world abound.

Consider for a moment the 'Mozart novel', of which there have been numerous examples over the years since his death.[24] We have observed some of the ways in which reference to 'real' music and musicians impacts upon the fictional world of the narrative, and we have noted that familiarity with musical texts cited in the narrative will have a bearing upon the reader's engagement with that narrative. The situation is complicated manyfold when a novel purports to be 'about' a figure from the world of music. Such a figure – Mozart, for example – would tend to be already in possession of an extratextual identity (developed over the period since his death through a diverse array of media) that in various ways impacts upon the character created in the literary text. What this means is that 'Mozart' has a presence beyond the immediate literary event, and that any literary representation of the historical figure has to engage with this presence to some extent. Moreover, a major component of that presence is the music that is attached to the composer's name and the meanings – contested and various though they may be – that are attached to that music. Thus, the 'Mozart novel' represents an engagement both with the meaning of the historical figure of the composer himself and with the ideas that circulate in relation to his music. These are precisely the issues that Anthony Burgess grappled in *Mozart and the Wolf Gang* (see Chapter 2). They also constitute a main point of interest in Janice Galloway's third novel, *Clara*, which is based on the life of Clara Schumann (née Wieck), who besides being wife to the celebrated German composer Robert Schumann (1810–56) was also a famous and successful composer-musician in her own right. The relationship between Schumann and Wieck provides one of the great romantic stories from the world of classical music. Schumann is widely regarded as a key figure in the development of post-Beethovian art music, a tragic figure who embodied (in terms of his work, certainly, but also because of an early death brought on by depression and disease) a Romantic sensibility which paved the way for later innovations, including the Wagnerian revolution (Worthen 2007). At the same time, Wieck's multifaceted career renders her somewhat of an emblematic figure within the history of women's art (Reich 2001). When one considers the other famous people hovering on the edge of the Schumanns' story (Mendelssohn and Brahms, for example), as well as the numerous historical and aesthetic issues of interest that are raised by a consideration of their work, it may be observed that there is a lot here for the biographical novelist to work with.

Clara represented a significant change in emphasis for Galloway, whose two previous novels – *The Trick Is to Keep Breathing* (1989) and *Foreign Parts* (1994) – were clearly inspired by the tradition of progressive Scottish writing launched by Alasdair Gray's *Lanark* (1981), which has also been an influence upon writers such as Iain Banks, James Kelman, Liz Lochhead, Irvine Welsh, Alan Warner, A. L. Kennedy and Tom Leonard.[25] Although foregoing a Scottish location or subject, Galloway's new departure continued to display the 'freedom with formal experiment' (Goldie 2005: 526) that was one of the recurring characteristics of the post-*Lanark* Scottish literary tradition. *Clara* is a difficult book in many respects: the widespread use of free indirect discourse produces a fluctuating narrative perspective, and if this in one sense echoes the Schumanns' overwrought relationship it makes at the same time for a challenging, not to say unsettling, read. Formal experimentation is extended to the realm of typography (again typical of contemporary Scottish writing); the result is a highly discursive text in which 'normal' novelistic discourse is offset by a range of different typefaces and styles of layout. It is in fact in respect of Galloway's typographical innovation that a key issue – not only for *Clara* but for music-fiction generally – emerges.

One of the central and recurring issues of this study has been the representation of music in literary form, and the various strategies that have been deployed by a range of authors in their attempts to communicate the meaning or the effect of musical sounds. In Chapter 1, for example, we observed how Jeanette Winterson included a long fragment from the score of the opera *Der Rosenkavalier* at the end of her novel *Art & Lies*, and we noted how this fragment appeared to be possessed of an aura of authority (or at least represented as such) that was at odds with the deconstruction of authority pursued in the properly literary parts of the text – that is, those parts using the resources of standard novelistic discourse (written language – sentences and paragraphs – presented in a uniform typeface). In *Clara*, we find that Galloway has likewise included numerous score fragments from the work of Robert Schumann; and yet the effect is very different to the one achieved in Winterson's novel.

Many contemporary Scottish novelists employ non-standard typographical layouts, and they do so in a variety of ways and for a variety of reasons. The overall effect, however, is always to place in the foreground the act of writing itself and to introduce discourses of contingency and irony that invariably bear upon the subject matter in some manner and to some extent. Galloway has transposed this inheritance into her biographical novel. This means that an important part of the book's meaning lies in the way it looks rather than the way it reads; for the author clearly believes that judiciously deployed typographical innovation can represent the vicissitudes of the Schumanns' passionate relationship more effectively than standard novelistic discourse.

The issue is complicated, however, by the fact that the passion of Robert and Clara was both experienced and expressed in terms of a musical discourse that so dominate their lives, in the various roles of composer, performer, conductor, administrator, critic, and so on. Galloway addresses this by incorporating musical notation into her novel, but in such a way as to make it an organic part of the narrative. Between pages 183 and 186, for example, a number of different typographical and narrative discourses are simultaneously invoked, including: translated extracts from the work of the German Romantic poet Heinrich Heine, many of whose lyrics were set to music by both Robert and Clara; extracts in the original Scots from the work of Robert Burns; score fragments (a musical staff with key signature and 'handwritten' notation); 'proper' third-person narrative discourse; extracts from letters written by Robert to Clara; untranslated lists of the German titles of song cycles composed by Robert; and stylised images that mark the breaks between different sections of the musical opus, as well as the end of this particular section of the novel itself. On the latter three of these four pages, moreover, the written language is superimposed over pages from the scores of three of the songs listed in the written text. The musical notation is faint but clearly discernible, and the effect is twofold:firstly, the extra-textual (which is to say, musical) life of this material is invoked, but not in such a way as to grant it any implicit authority or priority over its reproduction in this particular context. The literary text emerges neither as an addendum to nor an interpretation of the musical text; their co-existence within the same space is symbolic of what Benson calls 'the necessary dependencies of art' (2006: 117). The contingency of the language is of a piece with the contingency of music, and the score is revealed as a medium for the communication of meaning rather than a repository of the meaning.

Secondly, in these pages, Galloway gets closer than any novelist in history to achieving the supremely musical effect of counterpoint. The juxtaposition of various literary discourses (lyric, narrative, letter, song-list), the deployment of different signifying media (score fragments and section breaks), and the subimposition of musical notation combine to create a text in which various 'voices' are continually interacting to produce complex effects that do not so much symbolise as reproduce the effect of listening to contrapuntal music. Just as with a piece of music, one voice may in theory be isolated from the others for purposes of analysis or identification; to do so, however, would entail losing some of the potential of the text to create a range of meanings with which the listening (in this case, reading) subject may engage. The role of each voice may only be fully perceived as a function of its relationship with all the other voices. Thus, in the pages in question, Schumann's letter relates to the Germanic song-titles, which in turn relates to the lyric extracts and the score fragments and the third-person narrative, and so on.

In both these ways, Galloway adapted the experimentalism typical of the Scottish literary renaissance in order to confront the limits of the biographical novel and to address the perennial problem of using the resources of one medium – language – to represent another: music.

5
The Uses of Music in the Contemporary British Novel

Introduction

We turn away from matters of musical and literary genre in this final chapter to consider some of the other issues that emerge in relation to the contemporary British music-novel. It should be remembered that this 'turning away' is only tactical, as the question of genre persists in any response to the representation of music in fiction. The emphasis shifts at this stage, however, to a fuller engagement with some of the effects, experiences and emotions that we find represented time and again throughout the field.

Drawing on insights that have accrued over the course of the study thus far, in the first two sections we shall observe how the music-novel enables the question of temporality to be posed with particular resonance and in relation to two specific effects: the first being historicism, the second being nostalgia. The latter term entails a consideration of the vogue for semi-autobiographical fiction that deploys the popular music of the 1970s as a discursive element. The first term refers to the sense of history that bears upon our period (1990 to the present) and in particular to the array of social, political and cultural uses to which history has been put in Britain during this period. Harking back to earlier comments on the work of Marcel Proust, we shall observe that music is particularly suited to this task for a number of reasons, two of which are of immediate interest: firstly, its power to embody memory; secondly, its inherent temporal nature.

The third section of this chapter is a consideration of one of the most powerful of musical effects. Silence represents the apparent absence or temporary cessation of any organised or intended sound; as such it is linked with some of the most fundamental emotions and experiences of which the human subject is capable. Composers have long been aware of the power of silence to invoke such emotions and experiences, and this has historically been one of the effects of which writers have been most covetous. At the same time, we have noted that the novelist who would write about music has always been condemned to a form of silence: despite the brilliance of the metaphors or the range of the descriptive language or the extent of the experimental technique, it is simply not possible for written language to reproduce the sound of a piece of music. Silence, therefore, is implicated in some of the most pressing issues confronting the contemporary British music-novel.

The meaning of 'silence', of course, is always a partial effect of the context within which it occurs. The silence that exists between two subjects can likewise be troped in various ways – as an aggressive refusal to communicate, for example, or as an acknowledgement of an implicit empathy. This brings us to the subject of the final section of this chapter: 'love', and the many different ways in which such a notion bears upon an analysis of the contemporary music-novel. Now, it so happens that many of the people who 'love' fiction also 'love' music, and this remains an important consideration: commercially speaking, it will do your novel no harm if it incorporates references to music that is popular with (or at least familiar to) an eclectic culture-consuming demographic. Then again, one might observe that the tradition of music as an expression of (or as an accompaniment to expressions of) love is too powerful and too well established for the novel to ignore. Love and music, we might say, go together like a horse and carriage, and contemporary novelists have not been chary in exploiting the connection.

Questions relating to the role and representation of 'love' in the contemporary music-novel go further than considerations of commerce or tradition, however. How much further, and in what ways, we shall see in the section dedicated to its analysis. At this point it is enough to note two things: firstly, love – in one form or another – features without exception as a central element within all the texts considered in this study; and secondly, wherever love is, music is close by. The ubiquitous presence of love in human affairs (and more especially in stories about human affairs) may help to account for the frequent recourse to music in that most human of narrative forms, the novel.

The uses of history: Rose Tremain, *Music and Silence* (2000); Peter Ackroyd, *English Music* (1992); A. N. Wilson, *Winnie and Wolf* (2007)

History and music cross-fertilize at a number of points, some of which have already been invoked in this study. In texts such as de Bernières's

Captain Corelli's Mandolin (see Chapter 3) and Mitchell's *Cloud Atlas* (Chapter 1) we observed the representation of sustained musical themes over historical periods of greater or lesser duration. In Chapter 4 we noted the vogue for historical murder mysteries set in the world of classical music. Then again, famous figures from various musical milieux are also frequently made the subjects of fiction. There is also the trend (to be considered at length in the next section) for contemporary novelists to write about the period of their own childhood and adolescence, and to 'authenticate' their narratives with references to the popular music of the period. The Proustian notion of music as a spur to memory pervades such narratives, and is indeed discernible as a presence within all music-fiction set in the past, whether such a connection is overtly thematised or not.

There is also a kind of novel that focuses specifically on the past: 'historical fiction', which emerged during the early stages of the novel's evolution and has remained immensely popular down to the present day (Bradford 2007: 81–99; Shaw 1983). Like the thriller and the crime novel, historical fiction tends to straddle the divide between the 'popular' and the 'literary'. As with those genres, problems of definition abound, because any novel set in the past qualifies to be described as 'historical', and that includes contemporary literary texts (Kazuo Ishiguro's *The Remains of the Day*, for example, which won the Booker Prize in 1989) as well as popular texts from the past which have subsequently achieved literary status (such as *A Tale of Two Cities* [1859] by Charles Dickens). Even the recent past – the past of living memory, as in Arnott's *Johnny Come Home* (see Chapter 4) – is officially 'history', at which point any attempt to categorise a discrete 'historical' sub-genre ceases to have any real meaning.

And yet the historical novel remains in both critical and commercial currency. It would appear that the term is usually reserved for fiction set in periods beyond living memory, frequently in eras that, through an obscure critical process (involving incalculable factors such as fashion and visibility), have gained an extra-literary status of intrinsic importance or interest. There are many historical novels set during the Restoration or the Regency, or more recently the First World War, for example, but fewer are set in the 1520s or the 1760s or the 1830s – periods of equal importance and interest for the professional historian, no doubt, but ones that have never earned a dedicated sobriquet of their own.

Rose Tremain has earned a reputation as a literary writer of historical fiction. Her novels are widely reviewed in prestigious journals and newspapers; they attract serious critical attention; and she has won a number of prizes over the course of her career. (*Music and Silence*, for example, won the Whitbread Novel Award in 1999.) It is clear on reading her work, moreover, that Tremain retains ambitions beyond simply presenting accurate renditions of particular periods or creating an 'authentic' atmosphere through the use of exotic periods, locations or language. Tremain's books are heavily researched, it seems – like any historical novelist, she wants to get the details right – but such research remains at the service of a 'literary' vision that bears upon every aspect of the text: the choice of subject and setting; the development of a sympathetic narrative style; and the moral insights that are developed in association with the various characters and their relationships.

Music and Silence tells the story of a young English lutenist named Peter Claire who in 1629 takes up a post with the orchestra of King Christian IV of Denmark. Christian is depicted as the downhearted king of a demoralised country. Defeat at the Battle of Lutter (1626) three years earlier had signalled the end of Denmark's status as a major European power (although the King would continue to play power politics until his death in 1648, especially with his great rival Gustavus Adolphus of Sweden). Expeditions to a remote silver mine in Norway in order to revive the fortunes of the kingdom prove fruitless. Christian's domestic life, meanwhile, is in turmoil. For a number of years he has been estranged from his adulterous second wife Kirsten Munk, whom he married in 1616, four years after the death of his beloved first wife Anne, and with whom he had twelve children. As the King broods on his personal and political disappointments, Munk plots ruthlessly around the Danish court, indulging her monstrously lascivious nature and looking for weaknesses that she might exploit to further her ambitions.

Peter Claire is not quite the innocent 'angel' the King takes him for when he first arrives at Rosenborg. In a parallel plotline, Francesca, Countess O'Fingal, tells how she was wooed from her Italian home by the Earl, Johnnie, and brought to his estate in Cloyne in the west of Ireland. After ten years of happy marriage, the Earl becomes obsessed with a piece of music he dreamed of one night but which on waking found that he could remember no more than a short phrase. Johnnie is tormented to the point of insanity by the fact that every development of the phrase that he can compose seems to diminish rather than enhance it; soon his health, his estate and his family life start to suffer. Francesca hires Claire to help her husband with his musical search. Although the handsome young musician fails to discover the lost music, his physical beauty and serious manner attracts the Countess, who seduces him. On a trip to Dublin, Johnnie discovers that 'his' lost music was actually composed by the Italian Alfonso Ferrabosco (two composers of that name, father and son, were popular at the time – but Tremain does not specify which of these is referred to here), and he dies in agony after dismissing Claire. Francesca is left in Cloyne with her four children, a prey to guilt for the betrayal of her husband, to sorrow for his disastrous fate, and to desire for the man who had temporarily reprieved her.

The association of music with absence, betrayal and death in the story of Johnnie O'Fingall is at odds with the generally positive connotations that have attended the medium in western cultural discourse. And yet the potential for such a reading always existed – the flip side, as it were, of the representation of music as a quasi-divine echo of the perfection that awaits us beyond this mortal coil. Hints of such dangers may be found throughout the great canon of music writing – for example, in Plato's concerns regarding the disruptive power of music over both mind and body. As noted in Chapter 1, unacknowledged problems are certainly present in Rousseau's work, in which thought, music, voice and writing are locked into a complex moral hierarchy of communication systems and media.

In his dream, Johnnie perceives an image of that perfection before which the everyday world of work and family fades into insignificance. Despite the resources of his wealth and the aid of a professional musician, however, his quest to retrieve the memory is in vain – as it always must be; the human mind may imagine perfection, it seems, but it cannot be embodied in any material medium or form. The betrayal is exacerbated, moreover, by the fact that he was not the instrument through which the divine spoke but merely an imperfect conduit – subject to the vagaries of memory – of someone else's inspiration. Haunted by the dream of perfection, Johnnie fades into literal silence (he loses his voice) and death.[1]

One of Johnnie O'Fingal's literary forebears is Charles Swann (in Proust's *Swann's Way*; see Chapter 1), who is also haunted by absent music and then disappointed by his re-encounter with it. At the Danish court, meanwhile, Peter Claire is wrestling with his own demons, musical and otherwise. On leaving Ireland, he took up the post as lutenist with Christian's orchestra only to find that the principal performance venue is a cellar from where, by means of an ingenious system of pipes and ducts specifically designed for the purpose, the music is transmitted into one of the palace's reception rooms for the amusement of the king and his guests. Claire is attracted to another of the palace's 'invisible' servants, Emilia Tilsen, lady-in-waiting to the disgraced Kirsten who, although officially out of favour, is suffered to retain a retinue in a section of the palace. The narrative follows the twists and turns of their love affair, which is shown to be dependent upon the deteriorating relationship between Christian and Kirsten. In the end it is a whim of the latter that brings the young lovers together, although matters might just as easily have transpired otherwise.

In conversation with Claire, King Christian argues that music brings order to 'the silent chaos that inhabits every human breast' (29). Besides providing the title of the novel, this image of music and silence locked in eternal battle at both an historical and a personal level recurs throughout the text.[2] Christian brings musicians (including Claire) to Norway with him because he wishes to ward off the universe's 'uncaring silence' (59); 'There will be silence!' (66) thunders Johnnie O'Fingal, a statement which, in the light of his failure to rediscover the lost music, is both a command and a terrified realisation; back in England, Claire's father dreads the silence to which his children's absence (one through work, one through marriage) will condemn him. Silence is a paradox – a positive absence that resides in the time-space both before and after human endeavour. To put it another way: in the sonic morality of the text, silence equates to death.

Human endeavour, on the other hand, is invariably noisy, and it is in the context of this noisiness that music comes to function as a positive affirmation of the immemorial human emotions of hope and desire. Kirsten's antipathy towards music clearly affiliates her with the forces of silent chaos (453), while Emilia's dream of 'order and harmony' (163) takes the form of a concert by her would-be husband Peter Claire for their friends and family. Whereas Tremain associates music with the positive human experiences of love and desire, silence is represented as music's ineluctable other, a manifestation of fear and absence. The text dramatises some of the recurring complexities of musical discourse while at the same time revealing music's central historical role as a medium for the human understanding of its own paradoxical status.

Peter Ackroyd's representation of history in *English Music* (1992) appears somewhat impressionistic, one might even say incoherent, when compared with Tremain's approach. There is not just a stylistic difference, however: the former's discourse is the product of an integrated, radical literary vision in which history is more than just exotic backdrop or narrative pretext. Throughout his career, Ackroyd has developed a reputation as a writer (of novels and other literary forms, including historical biography and cultural geography) whose central theme is the past – specifically the English past – and its insistent relationship with the present. This 'almost compulsive interest' has combined with an interest in progressive literary technique to create, as the critic Richard Bradford describes it:

> an iconoclastic brand of historical fiction. The conventional history novel used and still uses traditional perceptions of history as a backdrop for, sometimes romanticized, invention. Ackroyd continually creates collisions between our sense of the past and our notions of ourselves. He plays with orthodox conceptions of history . . . and then creates a spiral of questions: the past and the present begin to become unnervingly similar and our notion of the present as a secure and, by implication, superior perspective is undermined.[3]

We may observe just such a process at work in *English Music*. The story is narrated by an old man named Timothy Harcombe, looking back at his youth in various parts of England between the two World Wars. The boy lived with his father, Clement, who is a kind of spiritual healer (not unlike John Rebus's father, in fact), but it is Timothy who emerges as the true visionary. Chapters of 'proper' narrative are interspersed with chapters in which the boy dreams that he has been transported back in time to meet various figures from English cultural history – some real (Charles Dickens, William Blake and William Byrd, for example), and some the creation of the English cultural imagination (Alice, Miss Havisham, Friday).

Music features as an important element of 'the present' – that is, the period of Timothy's youth that functions as the principal temporal 'reality' of the narrative, although it is surrounded by other time periods both in the future and in the past. Music's importance is signalled from the outset with the description of the manner in which Clement Harcombe would use the tension between music and silence in order to create a receptive atmosphere for his 'healing' performances (4). The motif is continued when a slightly older Timothy, now separated from his father, becomes interested in early English music, especially the music of William Byrd, in whose compositions (echoing Tim Bowler's *Starseeker* and Terry Pratchett's *Soul Music*: see Chapter 4) 'resounded the harmony of the universe' (198). In fact, music features in every 'real' chapter (those in 'the present' in which the narrative is advanced) as well as in every 'visionary' episode throughout the text.

What the reader learns over the course of the narrative, however, is that these musical references are symbolic of, not constitutive of, the 'English music' of the title. The latter appears to refer to a kind of spirit informing English history: more specifically a peculiar cultural imagination that apparently endures throughout history. It is Timothy's father who first introduces the notion, describing 'English music' as 'not only music itself but also English history, English literature and English painting' (21). Thereafter it is engaged and glossed by the various figures who populate Timothy's dreams. The informing idea is summed up by one such figure, Austin Smallwood, a detective from the recent past who clearly resembles Sherlock Holmes:

> [I] have made a curious discovery. It is perfectly clear to me now that English music rarely changes. The instruments may alter and the form may vary, but the spirit seems always to remain the same. The spirit survives. I supposes that is what we mean by harmony. (128)

English Music, in other words, is an integrated element of Ackroyd's wider scholarly programme, which would appear to be dedicated to revealing the continuities of English cultural history. There are three interrelated points worth making about the deployment of music (or the concept of music) in the present context.

Firstly, Ackroyd's title stands as an explicit rejoinder to a once well-known description of Britain as *das Land ohne Musik* – 'the land without music'. This telling insult (variously attributed although obviously Germanic in origin) drew on a prejudice prevalent among the continental intelligentsia since at least the late eighteenth century. Austria (so the story went) was the birthplace of modern classical music; Germany was the place where it was pursued most passionately and most imaginatively; France and Italy could offer brilliant variations (in the realm of opera, for example), while other countries (Russia, for example) were capable of producing valid responses to the classical idiom from within a local or national tradition. In all these areas, however, Britain was deficient; in terms of composition, especially, the island did indeed appear to be silent.

This jibe originated from a period before the great flowering of modern British compositional talent as represented by the likes of Edward Elgar (whose work only began to impact upon the European musical imagination in the early decades of the twentieth century), Ralph Vaughan Williams and Benjamin Britten. It also overlooked the astounding cultural renaissance that occurred in Britain during the early modern period which produced composers such as Thomas Tallis, William Byrd and Henry Purcell. Nevertheless, a sense of (classical) musical inferiority was widely felt and has indeed continued to impact upon the general cultural confidence of the island in various ways down to the present day.

To entitle one's novel *English Music* represents an aggressive rhetorical intervention within this discourse. On one level, Ackroyd's book carries the message that there clearly is a long-established national music tradition in England and that it does represent a fruitful exchange between international and national traditions. Moreover, within the novelist's vision the music thus produced – English music – takes on a symbolic weight with regard to national history, which gives the lie to this particular example of Brit-baiting.

The second point I want to make in relation to this novel is that music provides a powerful and endlessly adaptable metaphor with which Ackroyd can dramatise the notion of continuity through time. Musicological discourse reveals that a particular theme may persist in essence throughout the course of a composition; even when refined (in terms of texture, volume or any other musical effect) it continues to exercise an influence over the meaning – indeed, the identity – of that composition. *English Music* is 'musicalised' in the sense that the 'theme' introduced in the opening section is revisited (albeit in different form and to different effect) in each subsequent section. Thus, the Blakean poem that constitutes Chapter Sixteen (349–59) is a reconfirmation in a different discursive register of the theme that was first introduced in Chapter 1 relating to the existence and the value of 'English music'. Both these effects, moreover, appear to confirm an immemorial cultural pattern whereby the past continues to exercise an implicit influence upon the present, even if those marooned in the present happen to be ignorant of that influence. In this way, music, literature and history are implicated in a symbiotic formal process whereby the 'truth' of one reinforces, and is in turn reinforced by, the 'truth' of the others. But what is this 'truth'? What is the meaning of 'English music' that remains the essential component of the various iterations dispersed over history?

This brings me to the final point. The notion of an 'English music' that persists over time and which remains the same in essence across numerous discursive contexts would appear to be fundamentally at odds with a model – invoked time and again in the novels featured in this study – that regards music as radically contingent and dialectical: where the meaning of a piece of music is always a function of the relationship between compositional intention, performance dynamic and listening context. The appeal to essence – to an endless English music 'in sweet notes interlinked from age to age' (392) – belies both the use to which a particular sound may be put in different contexts, as well as the way in which a meaning attributed to that sound will mutate as an effect of its realisation in the present (whenever and wherever that present may happen to be). The epiphany towards which Timothy Harcombe is moving throughout the narrative is encapsulated in the final line of the text: 'I have heard the music' (400). Such an apparently simple statement comprehends an array of complex historical and political processes, however, and is at odds with the discourse of essence that permeates the text and which is replicated in emblematic form in this final statement. Music, in other words, will not serve the ends for which the author has invoked it in this instance: the 'Englishness' of 'English music' is always going to be a signifier under erasure.

Similar issues are raised by A. N. Wilson's *Winnie and Wolf* (2007), a novel based on the relationship between Adolf Hitler and Winifred Wagner, the English-born daughter-in-law of the great composer. History records that Hitler was somewhat of an opera buff who seriously considered a career in set design during his youth in Vienna. He came to regard Richard Wagner as the seminal expression of a German spirit which modern history had conspired to suppress, and saw it as his task to revive that spirit in all its possible manifestations. Winifred Wagner, meanwhile, had managed the annual Wagner festival at Bayreuth since the death of her husband, Siegfried. She met Hitler during the early 1920s at a time when Germany was suffering in the aftermath of the First World War and the punitive measures enacted by the Treaty of Versailles. They developed a close friendship which Wagner honoured until her death in 1980, thirty-five years after the revelation of the unspeakable excesses of the Hitler regime.

Wilson's novel follows history closely up to a certain point. The deprivations of interwar Germany and the milieu in which Hitler's political creed evolved and thrived are vividly represented. Likewise, the political machinations of the Wagner 'industry', in which aesthetics are constantly mitigated by economic considerations and the egos of the principal agents, are closely observed. The 'fictional' element of the text lies in the proposition of a daughter born to the eponymous couple in 1932, at a time when (the novel suggests) Hitler's burgeoning political career put paid to the possibility of anything more than a platonic friendship. All this is seen through the eyes of an impressionable young narrator whose own life is closely enmeshed with the historical figures around him. Herr N— finds himself in the eye of an extended political storm but manages (or purports to manage) to avoid implication in any of the morally reprehensible attitudes or practices associated with Nazism. At the instigation of Winifred Wagner (whom he has always secretly loved),

Herr N— and his wife adopt the child, an act which becomes a source of great tension – and eventually animosity – between them. The story of the friendship between 'Winnie' and 'Wolf' effectively ends in 1940, although the narrator goes on to describe the last agonising period of the war in which Germany was once again destroyed.

Herr N— initially joins the Wagner organisation to facilitate his doctoral research which, as he explains at an early point in the text, was focused on the great composer's use of, and response to philosophy:

> All those dazzling operas, even the apprentice work in *Rienzi*, but certainly *The Flying Dutchman* and everything he had written subsequently, did not merely seem to me the most wonderful music that had ever been composed. They were also the most fascinating examples of philosophy transposed into art. They were dramatized ideas. (8)

This introduces what later emerges as the central issue of the novel: the relationship between culture and history and the validity of historicism as an hermeneutic strategy. The issue, moreover, is dramatised in a dialectical form that in itself symbolises the problem of history, and more particularly the manner in which music is implicated in that problem.

On the one hand, there is the possibility that despite the composer's well-documented anti-semitism (which, typically of the era, was casual and opportunistic), Hitler's use of Wagner's music to expedite a political agenda represented an act of violent appropriation that is belied by the music itself. Hitler, in order words, translated the organic unity of the art object (or at least his perception of organic unity) into a political idiom, finding confirmation of Nazi political policy in Wagner's integrated music dramas. This, of course, is entirely typical of the politics/ culture interface throughout human history: the past becomes a function of the politics of truth obtaining in the present. Wagner was perhaps only the highest-profile victim of Nazi cultural policy, however, which rendered all of history susceptible to reinterpretation in terms that bolstered the apparently manifest destiny of the Third Reich.

At the same time, it seems clear that Hitler was profoundly influenced by Wagner's music, and that his world view – which found political expression in the institution of National Socialism – represented a bastardised version of the ideas expressed in that music. As Nazism was remaking Wagner, then, Wagner was, at least to some degree, making Nazism – informing, through its leader's peculiar matrix of experience and prejudice, the political creed that entranced a nation. Even as the present looks to remake the past in its own image, in other words, so it is, in some manner and to some degree, in itself always already an effect of the past. This is the central paradox of historicism – and indeed of hermeutics; in this instance it is what continues to fuel the debate regarding the contribution of a radical nineteenth-century composer to a devastating twentieth-century political philosophy.

The problems of history and historicism are replicated at a formal level in *Winnie and Wolf*. Of course, the reader is always aware that this is a 'novel' written by a well-known British novelist named A. N. Wilson. Within the fictional world created by the author, however, formal issues of authenticity, structure and reliability are foregrounded. These issues, moreover, are clearly and directly linked both to the problem of historicism, which forms the principal theme of the narrative, and to the practice of music, which forms the principal means whereby that theme is explored.

The status of this document is signalled as an issue from the outset. The main text takes the form of a confessional narrative written by Herr N— in an unnamed town in the former Communist state of East Germany (whence he and his family fetched up after the war) some time after his adopted daughter defected to the West in 1960. Under the name of Senta Chrisiansen, she moves in 1968 to Seattle in the United States, where she works as a professional musician. She receives the text from Herr N— in 1982, at which point she changes her name to Winifred Hiedler. She passes the text on to a local Lutheran pastor named Hermann Muller some time before her death in 2006. He translates and 'edits' the text, providing various footnotes and also a preface in which he speculates as to its authenticity even as he avows belief in the central proposal that Winifred Hiedler was indeed the daughter of Winifred Wagner and Adolf Hitler.

The refracted nature of the text is echoed by various formal and structural devices. The narrative is organised into roughly chronological sections running from 1925 to 1945, with each section taking its title from one of Wagner's works, starting with *The Flying Dutchman* (7–67) and ending with *Götterdämmerung* (*The Twilight of the Gods*) (329–61). As with all such references, however, the reader's engagement with the narrative depends at least to some extent on the level of their extratextual familiarity with the 'real' music represented by those titles. The narrator goes out of his way to draw parallels between life in interwar Germany, Wagner's own experiences in the mid-nineteenth century, and the stories contained in his music dramas. It is clear, for example, that Hitler regards himself as the modern personification of Parsifal; but while it is possible to describe Wagner's treatment of the Parsifal legend in linguistic terms, it is not possible to reproduce the music (either the actual sound or the emotional effect) with which that treatment is realised. It is down to the reader to supply a cognitive substitute for the experience signified by the title of Wagner's music drama. That substitute will then determine in large part both the level and the kind of the reader's engagement with the literary narrative.

Wagner's influence pervades the text in more subtle ways, however. For example, the narrative oscillates between a number of different strands: the life and times of Richard Wagner himself; the early career of Adolf Hitler; Wagner family politics in Bayreuth during the 1920s and 1930s; and the experiences of Herr N— and his family against the backdrop of the rise of Nazism. There is also, as we have seen, a discourse of philosophical speculation which is focused on the ways in which all these strands might relate – something which also links to the central theme of historicism. Now, this approach – in which multiple strands (or 'themes') are organised around a central theme – is in some ways very familiar. Among other things, it recalls the binary and tertiary structures of sonata form which were discussed in Chapter 1, with its model of theme and variation and its characteristic ABA structure. One of Wagner's achievements, as generations of commentators have revealed, was to introduce a radical hesitancy with regard to that model (McGee 2002). The famous chord that features in the prelude to *Tristan und Isolde* is unlike anything that preceded it in the canon of art music, not because the composer happened to hit upon a new combination of pitches or timbres but because he managed to embody in sonic form the dialectic of making and remaking – of past event bearing upon, while at the same time being enabled by, present interpretation. Every variation already exists in 'the chord' *in potentia*, but the meaning of 'the chord' will change with each new variation: that is the paradox upon which Wagner built his art. In essence it is the same paradox which is at the heart of the human experience of time.

Winnie and Wolf attempts to replicate this paradox by blurring the boundaries between distinct strands, and more directly by shifting the onus of distinction onto the reader. At a number of points, for example, it is not clear whether the narrative is referring to Wagner or Hitler (244ff); only when it does become clear may the similarities (and more significantly the differences) between the two figures be appreciated. At another point (273–6), a description of rehearsals for a festival production of *Parsifal* under the baton of Richard Strauss (another politically ambivalent figure) is interspersed with a description of the murder of various 'rogue elements' and political enemies during the so-called Night of the Long

Knives (30 June–2 July 1934). The high artifice of the one is blatantly – almost comically – juxtaposed with the brutal *realpolitik* of the other, thus seemingly reconfirming the long-held suspicion that Wagner's music and Hitler's political vision were indeed launched upon the same moral and philosophical continuum. Ultimately, however, Hitler's 'Wagner' is shown to be as arbitrary and as groundless as Wagner's 'Hitler'; and while the text reveals that the historical issue is one not of inheritance but of perspective, it shows also that music is the primary artistic discourse wherein such a realisation is both communicated and embodied.

The uses of nostalgia: Hanif Kureishi, *The Buddha of Suburbia* (1990); Jonathan Coe, *The Rotters' Club* (2004); Bill Broady, *Eternity is Temporary* (2007)

Nostalgia constitutes both a particular kind of historicism as well as a particular emotional response to absence. With regard to the first of these, history itself tends to be foreshortened in the discourse of nostalgia – restricted to the living memory of the subject who looks back upon periods and places from their own past that were formative of their present identity. The sense of absence, meanwhile, registers both temporally (the invocation of a qualitatively different period in the earlier life of the remembering subject) and spatially (the invocation of a landscape different in kind and quality from the one currently inhabited by the remembering subject). It is in this sense that nostalgia tends to be associated with a range of negative emotional responses – yearning, sentimentality and melancholy, for example. Such responses, moreover, are susceptible to a variety of discursive treatments – as John J. Su points out in the introduction to his *Ethics and Nostalgia in the Contemporary Novel*: 'What began in the seventeenth century as a physiological disease had become in the twentieth century a social ailment that leads to an obsession with kitsch and heritage in its most benign forms and fascism in its most extreme versions' (2005: 1). Although the faculty of memory appears not to be restricted to the human species, the propensity to experience the passing of time as loss may well be. In any event, nostalgia has come to be widely regarded as an inevitable, although somewhat indulgent, element of human experience.

The old joke maintains that nostalgia is okay but not what it used to be. There is a serious point here: although it persists as a quasi-universal human trait across time and space, in fact the meaning of nostalgia waxes and wanes in relation to a number of factors. It is, in other words, a fully politicised concept. One such factor is, unsurprisingly, the remembering subject: thus, a seventy-year-old and a thirty-year-old looking back from the same year (say, 1980) might be nostalgic for different eras (say, the 1950s and the 1970s respectively); or they might be nostalgic for the same era (say, the 1960s) but for different reasons.

Nostalgia is also quite clearly an effect of the (temporal and spatial) context in which it is invoked. It seems clear, for example, that around the time of the millennium Britain went through a period of intense remembering – a vogue for the backward glance that was in excess of the discourse of nostalgia that one might expect to encounter in most modern societies. Numerous possible reasons might be adduced for this, one of which was the onset of the millennium itself and the historical watershed that it appeared to represent. Another was the advent of the technological revolution that effected a fundamental change in a wide range of cultural practices. Social change, of course, has been endemic since the nineteenth century and the global hegemony of a capitalist system that depends on the constant renewal of markets and consumer demand; but the pace of social change (in Britain as elsewhere in the west) has been highly accelerated since 1980 by the widespread conversion from analogue to digital in core areas such as communications, education, media and entertainment.

The effect of this accelerated rate of change was to render the immediately preceding period (the 1970s) especially amenable for a discourse of nostalgia. Such a discourse, moreover, was particularly suited to the novel, and again for a number of recognisable reasons. As pointed out in the introduction to Chapter 3, one such reason was the coming to maturity of a generation of writers who had grown up during the 1970s and who had an appreciation of that decade's role and function in relation to modern British history (Garnett 2007). A more fundamental reason was the remorseless impact that digital technology has had upon the novel form itself, and the subsequent propensity of writers to reflect upon the changes that have overtaken their own medium. Certainly, the writing of a novel connoted something different after the invention of word-processing and the personal computer (although the influence of digitalisation on novelistic style has by and large yet to be considered).[4] Beyond this, however, developments in publishing, marketing, celebrity authorship, genre, media adaptation and so on have radically altered the social function of the novel over a relatively short period of time (Squires 2005). It should not be surprising that those novelists who have lived through this revolution would incorporate it in one form or another into their own narratives; nor that such a gesture should cross-fertilise with a discourse of nostalgia for the preceding era.

One of the principal attractions of the 1970s for later British novelists, however, would appear to be the opportunity to engage with the changes that were then overtaking contemporary popular music. It transpires that music is in fact a key resource for any discourse of nostalgia. Why this should be so is not clear (although see Botstein, 2000, and Strausbaugh, 2002); the links between mind, music and memory are still being discovered by researchers from a range of disciplines (Levitin 2007; Sachs 2007; Storr 1997). Even on an intuitive level, however, it may be observed that remembering subjects tend to associate particular periods with particular sounds – be they styles, genres or individual songs. This effect is especially noticeable in relation to the 1970s, for that was a decade in which a paradigm shift occurred in British popular music. It is true that many commentators have speculated as to the illusoriness of that shift, maintaining that the underlying patterns of popular music discourse remained the same, albeit repackaged for a new generation: 'We thought that everything would change,' thinks the disillusioned journalist Terry in Tony Parsons's *Stories We Could Tell* (2005), 'but it's the same old rock 'n' roll showbiz' (236). Despite this, there can no doubt that a revolution of sorts was perceived by contemporaries, nor that it left a profound impression upon those who lived through the period (Medhurst 1999; Sabin 1999).

Hanif Kureishi's *The Buddha of Suburbia* (1990) has proved extremely influential in terms of its representation of British-Asian identity. The critic Richard Bradford goes so far as to claim that it 'initiated a sub-genre, what I shall call the Assimilated Postcolonial Novel' (2007: 203). With a white mother and an Indian father, Karim Amir describes himself as 'a funny kind of Englishman' (3), and this 'funniness' (an attribute uncertainly situated between comedy and strangeness) has served as a paradigm in terms of which this modern 'hybrid' identity has measured itself. It is significant that Kureishi chose to dramatise this identity – its limitations as well as its integrity – in terms of a discourse of popular music. What that practice offers the Asian-British subject is a potent symbol of the attractions (and the dangers) of the world in which they live; it constitutes a form of cultural currency with which they can negotiate a sense of identity in a context of competing practices and values. At the same time, as we saw in relation to Suhayl Saadi's *Psychoraag* (see Chapter 3), music also offers an image of harmony, of reconciliation and love; music is a bridge across the hyphen that threatens permanently to sunder the modern hybridised subject from itself.[5]

Kureishi was perhaps the first British novelist to attempt to describe the milieu from which punk music emerged, as well as the impact that it had upon a generation of young British men.[6] The musical world described in the opening sections of *The Buddha of Suburbia* (1990) is one fundamentally still in thrall to a 1960s rock aesthetic dominated in large part by the Beatles, the Rolling Stones, Bob Dylan and their fellow travellers. It is, moreover, a world in which musical taste is a key element in the determination of cultural credibility; to support or even to be associated with the 'wrong' kind of music risks a form of social stigmatisation that is felt all the more keenly because of the relative youth of those involved. Thus, in an early scene the ultra-hip Charlie Kay dismisses Karim Amir's support for the Rolling Stones – a band which, even by the mid-1970s, appeared to many to represent the values of a bygone age. He extols instead the 'progressive' qualities of Pink Floyd and in particular the band's 1969 album *Umma Gumma* (14). Karim is suitably chastised and the social order is confirmed.

Charlie embodies the moment of pre-punk British popular music which, as we observed in relation to Jake Arnott's *Johnny Come Home* (in Chapter 4), was a volatile, confused period in terms of value and taste.[7] The pop music that made its way into the charts was denigrated by those who professed to take music seriously – especially by the contemporary music journals and the young male population that constituted its principal readership. At best, such music was harmless, throwaway fun; at worst it was pap for the culturally dispossessed. Meanwhile, the 1960s had left a legacy that many pursued still, in and out of the charts. In terms of serious contemporary rock music, however, two main (interrelated) trends dominated: the 'progressive' rock associated with the likes of Pink Floyd, and the 'art' rock that was in particular associated with Roxy Music and David Bowie. The latter, in fact, emerges as an important reference point in *The Buddha of Suburbia*, and indeed features as a key figures in many of the music-novels set in the 1970s.[8]

Coming from the same area of south London and having attended the same school as Bowie, Charlie aspires towards the status that Bowie has managed to achieve, which combines the serious intent of the artist with the adulation of the superstar (Stevenson 2006). Charlie lacks talent, however: his music is derivative; even his band's name, Mustn't Grumble, invokes a kind of fey, affected Englishness associated with the 1960s and hopelessly out of kilter with emerging tastes. In fact, the shift in focus from suburb to city coincides with the advent of punk – what the novel refers to as a 'renaissance' (153) in British music. Whereas Bowie and many established British acts (including the Rolling Stones and Pink Floyd) managed to ride out the punk wave, Charlie realises he must sink or swim. In an act that mimics the protean identity of Johnny Chrome in

Johnny Come Home, he transforms himself from a sensitive, middle-class artist to a crass, working-class punk overnight. This transformation is announced by a change of name: Mustn't Grumble becomes Charlie Hero and the Condemned – a 'shit' band who '[can't] play, can't sing, can't write songs, and the shitty idiot people love us!' (153).[9]

Kureishi's novel initiated many of the themes and tropes that were to feature in subsequent novelistic representations of the punk era. In particular, the transition from a 'prog' or 'pop' to a punk sensibility is frequently referenced in contemporary music-novels. For example, Tony Parsons's *Stories We Could Tell* details the adventures of three young music journalists over the course of one night in London in the summer of 1977, each of whom is, to some extent, coming to terms with the onset of punk. 'Classic' rock (that which was still influenced by the 1960s) is still in the frame, as indeed are other emerging forms (disco, for example) that would go on to exercise an important influence upon subsequent British popular music culture. Despite the occasional speciousness of the claims made on its behalf, however, it is punk rock that provides the key to the contemporary music scene; and this deference is something that is acknowledged to different degrees (and with different effect) in novels such as *Espedair Street* (1987) by Iain Banks, *One for the Money* (1994) by Carol Clewlow, *The Lonely Planet Boy* (1995) by Barney Hoskyns, and *Stars are Stars* (2007) by Kevin Sampson.

Punk also features significantly in *The Rotters' Club* (2001). Jonathan Coe's best-known novel to date (adapted for BBC television in 2005) is set in Birmingham and describes the adventures of the Trotter family and a number of associated characters during the middle years of the 1970s.[10] The narrative is book-ended by two small scenes set in 2003 (two years after the text was published) in which relatives of the principal characters provide a framework for the narrative proper. The characters from these framing scenes look back upon a period that was formative of themselves in a myriad of perceived and unperceivable ways. Among other things, such a device enables the author both to place nostalgia in the foreground and to question it as a discursive context with which to engage such a narrative.[11]

Typically, music features as a key element of the remembered world. It figures as a particularly crucial element of adolescent cultural exchange – as an early comment puts it: '[the] conversation drifted, as it always did, towards music' (26). Reference is made throughout to actual popular musicians (for example, Bob Marley and Eric Clapton) and, as always, the reader's engagement with the narrative depends at least to some extent on their familiarity with these figures and the values (musical and otherwise) associated with them. In the hypersensitive world of adolescent masculinity, musical taste provides the key to social status. And because the latter is regarded as a vital element of sexual standing, the importance of music is even further emphasised. Support for the 'wrong' band or style could be fatal both to one's reputation and to one's chances; at the same time, as Benjamin Trotter discovers, originality and independence of taste were valuable tactics in the never-ending battle to establish an acceptable profile among one's peers, even if was not as 'cool' as that of *The Buddha of Suburbia's* southerner, Charlie Kay.

As in Kureishi's novel, the established pre-punk scene has to be sketched in if the impact of punk is to be properly appreciated. The narrative proper commences on 15 November 1973, and the bands referenced in the opening pages include Black Sabbath, Status Quo, Led Zeppelin, Jethro Tull and Pink Floyd – all representatives of an aesthetic (with various wings such as 'prog' and 'metal') that was to become the target of punk and New Wave aggression in the latter part of the decade. The text's key musical reference, however, is to a semi-obscure psychedelic rock band from Canterbury named Hatfield and the North, and in particular their cult second album, *The Rotters' Club* (1975). With its long jazz-rock excursions and its ironic pop vignettes, this album encapsulates what many (post-punk journalists for the most part) would come to regard as the self-indulgence and complacency of contemporary British popular music. Such, nevertheless, is the milieu in which Benjamin and his musically inclined fellows find themselves; it is the milieu that encourages him to join a band entitled 'Gandalf's Pikestaff', and which gives rise to his soon-to-be-hopelessly-outmoded ambition 'to push back the boundaries of the three-chord song' and to compose a 'rock symphony' (45).

Benjamin's attendance at a Hatfield and the North gig elicits a response that in many respects sums up the significance of music for the sensitive male adolescent in contemporary British fiction:

> It was the world, the world itself that was beyond his reach, this whole absurdly vast, complex, random, measureless construct, this never-ending ebb and flow of human relations, political relations, cultures, histories . . . How could anyone hope to master such things? It was not like music. Music always made sense. The music he heard that night was lucid, knowable, full of intelligence and humour, wistfulness and energy and hope. He would never understand the world, but he would always love this music. He listened to this music, with God by his side, and knew that he had found a home. (100)

Music (or at least a particular style of music) offers the young man a sanctuary; he is little aware of how fragile that sanctuary is, however, given the upheaval that lies in waiting. The first stirrings of an alternative aesthetic is introduced by Benjamin's friend Doug Anderton, whose inclinations tend towards music journalism rather than composition or performance. On a trip to London, Doug attends a gig (the Clash at Fulham Old Town Hall) and, as with Benjamin's experience at the Hatfield and the North gig, the performance he witnesses has a profound, long-lasting effect on him. After the concert he jostles at the bar for a drink, feeling 'wonderfully and unexpectedly at home' (162).

In a later section, Doug describes the moment at which the musical vision of Benjamin and his like-minded friend, Philip, is overtaken and rendered obsolete by punk. During a rehearsal, their fellow band members rebel against the proposed thirty-two-minute rock symphony that Benjamin and Philip have in mind and begin instead to play a 'ferocious . . . riotous three-chord thrash' (180). As with Charlie Kay's band in *The Buddha of Suburbia*, the transition is signalled by a change of name (Gandalf's Pikestaff becomes The Maws of Doom) and the advent of an alternative musical sensibility is symbolic of (and intimately linked with) a sea-change in contemporary British life. The middle-class Benjamin is incapable of Charlie's bad faith, however; while the latter remakes himself as Charlie Hero, the former embraces art music as the 'proper' medium through which to realise his ambition to write a symphony; accordingly, in the latter part of the text his points of reference become the likes of Vaughan Williams, Ravel and Sibelius rather than the pre-punk rock heroes who had fired his adolescent dreams.

The Buddha of Suburbia and *The Rotters' Club* are novels in which the music of the 1970s is incorporated as part of a wider discourse focused on the experience of British adolescents during a period of significant socio-political change. In Bill Broady's *Eternity Is Temporary* (2006), however, music itself becomes the central focus. The time and place (London, 1976) may match, but the musical issues extend far beyond the parameters of punk or indeed of any such minor 'blip' in the ongoing story of music's role in the human imagination.

The story concerns two young adults, Evan and Adrea, who take jobs in a residential home for the elderly in the London Borough of Camden during the famously long, hot summer of 1976. Evan, typically, is fully immersed in contemporary 'popular' music; like Charlie and Benjamin in the other two novels, his taste tends towards the esoteric and he disdains the inauthentic, which he perceives everywhere in the world of contemporary popular music. As with his fictional contemporaries, Evan plays in a band that is not very good. In fact it is 'terrible', comprised of 'scruffy hippies' who are almost entirely deficient of musical talent. Evan is not a competent musician himself; however, he does possess qualities (at least in Adrea's eyes) that set him apart from his band mates: 'They were all completely of their time' she thinks: 'modern, contemporary, utterly 1976 – whereas Evan wasn't' (88).

Eighteen-year-old Adrea is likewise musically inclined, although her tastes run to jazz and in particular the mid-twentieth-century African-American singer Billie Holiday. The music of 'Lady Day' appears to provide Adrea with a level of emotional expression that is missing from the popular music of the 1970s, and which she cannot access in her own life. Under Evan's tutelage, however, she is introduced to the world of pre-punk rock music, in which bands such as Blue Öyster Cult provide the soundtrack to their evolving relationship. Meanwhile, Mr Price, the deputy matron of the residential home, attempts to escape his duties by retiring to his room to listen to classical music. As with Adrea, Price compensates for the emotional life that he lacks in reality by listening to emotionally charged music – in his case, Mahler, Beethoven and Bruckner.

Eternity Is Temporary depicts a wide variety of musical practices and traditions in its opening sections, then. Formally, the various characters comprise a counterpoint that (as with other multi-stranded narratives, such as Coe's *The Rotters' Club*, Parsons's *Stories We Could Tell* or Arnott's *Johnny Come Home*) constitute 'voices' – competing, overlapping, harmonic – within the same narrative. In Broady's novel, this formal dimension 'leaks' in from a story line that is supersaturated with music. In defiance of the throwaway pop songs of the period ('If 1975 had been a bad year, then 1976 was shaping up to be even worse': 9), Evan subscribes to a discourse of 'authentic' music which, whatever its contemporary manifestation, had its basis in a rock aesthetic that was developed and came to its fullest expression during the 1960s. Although an artist such as Jimi Hendrix is considered 'better' than contemporary pop acts such as Sailor or the Brotherhood of Man – in ways and for reasons that have been described many times in many different ways – ultimately it is a matter of conviction: Evan feels the difference, and therefore knows it to be true. And although the musical objects and the emotional responses to those objects are different, this visceral engagement with music is something that he shares with Adrea and with Price.

The search for musical authenticity – 'the real thing' (102) – brings Evan and Adrea to the famous Roundhouse venue (in London) to see the Patti Smith Band. This episode is based on historical events: that particular American act did indeed play at that venue at that time, 'interpreting' (to the point of non-recognition) various rock classics as well as performing material from their own cult album *Horses* (1975). The performance was widely regarded as a crucial moment in the development of British punk. Initially, '[the] whole thing was a shambles' (113); and yet there is something about the content, the delivery and the attitude with which the music is performed that impresses Evan and the rest of the audience. Staggered by the energy and the absolute commitment of the performance, the young lovers wander out into the streets of London and make their way slowly back to the residential home. Later, in a phrase which recalls Charlie Kay's stunned response to his own first exposure to punk, Evan says: '*this was it*' (202, original emphasis).

Both the promise and the potential of the Patti Smith gig is belied just a short time later, however, by another concert at the same venue: the Ramones (another US 'punk' band) supported by the Stranglers and the Flamin' Groovies. Evan is shocked by the speed with which the radical energy of Patti Smith has been drained, and her liberating attitude – towards the audience, towards the artistic medium in which she was engaged, towards herself – has been processed into a 'product': 'Joey [Ramone] and the boys were like cartoon characters,' thinks Evan, 'perfect for the Disney franchise . . . their stupidity was so calculated, so artful' (229). Inured to the difference between the 'artful' and the 'artistic', however, the Roundhouse audience lauds the two 'punk' bands while disparaging the intelligent, tuneful pop of the Flamin' Groovies.

For Evan it is as if the revolution has been hijacked before there has been an opportunity for its message to be disseminated. It is Adrea, however, who points out that every fashionable 'revolution' is susceptible to such a process of 'franchising', whereas real change can only be effected at the level of the individual (233–4). This (essentially hippy) notion accords with Evan's epiphany during the earlier Patti Smith performance when, noticing the singer's 'wattled skin', he had realised that 'being young had nothing to do with age' (116). Neither does it have to do with adherence to the currently fashionable, nor with belonging to the 'winning' side, as the Ramones' gig convinces him. 'Youth', rather, connotes an attitude towards the social, political and cultural circumstances in which the subject finds itself, regardless of their personal age or of the historical period in which they live.

This epiphany is encapsulated in the paradoxical title of the novel. Evan first encounters the phrase in a reproduction of an etching entitled *Eternity Is Temporary* by the seventeenth-century Italian artist Giovanni Castiglione, which Mr Price keeps on the wall of his room. Later, Evan claims to be writing a rock opera named *Eternity Is Temporary* when confronted by his former band mates at the Ramones gig. The extended form and the proposed instrumentation (synthesizers) of this piece are deliberately at odds with the guitar-based, two-minute songs rendered fashionable by the likes of the Ramones. Whereas the plans of Benjamin Trotter and Charlie Kay to make progressive 'art' had been outmoded overnight by the onset of punk rock, Evan embraces a deliberately retrograde form in order to resist the fashionable tide. It is entirely fitting, moreover, that the proposed work should be given a title alluding to the paradox whereby the timeless and the transient are symbiotically enmeshed. For just as the 'eternity' of the Patti Smith gig was in part a function of its 'temporary' nature, so (according to his taste and his way of thinking) the 'temporary' nature of punk differs fundamentally from the 'eternal' experience of authentic art.

In some ways, *Eternity Is Temporary* is merely a fictional vindication of a particular set of tastes: Patti Smith over the Ramones, the Flamin' Groovies over the Stranglers, and so on. In its indictment of what came to pass for 'punk' in British cultural history, however, it exposes contemporary nostalgia as a discourse which is, at least to some degree, complicit with the forces that conspired to eradicate punk before its promise was fulfilled.

One of the principal forms through which that punk moment of the 1970s continues to survive is the contemporary novel; and yet it presents for the most part an extremely partial vision of what punk was and what it represented. It would appear that there are things that are not being said, in order that what is said may come into clearer focus; likewise, there are certain noises that have been silenced so that certain other noises may resound all the more clearly. The relationship between silence and noise (invoked here in a socio-political sense) leads into the next section of this chapter.

The uses of silence: Angela Huth, *Easy Silence* (2000); Michel Faber, *The Courage Consort* (2002); Kazuo Ishiguro, *The Unconsoled* (1995)

By this stage it should be clear that one of the principal recurring strategies of this kind of fiction is the introduction of music as a palliative effect in a range of crisis situations. As Benson puts it: 'Music is valued for its singular powers of affect, and by these means, its powers of consolation. Put simply . . . music has the potential to heal, to make things better' (2006: 146). Quoting the musicologist Nicholas Cook, Benson goes on to point out that by far the majority of such texts 'replicate the conventionally aesthetic approach to music which predominates in the West, "an aesthetic which is essentially consumer-oriented in that music is treated as a kind of commodity whose value is realized in the gratification of the listener" (Cook, *Music, Imagination, and Culture* 8)' (Benson 2006: 149).

We may observe this pattern repeated again and again at a deep structural level in the music-novel, no matter its temporal or spatial provenance. Music's semiotic role in the text is to allude to kinds and levels of experience which can find no expression in established linguistic discourses. Its entry into the text invariably signals a shift in the emotional economy of the plot; eventually it comes to symbolise (sometimes to offer) forms of resolution and redemption that are not available in the 'real' world of the narrative. This composite effect is, moreover, categorically subject-oriented: music's significance always comes into focus as a means to modify the perspective (and thence the identity) of a character with whom the reader identifies to a greater or lesser extent. The promise is clear: music can change your life – to reprise Benson, 'to heal, to make things better'.

The role afforded music in this kind of novel is always invidious, however: always the product of a pact of bad faith shared (to a greater or lesser extent) by the author and the reader. The fact is that music in the novel is always intended by the author, or understood by the reader, to stand for something beyond itself, and this for the very simple reason that in a medium restricted to written language, music cannot stand for itself. Every music-novel, that is to say, realises a necessary silence – the silence of a sonic medium when transferred into a non-sonic medium. As we have seen throughout this book, this dilemma has functioned differently in relation to various theoretical and philosophical systems. At the same time, writers (poets as well as novelists) have developed several strategies to cope with the necessary silence of literary music – by the use of figurative language (especially metaphor), for example, or by incorporating musical references that exist outwith the literary text.

The resolute silence of the music-novel is quite clearly an effect of its condition as a literary form, then. A consideration of literary silence, moreover, necessarily encounters two other forms of silence with which its object is intimately related. The first of these is musical silence, which can on reflection function at a range of levels and take many different forms (Losseff and Doctor 2007). Musicology, for example, reveals that partial or complete gaps (the absence of an expected or possible sound) can have a profound effect upon the impact (and thus the meaning) of a piece of music. Then again, in some ways the unavailability of the final two movements of Schubert's Symphony no.8 in B minor (*Unfinished*) might be considered a form of silence, as the opening movements create a sense of narrative expectation that dissolves into nothingness. As the conductor and critic Daniel Barenboim (2006) has put it: '[Music] has a permanent, constant and unavoidable relation with silence . . . the beginning, the first sound, is already in relation to the silence that precedes it'.

Barenboim goes on to describe music as an intentional act that deploys human energy to displace, albeit temporarily, the surrounding silence: 'The note dies', he says, '[and] this is the beginning of the tragic element in music'. Here we have an intimation of the elementary discourse of silence from which all others (including the literary and the musical) derive. Against the ancient notion of an unfailing music of the spheres, the modern world has had to confront the possibility of silence as the truth underpinning all intentional sound, a silence that is waiting – after the 'dying fall' of human music – to reassert its remorseless, implacable presence. Silence is the ghost that haunts all music, although it is only since the late nineteenth century and the onset of Modernism that such a realisation began to have a systematic impact upon musical composition itself.[12]

Paradoxically, the silence confronted by Modernist musical discourse is of a piece with the silence that has characterised literary music since people first attempted to describe music with words. The intended musical act is surrounded by silence; silence is encoded into its very conception. At the same time, every music-novel is obliged to enact its own silence vis-à-vis the musical discourse it looks to represent. The literary text embraces music's promise of transcendence, only to find that such a promise is belied by both its own medium (writing) and the object of its discourse (music). Such is the critical context within which an analysis of the uses of silence in the contemporary music-novel must proceed.

Silence has featured as a significant theme in some of the novels already examined in this study, such as Alan Warner's *Morvern Callar* (see Chapter 3), Rose Tremain's *Music and Silence* (see above) and Adam Lively's *Sing the Body Electric* (see Chapter 4). 'The space next to me bristles with silence' says one of the narrators of Jackie Kay's *Trumpet* (1999: 12).

Angela Huth's *Easy Silence* (1999) is another text in which the paradoxically palpable quality of silence makes itself felt. The story concerns William and Grace Handle, a middle-class couple living in the south of England who are approaching old age together. William is the leader of the long-established and successful Elmtree Quartet; Grace stays at home working on a book of flower paintings. Their lives are disrupted by two new dynamic presences: a volatile young man named Lucien who forms an unlikely attachment to Grace and towards whom she feels a motherly protection (her own semi-estranged son is presented unsympathetically throughout); and an attractive viola player named Bonnie Morse who is recruited to replace a retiring member of the quartet. In different ways the couple become obsessed with these incomers. William begins to plot Grace's murder (his bungling attempts qualify the text to be described as a 'black comedy'); Lucien it is, however, who becomes the successful murderer when he brutally kills his own mother.

Easy Silence is a typical example of a kind of English novel set in a middle-class milieu and in which classical music features significantly.[13] Although it contains various generic traces (crime fiction and the novel of manners, for example), the text is essentially 'literary' in impulse and intent – a definition that carries both institutional and formal/stylistic implications. By and large, the music it refers to derives from the classical and Romantic periods of the western art tradition; Modernism, as usual, tends to get very short shrift.[14] Various well-known composers are referenced in the text where the extra-textual 'meaning' of their work is recruited to perform significant narrative tasks. Thus, at different points in the story William 'uses' Chopin to calm himself down (124) and Schumann to explore his feelings for Bonnie (227). The latter's dislike for Haydn (200) and Grace's love of Liszt (38), as well as William's response to each of these predilections, provide important clues as to the evolving emotional landscape of the narrative. Some of the characters perform music to a professional standard and most are capable of discussing musical matters (what it means, how it makes them feel, and so on). Those who cannot engage with such matters (such as Lucien) figure as problematic presences within the narrative; excluded from the discourse of music, they are likewise bereft of the moral capital that music represents.

Besides featuring so strongly at a conceptual level *Easy Silence* attempts to replicate musical form in a number of respects, although the analogies remain resolutely 'metaphorical'. The subplots concerning Grace and William form recognisable 'themes' which begin together, diverge as a result of different (although similar) experiences, continue to overlap at various points throughout the narrative, and then reconvene towards the end of the text in an act of reconciliation and closure. The narrative assumes an active life inasmuch as certain themes (the Bonnie/Grant relationship, for example) are anticipated before they fully emerge (28), while others (the Grace/Lucien relationship) are recalled – and modified – late in the piece in the light of new information (267).

Easy Silence is not self-consciously musicalised as in the manner of Jilly Cooper's *Appassionata* (see Chapter 4) or *Sing the Body Electric*, both of which employ symphonic form to structure their narratives. Nevertheless, these effects recall the manner in which certain kinds of music deploy contrapuntal themes and temporal displacement (anticipation and recollection) to create specific effects.

Huth's novel deploys yet another popular musical effect. The phrase 'easy silence' forms a leitmotif that is repeated at regular intervals throughout the text. Like any leitmotif, moreover, its meaning changes in relation to the surrounding text. Initially the phrase is used to describe the comfortable relationship between William and Grace, which obtains:

> the mutual charge of love and affection, garnered from so many years of happy marriage, that does not need words, queries, analysis. She and William both recognised, and were able to indulge in, the lazy silence of mutual knowing, the unspoken agreement that no effort had constantly to be made. (15)

This 'easy silence' is invoked at various points throughout the text as a positive, desirable quality – a kind of sonic reward for the deep trust born of familiarity that develops between people over an extended period of time. William even experiences it with certain members of the quartet (186) – at least, with the ones (Rufus and Grant) he knows well and with whom he feels no pressure to converse.

There are other forms of silence at large throughout the text, however – some of them far from 'easy'. Sometimes (as between Lucien and Grace) silence signifies egotistical self-preoccupation (15); sometimes (as at various points during the quartet's working trip to Prague) it signifies moodiness resulting from frustration and misunderstanding (179, 185). After the failure of his latest and final murder attempt, silence – 'natural' and 'familiar' (301) though it be – descends over William and Grace, although now it has minatory overtones, infused with regret and loss. It is only with the announcement of Bonnie's engagement to Grant and the return of William's perspective on his own life that he learns to value once again the long-established ratio of sound to silence that characterises his relationship with his wife.

The emphasis on silence is remarkable in a story in which music figures so significantly. Like many of the characters encountered in contemporary music-fiction, William is extremely sensitised to sound, and his conscious life is highly musicalised: that is to say, he hears the world, and organises his relationship with it, in terms of music. The great composers of the western art tradition provide William with a language through which he may understand and articulate his life. It is, for example, their mutual bond to music that encourages William to dream of an otherwise unlikely relationship with Bonnie (177); later, as I have already suggested, the music of Schumann provides him with both an opportunity and a language to explore his feelings for her (227). Silence plays an important role in this process: for one thing, it provides a necessary caesura between the intense emotional creations of the masters; for another, it obviates the sonic banalities that comprise day-to-day life. Huth deploys silence to indicate the intensified sonic experience of musicians such as William, and to illustrate a range of emotional states that result from such a way of experiencing the world. As yet, there is little sense of the medial self-reflection or the metaphysical anxiety that silence represents for certain other contemporary writers.[15]

One such writer is Michel Faber, whose short novel *The Courage Consort* (2002) encapsulates many of the issues relating to silence as a theme within contemporary music-fiction. The story concerns yet another group, a quintet of singers who (with the aid of a grant) retire to an isolated Belgian chateau for a fortnight in order to practice a particularly challenging new commission. The 'Courage Consort' is comprised of Julian (tenor), Ben (bass), Dagmar (contralto), Catherine (soprano) and her husband Roger (baritone); and as with all such arrangements, the internal politics between the members of the group provides much of the animus for the plot. Despite this, the text (unlike the group) is not an ensemble project. Although the others intrude upon the narrative to a greater or lesser extent, the principal focus remains upon the relationship between founding member and chief facilitator Roger Courage and his wife who, as the story opens, is contemplating suicide.

The Courage Consort resembles *Easy Silence* in as much as the troubled marriage between a musically inclined, middle-aged, middle-class English couple lies at the heart of each text. Indeed, Faber's novella is in some ways a straightforward piece of music fiction, rehearsing many of the formal and conceptual characteristics that we have come to associate with that particular literary genre. Reference is made throughout, for example, to a wide range of musical materials (texts, people, styles, etc.) from both the art and popular traditions. As always, such references have a bearing on the range of meanings available within the text and on the reader's response to it. Some of the characters experience the world as a predominantly aural phenomenon, with the ear (rather than the eye) providing the principal means of sensory engagement. Preparation for the performance of a particular piece constitutes the central device around which the narrative is organised. All in all, the novel serves as a quasi-realistic depiction of art music both as a profession and as a cultural force in the lives of various individuals and groups in the modern world.

Interesting differences begin to emerge when we observe the distance between the style of the musical text which the Courage Consort is rehearsing and the style of the literary text in which the group's experiences are narrated. The fictional *Partitum Mutante* is described as a '[devilishly complex]' (5) piece written by an avant-garde Italian composer named Pino Fugazza. It contains 'complicated and athletic melodies in perverse keys' (29), at least one passage that 'Roger . . . wasn't convinced was humanly possible to sing' (6), and other sections that appear to be mistranscribed (84). As with many such novelistic representations, there is a faintly parodic attitude towards contemporary art music and towards the people who compose it, in this case the comically obscurantist Italian.[16] In her enervated condition, Catherine suspects that '[a] bit of Bach or Monteverdi might be more healing than what this Pino Fugazza expected of her' (24). It is revealing that the performance of *Partitum Mutante* is cancelled after the death (from a heart attack) of Ben, and the text closes with the remainder of the group singing an old English round – 'Sumer Is Icumen In' – on the minibus while travelling back to the airport. The simplicity of the emotions articulated in the old song offers more in such testing circumstances, it seems, than the tortuous, over-refined insights of late or post-Modernism.

This contention between avant-garde aesthetics and an older artistic paradigm is replicated at a formal level in *The Courage Consort*. The book is in many ways resolutely 'realist': it introduces plausible characters undergoing plausible experiences in more or less familiar contexts; the prose style and the structure are accessible, featuring relatively short sections with plenty of dialogue and a judicious mixture of third-person reportage and free indirect discourse. It also features, however, a mystery that hovers around the edges of the narrative but which never comes to figure as a central element of the story, and which is left frustratingly unresolved at the end of the text. The strange cry heard by Catherine on at least two occasions from the wood surrounding the chateau (36, 83) could be made by an unfamiliar animal, or by the ghost of a baby that died in the forest towards the end of the Second World War (75); or it could be a figment of her 'hypersensitive' (27) state. The narrative makes it clear that the sound is related in some way or other to Catherine's perception of herself as a woman, as a wife and as a musician. As to the actual nature of that relationship, however, *The Courage Consort* is not forthcoming: whatever the cry represents cannot find representation within the text itself. While it remains predominantly realist in impulse, then, the novel retains an element of uncertainty at its core; and this element paradoxically links it with the avant-garde discourse that is eschewed at the level of the plot.

The standoff between different models of musical and literary representation are but local medial articulations of a much more fundamental division that is at the heart of the human experience, and which is represented in the text in terms of the relationship between music and silence. All the members of the Courage Consort notice the silence of the remote chateau in which they are rehearsing – the cosmopolitan Julian even complains that 'it wasn't natural' (27). It is Catherine, however, upon whom the absence of sound makes the most profound impact. From the outset she in particular experiences the silence as sinister, describing it as 'uncompromising' (25) and 'unearthly' (26). It represents a 'void' (31, 120) which Catherine feels compelled to fill with purposeful, organised sound as evidence of her continued human existence. It is against the '[awful, deadly] silence of Ben's absence' (120) that she breaks into spontaneous song at the end of the narrative, in which endeavour she is soon joined by the rest of the group. The silence, it seems, has been overcome, at least temporarily, and the narrative ends on an upbeat. The inevitability of silence remains, however.

Catherine feels 'unnerved by [silence]. It was if the whole universe had been switched off' (25). Such a notion speaks to primordial human fears of isolation, meaninglessness, death – fears that the fundamentally religious counternotion of a universal music was invented to offset. 'Nature', Catherine muses as she walks in the woods,

> meant the absence of people. It was a system set up to run without human beings, concentrating instead on the insensate and the eternal. Which was very relaxing now and then. But dangerous in the long run: darkness would fall, and there would be no door to close, no roof over one's head, no blankets to pull up. One wasn't an animal, after all. (50)

It is in such a context that the cry from the forest – itself so menacing in some respects – nevertheless represents a life force with which Catherine must come to terms if she is to regain a functional perspective on her life. There are in fact intimations throughout the text that the cry haunting Catherine during her stay in the chateau represents a projection of the baby for which her body is yearning. The terror of being responsible for another human life is as nothing, it seems, to the terror of the silence which signifies the complete erasure of human intention. Both in terms of its musical politics and its literary aesthetics, the text offers a stoical vision of human experience as a constant negotiation between an inevitable silence and a necessary music.

The principal musical text referenced throughout *The Courage Consort* is ultimately absent. The structure and the sound of *Partitum Mutante* are broached regularly; individuals' contributions at rehearsals are described at various points; the meaning of the musical text and of the style in which it has been composed are discussed; and so on – but the performance in which it was supposed to be experienced in its entirety for the first time is cancelled. A familiar structure – in which the narrative resolves itself in relation to some highly-charged musical text – is set in motion, but then abandoned. This explicit failure at the level of the plot mirrors the failure that is always implicit at the level of the medium, for we know that even if the performance of *Partitum Mutante* had gone ahead, the description of it in a literary text would still have been silent.

Benson makes a similar point in relation to Kazuo Ishiguro's *The Unconsoled* (1995) – a novel, he claims, which does

> not enter into the wager of literary music, opting instead productively to employ the silence of the text in the face of its music as an integral part of the construction of that music. The fictional music of *The Unconsoled* is difficult not only because it performs a Modernist refusal of conventional modes of address, but also because it is refused admittance to the text. It never really arrives.
>
> (2006: 155)

For these reasons, *The Unconsoled* is perhaps the strangest music-novel encountered in this study; it is certainly one of the most challenging. The story is narrated by an internationally renowned pianist named Ryder who, as the novel commences, has just arrived in an unidentified European city to play a concert. This plausible scenario is soon belied, however, by a series of bizarre episodes in which Ryder encounters various people (including his own wife and child) while also finding himself caught up in a civic dispute regarding the relative value and suitability of different musical traditions.

As Benson has noted, the style of *The Unconsoled* might be described as Kafkaesque in its disturbing fusion of the ordinary and the fantastic.[17] The city in which Ryder finds himself, for example, is typical in many ways, with its streets, squares, trams, its old quarter and so on. At the same time, the urban geography is distinctly odd, even wilfully frustrating, at times, as when towards the end of the text Ryder attempts to find the concert hall in which he is supposed to be performing (413ff). Places mutate into other places, distances dissolve and expand; the natural laws of time and space seem out of kilter. At an earlier point Ryder describes going to a cinema to see Stanley Kubrick's famous film *2001: A Space Odyssey*, but then incorrectly names Clint Eastwood and Yul Brynner as the starring actors (94). While the invocation of this particular film and the naming of well-known public figures work to locate the narrative in a familiar reality, the obvious errors work to undermine that familiarity: has Ryder or the author made the mistake? Or is this intended to represent an alternative reality in which, unlike the world of the reader, those actors actually did feature in that film?

The Unconsoled is both uncomfortable and difficult to read, then. The distortion (sometimes comic, sometimes grotesque) of familiar phenomena is unsettling while Ryder's increasing estrangement very rapidly communicates itself to the reader – who Ishiguro constantly risks alienating by the introduction of long passages the relevance of which to the 'main' story seems at best tangential. Alongside these alienating elements, however, Benson discerns something else: '*The Unconsoled* is pervaded by sadness and disappointment,' he writes, 'and therein resides the promise of its narrative: the enactment of consolation' (2006: 147). This picks up on something explicitly invoked in the text itself, when the conductor Brodsky refers to music as a 'consolation' for a wound that will not heal. What this particular wound might be is not specified. However, when Ryder suggests that Brodsky might expect to be healed by his romantic love interest, Miss Collins, he replies: '"She'll be like the music. A consolation. A wonderful consolation. That's all I ask now. A consolation. But heal the wound?" He shook his head . . . "A medical impossibility. All I want, all I ask for now is a consolation"' (313).

There is a sense in which every character in the book (including the narrator Ryder) is 'wounded' in some manner or to some degree, and that they are all searching for relief from this shared human inheritance of pain and sadness. They are all, in other words, in search of consolation – some form of experience or perspective that will enable them to carry on despite the 'wound' that each must bear. As Brodsky affirms, music traditionally offers such an experience and such a perspective: it presents the listener with a sense of resolution and closure, 'consoling' them in various ways; at the very least it maintains the possibility of consolation. Certainly, in terms of its constituent forms (sonata form, for example) and devices (key signatures, for example), western music of the Classical and Romantic periods might be regarded as a 'consoling' discourse, offering narrative shapes and narrative types through which the listening subject could assert a sense of identity and thus become 'real' to themselves. The live concert features as yet another element of this discourse. The performance of such music by artists of greater or lesser excellence represents perhaps the consummate 'consoling' opportunity – a narrative in which the vision of the composer and the genius of the interpretation combine to offer a sonic experience that wards off (albeit temporarily) the silent terror with which the human subject is otherwise surrounded.

This model of musical consolation is at odds with a Modernist conception of subjectivity as fundamentally alienated from itself; and this is where the echoes of Kafka in Ishiguro's novel begin to come into focus. The text's principal plotline sees Brodsky's Romanticism opposed to Christoff's Modernism, with different elements within the town supporting one or the other and Ryder the performer stuck in the middle.

All this is beside the point, however, and for two reasons. Firstly, there is the by now familiar argument that the ideas relating to music are represented through a non-musical medium that can never be satisfactorily reconciled with its object. Literature, to put it figuratively, cannot 'console' music, because they are categorically estranged. Secondly, the final consoling performance, in relation to which all the different models of music affectivity might be evaluated, never in fact arrives. The resolution which Ryder's concert promised throughout the narrative is not forthcoming, and the reader in search of meaning – of the book and of themselves in relation to the book – is in this sense left 'unconsoled'.

Ishiguro's novel ends with a hellish image of Ryder, recently estranged from his wife and child, sitting on a tram going round and round the unnamed city, eating a never-ending breakfast and swapping inanities with a stranger sitting opposite (532–5). Things are not quite as bad as they seem, however. The musician retains positive memories of sharing a recent bus journey with his son Boris when they were both happy and enjoying each other's company, and the food and conversation he shares with his new acquaintance offer an equally positive image of the perennial human faculty of empathy, as well as people's capacity to find comfort and pleasure in ordinary things and everyday situations. Ryder knows that he will at some point have to disembark to prepare for a flight to Helsinki and yet another concert date; in the meantime he is happy to stay on the tram, talking and eating with his new friend. The promise of artistic consolation has been compromised in the (post-)modern world, it would seem: consolation resides, if anywhere, not in the consummate moment of the artistic text (either musical or literary), but in the multitudinous moments which together comprise everyday life – not in the arrival, that is to say, but in the travelling.

On one level, *The Unconsoled* is about nothing more – and nothing less – than a series of failed relationships. Misunderstandings and muddles reign, despite the prolix lengths to which characters are willing to go to try to explain their problems, their motives, their desires. And yet the possibility of something else is retained: a more optimistic model of human intercourse. The concern shown by his companion for Ryder's happiness at the close of the narrative, and the latter's positive response to that concern, together comprehend an experience that might be described as 'love'. It is the concern of one person for another and a willingness to take trouble to care for their well-being; it is the articulation, in defiance of an apparently universal law, of something for nothing. It is the hope of such exorbitance, of such senselessness in relation to 'natural' law, that enables the human subject to subsist within a silence which would otherwise be overpowering. Silence infuses the music, perhaps; but love punctuates the silence, and this brings us to the final section of the chapter.

The uses of love: Nick Hornby, *High Fidelity* (2000); Anne Donovan, *Buddha Da* (2004); Billy Cowie, *Passenger* (2007)

We have encountered evidence of a connection between music and love throughout this study; novels such as *Captain Corelli's Mandolin* and *Music and Silence* are typical in the manner in which they incorporate music as an element of greater or lesser symbolic significance within a central love story.[18] Besides this, it is noticeable on an anecdotal level the frequency with which people tend to talk about how much they 'love' a particular composer or an individual work or a performer or a style. Even a cursory glance reveals that music tends to elicit strong – sometimes overwhelming – emotional responses among a range of subjects. Therein lies its power (or at least part of its power) as a recurring device within cultural history. At the same time, it seems clear that music is intimately connected with the human emotion of love: the feelings through which the many different experiences that we call 'love' manifest themselves find potent expression in musical discourse – hence their association in such great variety of cultural forms, practices and contexts throughout history.

Of all the many aspects to this association between music and love, two are of particular interest here. Firstly, we should consider the possibility of a formal correspondence between the two concepts – that is, the fact that each be regarded in certain key aspects as an analogue of the other. The 'process' of love, we might say, comprehends a strong emotional response on the part of a subject towards an object, the narrativisation of that response in generic terms, and the identification and occupation of subject roles within that narrative. Leaving aside the enormous canon of music that is self-consciously focused on love, we may still observe that even the simplest piece of music partakes, at least to some extent, of this 'process' in as much as it: a) comprehends a relationship of sorts between a subject (the sound) and a putative object (what the sound 'means' or 'represents'); b) realises a narrative trajectory with reference to a range of genres of greater or lesser familiarity; and c) in effect 'creates' the listening subject by offering them a variety of positions within that narrative. In short, the experience of love is a lot like the experience of music: both make demands and both offer rewards; ultimately, both offer the subject an opportunity 'to be' in a particular way.

Secondly, and in apparent contradiction of the previous paragraph, it could be suggested that these two concepts are united in their resistance to human attempts to understand them – which is to say, to categorise, organise and control them. We know that music is a 'discipline' which is susceptible to the strictures of instrumental knowledge: we know that one can study its component parts, its constituent practices, its histories; the student can track its fashions, trace its traditions, consider the impact of memory and technology and ideas. Music comprehends sociological, economic and physiological perspectives as well as aesthetic and philosophical ones. Like all disciplines, we might say, it provides a domain of knowledge from where one can address human experience.

As well as being a 'discipline', music is also many other things, one of the most valued being its recalcitrance vis-à-vis disciplinary discourse. This does not mean that we must fall back into mystification, or reject disciplinary knowledge as essentially misguided. It does mean, however, that we must recognise that different people feel moved by or drawn to different styles of music; and that although such responses are calculable in disciplinary terms, such calculations invariably miss something of the immediacy of the encounter between the music and the subject. Music, we might say, connotes not a 'process' but an 'event', the precise singularity of which belies the power of disciplinary knowledge. Much of the time, what tends to be especially valued about music is what it means to 'me', how it makes 'me' feel, how, in effect, it calls 'me' into consciousness; and such a value is always, in some way and to some extent, in excess of disciplinary discourse.

Again, the parallels with the concept of love present themselves – at least with that model of 'love' formulated in western discourse since the early modern period (with Shakespeare figuring as a key influence).[19] For one thing, love is a common experience that creates impressions of singularity. It is intensely subject-oriented, but is founded upon a relationship with otherness. Love may be strictly 'disciplined' (in sociology, psychoanalysis or religion, for example), yet it is not answerable to prescription: no-one can say why or how it occurs between certain people, nor account for its presence or its absence in certain contexts. The altruism which in some accounts constitutes its central defining feature is in violation of various 'natural' laws (natural selection and thermodynamics, for example); yet it is in itself a 'law' instituted and observed by all of human societies. Love, in short, is an affront to disciplinary knowledge – always the most desired, yet always the most elusive, of human experiences.

These connections between music and love – speculative though they be – bear upon our consideration of the representation of music in fiction, for the latter connotes formal exigencies, as well as a body of highly sophisticated disciplinary knowledge, that are proper unto itself. Because music maintains such a close bond with the concept of love, the latter is never far away in the music-novel – something proved time and again in the texts addressed in this study. The representation of that bond is complicated, however, by the literary medium itself, and more precisely by the complex relations (disciplinary and otherwise) that literary discourse maintains with both music and love. Love may find expression in music, or music may implicitly express the human conception of love: to attempt to represent these expressions in the form of a novel is to introduce new elements that (to employ a metaphor from science) can react with the other constituents to produce an unstable compound.

An intense love of music can in itself constitute a challenge to romantic love. In Nick Hornby's *High Fidelity* (1995), for example, the narrator, Rob Fleming, is a record shop owner and sometime DJ who is obsessed with music to the point at which it has cost him (or at least contributed significantly to the failure of) his relationship with Laura. Rob makes it clear that music is far too serious to function as a mere soundtrack to romantic love; to his way of thinking, it constitutes the site of 'the bitterest of all bitter battles between men and women' (200).

High Fidelity is representative of a genre of 'lad lit' that came to prominence during the 1990s, and was purveyed (besides Hornby) by contemporary British novelists such as Tim Lott, Tony Parsons and Simon

Armitage. In a rather unsympathetic account the critic Richard Bradford described the phenomenon thus:

> Typically, the main character or characters will be men who attained a degree of adulthood – one is reluctant to say 'reached maturity' – around the end of the 1980s and thereafter find themselves in a social milieu that is, as far as their sex drive is concerned, at once seductive and perplexing. Their female counterparts seem able to match them in terms of confidence, intelligence, social bravado and hedonistic endurance and many authors and characters treat this as a credible licence for the behaviour and stylistic traits which have come to characterize the subgenre.
>
> (2007: 143)

'Lad lit', Bradford notes, remains 'contentious because commentators are divided on whether it is a commendable examination of maleness or the perpetuation, thinly disguised, of its prefeminist manifestations' (143). So far as *High Fidelity* is concerned, this very contention – between a self-aware masculinity and a kind of 'prefeminist' or perhaps even anti-feminist impulse – is at the very core of the novel, and it is entirely fitting that music should provide the medium through which these impulses are articulated.

In *High Fidelity*, the narrator describes his attempts to accommodate the different impulses that bear upon his life, key among which are a need for romantic love and a need to express himself in terms of musical taste. Rob is a man for whom music represents not so much a lifestyle choice as an absolutely essential element of life itself, like food and water. Although his taste seems eclectic, his age reveals him as the product of a particularly influential period in British popular music history: the punk and new wave movements of the late 1970s and early 1980s. This was a period, as we observed earlier in this chapter, when many British male adolescents developed a commitment to popular music that bordered on the pathological. Changes in the socio-political fabric of British life combined with new technology to produce figures such as Rob Fleming – figures drawn (comically or tragically, depending on the treatment) towards an understanding of their lives with obsessive reference to popular musical discourse.

Rob 'loves' his music, then, and he uses it to make sense of his life. For one thing, he believes that a lifelong inclination towards sad songs might have had a detrimental effect upon his ability to forge long-lasting, happy relationships (18). Likewise, the tendency to organise phenomena (such as break-ups) into handy, mind-sized chunks is clearly linked to the penchant (featured at various points throughout the text) for making musical lists. Comparing his lists with those of Dick and Barry, his employees and fellow obsessives, enables Rob to demonstrate his knowledge and taste, and is thus a crucial part of the process whereby he asserts his identity within the competitive discourse of popular music fandom.

The inappropriateness of utilising such a technique in the context of interpersonal relations does not strike Rob at first. The fact is, however, that although he 'loves' music, he 'loves' Laura too; among other things, *High Fidelity* stages the complexity of the interrelations between these forms of love and poses a question as to their mutual exclusion or compatibility.

Rob's dilemma is that his 'loving' relationship with music remains adolescent in several key respects, and this militates against the development of a mature 'loving' relationship with someone whose musical tastes – whose very way of engaging with music – differ so radically from his own. Music for Rob connotes not just a particular array of sounds, but a particular array of techniques for engaging with and responding to the world. To mitigate that love, to introduce a competing love object, would be to risk giving up part of his identity – the part that enables him to cope with himself, or at least his current conception of who he is. Laura's musical taste, in so far as it can be acknowledged at all, is merely a function of Rob's relationship with her. Her taste is an affront to him: she likes the 'right' things (such as the song 'Got to Get You off My Mind' as performed by Solomon Burke, for example) for the 'wrong' reasons, and the 'wrong' things ('Bright Eyes' as sung by Art Garfunkel, for example) for no reason in particular other than that 'it's got a pretty tune' (201). The difference between these texts – which is absolutely fundamental to Rob – is incidental to Laura. The object may be identical but the means of engaging with it is radically distinct.

It is only when Rob begins to acknowledge Laura's taste – or more precisely her right to a taste of her own – that he can begin to move towards an accommodation of the different 'loves' that comprise his life. The narrative ends with him looking at Laura as she dances to 'Got to Get You off My Mind' and '[starting] to compile in my head a compilation tape for her, something that's full of stuff she's heard of, and full of stuff she'd play' (245). The discourse of taste is rehearsed – that which enables Rob to differentiate between 'good' and 'bad' examples of popular music and to reconfirm his own identity as part of that process of evaluation. Such a discourse has been mitigated, however, by an awareness that 'value' is a function of the uses to which it is put, and by an appreciation that different forms of love need to be accommodated and expressed in different ways.

Jimmy McKenna, from Anne Donovan's *Buddha Da* (2003), is another thirty-something character undergoing a crisis that lends itself to consideration in musical terms. Jimmy has been a happy-go-lucky, working-class Glaswegian up until the beginning of the narrative, a bit of a 'nutter' (1) according to his daughter Anne-Marie, but basically content with his work and his family. The parameters of his life are already set, on the whole: he is a painter and decorator, a father and a husband, and he engages with the things that contemporary working-class Scottish men are likely to engage with. As the novel commences, however, Jimmy has already started to wonder about his life – about the range of pleasures, experiences and emotions that his received identity has led him to expect. Finding no solace in the conventional Christian sects (Protestantism and Catholicism) that have traditionally dominated the Scottish religious imagination, he turns to Buddhism. His wife's amusement becomes bemusement and, soon after, resentment when she realises that this is not a joke: her husband is indeed undergoing a classic early- to mid-life crisis, one which cannot but have ramifications for her own lifestyle. More alarmingly, Jimmy's example raises uncomfortable questions about Liz's identity and her own expectations of happiness.

Donovan's novel is narrated by the three main characters, and these distinctive 'voices' weave around each other to create complex effects, often with the same events and experiences related from their different perspectives. This is a useful formal device in as much as the reader is enabled to enter into the action but at the same time does not become overly identified with any particular character. While this helps to maintain the underlying comic aspect of the narrative, it is also reflective of what is occurring at the level of the plot. Among other things, Jimmy's turn to Buddhism represents a search for an authentic personal voice amid the overwhelming cacophony of the modern world. Over the course of the narrative, however, he comes to understands the limits of 'authenticity' as a discursive principle, and the necessity for a counter-discourse based on the principle of harmony – the need to integrate his personal melody, as it were, with the music of the surrounding world.

This theme is developed in the narrative strand relating to Anne Marie. As the novel opens she is 'obsessed' (21) with the American pop star Madonna, reference to whose famous song 'Material Girl' carries obvious symbolic weight in the light of the novel's main themes. Anne Marie's relationship with music at this stage is typical of someone from her background; this reflects the 'comfortable' sense of identity with which the novel is taking issue. The musical dimension to this is broached in the first instance by Jimmy when, at a New Year's party, he attempts to re-indulge his youthful punk tastes. 'Scotland's answer to Johnny Rotten' (329) prepares for the evening by improvising a punk outfit and cavorting around the house singing 'I am an antichrist – I am an anarchist' (70) – the opening lines from the quintessential punk anthem, 'Anarchy in the UK' by the Sex Pistols. These words (which are usually interpreted in a public/political sense) possess an alternative potential that will soon emerge: Jimmy is 'an antichrist' in as much as he is rejecting traditional Christian teaching, and he is 'an anarchist' in respect of the systems with which a person such as he might be expected to make sense of the world. Jimmy is horrified, however, when he sees a recording of himself drunk at the party, miming to his favourite pop songs; his destruction of the videotape is symbolic of his rejection of those received cultural systems (including religion and music) which had set the limits on his way of being in the world.

Anne Marie undergoes a similar epiphany with reference to her own musical taste. Her friendship with Nisha is initially based on their mutual admiration for Madonna; the other principal musical influence in her life is provided by the perennial amateur favourite *Joseph and the Amazing Technicolor Dreamcoat*, by Tim Rice and Andrew Lloyd Webber, for which both she and Nisha are rehearsing at school. The performance of the latter, as well as a karaoke performance of selected Madonna songs at a millennium party, cements the friendship between the two girls. As the story develops, however, other influences begin to emerge; and with the technical assistance of Nisha's DJ/producer brother Gurpreet (a character who resembles the narrator of *Psychoraag* in a number of key respects), the two girls begin to look for a way in which to express these different influences. A television competition for a home-produced piece of music provides the opportunity, and the narrative shows Nisha and Anne Marie working hard to conceptualise a valid entry in terms of structure, content, production, and the myriad related matters that bear upon the creation of a musical text.

The resulting piece – entitled 'Salve Regina' and incorporating Latin, Buddhist and Punjabi elements, underpinned by contemporary dance beats – represents much more than an experiment in musical hybridism, however. Taken in the context of Anne Marie's home life, her co-creation represents nothing less than the persistence of love in the face of death, difference and enmity. The song she produces with Nisha 'contains', as it were, Anne Marie's relationship with her recently deceased grandmother,

her parents and her new friend, as well as a whole series of collateral associations which, taken together, actually comprise her identity and her life as a function of that identity.

In some ways, indeed, 'Salve Regina' is the musical equivalent of the extra-marital baby that Liz is carrying at the close of the narrative. Jimmy's response to each is linked; of the music, first of all, he thinks:

> Ah'd never been able tae get intae that kind of sampled stuff afore, always thought there was somethin kind of cheatin aboot it, but as ah walked alang ah kept listenin, beginnin tae feel how the rough voices of the lamas and the sweet high voices of the girls just fitted that perfectly, replayed it till it was fillin ma heid, blockin oot everythin else. (315)

Jimmy's characterisation of Anne Marie's musical hybrid as 'cheating' is typical of the punk discourse with which he is identified throughout the text, a discourse which tends to characterise 'computer' music as adulterated – that is to say, as an inauthentic form of music removed in impulse and expression from the individual genius who, by virtue of his skill and commitment, is capable of exciting empathetic responses in the listening subject. The use of 'cheatin' is revealing here, because to one (received) way of thinking, Liz's pregnancy is the result of her 'cheating' with another man. Jimmy's role as 'authentic' father has been compromised as a result of Liz's 'adultery', and yet he decides to assume responsibility for the unborn child and to reconfirm the family unit because of the love that he feels for his wife and daughter. His acceptance of 'Salve Regina' is thus linked to his acceptance of a child that is not biologically 'his': in defiance of established principles of 'authenticity' and 'adultery', both decisions respect the principles of difference, responsibility, freedom and mutual care on which the possibility of love is founded.

There are of course many different forms of love, and many different ways in which love may be experienced and expressed. In Billy Cowie's *Passenger* (2006), for example, a professional violinist named Milan Kotzia discovers that his body is hosting the undeveloped foetus of his own twin sister, conceived at the same time as himself but never born because of complications during pregnancy. After forty-two years of silence the foetus (which he names Roma) suddenly begins to communicate with Milan, tapping out the rhythms of classical music pieces on his back. Milan becomes romantically involved with a researcher named Murri who specialises in communication with the multi-sensory deprived. Under her tutelage, and using Morse code and rudimentary technology (tapping on his belt with a coin), Milan gradually learns to 'talk' with his sibling. Initially, their principal subject is music. Slowly, however, as their familiarity with the topic, with the medium and with each other grows, Milan and Roma become capable of highly sophisticated exchanges. Besides articulating emotions, opinions, requests, and so on, Milan is able to narrate the story of *The Heart Is a Lonely Hunter*, a novel by Carson McCullers about a deaf and dumb man living in the USA in the 1930s. Milan ends his relationship with Murri when he learns that she has been writing a thesis on Roma's case. Then, during an orchestra visit to Vienna, he wakes in a hospital bed after a serious accident to find that doctors have removed from his body what they refer to as a 'tumour'. Roma is 'dead' without ever having been officially 'alive', and the text ends with Milan grieving for the twin sister he had unwittingly carried throughout his life but known for only a year.

Roma has spent her entire life with the music to which her brother has unwittingly exposed her – the music that he listens to and which he himself plays. It is not only her physical existence that is entirely dependent on Milan, however; his cultural experiences determine (at least in the first instance) her world and her sense of identity in relation to it. It is therefore entirely natural that the parasite should use music as a means of communicating with the host; it is likewise understandable that the former's breadth of reference should initially mirror the latter's. Accordingly, Roma is constantly requesting pieces from Milan's performing or listening repertoire which – given his age and background – is predictably eclectic, encompassing both classical and popular traditions. She is particularly enamoured of Mozart's Clarinet Concerto, although it is in fact a popular song – Iggy Pop's 'Passenger', from which the title of the novel is taken – that Milan uses to characterise their relationship.

As with all such 'determined' relationships, however, the parasitic element eventually begins to challenge its limitations. Roma's aural imagination is restricted to what she can hear through Milan; her physical experience of music is likewise dependent upon his – the gestures he makes and the posture he adopts as he plays or listens to a piece of music. When she begins to compose her own work, however – tapping out the names of notes and performance directions for him to record – the relationship is reversed: he is now the conduit through which her musical imagination must be expressed. It becomes increasingly clear that Roma's emotional response to music is something over which her brother has no control; after her death, indeed, he suspects that despite a lifetime's immersion in music 'it wasn't him who liked it, who pumped the soothing chemicals into his blood stream on hearing a favourite piece. He was a surrogate musician' (129).

Passenger raises fascinating issues with regard to parent/child and sibling psychology, the viability of nature/culture transference, and the role and function of love in human experience. Milan is both brother to and parent of Roma; she is his forty-two-year-old twin but much of the time she behaves like an excited child, placing him in the role of responsible adult. The love he comes to feel for her is categorically different in kind and in quantity from the emotions he feels towards 'lovers' such as Murri. In fact, the relationship between these siblings realises in emblematic form the generally unacknowledged paradox on which the notion of human love has come to be established: the possibility of independence within a relationship of absolute dependence, or to put in another way, the (meta-)physical impossibility of getting something for nothing.

As pointed out in the introduction to this section, music provides in many ways the ideal concept with which to address all these issues, including the seminal paradox of love. The notion that music exists in nature as an ideal language of the emotions is tested in relation to Roma's literal interiorisation.[20] After all, she is denied a programmatic engagement with music in as much as she possesses no 'reality' within which to locate the sounds she hears. The famous Clarinet Concerto cannot 'suggest' or 'represent' or 'invoke' (or any other metaphor of transference) any existential equivalent from the world in which it was composed and in relation to which it possesses various interrelated meanings and values. For Roma, however, both the meaning and the value of Mozart's work lie inherent within the sounds themselves; meaning and value are not functions of the ability of those sounds to refer to something beyond themselves, because in Roma's case there is no beyond. For her, rather, music simply has to be what it already is; her response to music is therefore a confirmation of music's inherent signifying potential, as recognised and organised by the composer.

Cowie has developed a plausible phenomenon (the foetus in foetu, of which there are numerous instances in the medical record) in an implausible direction in order to tell a story about love and music. Roma represents what is in essence the ideal listener to music, uncontaminated by the world or by the myriad factors that bear upon the listening moment. Moreover, this role as ideal listener is clearly related to her role as ideal love object: she represents for her brother-host the impossible prospect of a recognisable 'other' who is nonetheless indelibly attached to the subject. *Passenger* works to show that, just as the ideal of love is embedded in the human consciousness, so the ideal of a perfect meeting between expression and understanding is embedded in music.

The latter is a proposition to which the present study, with its insistence on both the worldliness and the wordiness of music, is opposed. Indeed, the ideal 'love' is no more available than the ideal listening experience. It seems likely, rather, that both discourses emerged in response to certain historical developments, and both are just as likely to fade when historical circumstances alter. Nevertheless, such discourses have accrued force and exponential resonance over centuries of use, and both continue to exercise a strong influence over artists down to the present day. If music-novels such as *Passenger* represent a medium in which both ideals – the 'perfect' unmediated listening experience, the 'perfect' subject/object relationship – retain currency, they also provide a means whereby the highly contingent nature of such ideals might be exposed.

Notes

Introduction

1. Kramer 2003: 125, 130. This is in direct opposition to the influential view expressed by Kierkegaard: 'Music always expresses the immediate in its immediacy; it is for this reason, too, that music shows itself first and last in relation to language . . . Language involves reflection, and cannot, therefore, express the immediate. Reflection destroys the immediate, and hence it is impossible to express the musical in language' (1959: vol. I, 68).
2. The issue of Kramer's relationship to 'new musicology' and the cultural turn in ethnomusicology is contentious. See Cook (1998), Middleton (2003) and Scher (1999).
3. This decision has denied me the opportunity to discuss some remarkable music-novels, including Roddy Doyle's *Oh, Play That Thing!* (2004) and Bernard Mac Laverty's *Grace Notes* (1997).

1   The Music-Novel in Theory and Practice

1. Barry's study deals principally with poetry. He only mentions the novel in the final pages (1987: 184–5), where he suggests that the emphasis placed upon 'listening' by contemporary music theorists, as well as the notion of textual absence, influenced the 'constructive' aesthetic of novelists such as Fielding and Sterne – that is, the comic novelist's insistence that the reader should contribute creatively to developing the meaning of the text.
2. Christopher Norris (1990) has explored the contemporary theoretical context of Barry's study and locates its most profound influence in the work of Paul de Man.
3. The rise and function of nineteenth-century programme music will be examined in the remaining two parts of this chapter.
4. Bakhtin writes: 'It must be noted that the comparison we draw between Dostoyevsky's novel and polyphony is meant as a graphic analogy, nothing more. The image of polyphony and counterpoint only points out those new problems which arise when a novel is constructed beyond the boundaries of ordinary monologic unity, just as in music new problems arose when the boundaries of a single voice were exceeded. But the material of music and of the novel are [sic] too dissimilar for there to be anything more between them than a graphic analogy, a simple metaphor. We are transforming this metaphor into the term "polyphonic novel", since we have not found a more appropriate label. It should not be forgotten, however that the term has its origin in metaphor' (1984: 22).
5. Bakhtin in Morris 1994: 90. Morris suggests that '[it] is helpful to recognize a figurative terminology of seeing, hearing and spatiality underlying Bakhtin's sense of aesthetic activity' (1994: 88). Chanan (1994: 37–51) interestingly

discusses various aspects of music history and aesthetics in the light of Bakhtin's theories without, however, emphasising the derivation of 'polyphony' as a specifically musical term.

6. Although *A la recherche du temps perdu* bears obvious affinities with 'modernist' music in at least some of its variations, this 'Overture' is clearly Wagnerian in both inspiration and intention. On the question of the various periods into which musicalised fiction may be organised, see Lagerroth (1999), and Wolf (1999). Lagerroth also discusses the metafictional function of the little phrase and how this may be related to music's general role in interrogating or exposing the constructed nature of the literary text.

7. It should be understood from the outset that 'metaphor' in this instance refers to the literary, rather than the critical, discourse – which is to say, it refers to a tendency amongst novelists to invoke music within their work, rather than a tendency amongst critics to impute musical influence in a specific work of literature. This issue is taken up in the next section, 'Music and Form'.

8. It is this faith in the power of aesthetic experience that has led to Schopenhauer being labelled as 'the artist's, and more especially the musician's philosopher' (Budd 1992: 76). Regarding his musical exceptionalism, it might be said that Schopenhauer is both typically German and typically Romantic in his privileging of the ear as the primary human sense. Martin Jay notes: 'From the time of Schopenhauer and Nietzsche up to that of Adorno, music rather than painting has been the primary aesthetic model for many German philosophers. And the hermeneutic tradition dating back to the Reformation, with its stress on the word of God, has always privileged hearing and speech over sight, a bias still evident in contemporary thinkers like Gadamer and Habermas' (1986: 198).

9. Quoted in Breathnach 1999: 266. Brad Bucknell also quotes Valéry who, looking back on the Symbolist heyday of the 1880s, wrote: 'We were nourished on music, and our literary minds dreamed only of extracting from language the same effects, almost, as were produced on our nervous systems by sound alone' (2001: 11).

10. The most famous point of contact is probably *Prélude à l'après-midi d'un faune* (1894), Claude Debussy's musical adaptation of Mallarmé's poem *L'après-midi d'un faune* (1876).

11. Brown 1948: 208–18. See also Basilius, for whom *Tonio Kröger* represents 'probably . . . the highest possible degree of fusion of the two arts of music and literature which a consensus will support' (1981: 171).

12. On Mann's attitude towards serialism see Aronson (1980: 238ff), who concludes that: 'The possibility that Mann misunderstood Schönberg's musical message and saw cultural chaos and disintegration where others discovered a new musical vocabulary tending towards coherence and affirmation is not to be dismissed lightly' (244).

13. John Shepherd writes: 'The analysis of music that is carried out within [music theory and music analysis] has been almost synonymous with the analysis of musical notation, the musical score. This embodiment of music within a material form, that of the score, has in turn enabled musicology (as distinct from ethnomusicology) to conceive of classical music as something apart from the rest of the world, an art form somehow independent of the

social, economic, political, and cultural forces that constitute that world. Consequently, to the extent that music theorists think about the question of "meaning" or "significance" in music, they think of it as contained exclusively within music's sounds' (1999: 161–2).

14. See Wolf (1999: 54ff) for an attempt to classify the many and various ways in which music may feature in the novel.

15. Before commencing an analysis of the possibility of narrative in music it is crucial to differentiate between sound and score – that is, between the auditory event and the textual rendering of that event. The development of notation as a means to imagine and subsequently create any musical work longer or more complex than the human capacity to memorise has profound implications for the question of narrativity in music. See Shepherd (1999).

16. Such, in any event, is the burden of Eduard Hanslick's influential mid-nineteenth-century thesis in which he argued, against Wagner's evolving practice, for a variant of musical idealism: 'The power which music possesses of profoundly affecting the nervous system cannot be ascribed so much to the *artistic* forms created by, and appealing to the mind, as to the material with which music works and which Nature has endowed with certain inscrutable affinities of a physiological order' (1974: 123, original emphasis).

17. Aronson writes: 'Throughout the first half of this century the sonata form, whether employed in compositions for solo instruments, for chamber music, or large orchestral works, was taken as a significant parallel for fiction writing. Literary critics were almost unanimous in their appraisal of some of the outstanding novels of the age as "sonatas in words"' (1980: 65). See also Basilius 1981; Brown 1948: 161–3; Emerson Carlile 1981; Grim 1999; Smith 1981; Wolf 1999: 64–6, 204–7; Ziolkowski 1981.

18. Benson writes: 'It is with post-Beethovenian music criticism – beginning famously with E.T.A. Hoffmann's 1810 analysis of Beethoven's *Fifth Symphony* – that we first encounter sustained attempts to read the individual movements of the symphonic cycle as dramatically interrelated, in particular around some musicalized protagonist. Closely allied to such holistically-oriented readings are narrativized conceptions of the sonata and the symphony, both nineteenth- and twentieth-century' (2006: 35).

19. On the question of voice and its relevance for a consideration of musical narrative see Bernhart 1999: 27–8.

20. It was precisely the archetypal properties of sonata form, as developed in the Romantic symphony, that Berlioz exploited so brilliantly in his *Symphonie fantastique* (1830), so that the programme (a gothic narrative concerning a Byronesque hero, unrequited love, death and witchcraft) appears to emerge 'organically' from the form of the music itself.

21. This debate achieved heroic status during the second half of the nineteenth century in the extended exchanges between Hanslick and Wagner. Latterly, preoccupation with the relationship between music and narrative has become 'virtually a disciplinary subfield' (Kramer 1992: 235, cited in Seher 1999: 15); the issue may indeed be regarded, as Scher maintains, as 'an ideal hunting ground' for music-oriented literary criticism, as it is with reference to the question of narrative that 'the two media genuinely intersect' (1999: 15). See also McClary 2000, and Nattiez 1990.

22. 'The principal musical influence on the novel, and even the novelette, has been the adoption of methods of construction developed by Wagner' (Brown 1948: 209).

23. On rhythm in the novel see Brown (1967), who bases his study on Forster's *A Passage to India*. On the role of repetition in fiction see Hillis Miller, who describes two kinds of literary repetition: one, 'Platonic', based on similarity and 'grounded in a solid archetypal model which is untouched by the effects of repetition'; the other, 'Nietzschean', based on difference and giving rise to 'ungrounded doublings which arise from differential interrelations among elements which are all on the same plane' (1982: 6). See also Deleuze (1994), and the essay 'On repetition' by Said (1983: 111–25).

24. The literature is enormous, but besides the sources already referenced in this section see in particular Aronson 1980; Bauerle 1993; Bucknell 2001; Grim 1999; Kumar 1991; Smith 1981; Weaver 1998; White 1998; Wilson 1931.

25. Ayrs invites comparison with two other fictional composers: Adrian Leverkühn and Paul Clearwater – the latter featuring in the novel *Sing the Body Electric*, which we shall encounter in Chapter 4.

2   The Role and Representation of Music in the Novel

1. See, for example, Dorothea Brooke's dismissive attitude towards Moore's song 'The Last Rose of Summer' in *Middlemarch* (Eliot 1967: 89).

2. In so far as Heathcliff is a disruptive Irish presence within the stable world of the Heights, he might be regarded as a precursor of Michael Furey, the passionate young man in James Joyce's story 'The Dead' who dies for love.

3. The housekeeper Nellie Dean uses the term to describe the child's spirit (83); soon after Cathy 'sings' her father to sleep (84), only to discover that he has in fact died. This suggests that, because of her identification with Heathcliff, her 'music' has taken on the dangerous overtones associated with him.

4. The critical literature on this tradition is extensive, but besides da Sousa Correa, see Barry (1987), Benson (2006) and Thomas (1995). It is Mr Casaubon's ignorance of German intellectual history that causes Will Ladislaw to disdain his cousin's wish to write a 'key to all mythologies' (Eliot 1967: 240).

5. The debate over gender, technique and meaning was still being played out a generation later, as when the narrator of Proust's *Swann's Way* (1913) notes that the character Odette 'played vilely, but often the fairest impression that remains in our minds of a favourite air is one which has arisen out of a jumble of wrong notes struck by unskilful fingers upon a tuneless piano' (1957: 278).

6. The idea of the 'Wagnerian novel' – as well as the larger category of 'literary Wagnerism' – existed well before the onset of modern intermedial studies; see for example Blissett (1968) and Cave (1978).

7. Asquith 2005: 11. See also Grundy, who claims that 'Hardy's devotion to "Tune" was lifelong and . . . constant' (1979: 134).

8. Grundy draws parallels between *Jude the Obscure* and a different contemporary operatic master: Verdi. In particular, she claims, Jude's death scene is a reworking of the final act of *La traviata*: 'The parallel is with the Verdian "remembrance" motive rather than with the Wagnerian *leitmotiv*, for the

chief function of the bells is not to characterise Christminster but to remind us of the changed situation' (1979: 153). The bells never 'represented' Christminster in such a straightforward way, of course; rather, they invoke the abstract human emotions of desire, hope and happiness, and Hardy's treatment of them fully complies with the Wagnerian technique.

9. The word proliferates, with many different shades of meaning, during the scene where Mrs Wilcox tells Margaret Schelgel of her desire to leave Howards End (95).

10. See Lagerroth, who considers '[how] it is that a verbal text engages in musicalization as the practice for self-reflexivity' (1999: 208).

11. On the role of counterpoint in literature see Grim (1999), and Wolf (1999: 20 and *passim*).

12. Lothar Fietz, in a study of Huxley's fiction from 1969; quoted in Wolf (1999: 169).

13. In this, as well as in the general emphasis on music as a privileged key to the human condition, Huxley reveals the influence of Proust in particular.

14. As Dahlhaus writes: 'Around 1870, Beethoven's quartets became the paradigm of the idea of absolute music that had been created around 1800 as a theory of the symphony: the idea that music is a revelation of the absolute, specifically because it "dissolves" itself from the sensual, and finally even from the affective sphere' (1991: 17).

15. Rampion's dissent is ironic, in so far as it was his insistence on the common culpability of music snobs and 'God-snobs', and on the immorality of inauthentic responses to music, that precipitated Spandrell's 'suicide'.

3   Musical Genre in the Novel

1. The issue of the institutional status of music has been most forcefully (not to say self-consciously) pursued in relation to ethnomusicology, which as a discipline always functioned at a tangent to the western art tradition. See Cook (1998: 85–101).

2. Notable in this regard is the influence of various 'organic' intellectuals, such as Milan Kundera (1986, 1996) and Edward W. Said (2006), who have adopted a self-consciously intermedial approach to cultural matters, and for whom the music/literature nexus is absolutely implicit.

3. American writer Deborah Grabien has produced a series of novels – *The Weaver and the Factory Maid* (2003), *Matty Groves* (2005), *Cruel Sister* (2006) – based on folk ballads.

4. The question of musical genre (and thus of its fictionalisation) in Irish cultural history is especially fraught. Recent Irish novels incorporating elements of folk music include John B. Keane's *The Bodhrán Makers* (1986), Dermot Bolger's *Father's Music* (1998), and Patrick McCabe's *Winterwood* (2006).

5. Besides being a writer, de Bernières is also a musician and member of a successful group call the Antonius Players, which specialises in medieval and folk music.

6. Michael Ondaatje's *Coming through Slaughter* (1979) – based on the life of pioneer cornet player Buddy Bolden – predates Morrison's novel by thirteen years, and is arguably more successful (it is certainly more daring) in its use of techniques borrowed from jazz.

7. Along with American singer Karen Carpenter (who died in 1983), Zavaroni was one of the first high-profile victims of this disorder. It is now an established element of the British popular imagination (regularly invoked during the latter years of Diana, Princess of Wales) and the subject of frequent media-induced panics.

8. The myth was brilliantly captured in (rock) musical form on David Bowie's seminal album *The Rise and Fall of Ziggy Stardust and the Spiders from Mars* (1973), which dramatised the pop career (and demise) of the eponymous 'star'. Bowie's adoption (and subsequent abandonment) of the Ziggy persona offered a salutary lesson to aspirant 'stars' everywhere; as the roll-call of popular music victims reveals, however, it is a lesson that each generation has to relearn.

9. Rushdie was famously befriended by Irish rock group U2 during the 1990s, appearing on stage during the London leg of their *Zoo TV* World Tour in 1993. The group recorded a version of 'The Ground beneath Her Feet' for the soundtrack of the film *The Million Dollar Hotel* and for their album *All That You Can't Leave Behind*, both of which appeared in 2000.

10. See the section 'The uses of silence' in Chapter 5 below. See also 'Quasi Parlando II: Blanchot and the Silent Narrative', Chapter 4, in Benson (2006: 89–103), on the complex relations between sound, silence and subjectivity.

11. The problems are all too apparent in Dreda Say Mitchell's *Killer Tune* (2007), a novel whose reliance on (good and bad) stereotypes and coincidence constantly undermines the 'street' credibility it so assiduously pursues at the level of the plot.

12. The exceptions tend to be the more cerebral genres, such as folk, singer-songwriter and progressive rock, although in no case is empathetic movement categorically disbarred.

13. The tradition of transcribing Scots for literary purposes is at least as old as Burns, although the modern trend is most closely associated with writers such as James Kelman, whose novel *How Late It Was, How Late* won the Booker Prize in 1994, and Irvine Welsh, who published the enormously successful *Trainspotting* a year earlier. Both of these novels, interestingly, incorporate music as an integral thematic element.

14. Elements of ternary form subsist within the relationship between Zaf and the two significant (very different) women who feature in the narrative: his current girlfriend, Babs (white, Scottish-Irish, nurturing), and Zilla (brown, Scottish-Asian, predatory). These extremes introduce an emotional economy that Zaf tries to 'resolve' in typical novelistic fashion, although the text avoids traditional realist closure.

15. The pattern is even older, of course, and certainly more widespread; the movement from court to greenwood and back again provides, for example, the basic structure for much Shakespearean comedy.

4 Music and the Genres of Fiction

1. On the sound/silence connection see Chapter 5. The age-old connection between music and mathematics was consolidated in 2007 by the founding

of a new journal (Taylor & Francis, *Journal of Mathematics and Music*) dedicated to exploring the relations between the two fields.

2. Texts incorporating variations on such a scene include *These Demented Lands* (Alan Warner), *An Equal Music* (Vikram Seth), *Easy Silence* (Angela Huth), *The Concert Pianist* (Conrad Williams), *Starseeker* (Tim Bowler), *Soul Music* (Terry Pratchett), *The Ground Beneath Her Feet* (Salman Rushdie), *Morvern Callar* (Alan Warner), *The Lonely Planet Boy* (Barney Hoskyns), *Amsterdam* (Ian McEwan), *High Fidelity* (Nick Hornby) and *Buddha Da* (Anne Donovan). We shall observe how the climactic concert is broached but ultimately absent from two texts which might also be described as 'Kafkaesque' to some degree: *The Unconsoled* (by Kazuo Ishiguro) and *The Courage Consort* (by Michel Faber).

3. *Appassionata* is one of the 'Rutminster Chronicles', a series of novels set in a fictitious English county and featuring a number of recurring characters. Interestingly, *Score!* (1999) (which followed *Appassionata*) is a murder mystery set around the staging of Verdi's *Don Carlos*.

4. The notion of camp (usually referenced to a pioneering essay from 1968 by the US critic Susan Sontag) emerges from a broad postmodernist sensibility that is opposed to modernist aesthetics and its drive towards interpretation, but which is susceptible to accusations (like postmodernism itself) of political quietism.

5. The highest profile example of such a character in modern British fiction is Bridget Jones, who featured in two successful novels (by Helen Fielding) towards the end of the 1990s. The heroine's search for a significant male other in *Bridget Jones's Diary* (1996) leads her away from 'sex-and-shopping' towards the genre of romantic love, one enduringly influential version of which (Austen's *Pride and Prejudice*) is intertextually incorporated within the narrative.

6. It is interesting in this respect that the publication of *Appassionata* coincided with the emergence of the Spice Girls and the advent of 'girl power'.

7. The publication details list Rebecca Farnworth as co-author. It is not uncommon for celebrity authors to employ ghost-writers; and while this is unproblematical in relation to certain genres (sports autobiographies, for example), it places a question mark over any critical discourse (including the present one) that incorporates the notion of authorial intention as part of its analytical method.

8. Sarra Manning's *Guitar Girl* (2003) and Rachel Cohn's *Pop Princess* (2004) highlight the dangers of the pop world for slightly younger (and less sexually mature) females, while Carol Clewlow's *One for the Money* (1994) relates a tale of rock excess from the perspective of a central female character.

9. Tolkien might be regarded as a pioneer of 'filk' – a term referring to a style of music that began to emerge from science fiction and fantasy fiction conventions during the 1970s. Originally regarded as an amusing diversion, 'filk' has become a seminal element of the sci-fi and fantasy subcultures.

10. These publications included *The Time Machine* (1895), *The Island of Doctor Moreau* (1896), *The Invisible Man* (1897), *The War of the Worlds* (1898) and *The First Men in the Moon* (1901).

11. A key reference is *A Sea Symphony* by Ralph Vaughan Williams, first performed in 1910. Although the sea is a perennial theme in classical music

(as in all the arts), it seemed to enjoy a peculiar vogue around the beginning of the twentieth century, with dedicated compositions by the likes of Stanford, Elgar, Bridge and Debussy.

12. Whitman's 'I Sing the Body Electric' is included in *Leaves of Grass*, although the title and the line itself were not added until the edition of 1867 (see *Selected Poems*, 1991: 12–19). The phrase was also used for the title of a celebrated short story by American science fiction writer Ray Bradbury (2003). The latter (which was subsequently dramatised on the cult television programme *The Twilight Zone*) concerns the relationship between a child and her new 'Electrical Grandmother'; the parallels with Lively's novel (which also concerns the fate of human emotions in the face of new technology) are clear.

13. Parents in contemporary Britain will no doubt recognise the addictive nature of the gadget, especially given its interactive element.

14. The information included with the text of *Johnny Come Home* claims that it is being adapted as a television drama for Channel Four.

15. The Angry Brigade formed in London in 1967, although it was active as a terror organisation only between 1970 and 1972, being responsible for up to twenty-five bombings around Britain. The organisation attracted not only old-style political anarchists, but also adherents of new movements such as the Situationist International and radical feminism. The action of *Johnny Come Home* is set against the background of the trial of a number of Angry Brigade activists known as the Stoke Newington Eight, which effectively ended the organisation. See the materials collected at recollectionbooks.com/siml/library/AngryBrigade/.

16. On the relations between the cultural, political and musical transition between the 1960s and 1970s in Britain see Savage (2001) and MacDonald (1994: 1–34). On glam rock in particular see Hoskyns (1998) and Thompson (2000).

17. Pearson's status as a second-hand terrorist, as well as the depiction of a kind of haphazard political radicalism at large in British society, recall one of the prototypes of the thriller genre: Joseph Conrad's *The Secret Agent* (1907).

18. The list may be found at www.lib.washington.edu/music/mystery.html.

19. Some of the texts included in the present study that maintain echoes of this sub-tradition are Angela Huth's *Easy Silence* (see Chapter 5), Conrad Williams's *The Concert Pianist* (Chapter 1), Ian McEwan's *Amsterdam* (Chapter 3), Jilly Cooper's *Appassionata* (Chapter 4), Kazuo Ishiguro's *The Unconsoled* (Chapter 5), Andrzej Klimowski's *Horace Dorlan* (Chapter 4), and Michael Faber's *The Courage Consort* (Chapter 5). See also *Other Lulus* (1994) by Philip Hensher.

20. Philip L. Scowcroft has published two very useful online essays on the subjects of 'Crime Fiction and Music' and 'Murder in English Detective Fiction' (see Bibliography: 'Other Sources').

21. The entry may be found at www.ianrankin.net/pages/content/index.asp?PageID=104.

22. *Let It Bleed* (1995) and *Black & Blue* (1997) are named after Rolling Stones albums released in 1969 and 1976 respectively. The collection entitled *Beggars Banquet* (named for an album of 1968) also features some Rebus stories. Rankin claimed that Rebus was loosely based on Scottish rock musician Ian Stewart, whose long association with the Rolling Stones earned him the title

of the 'sixth Stone'. Rankin wrote a lyric of that title that was recorded by musician Aidan Moffat for an album entitled *Ballads of the Book* (2007) featuring collaborations between musicians and writers from Scotland. See also the collection entitled *Blue Lightning* (1998), edited by John Harvey, which features eighteen short crime stories (including one by Rankin) inspired by music of various kinds.

23. On the commonalities between historiography (including biography) and fiction see Hayden White (1978) and (1987).

24. The Mozart theme in fiction is almost as old as the composer himself. Besides Burgess (whose novel was considered in Chapter 2), since 1990 there have been treatments by Bastable (1995), Bauld (2006), Cowell (2003), Dracup (1996), Montanno (1995), Morpurgo (2008), Moser (2006), Neider (1991), Nickel (1996), Prantera (2001), Rudel (2001), Waldron (2005), Wolff (1999) and Wyatt (1995). See the 'Writings of Fiction' collected at www.themozartcafe.net/library1.html; and also Alma H. Bond's *The Autobiography of Maria Callas* (1998) – a 'novel' that complicates the matter still further by introducing yet another form.

25. See March (2002). The influence of this tradition on Suhayl Saadi, author of *Psychoraag*, was noted in the Chapter 3.

5   The Uses of Music in the Contemporary British Novel

1. O'Fingal's fate is obviously related to that of the narrator of Adelaide Anne Proctor's poem 'A Lost Chord' (1860) who, idly playing the organ one day, 'struck one chord of music, / Like the sound of a great Amen . . . I have sought, but I seek it vainly, / That one lost chord divine, / Which came from the soul of the organ, / And entered into mine. / It may be that death's bright angel / Will speak in that chord again, / It may be that only in Heav'n / I shall hear that grand Amen.' It is ironic that in 1888 this paean to the inadequacies of mortal music became, in Arthur Sullivan's setting (entitled 'The Lost Chord', 1877), one of the first pieces of music to be recorded on Thomas Edison's phonograph.

2. These comments anticipate the section on 'The uses of silence' below.

3. Bradford (2007: 83). Ackroyd's interest in the past is evidenced in texts such as *Dickens* (1991), *London* (2000), and the more recent *Thames: Sacred River* (2007). The non-fictional work closest in ethos to *English Music* is *Albion: The Origins of the English Imagination* (2002).

4. There is nothing in Bradford (2007), in Lane, Mengham and Tew (2003), or in Shaffer (2005) on the impact of modern digital technology on the evolution of the novel.

5. Kureishi pursued all these subjects further in *The Black Album* (1995), a novel whose title (invoking the Beatles' *White Album*) and story self-consciously engage with British and African-American popular music and its relevance to British-Asian identity.

6. Kureishi co-edited (with Jon Savage) *The Faber Book of Pop* (1995), and all his writing (for screen and stage as well as fiction) demonstrates an appreciation of the role of music in wider cultural concerns. In a discussion of the social influences on *The Buddha of Suburbia*, Kureishi wrote: 'Music is very important

in this book . . . It was my obsession when I was growing up, as it was for many people of my generation' (2008).

7. Savage (2001) offers a compelling account of the world of British popular culture in the years immediately preceding punk. See also Hebdige (1987), Hoskyns (1998) and Thompson (2000).

8. Besides *Johnny Come Home* and the other texts mentioned in this section, Bowie features as a key reference in Iain Banks's *Espedair Street* (1987) and Kevin Sampson's *Stars Are Stars* (2007). In *Gabriel's Gift* (2001), Kureishi depicts an aging rock star (Lester Jones) whose career resembles Bowie's in many respects, especially in his interest in visual art. This latter novel also features a cameo role for Karim Amir, while Charlie Hero pops up in both *Gabriel's Gift* and *The Black Album* (1995).

9. Charlie Hero would appear to be a thinly disguised depiction of the British 'punk' Billy Idol who, along with Siousie Sioux, was a member of the so-called 'Bromley Contingent'. This was the name given to a group of fans of the Sex Pistols who, like the characters Karim and Charlie, hailed from that part of Greater London.

10. Coe's third novel, *The Dwarves of Death* (1990), also has a music theme. Besides a storyline featuring a cult post-punk band and a troubled rock auteur, each chapter is prefaced by a quote from Morrissey (singer and lyricist, formerly with the Smiths), while the narrative itself is structured in the shape of a pop song.

11. Sophie and Patrick, the characters from these framing scenes, feature in a sequel entitled *The Closed Circle* (2004).

12. For an assessment of the relationship between silence and noise see Attali, who associates silence with forms of knowledge that are abstract, scientific and elitist. He writes: 'Our science has always desired to monitor, measure, abstract, and castrate meaning, forgetting that life is full of noise and that death alone is silent: work noise, noise of man, and noise of beast. Noise bought, sold, or prohibited. Nothing essential happens in the absence of noise' (1985: 1).

13. We have already encountered examples of this trend with Conrad Williams's *The Concert Pianist* (Chapter 1), Lively's *Sing the Body Electric* (Chapter 4) and Ian McEwen's *Amsterdam* (Chapter 3); other examples included Michel Faber's *The Courage Consort* (see below), Kazuo Ishiguro's *The Unconsoled*, Billy Cowie's *Passenger*, Vikram Seth's *An Equal Music* and Philip Hensher's *Other Lulus*.

14. Benson describes the 'common . . . strategy employed by Vikram Seth in *An Equal Music*, according to which contemporary art music represents only a decadent and dessicated Modernism, an atomized intellectualism at odds with the organic physicality of our natural musical condition' (2006: 143).

15. There is a hint of such self-reflection when, thinking about his attraction towards Bonnie, William considers 'the inadequacy of words' (157) – something which obviously relates, in such a context, to the ability of language to describe music.

16. As Benson has suggested (see Note 14 above), modernism and postmodern experimentalism are routinely disparaged in contemporary British music fiction. Philip Hensher's *Other Lulus* (1994) is unusual in its focus on the work of the modernist Alban Berg, although its Berlin setting and its European

atmosphere clearly remove it from the type of novel of which *Easy Silence* is so representative.

17. The chapter in Benson is entitled 'Words Without Song: Kafka and *The Unconsoled*', pp. 141–60. At one point Ryder catches a glimpse of himself in a mirror and sees that his 'face had become bright red and squashed into pig-like features' (240). The parallels with Gregor Samsa (who also turns into an animal) from Kafka's *Metamorphosis* are apparent, as indeed they were in Klimowski's *Horace Dorlan* (see Chapter 4), with which text *The Unconsoled* shares a certain air of stoicism in the face of absurdity.

18. Music and love are conjoined in one of the most successful music-novels of recent years: Vikram Seth's *An Equal Music* (1999). Of representative texts not treated in this study see also Russell Hoban's *My Tango with Barbara Strozzi* (2007), Carol Clewlow's *One for the Money* (1994), Alan Hollinghurst's *The Spell* (1998), and Kevin Sampson's *Stars Are Stars* (2006).

19. The critical literature on love in its many different aspects is extensive, but for representative debates see Barthes (2002), Bloch (1991), Derrida (1997), Foucault (1990) and Schuld (2003). In relation to Shakespeare in particular see H. Bloom (1994), 45–75, 371–94; A. Bloom (2000) and Line (2004).

20. Roma's fate resembles that of the character of Buster in Bernice Rubens's *Spring Sonata* (1981) – a novel narrated in part by a musically-inclined foetus who refuses to leave his mother's womb.

Bibliography

(All texts published in London unless otherwise stated.)

Peter Ackroyd, *Dickens* (Mandarin, 1991)
———, *London: The Biography* (2000; Vintage, 2001)
———, *Albion: The Origins of the English Imagination* (2002; Vintage, 2004)
———, *Thames: Sacred River* (Chatto & Windus, 2007)
Theodor Adorno, *Philosophy of Modern Music* (1948; trans. Anne G. Mitchell and Wesley V. Blomster; Sheed & Ward, 1973)
———, 'On Popular Music', in John Storey (ed.), *Cultural Theory and Popular Culture: A Reader* (Hemel Hempstead: Harvester Wheatsheaf, 1994), 202–14
David Ake, *Jazz Cultures* (University of California Press, 2002)
Richard N. Albert, *An Annotated Bibliography of Jazz Fiction and Jazz Fiction Criticism* (Westport, CT: Greenwood Press, 1996)
James Anderson Winn, *Unsuspected Eloquence: A History of the Relations between Poetry and Music* (New Haven and London: Yale University Press, 1981)
Alfred Appel, *Jazz Modernism: From Ellington and Armstrong to Matisse and Joyce* (New York: Alfred A. Knopf, 2002)
Alex Aronson, *Music and the Novel: A Study of Twentieth-Century Fiction* (New Jersey: Rowman and Littlefield, 1980)
Lucie Armitt, *Fantasy Fiction: An Introduction* (New York: Continuum, 2005)
Mark Asquith, *Thomas Hardy, Metaphysics and Music* (Basingstoke: Palgrave Macmillan, 2005)
Jake Arnott, *Johnny Come Home* (2006; Sceptre, 2007)
Jacques Attali, *Noise: The Political Economy of Music* (1977; trans. Brian Massumi; Manchester: Manchester University Press, 1985)
M. M. Bakhtin, *Problems of Dostoevsky's Poetics* (1963; trans. C. Emerson; Minneapolis: University of Minnesota Press, 1984)
Kevin Barry, *Language, Music and the Sign: A Study of Aesthetics, Poetics and Poetic Practice from Collins to Cambridge* (Cambridge: Cambridge University Press, 1987)
Roland Barthes, *A Lover's Discourse: Fragments* (1977; trans. Richard Howard; Vintage, 2002)
H. A. Basilius, 'Thomas Mann's Use of Musical Structure and Techniques in *Tonio Kröger*' in Cluck (1981), 153–71
Charles Baudelaire, *Flowers of Evil and Other Works* (New York: Dover, 1992)
Ruth H. Bauerle (ed.), *Picking up Airs: Hearing the Music in Joyce's Text* (University of Illinois Press, 1993)
Tony Bennett, Simon Frith, Lawrence Grossberg, John Shepherd and Graeme Turner (eds), *Rock and Popular Music: Politics, Policies, Institutions* (Routledge, 1993)
Stephen Benson, *Literary Music: Writing Music in Contemporary Fiction* (Ashgate 2006)
Walter Bernhart, 'Some Reflections on Literary Genres and Music' in Bernhart, Scher and Wolf (1999), 25–36

Walter Bernhart, Steven Scher and Werner Wolf (eds), *Word and Music Studies: Defining the Field* (Amsterdam: Rodopi, 1999)

Andrew Blake, *The Land Without Music: Music, Culture and Society in Twentieth-Century Britain* (Manchester: Manchester University Press, 1997)

William F. Blissett, 'George Moore and Literary Wagnerism' in Owens (1968), 53–76

Howard R. Bloch, *Medieval Misogyny and the Invention of Western Romantic Love* (Chicago: University of Chicago Press, 1991)

Allan Bloom, *Shakespeare on Love and Friendship* (Chicago: University of Chicago Press, 2000)

Harold Bloom, *The Western Canon: The Books and School of the Ages* (Harcourt Brace & Company, 1994)

Leon Botstein, 'Memory and Nostalgia as Music-Historical Categories', *Music Quarterly* 84 (2000): 531–6

Richard Bradford, *The Novel Now: Contemporary British Fiction* (Oxford: Blackwell, 2007)

Mary M. Breatnach, '*Pli selon Pli*: A Conflation of Theoretical Stances' in Bernhart, Scher and Wolf (1999), 265–76

Joseph Bristow, *Empire Boys: Adventures in a Man's World* (Harper Collins, 1991)

Bill Broady, *Eternity is Temporary* (Portobello Books, 2006)

Calvin S. Brown, *Music and Literature: A Comparison of the Arts* (Athens, GA: University of Georgia Press, 1948)

E. K. Brown, *Rhythm in the Novel* (1950; Toronto: University of Toronto Press, 1967)

Terence Brown, 'Music: the cultural issue', in Pine (1998), 37–45

Brad Bucknell, *Literary Modernism and Musical Aesthetics: Pater, Pound, Joyce, and Stein* (Cambridge: Cambridge University Press, 2001)

Malcolm Budd (ed.), *Music and the Emotions: The Philosophical Theories* (1985; Routledge, 1992)

Judith Butler, *Gender Trouble: Feminism and the Subversion of Identity* (Routledge, 1999)

Richard Cave, *A Study of the Novels of George Moore* (Gerrards Cross: Colin Smythe, 1978)

Michael Chanan, *Musica Practica: The Social Practice of Western Music from Gregorian Chant to Postmodernism* (Verso, 1994)

Peter G. Christenson and Donald F. Roberts, *It's Not Only Rock & Roll: Popular Music in the Lives of Adolescents* (New Jersey: Hampton Press, 1998)

Marcia Citron, *Gender and the Musical Canon* (Cambridge: Cambridge University Press, 1993)

Martin Clayton, Trevor Herbert and Richard Middleton (eds), *The Cultural Study of Music: A Critical Introduction* (Routledge, 2003)

Nancy Anne Cluck (ed.), *Literature and Music: Essays on Form* (Provo, Utah: Brigham Young University Press, 1981)

Nicholas Cook, *Music, Imagination, and Culture* (Oxford: Clarendon Press, 1990)

———, *Music: A Very Short Introduction* (Oxford: Oxford University Press, 1998)

Mervyn Cooke, *The Chronicle of Jazz* (Thames & Hudson, 1997)

Carl Dahlhaus, *The Idea of Absolute Music* (1978; trans. Roger Lustig; University of Chicago Press, 1991)

Lawrence Davies, *César Franck and his Circle* (London: Barrie & Jenkins, 1970)

Gilles Deleuze, *Difference and Repetition* (1968; trans. Paul Patton; Athlone Press, 1994)

Jacques Derrida, *Politics of Friendship* (1993; trans. George Collins; Verso, 1997)

Delia de Sousa Correa, *George Eliot, Music and Victorian Culture* (Basingstoke: Palgrave Macmillan, 2003)

Roddy Doyle, *Oh, Play That Thing!* (Jonathan Cape, 2004)

Terry Eagleton, *The Ideology of the Aesthetic* (Oxford: Basil Blackwell, 1990)

Terry Eagleton, *Heathcliff and the Great Hunger: Studies in Irish Culture* (Verso, 1995)

T. S. Eliot, 'Tradition and the Individual Talent' (1919) in Selected Essays (Faber and Faber, 1999), 13–19

Robert Emerson Carlile, 'Great Circle: Conrad Aiken's Musico-Literary Technique' in Cluck (1981), 187–94

E. M. Forster, *Aspects of the Novel* (1927; Harmondsworth: Penguin, 1981)

Michel Foucault, *The Will to Knowledge: The History of Sexuality – Vol. 1* (1976; trans. Robert Hurley; Harmondsworth: Penguin 1990)

Carl Freedman, *Critical Theory and Science Fiction* (Hanover, NH: Wesleyan University Press, 2000)

William Freedman, *Laurence Sterne and the Origins of the Musical Novel* (Athens, GA: University of Georgia Press, 1978)

Simon Frith, *Sound Effects: Youth, Leisure, and the Politics of Rock 'n' Roll* (New York: Pantheon Books, 1981)

Mark Garnett, *From Anger to Apathy: The British Experience Since 1975* (Cape, 2007)

John Garth, *Tolkien and the Great War: The Threshold of Middle-Earth* (HarperCollins, 2003)

Ken Gelder, *Popular Fiction: The Logics and Practices of a Literary Field* (Routledge, 2004)

Stuart Gilbert, *James Joyce's 'Ulysses': A Study* (1930; 2nd edn. Faber and Faber, 1952)

Gerard Gillen and Harry White (eds), *Irish Musical Studies: I – Musicology in Ireland* (Dublin: Irish Academic Press, 1990)

Joscelyn Godwin, *Harmony of the Spheres: Source Book of Pythagorean Tradition in Music* (Rochester, Vermont: Inner Traditions Bear and Company, 1993)

David Goldie, 'The Scottish New Wave' in Shaffer (2005), 526–37

William E. Grim, 'Musical Form as a Problem in Literary Criticism' in Bernhart, Scher and Wolf (1999), 237–48

Joan Grundy, *Hardy and the Sister Arts* (Macmillan, 1979)

Jean H. Hagstrum, *The Sister Arts: The Tradition of Literary Pictorialism and English Poetry from Dryden to Gray* (Chicago: University of Chicago Press, 1958)

Eduard Hanslick, *The Beautiful in Music: A Contribution to the Revisal of Musical Aesthetics* (7th ed. 1885; trans. Gustav Cohen; New York: Da Capo Press, 1974)

Leon Harkleroad, *The Math Behind the Music* (Cambridge: Cambridge University Press, 2006)

Dick Hebdige, *Subculture: The Meaning of Style* (1979; Routledge, 1987)

Philip Hensher, *Other Lulus* (Flamingo, 2003)

J. Hillis Miller, *Fiction and Repetition: Seven English Novels* (Oxford: Basil Blackwell, 1982)

bell hooks, *Yearning: Race, Gender and Cultural Politics* (Turnaround, 1991)

Bruce Horner and Thomas Swiss (eds), *Key Terms in Popular Music and Culture* (Oxford: Basil Blackwell, 1999)

Barney Hoskyns, *Glam Rock* (Faber and Faber, 1998)

Barney Hoskyns, *The Lonely Planet Boy: A Pop Romance* (Serpent's Tail, 1995)

Jeffrey H. Jackson, *Making Jazz French: Music and Modern Life in Interwar Paris* (Durham, NC: Duke University Press, 2003)

Jamie James, *The Music of the Spheres: Music, Science and the Natural Order of the Universe* (Abacus, 1995)

Martin Jay, 'In the Empire of the Gaze: Foucault and the Denigration of Vision in Twentieth-century French Thought', in David Couzens Hoy (ed.), *Foucault: A Critical Reader* (Oxford: Blackwell, 1986), 175–204

James Joyce, *Dubliners* (1914; Oxford Worlds Classics, 2000)

Søren Kierkegaard, *Either/Or*, 2 vols. (1843; trans. David F. Swenson and Lillian Marvin Swenson; New York: Anchor Books, 1959)

Peter Kivy, *Music Alone: Philosophical Reflections on the Purely Musical Experience* (Ithaca, NY: Cornell University Press, 1990)

Lawrence Kramer, 'Review of Robert K. Wallace, *Jane Austen and Mozart: Classical Equilibrium in Fiction and Music*, in *Nineteenth-Century Music* 8 (1985), 277–9

——, *Music as Cultural Practice, 1800–1900* (Berkeley: University of California Press, 1990)

——, *Classical Music and Postmodern Knowledge* (Berkeley: University of California Press, 1995)

——, 'Subjectivity Rampant! Music, Hermeneutics, and History' in Clayton, Herbert and Middleton (2003), 124–35

Udaya Kumar, *The Joycean Labyrinth: Repetition, Time, and Tradition in Ulysses* (Oxford: Clarendon Press, 1991)

Milan Kundera, *The Art of the Novel* (1986; trans. Linda Asher; Faber, 2005)

——, *Testaments Betrayed* (1993; Faber and Faber, 1995)

Hanif Kureishi, 'The social influences on *The Buddha of Suburbia*', *The Guardian: Review* (26th January 2008), 7

Hanif Kureishi and Jon Savage (eds), *The Faber Book of Pop* (Faber and Faber, 1995)

Bernard Mac Laverty's *Grace Notes* (1997; Vintage, 1998)

Ula-Britta Lagerroth, 'Reading Musicalized Texts as Self-Reflexive Texts' in Bernhart, Scher and Wolf (1999), 205–20

Richard J. Lane, Rod Mengham and Philip Tew (eds), *Contemporary British Fiction* (Cambridge: Polity Press, 2003)

Scott Lash, *Sociology of Postmodernism* (Routledge, 1990)

Daniel J. Levitin, *This Is Your Brain on Music: Understanding a Human Obsession* (Atlantic, 2007)

Jill Line, *Shakespeare and the Fire of Love* (Shepheard-Walwyn, 2004)

George Lipsitz, *Dangerous Crossroads: Popular Music, Postmodernism and the Poetics of Place* (Verso, 1994)

Adam Lively, *Sing The Body Electric: A Novel in Five Movements* (Chatto and Windus, 1993)

Judy Lochhead and Joseph Auner (eds), *Postmodern Music/Postmodern Thought* (Garland, 2001)

Suzanne M. Lodato and David Francis Urrows (eds), *Word and Music Studies: Essays on Music and the Spoken Word and on Surveying the Field* (Amsterdam: Rodopi, 2005)

Nicky Losseff and Jenny Doctor (eds), *Silence, Music, Silent Music* (Abingdon: Ashgate, 2007)

Cristie L. March, *Rewriting Scotland, Welsh, McLean, Warner, Banks, Galloway and Kennedy* (Manchester: Manchester University Press, 2002)

Susan McClary, *Feminine Endings: Music, Gender, and Sexuality* (Minnesota: University of Minnesota Press, 1991)

———, *Conventional Wisdom: The Content of Musical Form* (Berkeley: University of California Press, 2000)

Ian MacDonald, *Revolution in the Head: The Beatles' Records and the Sixties* (Fourth Estate, 1994)

Bryan McGee, *The Tristan Chord: Wagner and Philosophy* (New York: Own Books, 2002)

Andy Medhurst, 'What Did I Get? Punk, Memory and Autobiography', in Sabin (1999), 219–31

Rod Mengham, 'General Introduction: Contemporary British Fiction' in Lane, Mengham and Tew (2003), 1–7

Richard Middleton, 'Music Studies and the Idea of Culture' in Clayton, Herbert and Middleton (2003), 1–15

Terry Miller and Andrew Shahriari, *World Music: A Global Journey* (Routledge, 2005)

Hilary Moore, *Inside British Jazz: Crossing Borders of Race, Nation and Class* (Aldershot: Ashgate, 2007)

Joe Moran, *Interdisciplinary* (Routledge, 2001)

Pam Morris (ed.), *The Bakhtin Reader: Selected Writings of Bakhtin, Medvedev, Voloshinov* (Edward Arnold, 1994)

Anja Müller-Muth, 'A Playful Comment on Word and Music Relations: Anthony Burgess's *Mozart and the Wolf Gang*' in Bernhart, Scher and Wolf (1999), 249–61

Jean-Jacques Nattiez, 'Can One Speak of Narrativity in Music?', *Journal of the Royal Musical Association* 115 (1990): 240–57

Christopher Norris, 'Music, Language and the Sublime' in *What's Wrong With Postmodernism: Critical Theory and the Ends of Philosophy* (Hemel Hempstead: Harvester Wheatsheaf, 1990), 208–21

Christopher Norris, *Derrida* (Fontana Press, 1987)

Graham Owens (ed.), *George Moore's Mind and Art* (Edinburgh: Oliver and Boyd, 1968)

Catherine Parsonage, *The Evolution of Jazz in Britain, 1880–1935* (Aldershot: Ashgate, 2005)

Walter Pater, 'The School of Giorgione' (1877), in *The Renaissance: Studies in Art and Poetry* (1873; Macmillan, 1910), 130–54

Morse Peckham, *Beyond the Tragic Vision: The Quest for Identity in the Nineteenth Century* (New York: George Braziller, 1962)

Richard Pine (ed.), *Music in Ireland 1848–1998* (Cork: Mercier Press, 1998)

Plato, *The Republic*, ed. Melissa Lane, trans. H.D.P. Lee and Desmond Lee (Penguin, 2007)

Eric Prieto, *Listening In: Music, Mind, and Modernist Narrative* (Lincoln: University of Nebraska Press, 2002)

Nancy B. Reich, *Clara Schumann: The Artist and the Woman* (1985; Ithaca: Cornell University Press, rev. ed., 2001)

Neil V. Rosenberg, *Transforming Tradition: Folk Music Revivals Examined* (Urbana: University of Illinois Press, 1993)

Jean-Jacques Rousseau, 'Essay on the Origin of Languages' in John Hope Mason (ed.), *The Indispensable Rousseau* (Quartet Books, 1979), 89–103

Roger Sabin (ed.), *Punk Rock, So What? The Cultural Legacy of Punk* (New York: Routledge, 1999)

Oliver Sachs, *Musicophilia: Tales of Music and the Brain* (Picador, 2007)

Edward W. Said, *The World, The Text and The Critic* (1983; Vintage, 1991)

———, *On Late Style: Music and Literature Against the Grain* (2006; Bloomsbury, 2007)

Jon Savage, *England's Dreaming: Sex Pistols and Punk Rock* (1991; Faber and Faber, 2001)

———, 'The Simple Things You See Are All Complicated' Kureishi and Savage (1995), xxi–xxxiii

Margaret Scanlan, 'The Recuperation of History in British and Irish Fiction' in Shaffer (2005), 144–59

Steven Paul Scher, 'Melopoetics Revisited' in Bernhart, Scher and Woolf (1999), 9–24

Arthur Schopenhauer, *The World as Will and Representation*, 2 vols. (trans. E. F. J. Payne; New York: Dover, 1969)

———, *The World as Will and Idea: Volume III, Containing Supplements to Part of the Second Book and to the Third and Fourth Books* (trans. R. B. Haldane and J. Kemp; Kegan Paul, Trench, Trübner, 1891)

J. Joyce Schuld, *Foucault and Augustine: Reconsidering Power and Love* (Notre Dame, IN: University of Notre Dame Press, 2003)

Brian W. Shaffer (ed.), *A Companion to the British and Irish Novel 1945–2000* (Oxford: Blackwell, 2005)

Harry E. Shaw, *The Forms of Historical Fiction: Sir Walter Scott and His Successors* (Ithaca, NY: Cornell University Press, 1983)

John Shepherd, 'Text' in Horner and Swiss (eds) (1999), 156–74

Dom Noel Smith, 'Musical Form and Principles in the Scheme of *Ulysses*' in Cluck (1981), 213–24

Claire Squires, 'Novelistic Production and the Publishing Industry in Britain and Ireland' in Shaffer (2005), 177–93

Nick Stevenson, *David Bowie: Fame, Sound and Vision* (Polity, 2006)

John Storey, *An Introductory Guide to Cultural Theory and Popular Culture* (Hemel Hempstead: Harvester Wheatsheaf, 1993)

Anthony Storr, *Music and the Mind* (HarperCollins, 1997)

John Strausbaugh, *Rock Til You Drop: The Decline from Rebellion to Nostalgia* (Verso, 2002)

John J. Su, *Ethics and Nostalgia in the Contemporary Novel* (Cambridge: Cambridge University Press, 2005)

Downing A. Thomas, *Music and the Origins of Language: Theories from the French Enlightenment* (Cambridge: Cambridge University Press, 1995)

Dylan Thomas, *Under Milk Wood: A Play for Voices* (1954; Dent, 1995)

Dave Thompson, *Glam Rock* (Collector's Guide Publishing, 2000)

David Trotter, *The English Novel in History 1895–1920* (Routledge, 1993)

Robert K. Wallace, *Jane Austen and Mozart: Classical Equilibrium in Fiction and Music* (Athens, GA: The University of Georgia Press, 1983)

———, *Emily Bronte and Beethoven: Romantic Equilibrium in Fiction and Music* (Athens, GA: The University of Georgia Press, 1986)

Timothy Warner, *Pop Music – Technology and Creativity: Trevor Horn and the Digital Revolution* (Aldershot: Ashgate, 2003)

Jack W. Weaver, *Joyce's Music and Noise: Theme and Variation in His Writings* (University Press of Florida, 1998)

Robert Welch (ed.), *The Oxford Companion to Irish Literature* (Oxford: Clarendon Press, 1996)

Harry White, *The Keeper's Recital: Music and Cultural History in Ireland, 1770–1970* (Cork: Cork University Press, 1998)

Hayden White, *Tropics of Discourse: Essays in Cultural Criticism* (Baltimore: Johns Hopkins University Press, 1978)

———, *The Content of the Form: Narrative Discourse and Historical Representation.* (Baltimore: Johns Hopkins University Press, 1987)

Sheila Whitely, *Women and Popular Music: Sexuality, Identity and Subjectivity* (Routledge, 2000)

Walt Whitman, *Selected Poems* (New York: Dover, 1991)

Edmund Wilson, *Axel's Castle: A Study in the Imaginative Literature of 1870–1930* (1931; Fontana, 1961)

A.N. Wilson, *Winnie and Wolf* (Hutchinson, 2007)

Werner Wolf, *The Musicalization of Fiction: A Study in the Theory and History of Intermediality* (Amsterdam: Rodopi Press, 1999)

John Worthen, *Robert Schumann: Life and Death of a Musician* (Yale University Press, 2007)

Theodore Ziolkowski, 'Hermann Hesse's *Steppenwolf*: A Sonata in Prose, in Cluck (1981), 196–212

Fiction

Peter Ackroyd, *English Music* (New York: Alfred A. Knopf, 1992)

Kingsley Amis, *Lucky Jim* (1954; Penguin, 1976)

Jane Austen, *Pride and Prejudice* (1813; Harmondsworth: Penguin, 1972)

Dorothy Baker, *Young Man With A Horn* (1938; The Jazz Book Club, 1957)

Christine Balint, *Ophelia's Fan* (W. W. Norton & Co., 2004)

Iain Banks, *Espedair Street* (1987; Abacus, 1990)

Bernard Bastable, *Too Many Notes, Mr. Mozart* (Little, Brown, 1995)

Alison Bauld, *Mozart's Sister* (Alcina Press, 2006)

Dermot Bolger, *Father's Music* (Flamingo, 1998)

Alma H. Bond, *The Autobiography of Maria Callas: A Novel* (Birch Brook Press, 1998)

Tim Bowler, *Starseeker* (Oxford: Oxford University Press, 2002)

Ray Bradbury, *I Sing the Body Electric* (1969; Avon Books, 2003)

Emily Brontë, *Wuthering Heights* (1847; Harmondsworth: Penguin, 1965)

Anthony Burgess, *A Clockwork Orange* (1962; Penguin, 2000)

———, *Napoleon Symphony* (Jonathan Cape, 1974)

———, *Mozart and the Wolf Gang* (Vintage, 1991)

Gordon Burn, *Alma Cogan* (1991; Faber and Faber, 2004)

Carol Clewlow, *One For The Money* (1994; Penguin, 1995)

Jonathan Coe, *The Dwarves of Death* (1990; Penguin, 2001)

———, *The Rotters' Club* (2001; Penguin, 2002)

———, *The Closed Circle* (Viking, 2004)

Rachel Cohn, *Pop Princess* (Simon & Schuster, 2004)

Jackie Collins, *The Stud* (1969; Pan, 1984)
Joseph Conrad, *The Secret Agent* (1907; Harmondsworth, Middlesex: Penguin, 1965)
Jilly Cooper, *Appassionata* (1996; Corgi, 1997)
———, *Score!* (Corgi, 1999)
Stephanie Cowell, *Marrying Mozart* (Penguin, 2003)
Billy Cowie, *Passenger* (Brighton: Idiolect, 2006)
Louis de Bernières, *Captain Corelli's Mandolin* (1994; Minerva, 1995)
Charles Dickens, *A Tale of Two Cities* (1859; Penguin, 1994)
Anne Donovan, *Buddha Da* (2003; Edinburgh: Canongate, 2004)
Arthur Conan Doyle, *The Penguin Complete Sherlock Holmes* (1930; Harmondsworth, Middlesex: Penguin, 1981)
Angela Dracup, *Mozart's Darling* (Robert Hale, 1996)
Jessica Duchen, *Alicia's Gift* (Hodder and Stoughton, 2007)
George Eliot, *Middlemarch* (1871–2; Penguin, 1967)
Michel Faber, *The Courage Consort* (Edinburgh: Canongate, 2002)
Helen Fielding, *Bridget Jones's Diary* (1996; Picador, 1997)
———, *Bridget Jones: The Edge of Reason* (1999; Picador, 2000)
E. M. Forster, *Howards End* (1910; Harmondsworth, Middlesex: Penguin, 1960)
Janice Galloway, *The Trick Is To Keep Breathing* (1989; Minerva, 1991)
———, *Foreign Parts* (Jonathan Cape, 1994)
———, *Clara* (2002; Vintage, 2003)
William Gibson, *Neuromancer* (1984; New York: Ace Books, 1995)
Deborah Grabien, *The Weaver and the Factory Maid* (New York: St Martin's Minotaur, 2003)
———, *Matty Groves* (New York: St Martin's Minotaur, 2005)
———, *Cruel Sister* (New York: St Martin's Minotaur, 2006)
Thomas Hardy, *Jude the Obscure* (1895; Penguin, 1985)
Fraser Harrison, *Minotaur in Love* (Hexham: Flambard Press, 2007)
John Harvey (ed.), *Blue Lightning* (Slow Dancer, 1998)
Robert A. Heinlein, *The Green Hills of Earth* (1951; New York: Baen, 2000)
Russell Hoban, *My Tango with Barbara Strozzi* (Bloomsbury, 2007)
Alan Hollinghurst, *The Spell* (1998; Vintage 1999)
Nick Hornby, *High Fidelity* (Penguin, 1995)
Mark Hudson, *The Music in my Head* (Vintage, 1999)
Angela Huth, *Easy Silence* (1999; Abacus, 2000)
Aldous Huxley, *Point Counter Point* (1928; New York: Harper & Row, 1965)
Kazuo Ishiguro, *The Remains of the Day* (1989; Faber and Faber, 2005)
———, *The Unconsoled* (Faber and Faber, 1995)
James Joyce, *Ulysses* (1922; Oxford: Oxford World Classics, 1993)
Franz Kafka, *Metamorphosis and Other Stories* (Penguin, 2007)
Jackie Kay, *Trumpet* (Picador, 1998)
John B. Keane, *The Bodhrán Makers* (1986; Dingle: Brandon, 2002)
James Kelman, *How Late It Was, How Late* (1994; Minerva, 1995)
Andrzej Klimowski, *Horace Dorlan* (Faber and Faber, 2007)
Hanif Kureishi, *The Buddha of Suburbia* (1990; Faber and Faber, 1999)
———, *The Black Album* (1995; Faber and Faber, 2000)
———, *Gabriel's Gift* (2001; Faber and Faber, 2002)
Edwin Leather, *The Mozart Score* (Macmillan, 1979)

Toby Litt, *I Play the Drums in a Band Called Okay* (Hamish Hamilton, 2008)
Colin MacInnes, *Absolute Beginners* (1959; Allison & Busby, 1992)
Patrick McCabe, *Winterwood* (Bloomsbury, 2006)
Ian McEwan, *Amsterdam* (1998; Vintage, 1999)
Thomas Mann, 'Tonio Kröger' (1903) from *Death in Venice and Other Stories* (Vintage, 1998), 137–94
———, *Doctor Faustus: The Life of the German Composer Adrian Leverkühn as Told by a Friend* (1947; trans. H. T. Lowe-Porter; Secker & Warburg, 1976)
Sarra Manning, *Guitar Girl* (Hodder, 2003)
David Mitchell, *Cloud Atlas* (Sceptre, 2004)
Dreda Say Mitchell, *Killer Tune* (Hodder & Stoughton, 2007)
Mary Montanno, *Loving Mozart: A Past Life Memory of the Composer's Final Years* (Cantus Verus Books, 1995)
Clare Morrall, *The Language of Others* (Sceptre, 2008)
Michael Morpurgo, *The Mozart Question* (Walker, 2008)
Toni Morrison, *Jazz* (1992; Vintage, 2001)
Nancy Moser, *Mozart's Sister* (Grand Rapids MI: Bethany House Publishers, 2006)
John Murray, *Jazz Etc.* (Hexham, UK: Flambard, 2003)
Charles Neider, *Mozart and the Archbooby* (Penguin, 1991)
Barbara Nickel, *The Secret Wish of Nannerl Mozart* (Toronto: Second Story Press, 1996)
Jeff Noon, *Vurt* (1993; Pan, 2001)
———, *Needle in the Groove* (Black Swan, 2001)
Andrew O'Hagan, *Personality* (2003; Harvest, 2004)
Michael Ondaatje, *Coming Through Slaughter* (1979; Picador, 1984)
Tony Parsons, *Stories We Could Tell* (2005; HarperCollins, 2006)
Amanda Prantera, *Don Giovanna* (Bloomsbury Publishing, 2001)
Terry Pratchett, *Soul Music* (1994; Corgi Books, 1995)
Katie Price, *Crystal* (Century, 2007)
Marcel Proust, *Swann's Way* (1913; trans. C. K. Scott Moncrieff; Penguin, 1957)
Ian Rankin, *Exit Music* (Orion Books, 2007)
Andromeda Romano-Lax, *The Spanish Bow* (Heinemann, 2008)
Bernice Rubens, *Spring Sonata* (1981; Abacus 1986)
Anthony Rudel, *Imagining Don Giovanni* (Atlantic Books, 2001)
Salman Rushdie, *The Ground Beneath Her Feet* (1999; Vintage, 2000)
Suhayl Saadi, *Psychoraag* (Edinburgh: Chroma, 2004)
Kevin Sampson, *Powder: An Everyday Story of Rock 'n' Roll Folk* (1999; Vintage, 2000)
———, *Stars are Stars* (2006; Vintage, 2007)
Vikram Seth, *An Equal Music* (Phoenix, 1999)
Mary Shelley, *Frankenstein: Or, The Modern Prometheus* (1818; Penguin, 2004)
Zadie Smith, *On Beauty* (2005; Penguin, 2006)
Lawrence Sterne, *Tristram Shandy* (1760–7; New York and London: Norton, 1980)
Irving Stone, *Lust for Life* (1934; Arrow Books, 1990)
———, *The Agony and the Ecstasy* (1961; Arrow Books, 1990)
Adam Thorpe, *Between Each Breath* (Jonathan Cape, 2007)
J. R. R. Tolkien, *The Lord of the Rings* (1954–5; HarperCollins, 1995)
Lindsay Townsend, *Voices in the Dark* (Hodder & Stoughton, 1995)
Rose Tremain, *Restoration* (Viking, 1990)

————, *Music and Silence* (1999; Vintage, 2000)

Juliet Waldron, *Mozart's Wife* (Amherst Jct. WI and online: Hard Shell Word Factory, 2005)

Alan Warner, *Morvern Callar* (1995; Vintage, 1996)

David Weiss, *Sacred and Profane: A Novel of the Life and Times of Mozart* (William Morrow, 1968)

————, *The Assassination of Mozart* (Hodder & Stoughton, 1971)

Irvine Welsh, *Trainspotting* (1993; Vintage 1999)

Conrad Williams, *The Concert Pianist* (Bloomsbury, 2006)

Jeanette Winterson, *Art & Lies: A Piece for Three Voices and a Bawd* (1994; Vintage 1995)

Virginia Euwer Wolff, *The Mozart Season* (Topeka, Kansas: Sagebrush, 1999)

Charles Wyatt, *Listening to Mozart* (Iowa City, Iowa: University of Iowa Press, 1995)

Jane Yardley, *Dancing with Dr Kildare* (Doubleday, 2008)

Other Sources

Daniel Barenboim, 'In The Beginning Was Sound', Reith Lectures 1 (April 7, 2006), www.bbc.co.uk/radio4/reith2006/lectures.shtml

recollectionbooks.com/siml/library/AngryBrigade/

www.themozartcafe.homestead.com/library1

www.lib.washington.edu/music/mystery.html

www.ianrankin.net/pages/content/index.asp?PageID=104

www.lib.washington.edu/music/mystery.html

Index

Printed and bound by CPI Group (UK) Ltd, Croydon, CR0 4YY